Iron

Robin L. Cole

First Edition.

Copyright © 2015 Robin L. Cole

All rights reserved.

This is a work of fiction. Any resemblance to actual persons living or dead, businesses, events, or locales is purely coincidental.

No part of this publication may be reproduced, distributed, or transmitted in any form or by any means, including photocopying, recording, or other electronic or mechanical methods, without the prior written permission of the publisher, except in the case of brief quotations embodied in critical reviews and certain other noncommercial uses permitted by copyright law.

The author greatly appreciates you taking the time to read her work. Please consider leaving a review wherever you bought the book, or telling your friends about Iron, to help spread the word.

Thank you for supporting my work.

FOR

For Valerie, my writing buddy and Mistress of Critiques, who never hesitated to poke me with a cattle prod whenever I fell behind in my duty of feeding her inbox with new material.

And, of course, for Phil, my amazing husband who supports me in everything I do, no matter how weird or wild. You're my best friend and partner, and I love you from the bottom of my heart. I couldn't have done this without you.

CHAPTER ONE

Any woman who says she didn't freak out over turning thirty is a damn liar.

Maybe she didn't do it all grand and flashy—you know, like that one friend who had to be peeled, bawling, off the bathroom floor in the middle of her own birthday party. Maybe she did it quiet-like, when she was all alone in her apartment with a glass of wine after everyone went home. Maybe she had herself a nice, long "I thought my life would be different by now" mope if not an all-out "where the hell is my life going" cry.

One way or another, at one time or another, though? She did it.

It's inevitable. It's a cruel twist of fate. Like reaching for the milk to make that first cup of coffee you absolutely need to help you face the day... only to realize said milk expired two weeks ago... and that might explain why your Oreos tasted funny when you were dunking them in a big glass of it last night. Turning thirty is like hitting your own expiration date. It's the end of those years where it's okay to be a little wild, a little lost—hell, even a little stupid. Thirty marks an end to that time when you could make bad decisions and change your mind a zillion times, because you were young and hadn't found your way yet; hadn't found yourself yet. You had all the time in the world to get it all figured out. You know; time to build your career, meet Mr. Right, get married, buy a cute little starter house, and maybe even get a dog. All that was what your thirties were for.

Only, one day you turned around to see that thirty was on the horizon and at that very moment you realized none of that stuff had fallen into place. Instead of having any—never mind *all*—of it figured out, you're still single and living alone in a crappy, over-priced New Jersey apartment, working a dead-end 9 to 5 office job with no clue what to do next. So, as those final minutes tick down to the dreaded 3-0, you think back to all those little things you should have done differently. Like, maybe you should have finished college instead of blowing it off, thinking you could just work your way up in the real world. Maybe you should have tried harder to build a nest egg instead of buying that cute little burgundy leather jacket that cost you a full week's pay last winter. Maybe you should have spent more time planning for the future instead of out partying with your bestie, telling yourself tomorrow was "Future Caitlin's" problem.

Or maaaaaybe that was the fourth glass of wine talking.

It was the dreaded night of the birthday-that-shall-not-be-named. An undertow of depression had me in its clutches as I sat there at the bar, knocking back a few glasses of particularly fine Riesling and waiting for that inevitable moment when the clock would strike midnight. As if turning thirty wasn't bad enough, I had the doubly bad luck of doing so on a drizzly Tuesday, the night before Halloween. Let's be honest. No one wants to stay up late to celebrate when they have to get up early and go to work the next day. (Not that I had much of a social circle, really.) So, there was no festive gathering to mark the big moment—or to distract me from it. There was just little getting-old me, parked in my usual seat at Gilroy's with a magically refilling wineglass, and a bird's eye view of a timepiece hell-bent on the destruction of my youth.

Okay, that's not completely true. The glass wasn't magic nor was it refilling itself with free booze. If either case was true, I'm pretty sure Gilroy's would have been the most popular bar in Riverview, if not all of New Jersey, instead of being a locals only sort of hole in the wall. I wasn't completely alone either. Jenni Fisher, bartender extraordinaire and my partner in crime since the era of diapers and the Muppet Babies, was doing an admirable job of keeping her bestie on the edge of sobriety. She was the one who had convinced me to come out to Gilroy's in the first place when she wasn't able to get the night off to celebrate with (i.e. babysit) me. I had tried to beg off, but she had made it very clear that my plan of hiding out in my apartment with a pint of rocky road ice cream, wallowing in my birthday blues while watching P.S. I Love You for the fiftieth time, was pathetic with a capital P.

Damn her and her knowing-me-all-too-well logic.

All the same, as I sat there alone at the corner of the bar, I regretted acquiescing. It was close to midnight and Gilory's was empty of the all but the hardcore regulars. What, exactly, did it say about me if I was among them? The thought of being curled up on my squishy couch in my crappy one-bedroom, slurping down the melty remains of chocolaty-marshmallow goodness while wibbling over some lovey dovey chick flick had a nostalgic charm about it. It certainly seemed more fitting, and a damn shade less sad, than feeling a little too flushed and wondering how steady I'd be in my borrowed stilettos when it came time for me to leave my barstool. At home I also could have covered the glowing digits on the cable-box and ignored the slow countdown to the witching hour. *My* witching hour. One step closer to being a lonely old crone for Caitlin Marie Moore.

"Uh-oh. I know that look. Come back from the dark side, Cat."

I looked up, realizing at that moment that I had been giving my empty glass a particularly evil scowl. Jenni stood on the other side of the bar, hands on her hips and a stern look on her face. The "tsk-tsk" after her words was silent but we both knew it was there. Another downside to being attached at the hip for more years than I currently cared to count. There was no point in trying to play it off. She knew I was one more glass and ten minutes away from a major melt-down, the public eye be damned. However, I held it as a point of pride that there was pretty much nothing I could do that would ever come near to her own Getting Old Breakdown. (Refer back to the aforementioned peeling of said friend off of a club's scummy bathroom floor.) So, instead of saying that I was fine and forcing a smile both of us would know was fake, I pouted and whined. "Getting older suuuuuuuuuucks."

"Don't I know it, darling. But wasn't a certain someone singing the 'thirty isn't old' tune just a few months ago?" She drew out the "*old*" with righteous derision. At a full three months and four days older than myself, she had no pity for me when it came to the marching orders of Father Time. Instead of consoling me, she picked up my empty glass and wagged it in the air. "Care for another?"

It's a sad day when a woman's best pout goes unnoticed. I tilted my head to one side and waited a few seconds for the world to catch up with me. There was a little too much of a delay there for my liking. "Nope, I think it's time you cut me off, barkeep." An involuntary glance at the clock made me regret the words as soon as they were out of my mouth. Only five minutes left until midnight. I thought I was supposed to be having fun for time to fly so fast.

Jenni imitated my pout far too well. "Then how about a coffee for the road? Wouldn't want you passing out in the cab on the way home."

She had arranged cab rides to and from my apartment for me, in addition to plying me with wine all night. Have I mentioned that I have the world's best bestie yet? Her refusal to console my irrational fear of aging aside, of course. I heaved a dramatic sigh, hoping it had the sound of one long in suffering, and rolled my eyes heavenward. "Yeah, I guess so."

I must have perfected my look of utter and complete misery, because she leaned forward and pinched my chin between her thumb and forefinger. She tilted my head down and laid a sloppy kiss on my forehead. "Cheer up, buttercup. It's not so bad. I survived it. Odds are you will too."

I scrunched up my nose in reply but she ignored me and disappeared into the kitchen to get me my coffee. I used the damp napkin my wineglass had been sitting upon to wipe the bubblegum pink imprint of her lips off my face. She had survived. Sure; it was easy for her to say that. Spectacular breakdown on the night of the momentous birthday aside, Jenni had her life a hell of a lot more figured out than I did. She wasn't the one questioning all of her life choices as the clock ticked down. Like a damn magnet, my eyes were drawn to its cruel face once again. Three minutes to go.

Balls.

I glanced over my shoulder (maybe, unconsciously, to see if I could make a beeline for the door and out run time) and felt my breath catch. Now, I'm not a gal to be too taken by a pretty face. My luck with the male half of the species has always been spotty. My most recent string of good on the outside but rotten on the inside online dating hook-ups had caused me to swear off the other half of the species entirely, for the time being. While I accepted my self-imposed perma-single status with cranky resignation, that hadn't affected my ability to appreciate a fine specimen when I saw one—and the finest I had ever laid eyes upon had just walked in the door.

He must have been at least six foot two, long and lean like a swimmer, and was dressed with that kind of bad boy edge that never fails to make me do a double-take. Worn brown leather bomber jacket? Check. Ass-kicking combat boots? Check. Dark denim that hugged him in all the right places? Double check. Thick, caramel colored hair fell in waves down to his shoulders, framing out high cheekbones and a pouty set of lips that could easily have graced the cover of a romance novel. This guy was the stuff of most red-blooded women's fantasies. Or, this red-blooded woman's fantasy, anyhow. His head was turned away from me as he scanned the bar, as if searching for someone, so I let myself stare for a moment. Hell, it was my birthday and I was half in the bag; I could oogle the man-candy if I wanted to.

Unfortunately, he wasn't alone. A petite little thing peeked out from behind him, her eyes also roving the room. As if she felt me looking at them, her head jerked in my direction and I was surprised to see how young she was. In addition to being short and rail-thin, she had long, pale blonde hair with blunt cut bangs, which made her heavily lined eyes stand out all that much more—and the look those eyes gave me was downright suspicious. I returned her stare with an incredulous look of my own. She didn't look anywhere near old enough to be that guy's date, let alone old enough to be out in a bar at midnight but; whatever. I got the hint. It wasn't my business anyhow. I jerked my head in the distracted man's direction and gave her an appreciative wink. Her eyes widened and her hand gripped his arm. From where I was sitting, she sounded high and breathy, which only reinforced my opinion of her age. "Kaine, I think that woman can see me!"

I looked away and choked down a laugh. It was a little late for her to be worrying about being caught sneaking in, under age. How had she even gotten past the door in the first place? I glanced over at the door. Rodrigo had his back to me but; nope, he hadn't left the gate unguarded. If he was getting lazy with checking the IDs again, he was going to be in some deep shit. I rose a fraction of an inch off my stool, full of good intentions, but a clatter on the bar in front of me drew my attention. Mr. Hottie, his jailbait companion, Rodrigos's laziness—all were forgotten. Jenni had returned but instead of a steaming cup of coffee, she had brought out a big cupcake, complete with a lit candle sticking up from its mound of buttercream frosting. "Happy birthday bestie! Make a wish!"

I glanced up at the clock, open-mouthed with the intent to protest, and froze. The minute hand had already struck midnight. As I watched, it clicked over to 12:01.

I felt my stomach drop.

"Jesus, Cat! You're white as a sheet—are you all right?"

For a moment, everything threatened to go dark. I kept a firm grip on the edge of the bar while the wave of dizziness washed over me. The room suddenly felt thirty degrees warmer, though a cold sweat had broken out on my palms. A pounding headache slammed into me all like a freight train. The dim mood lighting seemed to grow a million times brighter for just a brief second, lining everything and everyone in a strange, fuzzy golden glow. My stomach churned and, for a moment, I feared it was ready to return Jenni's generous alcoholic gifts—but I certainly wasn't going to admit that. I'm no stranger to the Porcelain Goddess and have had my share of nights bowing before her, praying for her to do away with my sorry ass quickly, but I'd never had trouble handling a few drinks. If I wasn't able to keep down four measly glasses of wine, I would just have to take myself out into the woods and shoot myself.

So, instead of confessing to the wussy way I was handling turning thirty—or, even worse, to holding my liquor—I flashed her a weak smile. "Yeah, I'm fine. Just a little shock to the system, hittin' that big 3-0. Guess I know now why you spent the first twenty minutes of your birthday locked in a stall at eXstasy."

Jenni's eyes narrowed and her lips pursed. Despite the glare, her tone was playful with resignation. "You are *never* going to let me live that down are you?"

My answering smile aimed for angelic, complete with a batting of the eyelashes. "Nope, not until you do something even more pathetic on your fortieth."

She rolled her eyes and chuckled. "Bitch. Make a wish and blow out your candle before you get wax in the yummy frosting."

I've always taken things like wishes very seriously. I've probably wished on the first star I see in the evening hundreds of times over the years, and I've always given a lot of thought to the last thing that crosses my mind before blowing out the candles on my cake—or in this case, the delicious red velvet cupcake. I can remember quite a few birthdays in my youth where my mother would get exasperated over how long I was taking to make the big blow, holding the whole family up from devouring the slowly melting ice cream cake. (That never mattered much to me, as I was never a fan of ice cream cake. I only ever enjoyed the chocolate crunchy bits they used to separate the vanilla and chocolate layers.)

So, making a wish on one of the landmark birthdays in my life wasn't easy. Especially when there were dozens of things I wanted. It was probably a little late to wish to be taller, but it would be nice to have a car that didn't rattle like it was going to go to pieces whenever I turned a corner. Or to have a boyfriend who lasted for more than a few months and who wasn't constantly between jobs, begging me for gas money every week. Oh—and it would be nice if he didn't call me Lisa on our last night in bed together. That would be great. Maybe even a new job, where my boss wasn't a useless asshat and I wasn't bored to tears every day. Or, at the very least, a raise so I wouldn't have to live off ramen noodles every summer when the office cut back our hours.

So many choices. None of them were really all that realistic, of course, but all were equally important to me. Besides, wishing for a sale at Coach so I could get that cute little red patent leather bag I'd been mooning over for months didn't really feel like an appropriate wish for such a momentous occasion. Feeling a little reckless—and not to mention still a bit dizzy—I left it up to that bitch called Fate and let my thoughts coalesce on their own as I closed my eyes and blew out the tiny flame: *Please let me figure out who I am.*

CHAPTER TWO

Huh. Where did that come from?

That had been rather a surprising summation to my litany of pie-in-the-sky wishes. Of course, it made perfect sense, even without the hindsight. Being lost in the proverbial forest of life minus a helpful trail of breadcrumbs was pretty much my M.O. Having a clue what to do next, to maybe finally improve my boring, broke-ass life would be nice. I could be satisfied with a birthday wish like that.

Jenni produced a knife from under the bar. She plucked the extinguished candle out with one hand while the other neatly sliced the cupcake in two.

"Mmm, this is totally the best part of birthdays," she proclaimed around a mouthful of the sweet treat.

I took a tentative bite, making sure not to miss out on all that gooey frosting, and was thankful that my settling stomach welcomed its deliciousness. The cake was soft and moist, with just a hint of cocoa, and I was a sucker for all that rich, sinfully sweet vanilla buttercream. My half was devoured in a shameful amount of time. "Holy crap that was good. Calories don't count on birthdays, right?"

"Nope." To prove her point, Jenni licked the remaining icing off of the candle. Her mouth thinned into a line as she looked at me. "You're still a little pale. Are you sure you're all right?"

I shrugged and made a show of looking down at my arms. "Me, pale? How could you tell?" She rolled her eyes at me again but that frown didn't go away. I said, "I'm fine. Promise. Apparently I'm just too old to be out drinking past midnight anymore."

"Psh—there's no such thing. I'm living proof. It's like riding a bicycle or something. You fall off? You just get right back on."

"I think that one is about never forgetting how to do something or other, but close enough." My stomach was happy now that is was filled with the fuel of a major sugar rush, but my headache dug in its heels, threatening to split my cranium open if I moved too fast. The freaky migraine-halo glow around everything had died down, but I sensed a date with a hefty dose of Excedrin in my future.

Jenni disposed of the plate and pulled out a damp rag to wipe up the evidence of our little calorie splurge off the bar. "Can I get you that coffee or do you need to go?"

I pulled my cellphone from my pocket and considered my options. Tomorrow was going to suck, no two ways about it. My boss was going to be her usual useless self, talking about her damn kids all day to whatever poor soul she could waylay, while the rest of our tiny four-person department answered a zillion phone lines. Nothing would change that. An extra hour or two of sleep might help keep me from strangling her with her own headset for another day, however. I shook my head. "Nah, I better go. Besides, I think the shock of getting old has sobered me up."

Her mock-pout still lacked the sympathy I thought I deserved. She said, "Not old, just older. Gimmie a sec. I'll call you a cab."

I turned around in my seat and slowly scanned the bar in hopes that I would catch another glimpse of the nearly forgotten Mr. Hottie's backside one more time. No dice. It appeared that he and his little friend had ducked out while I had been busy trying not to yack on my birthday cupcake. Perhaps his little friend had gotten cold feet. Fake ID or no, she hadn't been fooling anyone. Well, except maybe Rodrigo. Which reminded me...

I slipped off my stool and took a moment to curse myself for wearing heels. They were so not my thing—give me sneakers any day—and Jenni's insistence that I wear them seemed even dumber now, since they certainly hadn't helped me land any male companionship throughout the night. I retrieved my cute little burgundy leather jacket from the rack at the end of the bar and waved her back over before shrugging into it. "I'm gonna go to talk to Rodrigo for a minute, then I'll wait outside. Some fresh air might not be the worst idea."

She came around the bar and engulfed me in a big hug. "Okay. Text me when you get home so I know you got there safe, okay?"

I planted a big ol' sloppy kiss on her cheek before letting her go. "You bet. Thanks for everything. You're the best."

She batted her eyelashes and held a hand to her forehead in her best swooning damsel impression. "I know. I am, aren't I? You're just so darn lucky to have me."

"Totally am. Talk to you later." After another quick hug, I made my way carefully to the door, stopping to lean casually against the wall of the alcove where Rodrigo was glued to his phone. The sight of a big, burly guy who was tattooed from head to toe playing Angry Birds with furious concentration made me smile. I cleared my throat. "That's a dangerous game you're playing there. I've heard it's a hard addiction to ditch once you start."

Without looking up, he smirked. "Damn right. Blame the wife. She put it on my damn phone." He scowled at the glowing screen. "Stupid game." He slipped the phone back into his pocket. "Hey, it's your birthday isn't it?"

I groaned. "Don't remind me."

He laughed. "Yeah, they stop being fun this late in the game don't they? Happy birthday anyhow." Despite my whining, I accepted his hug with good grace.

"Thanks." I liked Rodrigo. He and his wife Sarah were good people, and they had their first baby on the way. Mr. Gilroy was a pretty easy going boss, from what Jenni told me, but if he caught word of anyone underage in his bar, it would be Rodrigo's ass on the line. "Hey, I know it's none of my business, but what was the deal with that girl who came in here earlier? She looked waaaaay too young, no matter what her ID said."

He gave me a puzzled look. "What girl?"

"She was in here about five, maybe ten, minutes ago, with some tall, not-so-dark and handsome hottie." I described them both and watched his look of confusion deepen.

"I remember the dude, but he didn't have a girl with him."

"Really? Maybe she slipped in after him or something? It definitely looked like she was with him. She got all freaked out when she saw me looking at her." I was a bit lit, true, but I didn't think I was drunk enough to start imaging that sort of shit. I turned back to scan the bar again, hoping I had been wrong and they were tucked away at one of the tables in the dark corners. "Sorry, Jenni distracted me with a cupcake. Maybe they left after I spooked her."

"Shit, that's all I need right now." Rodrigo stood and gave my shoulder a squeeze. "Thanks for the heads up. I'll take a look around and make sure."

If he hadn't been so engaged in flinging little red birds at pigs, he might have been more up to speed on who was coming and going—but I kept that thought to myself. Feeling pretty noble for having my good deed of the night, I waved goodbye to Jenni and turned toward the door just as it opened inward. Perhaps if I had been one less sheet to the wind I could have avoided slamming head-on into the poor stranger who came through the door, but that was so not the case given my wobbly state. I grabbed a handful of the guy's coat to keep from bouncing off his rather solid chest and falling to the floor, though it was a near thing. I righted myself fairly quickly and tried to brush the tangled mess of my hair out of my eyes as I looked up at the newcomer. "Sorry about that! I'm usually not this cl—"

The words died in my throat. Fear alone kept me from jerking back and falling flat on my ass. I went rigid as my mind tried to process what it was seeing. Towering a good foot and a half above me, there was nothing human in the face that looked down at me. Ringed by a shaggy mane of thick, black hair, the proportions of his head were all wrong. The jaw hung too low and the forehead bulged like a shelf above deeply sunken, piggy eyes. His deeply wrinkled skin was the mottled blue-gray of a week old corpse pulled from the river. My stomach dropped for the second time that night.

I looked back over my shoulder, trying to keep the panic off my face while hoping to see someone coming to my aid. Jenni and Rodrigo were chatting by the end of the bar, caught up in some tale that involved a lot of spastic arm-waving on Jenni's part. The couple seated at the closest table returned my stare with puzzled looks of their own for only a split second before returning to their intimate conversation. No one seemed phased by the hulking Neanderthal blocking my path.

My brain screamed *Oh my God, oh my God!* and tried to run and hide in the corner of my cranium, but a calm, collected center I was surprised to find I still had deep inside took over. It told me to keep my cool and not lose my shit. Something seriously fucked up was going down and, given the calm of everyone else in the bar, I had the inkling that that thing might be me. I turned back. My voice cracked, but I kept it from trembling too much. "Sorry there, sir. Didn't mean to run into you like that. I might have had a few too many tonight." It was a struggle to keep my ditzy grin from faltering, but I played it up like a champ.

He cocked his head to the side like a puzzled dog, and I took that moment to edge around him toward the door. He turned slowly, never letting me out of his sight. Those dark, piggy eyes seemed to be all pupils, with no whites to speak of. His massive nostrils flared as he leaned in and sniffed at me, jowls wagging with each deep breath. His mannerisms were so bizarre, so canine, that they made my skin crawl.

"That's a killer mask by the way. Super realistic." It had to be a mask, my piss-scared mind reasoned. He was just a day early, that's all. Must be a real Halloween lover. A pasty, stinky, seven foot tall Halloween lover. All of that was thought in the most hysterical tone an internal monologue can muster, I'm sure. And, of course, I didn't believe a word of it. It seemed to take forever before I felt the reassuring solidity of the door against my palms. I yanked it hard and kept that smile plastered on my face. "Happy, uh, pre-Halloween. Sorry again for, you know, running in to you and all. Have a nice night!"

I backed out on to the sidewalk and yanked the door shut as quick as I could. My hands remained clenched on the handle, like I was somehow going to hold the damn thing shut against a hulking Goliath like that. My head whipped about, frantically searching for the cab, a cop, a passerby—

anything. My former tipsiness was good and gone but my legs were shaking like they would give out at any moment. My fortitude was so not improved by the utterly fucking vacant state of the street. Just me, a handful of empty, parked cars and two street lamps for as far as the eye could see.

Shit, shit, shit.

The door was pulled open and I let go to avoid being sucked in with it. I stumbled back, forgetting my already precarious balance, and tripped over my own feet in a pathetic attempt to keep myself upright. I went down on my ass, yelping from both from the pain and the cold wetness of the puddle I had landed in as it instantly seeped through my jeans. Goliath stood over me and I got a real good look at his Herman Munster sized shit-kickers. He glared down at me with those black, beady eyes. Huge, jagged teeth were revealed as it barked something at me. His voice sounded like marbles being crushed in a steel vice. I wanted to throw up. I couldn't make out a damn word but I was pretty sure he wasn't speaking English.

I scooted myself back inch by inch toward the street, pain forgotten, trying to put distance between myself and the demonic pyscho. If my eyes had widened any more, my eyeballs would have fallen out of my skull. I was pretty sure if I showed fear in the face of this thing, it would be just as bad as showing it to a wild animal, but I failed to keep the shrill note of hysteria out of my voice. "Look, I'm really sorry but I can't understand you. I don't speak... whatever the hell it is you're speaking!"

Panic, apparently, did not do a damn thing to temper my smart-ass gene.

He let out a deep Rottweiler-like growl and took another step forward. He straddled me with ease and this time there was obvious rage in his tone, though his fast, guttural words were no clearer. I shook my head in small, quick jerks, afraid to take my eyes off him for too long. The remaining foot and a half to the street seemed miles long. Where the fuck was that cab? "I said I can't understand you, buddy. Please, just let me go. Whoever you are, I don't want any trouble. I can forget I ever saw you, trust me!"

With another low, angry sounding growl, he reached down for me. A hand the size of a dinner-plate grabbed me by the front of my jacket and hauled me up into the air like I weighed nothing at all. I screamed long and loud, hoping someone—any-freaking-one—would hear me and come to my rescue. I clenched my hands in the lapels of my jacket and yanked on them, struggling to keep it from tightening around my throat. My legs dangled in the air and I kicked at him with all my strength, but it was like kicking a brick wall. I was pretty sure I hurt my foot more than I hurt him.

The creature held me up, his face only inches from mine, and I gagged at the rotten meat stench of his breath. Those large, canine-like teeth appeared again as his fleshy lips spread into what I can only describe as a grin. A horrible, predatory, movie monster grin. The world was spinning. I closed my eyes and held my breath, trying to work up another scream.

"Put her down."

Goliath turned his head, his ragged, matted mane of coarse black hair blocking my view of whatever brave soul had come out of the shadows. A dark, ugly rumbling rose from inside the beast and it took me a moment to realize that he was laughing. I squirmed with renewed vigor, trying to free myself from my coat while it was distracted, but it was no use. I had the upper body strength of an inchworm and he had me held tight. It was getting hard to breathe. I gasped out, "Please, get help! Call the police!"

Goliath said something again in that broken glass voice, and this time I could have sworn it sounded like he was mocking my unseen knight in shining armor.

The out-of-view stranger was not deterred. "I said, put her down. Now."

Oh brave, stupid soul. I had the sinking feeling we'd both meet our ends soon, smeared across the sidewalk by this crazy freak of nature. As if some part of my thoughts were heard—and not the good part, either—the meaty paw that held me up in the air opened and let me go. I fell to the concrete in a heap and felt a burst of agony blaze as my head bounced off the ground.

Then everything went dark.

CHAPTER THREE

Waking up from taking a knock to the head wasn't anything like I expected it would be. In the movies, our plucky hero (or the swooning damsel; take your pick) comes to slowly; blinking groggily, with everything before their eyes all bright and fuzzy. Maybe they moan a bit from the pain in their head, maybe not; depends on the flick. Then, as they blink faster, the colors deepen and the details around them start to come into focus. Someone appears from downstage to cluck and coo, telling them to remain still because they've just taken a nasty spill. Of course that person either is a doctor or someone will shortly leave to get our hero the doctor…

Yeah—so not how it happened.

There was no gauzy curtain that had to be cleared from my lens; not even a sad, pathetic whimper to alert my awaiting friend/lover/doctor to my awakening. Instead, my eyes sprang open and I found myself staring up at a white ceiling. A section just a few inches to the right of me was peeling in a familiar diamond-shaped pattern. It made sense that it was familiar, as it was the ceiling above my bed in the crappy little apartment I had lived in for the past six years. I tilted my head slowly to the side. Ever so slightly, mind you—the teeny-est, tiny-est movement—and waited for that runaway train impact of pain in the back of my skull.

Only, none came. I raised a hand and tucked it under my head. I felt around with gentle fingers, expecting a lump or some icky, sticky blood or something but… Nope. Nothing but regular, old sleep-tangled hair. I scrunched my nose up in confusion and muttered, "What the…?"

I was in my own bed, without any evidence of having gotten the crack to the head I clearly remembered getting. I laid there for a good minute and recounted the events of the night. No one in Gilroy's had shown any interest in the ugly brute as he came through the door. Even the people closest to me had just given me a weird look, like I was that crazy girl at the bar making a scene. I wondered if, perhaps, I had been. Maybe I had hallucinated the whole thing. Jenni's hand had been the only one to touch my drinks other than my own, which ruled out someone having slipped me something, but there was that sudden, explosive migraine that had nearly knocked me off my barstool. It, like my earlier buzz, was also gone (of course) but I remembered *that* pretty clearly. Had I suffered a bursting aneurysm or something? Did those even cause hallucinations? At one in the morning, after the night I had just had (or maybe only thought I had just had) the possibility of a solid medical reason for my bizarre night seemed strangely comforting.

I pushed myself up on my elbows and looked around. I was still fully dressed, the rumpled sheets beneath me just as I had left them that morning. My purse and Jenni's God-awful stilettos were on the floor by the nightstand, as if carelessly tossed. Granted, that was not as neat as I normally would have been with my expensive bag and borrowed goods, but it was not out of the realm of possibility given the combination of liquor and brain bleed. (The likelihood of having suffered some sort of hemorrhage was all but certain to me at that moment.) The room around me was mostly dark—a sidelong glance saw the deep of night outside the window—but the lamp on my dresser was casting a dull circle of light across the foot of the bed. A faint glow reached down the hallway outside my wide-open bedroom door and I recognized it as the familiar blush of my living room lamp left on. The faint murmur of voices told me that I had left the TV on as well.

I swung my legs over the edge of the bed and sat up, scowling. I had a lot of unanswered questions. How the hell had I gotten home? Had I passed out on the street like a drunk? Had someone peeled me up off the sidewalk and poured me into the cab? Or had I somehow stumbled into it on my own, barely coherent? Had the cabbie had to endure some freaky ranting about a terrible super-goon the whole way home? I scrubbed my face with my hands. I couldn't even face the worst question of them all: how bad would Jenni rip into me after she heard about this?

I couldn't make sense of it all. The harder I tried to wrap my brain around it, the less I cared. I was alive. I was home. And while it was probably a good idea to call my doctor in the morning for the next available appointment to get my noggin looked at, the danger I had thought I had been in appeared to have been all in my head. (Because as much as I kind of sort of wanted to believe my brain had gone all loopy on me, my gut told me I'd be feeling a hell of a lot worse if I were in that sort of mortal peril.) I was exhausted. The mere thought of the alarm going off in just a few hours made me want to weep big, fat baby tears. Whatever had happened, it was likely to result in embarrassment of monumental proportions, and I wasn't up to the amount of self-loathing such antics deserved at the moment. I could chastise myself over my morning combo of coffee and cereal.

I briefly considered a shower—I felt gross—but the will to follow through did not manifest. I resigned myself to an extra-large helping of self-reproach over breakfast and shrugged out of my jacket. A hanger seemed too difficult to unearth; the doorknob would have to do for one night. As I watched its weight settle against the door, I pulled out my earrings and tossed them on the dresser. The rest of my jewelry quickly followed, forming a small heap. My sweater was tossed in the corner that doubled as a hamper, leaving me in a tank top and leggings; close enough to pajamas for me. Getting to the bra was too much work though. I was going to hate myself for all sorts of things come morning—what was another smidgen for pulling an all-nighter going to matter? The living room light beckoned, though the TV had gone quiet. Maybe I had had the forethought to set the sleep timer. That would be just like me; too messed up to take off my damn coat but remembering to preserve the sanctity of my cherished 42" flat-screen.

I turned right and checked the front door first, shocked to find I had had the wherewithal to throw both locks on the door. Mentally patting myself on the back, I padded back down the hall, past the bedroom and darkened kitchen doorway, making a pit stop in the closet-sized bathroom. A look in the mirror only brought more bewilderment to the party. Though I had expected raccoon eyes and a smudge or two of sidewalk grime, my face was clean. Apparently I had also had the presence of mind to wash up before passing out fully clothed. That pretty much clinched the Leaking Blood Vessel In My Cranium hypothesis. Never on a stumble-drunk night had I ever remembered to take off my mascara before falling into bed. Come to think of it... I looked down at my hands. Yup; they were clean as a whistle too. This was getting weirder and weirder. Maybe I hadn't passed out on the street after all. Hell, maybe I had never made it to the street. Oh good God, what if I had passed out *in* the bar? I could forget a few years of mockery. Jenni would be regaling my grandchildren with the Tale of Granny Cat's Wild 30th B-day Meltdown.

I could hardly blame her. I had been ribbing her mercilessly about her own antics for months and months. I knew it was wrong but I couldn't help myself. She was just so much damn better than me at everything that I kind of had to latch on to the one moment of fail I could tease her with. She was my bestie and I wasn't supposed to feel so bitter about how much more pulled together her life was when compared to mine, but I couldn't help it. While not glamorous by any means, she had a decent thing going at Gilroy's. It paid the bills and gave her the time she needed to follow her real dream—singing. I had known since we were teenagers that she would be something big one day. She had a glow about her that attracted people in droves, including Anthony, the handsome and devoted marine whom I had a hunch would be presenting her with a ring when he returned from overseas. And why not? She was all around awesome. Friendly. Loyal. Easy-going. Fun. Not to mention a natural blond with gorgeously tanned skin and a rack I would kill for. Maybe if I had known what a talented knock-out that gangly teen with braces would grow up to be, I would have reconsidered my choice of a best friend in high school.

That's a load of crap, of course, but I'd be lying if I said that evil little thought hadn't crossed my mind once or twice over the years, usually while staring morosely in the mirror. After all, I came in at a whopping 5'3" with the complexion of our ghostly friend Casper and was almost embarrassed to let the ladies at Victoria's Secret see the lack of cup sizes I was buying. I glared at my reflection. My face was just a little too long, my nose a touch too thin. Mousy would be an accurate word to describe me, and it certainly felt fitting.

Sure, some called my pale blue eyes, with their thick, dark lashes and my equally black hair striking, but I had always thought it was a combination more suited to those creepy porcelain dolls than a living, breathing person. That unintentional goth-girl look was the source of the "black sheep of the family" jokes my dad had been telling for longer than I cared to remember. (Was goth even a thing anymore? Was I aging myself even more by saying that?) Those darling quips had fallen flat years ago—probably right around the time I became an awkward teen who realized there was no growth spurt in sight and I that I was getting no curves to speak of—but it was hard to deny, however bad the pun. Aside from having inherited his fair Irish complexion and the inherent inability to tan, I looked nothing like him. Or my mom. Or my curvy, spitting image of mom and dad could-do-no-wrong little sister, Emma.

There was that dark side again. Good going brain. I splashed my face with another round of cold water, ignoring the sting in my eyes. I could chalk those dark, depressing emotions and the tears they summoned up to the booze I had pounded back all evening, but I wasn't fooling anyone. Especially myself. I pulled a face at myself in the mirror as I clicked the light off. I stuffed my feet in the worn, plush froggy slippers I kept by the linen closet—the hardwood of the living/dining room was unbearably cold in the morning—and shuffled into the living room. I reached up for the pull-cord of the floor lamp behind my couch and froze as my poor, abused brain wracked itself to make sense of the scene in front of me.

My couch was not empty. Nor, a quick glance determined, was the battered old recliner under my window. And hell, why not add the dude standing in front of my fireplace to the tally? My eyes bounced back and forth between the three strangers like a ping-pong ball, my mind refusing to catch up. It took a moment before I recognized the girl in the chair and the guy leaning against my mantle as Mr. Hottie and jailbait; the couple I had seen earlier at Gilroy's.

Right before they disappeared mysteriously.

And I was attacked by Goliath the monster.

Lovely.

The woman on the couch was the only one I didn't recognize. She was middle aged; gentle and motherly looking in her violet cardigan and dark blue jeans. As she peered up at me, her heart-shaped face framed by waves of rich brown hair that matched her big, doe eyes, an unexpected calm filled me. I lowered my hand from the lamp cord, leaving the light on. Of course, the urge to run for the phone, screaming bloody murder crossed my mind but—somehow—it didn't seem to be the appropriate course of action. Maybe it was the desire to find the missing puzzle piece of how I had gotten home from the bar that overrode my fight-or-flight instinct. Maybe it was that not one of them had moved or spoken, and that all three looked just as uncomfortable as I thought I should feel. Or maybe I was still half-convinced my brain had sprung a gasket and I was hallucinating. Again.

Whatever the reason, instead of losing my shit I calmly gripped the back of the couch to steady myself and said a prayer of thanks that I hadn't stripped down to my panties before coming out of the bedroom. (Score one for skanky laziness.) I looked at them each in turn once more and cleared my throat. "So. Someone want to catch me up on what's going on here?"

Maybe if the situation had been just a little less weird I would have found the baffled looks the three of them exchanged comical. I understood their surprise. Really, I did. No one in their right mind would expect a single gal not to freak out if she awoke from a nap to find a trio of strangers in her living room. Of course, I don't know if anyone in their right mind would put themselves to be in the position of being said strangers either. I mean, what if I had been some gun toting right-wing nutbag? Riverview wasn't a rough city, per say, but there was a high enough crime rate that the idea had crossed my mind once or twice.

Finally, it seemed that the burden of answering me fell upon the older of the two women. She twisted around on the couch, once again looking up at me. Her smile was hesitant as she said, "Please, do not be frightened." Her voice was low and soft, like verbal velvet. "My name is Seana." She gestured to the others in turn. "The young lady is Mairi, and the gentleman over there is Kaine."

I digested those names for a moment. Weird ones, to be sure, but it was a weird situation all around so they almost seemed fitting. I might have been more surprised to find a Bob, Carol and Suzy waiting around for me to wake up, like we were old friends. Seana had fallen silent and I realized that all three of them were staring at me again, as if I were expected to do some sort of trick. I cleared my throat. "Well, that's great. Nice to meet you all. I'm Catlin, but I have the feeling one of you took a look in my wallet—

which better still have the last three dollars I have to my name in it—and you already knew that."

"Yes, ah, we did." Seana's cheeks colored a bit. She was one of those women who could blush prettily. "We crossed paths with you outside of the bar. After Kaine scared off the troll, we tried to rouse you but you were unconscious from the spill you had taken. When the taxi arrived, we thought it best not to send you off alone in such a state."

"That's nice of you." That right there put a big hole in my hallucination theory. If they had seen the… "Wait, did you say the *troll?*"

Seana didn't so much as blink. "Yes."

My stare had to have accused her of having three heads, but she didn't look the least bit ruffled. I, on the other hand, had begun to regret not making a beeline for the phone straight off. "Okay," I said slowly, drawing out the word. "You mean 'troll' as in the whiny Internet variety, right?"

"I'm sorry?" Her brow furrowed in a delicately befuddled sort of way. "I'm afraid I do not understand."

"I guess not then." I wondered what word was tripping her up. I had the sinking feeling that this gentle, motherly looking woman had no inkling of current slang. Hell, she might not even be aware of the existence of the Internet. "You said that freak who attacked me was a troll."

Seana nodded. Both of her companions were watching me with matching deadpan stares. If this was a joke of some sort, they were playing along remarkably well. Somehow, I didn't think they were acting. "And by that you mean an actual 'lives under a bridge, threatening to eat poor little billy goats' kind of troll?"

Her smile was the sad sort usually reserved for mental patients, making me feel like the crazy one for having to clarify what kind of troll she was talking about in the first place. She patted my hand where it rested on the back of the couch. "As you have seen from the one that crossed your path, trolls are a nasty sort, though they do not commonly stray from their colonies. Their rarity in these lands is a boon, seeing how easily they are given to violence. They often seek out… *larger* prey than the livestock featured in the myths your people tell."

"My people." She nodded again when I paused, as if in encouragement. My knees were starting to feel a bit weak and I wondered if I should have taken my head wound—missing state notwithstanding—a bit more seriously. "And that would make you…?"

"We are Aos Sí, the descendants of the Tuatha Dé Danann." It was the young woman who spoke; the pale waif Seana had called Mairi. She sat statue still in the exact center of my recliner, perched on the very edge of its seat with her hands folded in her lap. Teenage looks aside, when she met my stare it was with unwavering sureness. There was something frighteningly old about the eyes that gazed back at me. As I stared her down, her eyes seemed to change colors, flashing from hazel to a shimmering yellow. A chill ran down my spine.

Not wanting to stand there with my mouth hanging open like a complete tool, I managed, "That's, uh, Irish right?"

"Yes, of a fashion. Mairi speaks the truth. We are the descendants of an ancient race who once lived side by side with the ancestors of humanity, most notably on the Emerald Isle. It has been many ages since those days. So long, I'm afraid, that your people have long since come to think of us as myth. Those who remember us call us fae," Seana said.

"Fae." The word sounded ridiculous coming out of my mouth. "Like…faeries?"

She bristled. Her disapproval seemed to ripple around the room in a wave through the others. "Yes, if strictly speaking, but there are many connotations with that word that we would rather avoid. We much prefer the term 'fae,' please."

"Oh, sorry. I guess that makes sense. I mean, who in their right mind would want to be associated with Tinker Bell, right? And I don't see any wings or a bag of magic pixie dust on any of you." My mouth was getting ahead of my brain again. The nervous giggle that escaped me probably wasn't helping my cause much.

Seana's smile seemed a tad bit forced, which I assumed meant my jokes were not going over well. "Ah, yes. I'm afraid your modern culture has some skewed perceptions of us. We have been relegated to bedtime stories and cartoons. Too few remember the old myths these days, which are much closer to the truth."

"And that… 'troll'? He was also fae?" Good lord, those words sounded crazy rolling off my tongue.

She nodded. "Fae is what one might call our entire species, much as you are human. Trolls, shape-shifters, elves, merfolk, ogres, Aos Sí —we are all faekind. Such races had interbred with our own over the centuries, giving many of us mixed heritages, again much like modern-day humanity. Some of us may pass for what you would think of as human, even without a glamour, while others… Well, they cannot walk among humanity without it."

"Sure, sure." My eyes darted around the room. Not a single smirk or knowing wink among them. They were all damn near expressionless; as serious as the brain tumor I was so wishing I had.

Have you ever had that sudden, sinking feeling in the pit of your stomach when you realize someone you formerly thought was messing with you… wasn't? Or, maybe you even just had hoped that they were deluded and grasping at straws? You know; that gut churning, I just ate too much fast food kind of feeling that hits you when it becomes crystal clear that they really believe what they're saying. No matter how sad or wrong or just plain bat-crap crazy it sounds to you, they believe every single word that has come out of their mouths. Of course, that means you only have two choices: to be the dream-smasher who breaks the cold hard reality to them, or to be the poor sap who keeps a big fake-ass smile on your face while nodding agreeably and looking for the nearest exit before shit gets ugly.

This situation had obviously just become the latter.

CHAPTER FOUR

Saviors or not, the whole situation was too weird for me. I was only partially aware of my death-grip on the back of the couch as I berated myself for having failed to panic earlier, when it might have done me some good. (Obviously, I had never been good at making the correct life decisions.) As they watched me digest Seana's little speech about their freaky mythical nature, I wondered just how much of a chance I stood if I were to turn tail and tear-ass down the hall. Could I reach my phone before one of them tackled me? Who would I even call if I did? Would 911 send someone to the rescue of a girl being held hostage by fairies?

"She doesn't believe you." Mairi's breathy little voice was maddeningly calm. Her eyes bore into me. There was something hypnotic about that shifting gaze. It was almost inhuman in its detachment. I felt naked. "She is frightened of us."

Goddamn, she gave me the shivers. Faeries or crazies, there was definitely something beyond weird about these people. I blurted out, "Can you read my mind?"

Mairi cocked her head to the side, the corners of her mouth upturning in the tiniest of smiles. "I read emotions, not thoughts. My gift doesn't work on you but I don't need it, to tell what you're thinking. You look scared."

"Oh." Well, duh. While that didn't make me feel any better, it was probably true. Having never been cornered by fae folk in my own home before, I suppose my poker-face wasn't up to snuff for such a situation. Trying to tread waters that had gone way above my head, I settled for dumbly echoing the things my slow human brain wasn't capable of processing on its own. "What do you mean you 'read emotions'?"

"Mairi is an oracle," Seana said, pulling my attention back over to her. "She sometimes sees events that have yet to pass. Her gift also makes her sensitive to the emotions of others, allowing her to interpret them as easily as you and I converse with words."

"Well, that sounds…" I struggled to find the right word. Interesting? Unique? Downright crazy? "Nifty. And are you all…?"

"Not precisely. All Aos Sí possess such powers, passed down through our ancestral bloodlines, but there are many different Gifts. I myself am a Healer." I raised a hand to the back of my head as she said that. She smiled and nodded. "I took the liberty of taking care of that lump you took while you were sleeping." A chagrined look came over her face. "I hope I did not overstep in doing so."

"No, uh, thanks. You'll never hear me complain about not waking up with a concussion." Mairi was still staring at me and I found my gaze drawn back to her. "You said your gift wouldn't work on me. Why?"

"You have the Warding."

I stared at her blankly. That explained absolutely nothing. I took a deep breath and tried to keep calm. Trying to make sense of this nuttiness, trying to understand these three wackos, was about as easy as pulling teeth and I had never been the most patient gal. "And that would be…?"

"It's your Gift. It prevents mine from working on you," she said as calmly as someone stating the irrefutable fact that the sky was blue.

Okay. So, that water wasn't just only over my head; it had gone ball-shriveling cold. I felt the hair on my arms raise as a chill swept over me. "Excuse me—did you just say *my* Gift?"

"It was how we knew you were the one we have been searching for. You saw through my glamour inside the pub, and again through that of the troll." Mairi smiled. "Only someone Gifted with the Warding could do that."

I phrased my come back with delicate deliberateness, "And what the flying fuck, may I ask, is 'the Warding'?"

"It is our most rare Gift, one that has all but died out among our people. Other fae Gifts cannot be used upon a Warder—such as your being able to see through the magic that should have kept Mairi hidden from sight, or the similar enchantment that would have made that troll look human to those who laid eyes upon him," Seana explained. "In the days of old, Warders were the right hand of royalty. They guarded the king from magical subterfuge and advised him on many matters of great importance. Given its power, those who possessed the Warding were long ago hunted to extinction. Or so we thought."

"Hunted." Well, wasn't this fairytale getting better and better? I cleared my throat. "Lovely. Dare I ask by who?"

Seana looked away, chagrin writ on her all too expressive face. "Our people were not always united as they are now. Once, there was some credence to the common misconception of the fae being divided into warring factions of good and evil. Granted, as with much, things may not have been so clean cut but there were a great many years of unrest among us. The Warders of old became mistrusted by both sides, for the immunity their bloodline gave them. Those who were not killed in the Great War fled across the Veil, to hide here among the humans."

My stomach tightened up in knots. I desperately wanted to call bullshit on the wild story they were weaving but something made me hold my tongue. Instead, I choked out, "Well, isn't that just great."

"They were dark times, thankfully long past. Many believe the Warders died out entirely during the wars, but Mairi had a vision that caused us to believe otherwise. She knew we would find one of their bloodline here, in your world."

"Which just happens to be little ol' me."

Mairi was gazing off into space as she mused aloud, "And you just might be the last of your line. We have been searching for years, but you're the first Warder we've found."

Just what I wanted to hear. "Wonderful. And that—this 'Warding'—is why she can't read me?"

Seana nodded. "Precisely."

Again I touched the back of my head with a tentative hand. "But then how—?"

"Gifts are a power born unto themselves. They have limitations, especially when newly formed. Your Gift is very new; a raw talent that needs to be honed. Right now, it is much like a child that slumbers deeply after a powerful exertion and, as such, it is active only when you are. The Gift does not yet know how to work when you are unconscious. Thus, I was able to heal you while you slept."

"Well that's a crap Catch-22," I said dryly.

"It will change, over time. As your mind adapts and learns to use the Warding unconsciously, the Gift will begin to strengthen. There will come a day when even sleep will not stop its protections—no fae magic will be able to work upon you."

I couldn't believe I was even entertaining the possibility of believing them, but the words kept tumbling out of my mouth without stopping to check in with my brain. "And just how would I have inherited this awesome and rare Gift?"

"Are you sure you're human?" Mairi asked, forehead scrunched up as she scrutinized me like a bug caught inside a glass jar.

"Mairi! That was rude." Seana's tone was that of a scolding mother. Mairi didn't look at all chastised, though she shrugged and mumbled something that could have been an apology. Seana flashed me an apologetic smile. "Someone in your family line was fae. The Gifts rarely emerge in children of mixed blood, especially in generations further away from the original source, so it is likely that it was someone quite recent."

"So you're telling me grandma was probably banging a fairy. And, thanks to her interspecies hanky-panky, I have some really nifty superpower that millions of people would kill me for—oh, and right now it doesn't do jack shit for me if I take a nap. Yet, somehow, I've gone my whole life without ever having the teeniest tiniest hint of being so super special and it just happens to happen to me twice in one night, right when you guys show up. Am I getting all this?"

"You turned thirty today."

My head whipped around. Kaine stood with his back to my mantle, staring at me with the most unsettling turquoise blue gaze I had ever seen. His golden-gravel voice resounded with the deep profoundness of a church bell, clearing the room of all conversation with just four words. It was the first time he had spoken all evening. In fact, I had almost—somehow—forgotten that he was there at all while his lady friends bombarded me with weirdness. My voice came out as a breathy rasp. "How did you know that?"

"Thirty is the age of majority for us. We live longer and age slower than humans," Seana explained, her eyes also on Kaine. He turned and went back to gazing out the window as if we were no longer in the room. "Our gifts first manifest when we come of age."

"You have got to be shitting me." They had finally maxed out my bullshit tolerance. I threw my hands up in the air. "How the hell can you expect me to believe *any* of this?"

"I know this must all sound very strange to you." Seana bit her lip. "You saw the troll for yourself—"

"No, I don't know I saw a 'troll.' I know I saw some hideous, psychotic chud, but he could have been some freaking inbred mountain man come down to the city to get his kicks for all I know." Rage made me oh-so eloquent. "Look, I don't know what the fuck this is or what crazy shit you guys are on, but this?" I waved my hands and gestured to all three of them. "This has stopped being funny."

Seana frowned, her June Cleaver face wrought with confusion. "I do not understand. No one here has made any jokes."

I stared at her for a good thirty seconds, mouth gaping open. She was gazing at me with innocent puzzlement, as serious as a heart attack. Was sarcasm foreign to her? My voice broke hit a hysterical octave and my hands flapped in the air, doing their own spastic freak-out dance. "I don't know what kind of sick game this was supposed to be but I've had enough. If you're going to splatter-paint the room with my guts, I'd rather you just got on with it!"

"Please, hear us out," she begged, spreading her hands in what I assumed was supplication. "I know this is a lot to take in and much of it must sound mad to you, but I assure you every word we speak it true. The awakening of your Gift may be frightening but I promise you we mean you no harm. We have spent many years searching for a Warder. I beg that you let us explain our plight."

I scrubbed at my face with both hands, fighting back the urge to scream in frustration. I wanted to say that this couldn't be happening to me—but it obviously was—or that they were out of their freaking minds—which was highly likely but debatable given the unusual and otherwise unexplainable events of the evening. Still; I couldn't swallow the pills they were selling. I crossed my arms across my chest and channeled every bit of do-not-fuck-with-me energy I had into my face. "Why the hell should I listen to one more insane word of this? Give me one good reason why I should believe anything you've said. Just give me one, *solid* thing that I can't chalk up to you all being bat-crap crazy!"

Seana took a deep breath. She looked down at her hands, clasped in her lap. Three heartbeats passed before she said, with that maddening, infinite calm, "Show her, Mairi."

The blonde girl scrunched up her nose and whined, "Do I have to?"

"Do as she asks." There was no room for arguing with Kaine's clipped tone. Another three words, yet he cleared the air in the room like a gong strike. Freaky.

"Fine," she agreed with a huff. She closed her eyes and the world around her went wonky. Like a shimmer of heat rising from the horizon on a sweltering summer day, the air around her suddenly seemed to move all on its own, going all fuzzy and weird in a way that made my eyes hurt. There was no light, yet it stung like someone had shined a flashlight in them. I turned my head and squinted, raising a hand to shield them from whatever was threatening to sear my retinas. I started to open my mouth to protest but my thoughts found themselves jumbled up like a train wreck in my mouth. There was no longer a young girl seated on my recliner. Instead, a run-of-the-mill calico kitty stared back at me with luminous amber eyes. The tip of it long tail flicked back and forth lazily.

You know that feeling you get when you're on a roller coaster and it crests that first huge hill and starts hurtling downward, throwing your insides into free-fall?

Yeah—that moment had nothing on this. My voice sounded small and distant to my own ears. "Well. Kind of hard to argue with that."

"Mairi's mother is Aos Sí but her father is a shape shifter, an ancient fae race that predates even ours. As you can see, she has inherited his abilities as well," Seana said, as if that particular tidbit needed any further explanation. "We have told you no lies this evening, Caitlin. We are everything we have said we are, and more. I know this is all very strange and likely frightening for you to witness, but I ask again: will you please hear us out?"

What arguments did I have I left? I rounded the couch unhurriedly, hoping my gait looked graceful and deliberate rather than snail-slow to prevent my shaky legs from giving out. I took a seat, putting equal distance between myself, Seana and the impossible feline who had curled up contentedly on my chair, purring loudly. Kaine stood directly in front of me, once again silent and fixated on the dark, empty street outside my second-story window. For a fleeting moment I wondered, if the little one could read my emotions, see the future, *and* turn into a freaking cat, just what the hell could he do?

His eyes flicked back to me, boring in to my own with a chilling confidence for half a second before ignoring me once again. On second thought, maybe I was better off not knowing.

I took a deep breath and readied myself for the plunge. "Okay, I'm listening."

CHAPTER FIVE

I'm not sure how I managed to get to work the next morning, fully dressed and looking like my world hadn't just been shattered into tiny, pixie-dust covered pieces. 7am saw me bleary-eyed and rattled; short on sleep and high on nerves. I poured creamer into my cereal instead of into my coffee when I tried to force myself to down some breakfast—and that was only after burning my toast so bad I was forced to resort to said stale cereal. I had completed the morning by knocking my coffee off of the counter, breaking my favorite mug. Red letter start to the day, it was.

Luckily, those breakfast snafus were between me and the four walls I wasn't entirely certain I'd ever feel safe in again. After cleaning up my messes, I pulled on my big girl pants and tried to pretend it was any other day. I hadn't driven into the river on the way to work (though it might have crossed my mind once or twice) and I managed to punch in on time. I even smiled and told my boss that everything was just peachy when she pretended to care. No, I didn't mind working on my birthday one bit. Of course I wasn't offended that she had forgotten to get me a card. I'm pretty sure my laugh at her "who wants to be reminded that they've turned thirty anyway" joke was convincing. It got her to leave me alone in any case and, really, that was all that mattered.

I managed to lose myself in the mindlessness of the office grind, though I knew I was only half present in the dreary gray little world of my cubicle. One good thing about my job—at that moment, at least—was that it didn't require much brain power. I was a glorified switchboard, though I think the company had given my position some self-important (and wholly bullshit) secretarial title like Customer Service Specialist. Whatever you called me, I was an office grunt. A monkey probably could have done my job if it had legible handwriting and a pleasant speaking voice. I had been working there long enough that routing calls and pretending to care had become routine.

Oblivion proved short-lived, however. When the lunch-time slowdown hit and the phones stopped ringing, reality crept back in on quiet cat-feet.

God, that was *such* a bad metaphor, given the night I had just had. I hated myself for even thinking it.

Taking a deep, shaky breath, I slipped my hand into my purse and pulled out the neatly folded piece of paper tucked safely behind my phone. I must have told myself to throw that paper out half a dozen times while I sat on my couch, every lamp blazing deep into the early hours of the morning. I know I had told myself to throw it in the trash at least once more as I stood in my kitchen, staring at the garbage can while I poured Coffee-Mate into my bran flakes. I didn't need their brand of crazy in my life. I wasn't buying whatever it was they were selling. I couldn't write them off as wackos, given the furry antics I had witnessed with my own two eyes, but I didn't need shape-shifting and faerie bullshit in my life. That sort of crazy could only bring trouble. I didn't care what kind of super powers they claimed I myself had.

"Your Gift allows you to see through the glamours of even the most powerful fae, and that is a Gift we are in need of." Seana's pleas rang in my head. *"There is a Secret Keeper we must find, but he remains hidden from us. Our sources say he resides somewhere here, in Riverview. It cannot be a coincidence that we have found you here as well. Only with your help do we stand any chance of locating him."*

I certainly didn't give a rat's ass that I was their Obi Wan. I had never asked to be their only hope in some war being fought in some far off realm where trolls and elves ran free.

"Our High King is mad. He sees enemies around every corner; even in the face of those he once called friends. He no longer trusts anyone—even the words of his own advisers fall on deaf ears. Anyone who dares speak against him is banished, or worse. His younger brother tried to reason with him and voice the concerns of the people. He too was cast aside, a victim of Tiernan's mounting jealousy.

"We too have been exiled. The High King has placed a powerful geis upon us that prevents us from returning home. We are trapped here in your world, helpless, and can only listen as others tell us tales of how our homeland suffers. We need to find a way to break this binding, so that we may return home and join the fight to save our people from the High King's neglect before we no longer have a home to return to."

I blinked and looked down. The paper was unfolded, the edges crimped where I clenched it with my shaking hand. Written neatly in the center was a phone number. No identifying name was needed. They knew I wouldn't be forgetting any of them anytime soon. Honestly, I was kind of surprised—and maybe a touch disappointed—that they had given me something as mundane as a regular ol' phone number to reach them at. Shouldn't exiled faeries have had some sort of crystal ball messaging system or specially trained owls to deliver their mail?

My refusal to become embroiled in whatever mess they were in had been met with surprising calmness. Seana had insisted that I take that note, in case my mind somehow changed or I found myself in need of them, but then they had filed out; quick and quiet-like. Kaine never spared so much as a glance in my direction. Seana's parting hug and kiss upon the cheek left me feeling awkward, like I had just let down my long-lost aunt down. Mairi had brought up the rear, pausing in the doorway. Her words haunted me now, as they had all through my sleepless night.

"The troll has seen your face, but worse he knows that you have seen his. There isn't a fae alive who has forgotten what that means. If he travels back across Veil and tells others that a Warder lives in Riverview, you could be in grave danger. He may come looking for you, Caitlin. Please, be careful."

I crumpled up the paper and tossed it across my desk, watching it bounce off the fabric-covered wall and roll to a stop next to my untouched glass of water. My mouth was dry, making it hard to swallow, but I had no desire to drink. I felt shaky. I could have chalked that up to the three cups of coffee it had taken to get me functioning this morning, but I knew better. Some things, once seen, just cannot be unseen no matter how badly we wished them to be.

Sitting around staring moodily at a wad of paper wasn't going to give me back my peace of mind, in any case. I had no good explanation for what I had seen and even less reason to deny Seana's ludicrous version of reality. It certainly made more sense than anything I had come up with. All in all, it sucked but there it was—shit had gotten too real, too fast and now all I could do was take deep breaths and try to make it through the day. Preferably without thinking about how vulnerable I would feel walking to my car after work. Or scampering the few feet from my parking space to my front door, through an empty parking lot set down off the street.

Funny, I had always loved the seclusion that came along with my overpriced little apartment. Living above a shop that was closed by the time I returned home every evening and closed on Sundays gave me the luxury of privacy that not many in Riverview had. Being set back from the main road had always made it that much sweeter; not even Saturday traffic bothered me. Today, those assets had lost their luster. The thought of the sun setting with me alone, deadbolt or no deadbolt, was not a comforting one. I had the feeling my electric bill would be sky-high by the end of the month. The Ramen Days were coming early this year. Yippie.

I looked down at the clock on my computer screen. 12:45. Life around the office would be picking back up shortly, and while I still felt like a nervous squirrel was lodged in my gut, I had to try to eat something. I dragged myself up out of my chair and headed toward the kitchen. Perhaps staring at my yogurt instead of that note would guilt my stomach into letting me ingest something semi-solid. I gave Bernice, the co-worker one cubicle over from mine, the pantomime of eating and smiled at her affirmative thumbs up. There was no feeling in that smile, but maybe hers was just as bogus as mine. I couldn't see anyone actually liking the sterile gray world we worked in.

I kept my eyes trained on my fingernails like they were the most important thing in the world as I traversed the path to the break room. One or two nods at passing co-workers seemed to suffice, which was a relief. I was in no mood to make small talk. I had the feeling that the generic "What's new with you?" would send declarations of fairies among us spilling from my lips in shrill, hysteric tones. A trip to our dour HR man and the all too likely company mandated follow-up with a shrink was not the way I wanted to end my day. Instead, I kept my lips clamped tight and made a beeline for the refrigerator. Digging through that wasteland of precariously stacked items—and avoiding the land-mines of forgotten food—took a deft hand. I was consumed with that task when a voice behind me said, "Hey Caitlin, isn't it your birthday today?"

I knew without looking that that would be Marc, from the billing department. He had one of those voices that oozed confidence. He was the self-admitted "ladies' man" of the office, having declared himself God's gift to my half of the species on more than one occasion. Ugh. He was a nice enough guy, beneath the boasts and never-ending stream of cheesy pickup lines, but I had long thought he should consider himself lucky to work in a place where the adherence to professionalism was so lackluster. Anywhere else, he probably would have had a sexual harassment lawsuit or three on his hands. Some slightly inappropriate comment would somehow worm its way into our conversation, even if it only lasted two minutes, but I didn't have the energy to think of an excuse to avoid it.

"Yup, it is." I located my wayward cup of blueberry-on-the-bottom as I said it and snagged it out of the path of a particularly fuzzy looking container of... Well, it might have once been lasagna. I couldn't quite suppress a shudder. Some of the people in the office were utter savages. I plastered on a fake smile as I closed the fridge and turned around, the "thank you" dying on my lips.

Marc leaned in the kitchen door-frame, sipping a cup of coffee. As usual, he was dressed in khakis and a brightly coral polo. Unlike usual, he was sporting a pair of large, curling horns, one on each side of his furry face. That face was still human—sort of. His grin was far too toothy beneath a protruding nose that looked distinctly snout-like. His bare arms sported the same dark, wiry fur as his face and his stubby fingers grasped a steaming paper cup with surprising deftness. A wave of dizziness washed over me.

Holy hot staggering fuck. One of them was in my office. *In my office.* My extremities all seemed to go numb while the moment of panic played out in my brain. I heard the clatter as my unopened yogurt dropped to the floor.

His brows—now nearly indistinguishable from his wild mane and fur-covered forehead—rose. "Hey, you okay there?"

A million responses ran through my head.

Oh, great. Spectacular even. Just didn't expect your wicked 5 o'clock shadow there.
Well, I guess this explains why you're such a horn-dog.
Are you fucking kidding me? You're a FAIRY!

Obviously, none of those was appropriate.

Instead I stooped to pick up my yogurt, trying hard to school my face into something resembling normal, and tried to sound glib. "Oh yeah. Fine, fine. Seeing your cup of, ah, coffee there just made me realize that I forgot to turn my coffeepot off this morning." I flashed him a weak smile, eyes darting around as I tried so very hard not to take in all that fur and horns. I flung an arm out toward the hallway—thankfully not the one struggling to keep a grip on my yogurt—and stammered, "I better go call… somebody. You know, before my, ah, apartment burns down or something."

Thankfully, my high-pitched babble struck him dumb. He made no attempt to stop me as I shot past him through the open door. I was shaking from head to toe, my heart beating so fast I thought for sure it was going to burst out of my chest like an alien parasite. Somewhere deep down inside I had known there was no ignoring what had happened to me last night. I mean, you really just can't deny it for very long once you've seen Little Miss Muffet turn into a cat on your recliner. Maybe there was even a tiny part of me that had already come to grips with the fact that if I had seen such crazy shit once, it would happen to me again—but good goddamn. I had not expected it to happen again so soon. The bar, my apartment, now at work too? Was no place safe?

A nervous sweat bathed my forehead. A full-blown panic attack was seconds away from crashing down on me. I felt like I was going to fall to pieces but held on with an iron will as I scurried down the hall toward my cubicle, telling myself to keep breathing though my chest felt squeezed flat. I was afraid to look up from my feet; afraid of what I might see in the face of someone else I had trusted to be a normal, everyday member of the human race. I could have a nice, wheezy little fit and get a grip on things once I made it back to my desk. I could cower in the safety of those bland, gray walls for another four hours, trying to make as little contact with anyone as possible. Maybe then I could keep my tenuous grip on sanity for one more day…

"Caitlin, are you okay?"

Or the universe could bend me over one more time.

I froze mid-step, teetering on one foot, in front of the boss's office. I looked a mess, and I knew Marc would be gossiping about my odd behavior to anyone who would listen in no time. The chances at brushing this one off were pretty slim. I gave Allison my best smile and cleared my throat. "I've been better?"

The look she fixed me back with was of the no nonsense variety. She jerked her chin in the direction of the chair in front of her desk. "Come in. And close the door."

How could I refuse such a gracious invitation? Mentally cursing, I did as she asked. I settled myself into the seat across from her and tried to take a deep breath. This was pretty much bound to suck, no matter how I played it.

Allison sat forward, hands folded neatly in the center of her desk blotter. She was a tall, thin woman in her middle forties; nondescript brown hair pulled back in a ponytail, wire-frame glasses perched on her nose. A real type A, with a submissive husband and two young kids. I was pretty sure there was a dog—and a maybe even a minivan—in that equation somewhere, just to round out her image as the All-American Suburban Power Mom. As I found myself pinned under her best concerned-boss/sympathetic-mom stare, I felt for her kids. It was going be hard for them to pull one over on her one day. She said, "I've noticed that you haven't been yourself today, Caitlin. Are you okay? Is there something going on? Something that you would like to talk about?"

Yup, just as I had feared: pop psychology from the boss-lady. Oh goodie. Just what one wants when they're staving off a major meltdown. I bit my tongue and studied the sagging tiles of the ceiling above her desk intently. I tried to choose a good excuse from the chorus line running through my brain but they all sounded fake or downright crazy. All of a sudden, words started tumbling out of my mouth. Perhaps my traumatized psyche was so desperate to tell someone something about the night it had just been subjected to that even a grossly abbreviated version was better than holding it in one second longer. I spewed out words like "mugged" and "scared shitless"—hell, maybe even a dramatic "certain death" got thrown in there too. I felt myself grow more and more hysterical with each second. I'm pretty sure I let slip a "troll" or two, but I was so emotional that I was pretty sure it fit in context if I had.

By the time I had finished with my miraculous rescue by a few strangers on the deserted street, I was on the verge of sobbing. I took a deep, shaky breath to choke back the tears and stared at my hands. They were clenched together in my lap, going numb from the force of my own grip. Part of me couldn't believe I had just opened the emotional floodgates to my boss, of all people.

The rest of me just didn't give two shits. It felt so good to say *something*, finally. I had avoided Jenni's calls all morning, finally staving her off with a non-committal "tell you later" text. Maybe it would be easier to talk to her if I considered this a dress rehearsal for my later lie. Close as we were, I couldn't burden my bestie with my fucked up fairy tale. It was too damn weird, even for someone who had stuck by my side through my stinky incense and funny chanting hippie-pagan phase. Of course she would probably try to have herself committed right alongside me if I did tell her, just so I'd have company in the loony bin but, still. That was too much to ask for from a friend.

When I finally had the courage to look up, Allison was regarding me with a look of co-mingled shock and pity. Something about that look made my throat tighten until I wanted to throw myself into her arms and bawl like a baby. She asked me the expected questions: are you okay? Did you file a report with the police? Did you go to the hospital? I gave all the expected let's-not-make-waves answers. I belatedly wondered why I hadn't done those things, upon waking this morning. Wouldn't any sensible person have wanted to make sure they were healthy and sane? Had my subconscious already accepted that the boys in blue would be no help against gigantic monsters from another dimension? I had to swallow a hysterical giggle in a wet cough.

Good god, my life was a mess.

"...and you have the vacation time. Why don't you take the rest of the week off and rest?"

I blinked and stared at her for a moment, as if she had been speaking in Swahili. Allison, the attendance Nazi was *telling* me to take some time off? She had been known to argue the importance of silly little things like doctor's appointments and kids' graduations when they dared interfere with the well-oiled machine of her workplace. Her kindness in the face of my shaken state was uncharacteristically understanding. Granted, it wouldn't do me a whole lot of good, considering all the details I had been forced to leave out of my "mugging" story, but; still. It was strangely comforting to get even a small dose of sympathy from someone generally considered to be slave-driving and heartless.

Her suggestion had merit. I was less than useless in my current state and didn't see it improving much in the next day or so. A little vacation from responsibility might be just the pick-me-up I needed whilst sorting out the pile of crazy that had just been dropped in my lap. I accepted her offered tissue, dabbing my eyes as I nodded slowly. "Yeah, maybe that is a good idea."

And it did seem like a good idea. Right up until the moment I got in my car and realized the only place I could go was home. I wasn't ready to face Jenni and being in the public eye felt far too vulnerable—yet, my apartment no longer struck me as the welcoming bastion of comfort either. Locks were well and good (and living on the second floor was even better) but a door wasn't going to stop something like Goliath. Hell, if I had just seen a horny faun in the break room there was always the chance that some winged sprite would stop by at my bedroom window to ask for directions to Albuquerque.

Fuck. I thumped my forehead against the steering wheel and cursed whatever cruel deity had taken control over my life. What the hell was I going to do?

CHAPTER SIX

I would like to say I enjoyed my impromptu vacation. You know; that I indulged in a little Entering My Third Decade pampering. Perhaps that I got a much needed massage or had a fresh mani/pedi to brighten my mood. Given the gravity of the weirdness infiltrating my life, a day of drunken debauchery would have been just as fitting. Or, even if I had not had the gumption to go that far, that I had at least spent those days relaxing and recuperating, straightening out my head and making sense of the crazy train I had so recently boarded.

Yeah… I wish.

While I did get a lot of research done over those few days, it was done in the most bat-crap crazy fashion possible. I didn't leave my apartment. I kept the doors locked and the shades drawn. Every light in every room blazed like the sun 24/7, electric bill be damned. I lived off of coffee and a stockpile of Chinese take-out while I scoured the Internet for every bit of information I could find on the fae. Trust me, when I say "everything" I mean, *everything*. I went far past Google's top picks as I combed through every single little thing I could find: Wikipedia entries, Irish folklore, mythology essays, references in children's books, long diatribes on pagan theology. I read it all, right on down to a few eye-searing websites that looked like the proprietor had gone GIF happy when they were created back in the mid-90's. I even spent the better part of my Friday night reading some weird-ass PDF on Red Caps before I realized it was just some role-playing game guidebook.

Three marathon-long days of searching for some sort of sense—some teeny tiny crumb for my wobbly sanity to cling to—and do you know where it got me?

Nowhere.

Even after sifting through all the chaff, I was left grasping at straws.

Every site seemed to contradict the last. The dizzying variations to all the theories of the "truth" behind the fairytales made my brain ache. Not to mention that, in the end, I was just as lost as when I started. Sure, there were people out there who believed that the fae were real. Some of them even managed to not sound completely certifiable while stating their reasons. Hell, there were even some who claimed to have met them, in various places and fashions over the years. Yet, no one I could find had an experience quite like mine.

It took me nearly an hour of figuring out that something that sounded like "es she" was nowhere close to how it should be spelled. Damn Irish, with their mouths full of marbles. Even after translating phonetics into dialect, it did me no good. I could find only the barest mention of the Aos Si and knowing that they were thought to be a supernatural—but equally mythical—race like the sidhe and the near-godlike Tuatha Dé Danann did me no good. Those gobblety-gook words meant nothing to me. I needed facts that just didn't seem to exist.

Furthermore, I couldn't find a damn thing about the Warding I supposedly had. Not a single word. A lot of strange, supernatural abilities were attributed to faerie-kind, but that one? Not so much as a whisper. And don't even get me started on what freaky shit I found when I dared to look up information on "shape shifters."

Saturday afternoon arrived in the blink of an eye and by that time, I was officially out of steam. My eyes burned from staring so long at the computer screen and the thought of looking at one more website made me physically nauseated. (Or maybe that was last of the pork lo mein that I had eaten for lunch. Cold.) My back ached. I had fallen asleep on the couch with my fireplace poker near at hand two nights running. I wasn't sure if all the claims about cold iron being lethal to the fae were legit, but it gave me a little peace of mind to think I wasn't totally defenseless if Goliath showed up on my doorstep.

All in all, I was feeling grungy, cranky, and pretty damn stupid. I slammed my laptop shut and shoved it away from me, sending a cascade of empty soda cans and cardboard take-out containers off the other side of the coffee table.

The shrill, ringing chime of Jenni's text tone knifed into my self-loathing and made me jump. The realization of how silent the world around me was—and had been for days—only further drove home the level to which I had sunk. I picked my phone up off the couch at my back and read, "*You up yet sleeping ugly?*"

It felt foreign to smile. I replied, "*Bitch. Been up since 7 thank you very much.*"

"*Never know with you, old lady. You've really taken to this spinster-hermit thing. We still on for tonight?*"

I groaned. Saturday had been the date set in stone for our belated birthday bar hopping. I bit my lip and tried to think of a good excuse. How on earth could I go out drinking now, pretending everything was normal when it felt so...not? My thumb hovered over the digital keyboard as another text came in; *"You're thinking of ways to keep avoiding me aren't you? L What happened at Gilroy's was all my fault; I'm so sorry. I never should have let you go outside alone."*

I hated that she blamed herself for my "mugging." I had reassured her multiple times over the past few days that it wasn't her fault, but the guilt remained. God damn it felt shitty to lie to her. I texted back quickly, *"Stop that. It's totally not your fault so please stop blaming yourself. I'm okay. That asshole didn't hurt me. Scared me, yeah, but I'm tougher than that."*

The eye-opening realization struck me like a bolt of lightning, giving me the shivers.

I had just wasted a gift-horse of a vacay locked in my home, running up my electric bill while sucking down quarts of greasy carbs and fatty pork bits. Why? Because I was scared of fairies? I scowled. I was starting to hate the very word. The "me of a few weeks ago" would have laughed and called the "me of that moment" a pathetic loser. In fact, I muttered out loud, "Loser."

A few days space had started to leave me questioning what I had seen. Could that really have been a troll? I mean—come on. It was crazy enough that three strangers had slipped into my apartment and made me entertain their wacked out story; what were the chances that they had slipped me something that made me hallucinate the woman-turned-cat-turned-back-to-woman act? Maybe I was being a total ass, even trying to convince myself otherwise. How could I start believing in all this crazy magical crap thirty years into my life? Why on God's green earth would I, of all people, have ever been chosen to have some crazy rare mystical power like this completely untraceable, no mention to be found anywhere in the whole wide world "Warding"?

It all seemed like utter horseshit. Even Marc's goat-faced leer seemed less and less real to me now after my crusade through the Internet.

One look around at the mess of my living room and another down at myself to see the frumpy, stained sweatpants and faded tank top I was wearing—and had been wearing for days on end—and I made up my mind. Before Jenni could respond again, I texted, *"I'm still down. Just need to clean up and get pretty. Still meeting at your place at 8, right?"*

~*~

By 1 a.m. I was tipsy as hell and wondering why I had ever let myself become crippled by fear. Jenni and I had gone through one club, three bars, and enough liquor to make my liver weep. Though the night had started off with some jitters, I was glad I had forced myself out of my self-imposed fortress of solitude. The fresh air (and copious amounts of booze) had done me good. The world was looking brighter by the moment, my earlier fears becoming distant, crazy memories I was glad to leave behind.

Luckily, I managed to talk Jenni out of our usual last stop at Gilroy's. Discounted drinks or no, I just couldn't handle that place—not yet. I might have overdone it on my impassioned speech about how she shouldn't have to spend the end of her night off at her place of employment. I was half in the bag by that point so it's entirely possible. I'm not even sure if she really bought it or not but, either way, she let it slide.

Instead we wound up at Harbin's, a low key hole-in-the-wall down the block from Jenni's apartment. The bartender there had gone to 'tending school with Jenni and had a bit of a crush on her. That was both convenient—hello free drinks!—and awkward, since she happened to be very much taken and he knew it. Worse still, I knew that he knew it, and hated that he continued to hit on her anyway. I had the feeling I'd spend the remainder of the night running interference if he got too handsy but; whatever. It was still better than having to walk back through Gilroy's door. I wasn't sure I'd ever be able to look at that place the same way again.

Once in the bar, I shoved my coat into Jenni's arms and made a beeline for the bathroom. It was our usual ritual at the last stop of the night. I had a bladder the size of a pea, so she always procured us a table and a round of drinks while I dashed off to the ladies room. Thankfully there was an open stall, so I didn't leave her waiting long. I weaved my way over to the back corner, keeping an eye on my treacherous feet. I was glad that I had broken the rules of high fashion and worn flats—and even more glad that there wasn't much of a crowd in the bar to navigate, given how stumble-y I was.

When I made it to our table and slid into my seat, I was thrilled to see a full glass of wine awaiting me. Jenni was talking with Bryan, who had left his post at the bar to chat her up. Predictable. He loomed between us, a wall of determined stupidity. As usual his back was to me, so that all I could see was a wall of black fabric. I crossed my eyes and stuck my tongue out at him. Jenni stifled a laugh mid-sentence, giving me the mean little thrill of satisfaction I so longed for.

While they chatted, I rifled through my purse for some lip balm. Eventually she would ease my welcome into the break in conversation. Bryan would never acknowledge me himself. I was pretty certain he saw me as the final hurdle in his on-going quest to get her in the sack. He should have realized how lucky he was to be dealing with my puny five-foot-four ass. If not for me, he would have been facing down six feet of angry, muscled marine.

I heard the scrape of the chair between us being pulled out. "—the new girl, Ramona. I've got to stick around to keep an eye on her, but she's got this. I can hang for a bit."

Balls.

My stint as No Touchy Referee was starting early. Lucky me. The depths of my purse had just become the most interesting place in the world. Anything—even handbag lint—was interesting if it kept me from having to make eye contact and small talk with that douche-nozzle. The joy must have showed on my face, because Jenni chimed in brightly, "And you remember my friend Caitlin, right? We're celebrating her belated birthday tonight!"

Traitor. I took my sweet time turning away and hanging my purse on the back of my chair. I even rolled my eyes and snarled silently. I was *so* not in the mood for faux fawning tonight, but a girl's got to do what a girl's got to do. She would owe me big for this.

"Of course I do. Happy belated birthday, Cat." There was only the bear minimum of friendliness in his voice. It was pretty clear he was as sick of my fake flirtations as I was, but if he insisted on playing the same game over and over, I sure as hell wasn't turning in my cards early. It irked me to hear him call me Cat. Nobody but Jenni and my father did that. We certainly weren't on chummy enough terms for him to be using nicknames. Still, I plastered a smile on my face as I turned back to the table.

My overly cheerful greeting shriveled up and died on my tongue. Instead of saying anything, I gaped. There's no other way to describe it. I sat there, mouth hanging open like a hooked trout. I blinked rapidly, like that was going to change something. Like there was a film over my eyes, making me see something straight out of a nightmare not two feet away from my face.

Now Bryan was sitting eye-level with me, facing me—or, what I had once thought of as Bryan was. Though it remained man-shaped, there was little else about the thing before me that could be considered even remotely human. Its gray flesh was almost translucent, with a strangely pearlescent sheen, like a large wax doll. Milky whiteness seemed to roil beneath the surface of its skin, like smoke. The gaunt, oval face I stared into was all but featureless. It was like someone had quickly made the barest impressions of a human face in the wax, smearing thumbprint indentations where the eyes and mouth would have been and nothing else.

I glanced down, away from that horribly blank stare and saw that the clothing it wore hung off its emaciated frame, rippling with its every movement. How had I not noticed that sooner? The hand that rested upon the table was skeletally thin, its knobby, elongated fingers sheathed in the same strange, waxy skin.

I wondered—*hoped*—briefly, that I was seeing things. That maybe my days on end of paranoia were causing my brain to project something for me to fixate on. Unfortunately, rapidly fading buzz or no buzz, that made no sense. All night I had been looking over my shoulder, afraid I'd see horns or wings or fur on some stranger, but nothing had caught my eye. Not a single fairy in all of Riverview, until I let my guard down in a place I had pretty much trusted to be safe.

What the fuck was with the creepy-ass fae and bars?

I couldn't tell what kind of look the Wax Man formerly known as Bryan gave me during my long pause. (It's hard to read something with *no face*.) However, over its shoulder I could see Jenni giving me a wide-eyed "WTF?" look complete with mouthed query, so I scrambled to pull myself together. I faked a laugh—and let me tell you, it sounded pretty fake even to me—and forced myself to give the creature next to me a playful slap on the shoulder. Not caring how lame it sounded, I giggled and said, "Come on now, Bryan! Where are your manners? You should know better than to acknowledge a lady getting older!"

Whether or not they believed my previous shock to have been play-acting, they both laughed along with me. I kept that teasing smile on my face though my stomach was knotted tight. I wondered where that laugh was coming from. The pit-like indentation of its mouth didn't seem to move. How did it even have a voice?

Thankfully "Bryan" turned it's gaze back to Jenni, giving me a slightly less disturbing profile view. I knew they were having a pleasant enough sounding conversation without me—Jenni's tipsy laugh sounded genuine—but I couldn't follow the words. My mind was buzzing with fear and gibbering to itself that I should grab Jenni and run for the hills. She would think I was nuts if I did, of course. She obviously didn't see what I saw, otherwise she would never have tolerated it constantly brushing against her arm, her knee; touching whatever little bit of skin it could get away with without me butting in. It must have been throwing one of those glamours Seana had explained to me; the magic facade that it showed humans to keep them from seeing what it really looked like. If I made a run for it, I would be doubly screwed for having let yet another fae know I could see its true face. I didn't need two scary dudes out there, hunting me down for the so-called Gift that was ruining my life.

Shit. What the hell could I do?

I sat back in my chair, guilty over how glad I was that it wasn't flirting with me. I wasn't sure I could handle playing along if that *thing* touched me. When little more than the occasional nod or laugh was needed from me, I had nothing to do but look at it. My wine glass remained untouched, my stomach too sour to consider another sip of alcohol.

Instead, I studied the Wax Man in quick glances, all the while wondering what it was and what I should do. I mean, it didn't look all that dangerous. Creepy as hell, yes, but not out-right dangerous. Not like Goliath had looked, with his lion's teeth and ham fists. How could this thing be feeding off of humans?

Seana had made it sound like all of the bestial fae did in one way or another. Goliath was obviously one of the more carnivorous types. I was pretty sure I knew how he'd prey upon humans. This thing was different. With no physically frightening features to pinpoint—or features at all, really—I was at a loss for how this thing could eat...

A chill ran down my spine. It kept *touching* her.

My eyes darted down to the hand resting on the table near me. The angle was all wrong to get a good look, but I thought something about them was off. They didn't look human, with strange ridges peeking out at regular intervals, running down each finger to its hidden palm. I watched the hand it had casually rested against Jenni's. It's thumb stroked the back of her hand. That hand appeared to be glowing; pulsing faintly. I knew immediately that it wasn't a trick of the light. That milky mist under its skin was moving, swirling.

If I had thought my stomach felt knotted and sick before, I had had no idea the depths to which it could sink. It *was* feeding on her. It was sucking something out of her; some emotion or energy that wasn't visible to the human eye. Whatever the hell was making that smoke beneath its skin was something it sucked out of humans.

I had a feeling that this job was a smorgasbord for a creature like him—tons of contact with drunk, emotional ladies who never even knew that they were prey. Before the veil had been ripped from my eyes, I had seen what it had wanted everyone to see too: sandy blonde hair, hazel eyes, a slight cleft in the chin. Nothing over the top gorgeous but maybe that was what it wanted. Too good looking would have attracted too much attention or, perhaps, put some of the less inebriated women on guard. Maybe it wanted to be seen as cute but harmless run-of-the-mill boy next door. The kind of stranger that you could trust. The thought made my stomach roil with a whole new emotion: rage.

"...must get lonely though." I still had no idea where that voice could be coming from, but something about its husky, sympathetic tone made my ears perk up. It had Jenni's hand cupped between in its own. Judging by her empty glass and the forlorn look on her face, she wasn't in a great state of mind. While I had been trying to think of a game plan to use against our interloper, she had drifted into the danger zone. I wasn't the only one who noticed. "Bryan" sidled his chair just a little bit closer and that sparkle-swirl where their hands met increased. "You know, we close up soon. As soon as I show Ramona how to cash out and lock up, I could walk you home. We could watch a movie, talk a bit more—"

Oh. Hell. No.

Fueled by fury and the last dregs of my earlier buzz, I reached over and grabbed it's wrist. The cold, slick feeling of the flesh beneath my fingers made me want to recoil, but I stuck to my guns and pried it's hand off of hers. The moment their contact was broken, the glow beneath it's translucent skin died.

Jenni drew her hand back immediately, probably in surprise given the wide-eyed stare she leveled my way. The Wax Man's head whipped around and it didn't need eyes for me to know I was getting a vengeful stare from its human facade. I could feel its anger. That was fine by me. I was pretty pissed off too.

There was no playfulness in my voice when I said, "First off, you know she has a boyfriend. Second, the only person walking her home tonight is *me*. So why don't you knock off the act? We all know you're just trying to get in her pants, 'cause you've been trying for years. Not gonna happen, buddy, so I think it's about time for you to piss off."

I pushed its arm away with all the force I could muster and stood. My purse was already on my shoulder as I gathered up my coat. It was still staring at me—it was hard to think of it as "Bryan" when those two elongated black pits were trained on my face—but it made no move to get up. Belatedly, I wondered just what the hell I would do if it did. I ignored the shaking in my knees and held my ground. "Come on Jen. Let's go."

Jenni sputtered something that was probably an apology, quickly grabbing her own coat and purse up in her arms. I waited until she was past me, never taking my eyes off of the Wax Man's face, before I whipped around and marched out of the bar after her. People were staring but I kept a look of righteous fury on my face until the door slammed shut behind us. Those onlookers never knew those few feet were the longest in my life.

The bracing autumnal air outside felt good. I hadn't been aware of how flushed I was until it hit my skin and a chill of a whole 'nother sort ran through me. I shrugged into my coat and pulled out my cell phone, using my short phone call to the cab company to center myself. Jenni was waiting a few feet away, arms crossed. She didn't look happy with me. She fell into step beside me and waited until I slipped my phone back into my bag, ride secured. Then, she attacked. "Jesus Christ, Cat! What the hell was that about?"

Lucky for me there was some truth I could use to cover the revelation I couldn't even begin to explain to her. "He crossed the line. I don't like that scumbag trying to take advantage of you."

She snorted, brushing a stray ringlet of hair away from her face. "Oh please, that's bull. He's been much sleazier than that before. It never bothered you then. We could have gotten another free round or two out of him before I blew him off."

I shot her an incredulous look. It was so damn hard to argue with someone who hadn't seen what I had. I wished I could tell her, but that was flat out of the question. Instead, I quickened my pace and shot back, "Oh yeah? And what if he followed you home this time? He's enough of a shit to hit on a girl who has told him a zillion times she's got a boyfriend. Who knows what he might do when he finally snaps!"

"You're totally overacting Cat." She jerked to a halt. "You've played along every other time and we've laughed it off afterwards. You just made a big scene over nothing and made it pretty much impossible for me to ever step foot back in that place! What gives?"

I stood there for a moment, heart hammering, before I turned to face her. I half-expected to see him coming up behind us, but the street was clear of any familiar faces. We were close to her apartment now and, man, I really wanted to be safe behind those locked doors, but I knew that stubborn stance. She was determined to have it out with me then and there, public eye be damned. I loved my bestie, but man did she know how to make a scene—especially after tying one on. Since I couldn't very well tell her I was afraid of the monster a few doors down, I took a deep breath and apologized to my soul for the lie I was about to tell. "I like him."

She couldn't have looked more shocked if I had hit her in the back of the head with a board. Her voice was a disbelieving squeal. "*What?*"

I turned around and resumed my march toward her place. She caught up to me only a second later, still sputtering. "Are you serious? I thought you hated him! You're always saying how cheesy and pathetic he is. You just called him a scumbag not ten seconds ago!"

"Yeah well, it's called jealousy okay? I didn't want you to feel sorry for me, so I ragged on him instead. He's always been all over you anyway so it doesn't matter." I hid my face in my hands. It was to hide the pain of lying but she didn't need to know that. Let her think it was embarrassment. I hated myself more and more with every word. "But tonight I guess I was just cranky and drunk and, well, I acted stupid, okay? I'm sorry I made a scene."

"Aww, Cat!" She slung an arm around my waist, nearly knocking me off balance. "I'm sorry! You should have told me. I never would have suggested that we keep going there if I had known."

I accepted her sympathy mutely. My cheeks were flaming, growing warmer as she went on and on about how much she loved me and how I couldn't let my single-ness get me down; how I would find a wonderful man that made me as happy as Anthony made her one day. I let her think my blush was embarrassment rather than guilt. I had never told my bestie a lie before. I felt like a shit.

We dawdled on the porch outside her place for a few minutes. Thanks to liquor and plain old naivety, she spent the whole time rambling on about how great I was and how bright our future would be and how I should keep my chin up. It took everything I had not to shake her, darkening her happy little world with the truth of what we had just narrowly escaped. She was waxing poetic about the beautiful weddings we'd have one day, and how we'd screw up our children as badly as our parents had screwed us up, when the cab finally arrived. I had never been so glad to shoo her inside, climbing into the cab and locking the door behind me.

Thank God the cabbie was your regular run-of-the-mill human. Or maybe he was just a non-bestial fae that could pass for human. I pushed that thought out of my head and dug through my purse with singular determination.

"Where to ma'am?" he asked, in a tone that made me think it wasn't the first time he was posing that question.

"I—uh—I'm sorry. Just give me one minute to, uh, double check the address okay?" I retrieved the little ball of paper from the depths of my bag and smoothed it out once again. The hand that held the phone to my ear was shaking. I squeezed my eyes closed and prayed someone would answer, despite the late hour. It seemed to ring forever, until my heart sank and I was sure it was about to click over to voicemail—

"Hello?"

Relief flooded through me. A tear came to my eye. I couldn't keep my voice from trembling. "Hi Seana, its Caitlin Moore. I'm sorry for calling so late, but I think I need your help after all."

CHAPTER SEVEN

The address Seana gave me lead to a neighborhood I had never visited before, where the rows of brownstones sat with dignified grace. The stately windows and carved stone facades hearkened back to a forgotten era long before my own. I fell in love with them immediately. Even in the dark, guided only by streetlights, it was clear how they put my piddly little apartment to shame. It was also quiet on their street, which was about as close to suburbia as you could get without leaving city limits. We were the only car around, which seemed abnormal to me, even at such a late hour.

Thankfully I had enough cash on me to cover the cab fare. A trip to the edge of the city hadn't been part of my plans, but my mother's insistence that I keep an extra twenty tucked under the ID in my wallet (much like the importance of always wearing clean underwear in case I was hit by a bus) was deeply ingrained in my psyche. Having to borrow money from the people I had been avoiding would have made my night all that much more embarrassing. Thanks for the life lesson, mom.

I stood on the sidewalk and listened to the cab disappear into the distance. A minute or two passed before I could drag my feet up those graceful stone stairs and stare at the beautiful, dark wood of their door. I still couldn't quite believe what I was doing. I had been so adamant about staying far away from these people only a few days earlier. Now I was at their door in the middle of the night, heart beating like a drum. My need for their help warred with my pride. (And not a bit of me was scared shitless of what new and exciting freakishness awaited me beyond that door. Nope, not one bit.)

There was a light on over the porch, framing me in a puddle of pale gold as I stood there, full of doubts. I had to ask them for help. I had no other choice. I couldn't ignore whatever this Gift was that I had and I couldn't stand being so lost and afraid one moment longer. The image of that Wax

Man sucking the life out of my unsuspecting bestie was burned into my mind. I shuddered. Something had to be done about that. I couldn't—*wouldn't*—sit by, helpless, like that again. I had no option of retreat, not this time. I took a deep breath, gathered up my metaphorical balls, and knocked.

Seana opened the door. She looked so average, standing there. It baffled my mind. A creature who could banish head injuries with a wave of her hand should have been dressed in a grand gown or Grecian robes or something. Maybe even surrounded by a halo of light. Instead, she looked like your run of the mill suburban mom: barefoot, in dark leggings and an over-sized, ivory cable-knit sweater, with her hair pulled back in a ponytail. She had the eyes of a healer, though. They radiated concern as she ushered me into the dimly lit foyer. It didn't escape my notice that she scanned the street behind me before shutting the door, throwing more than one lock home.

I stood there, dumbfounded by the normalcy around me. Coats hung in a neat row along one side of the foyer, with a pair of muddy boots on the rack beneath them. The living room that opened up before me was cozy with a plush couch and matching loveseat, their rich brown color complimented by the thick pile of the carpet in the center of the room. A paperback lay over the arm of the couch, a cup of tea—still steaming—sat on the end table next to it. Dark woods echoed their lovely front door in the end and coffee tables. They were a nice contrast to the cream-colored walls. A flat-screen TV was mounted on the wall above a cluttered entertainment center that held a dizzying array of DVDs and gaming consoles.

I was speechless. I don't know what bothered me more: that these otherworldly creatures lived such regular, human-like lives or that they were obviously much better off than me. I mean, what did fairies do to make a living? They had to have some sort of income. I guess if illegal immigrants could manage it, so could otherworldly species, but their high-end neighborhood and décor were a step or three beyond minimum wage. Unless they were just using another of their mystical abilities to hoodwink their landlord and the nice folks at Crate and Barrel into free rent and all the furnishings they needed, of course.

Seana laid a hand on my shoulder. "Can I get you something?" Her other hand gestured to her abandoned cup. "Some tea, perhaps?"

I didn't trust my voice yet. The flighty feeling of being on the verge of a full blown panic attack has loosened its grip on the cab ride over, but it wasn't gone. I wondered if it would ever disappear, or if it had just become my new normal. I wasn't at all thirsty, but another moment or two to pull myself back together couldn't hurt. I nodded.

She squeezed my arm gently. "Make yourself at home. I will be right back."

I rounded the corner of the loveseat after she passed through the far door into what I assumed was the kitchen. I slid out of my coat and folded it over the arm of the couch, my purse tucked against it. There was no sign of Kaine or Mairi. (I even looked in the corners of the room for a hidden kitty.) Everything was quiet, except for the usual creaks and squeaks of an old house. If they were around, they were keeping mouse-quiet and letting Seana handle me. Not the worst idea, considering how unsettling I found both of them.

With a slowly exhaled breath, I sat on the edge of the seat. My hands fidgeted in my lap as my eyes roved the room, unable to find a place to settle. What was I doing? How on earth did I think coming here would make anything better? I had hoped to feel comforted. Safe, even. Instead, I felt more lost than ever. I had no clue what I was going to do; what I should say. I was pretty sure the deal I had refused days earlier still lay on the metaphorical table between us, but unless I accepted it, their help would not be given freely. I was no keener now than I had been then on the prospect of being used as a pawn in their little struggle for fairy power, but perhaps I was more open to bargaining. While I hadn't thought so at the time, I had come to realize that there were things I wanted from them in return.

When Seana returned, I was a bit more composed. I took the tea with a smile and a thank you. A sip told me it was chamomile. Ick. I thought it tasted more like warm bathwater than a beverage, but the attempt to imbue me with some calming properties was a kind gesture. I cupped it in one hand and rested it on my knee. "Thank you for letting me come here. I know it's insanely late." Not to mention flat out insane, I added silently.

She tucked herself back into the previously occupied corner of the couch, legs folded beneath her. She waved a hand at the book on the end table. "It is no trouble. As you can see, I am not the best sleeper."

"Still, you must think I'm ballsy, calling you at two in the morning. Especially the way I acted when we last spoke." My face flushed at the memory. I hadn't been the most gracious about asking them to exit my apartment. I think the words "freak" and "nutcase" might have been tossed around a little more liberally than I now cared to remember. "I'm sorry I was such a bitch."

Her chuckle was soft; musical. "You had had a very rough night. Your short temper was completely understandable."

I snorted. "That's a nice way to put it. 'Rough nights' seem to be my thing lately."

"I thought that might be the case." She took a slow sip of her tea and regarded me with that concerned mother stare of hers. "Would you like to talk about it?"

Everyone had been handling me with kid gloves lately. I knew they meant it to be kind, but instead it just made me feel worse. It made me feel defective. Since I didn't want a repeat of the hysterics that had taken place in Allison's office, I kept my story short and to the point. Even when I stuck to the facts, images of that horrible creature feeding off Jenni flashed before my eyes.

My hands had begun to tremble by the time I finished recounting my evening. I placed my teacup down on the coffee table before I did something stupid like spill it all over their expensive looking rug. Thankfully, my eyes remained dry.

"I am so sorry that you had to witness such a horrific thing." I searched her face carefully, noting every little bit of shame and concern writ there. Her expression told me volumes more than her carefully worded apology. There was a deep, all-knowing sort of fear lurking beneath her patented blend of motherly distress.

"So I'm not crazy? You know what that thing was?"

"Unfortunately, I do. They are abhorrent, soulless creatures called Shades. They are reviled, even among the bestial fae." Her disgust was clear. "As you saw, they feed on the happiness that can be found in others. Many turn feral, ruled by their hunger alone. You are lucky this one showed such restraint. Many drain their prey dry."

I tried to swallow the slick lump in my throat. "What happens then?"

She looked down and shrugged uneasily. "Some recover, in time. Others are not so lucky. They themselves become lost, their light dimmed or extinguished completely. Some are consumed by the darkness and lose the will to carry on. Others are driven mad. There are many in asylums the world over who have been forever changed by the touch of a hungry Shade."

The thought of Jenni locked away in some padded room—or worse, throwing herself off some bridge in despair—rekindled my earlier rage. "And you're telling me those things, those Shades, just walk around feeding on us at will? That they're basically killing people with their touch every damn day and no one is trying to stop them?"

"In High Queen Isobail's day they were banned from this world, as were most of the bestial fae. Shades have long been distrusted and the havoc a single one can wreak if left unchecked was too dangerous for both your kind and mine. If one disobeyed the law and crossed the Veil, it was considered an act of treason. Do you know what that means?"

"I watch the History channel," I replied tartly. "Let me guess. It's punishable by death?"

"Yes. Isobail took such things very seriously. She upheld the tradition of protecting this realm against our darker brethren. Like those before her, she engaged Hunters to track down law-breakers on either side of the Veil, and they would have been sent to stop any fae who dared defy the law, Shade or otherwise." Seana's anger was a quiet thing, but there was a fierceness in her eyes that made me sit back just a bit. "Now you have witnessed the folly of High King Tiernan's carelessness first hand. The Hunters no longer safeguard your world. I can only assume they are no longer playing their role in mine as well. I had not thought the situation so bad." She looked down at her lap again, where her hands were wringing one another in worry. I thought I heard a catch in her voice. "His madness is truly destroying the world."

What the hell was I supposed to say to that? It wasn't just her world she was talking about; some far off mystical green fields where sylphs and satyrs frolicked the day away. Without High King Nutbag over there doing his job, the creepy crawlies that they kept locked away in the dark corners of their shining cities were just going to keep coming into mine. And who could blame them? If their own people hated them so much, of course they'd come on through to a place where they could get a free meal and a hefty dose of anonymity.

Of course that also meant if she was right—and God damn me, it certainly sounded like she was—I was the one and only key to stopping them. I was the only one who could help them find their Secret Keeper and their way home, so they could put a firm hand back on the throne.

Talk about fucked between a rock and a hard place.

"All I've wanted from the second this all started was to ignore it. To go back to my normal life, where crazy shit like this doesn't happen. I don't even care how boring it was now. I just want things to go back to the way they were before I realized I had this shitty 'Gift' so I can walk outside and go to work and have a night out without seeing some monster in the corner that no one else can see." I sank back in the loveseat, defeated. I knew the answer even before I asked the question. "But that isn't going to happen, is it?"

She shook her head. "No, it won't. A Gift, once awoken, will not slumber again. Some may be suppressed for a time by extreme means, but I do not believe one such as yours could be made to do so, given its very nature to resist other magics. Even now, in its fledgling state, you were able to see through three glamours and that is no small feat. Glamours are one of the most deeply ingrained fae magics. They are learned from the cradle and practiced by many until they become as natural as breathing."

That was *so* not what I wanted to hear. Then again, it wasn't exactly a surprise either. Even if she had a way to make me to stop seeing the hard truth of what was out there, I couldn't forget what I had already seen. I was good at making stupid mistakes and telling myself little white lies, but even I had limits. It was one thing to tell myself that I would start my diet again tomorrow while scarfing down a greasy bacon cheeseburger. Pretending that I had never seen Jenni's happiness getting sucked out by a creature straight out of my nightmares? Or that I hadn't smelled Goliath's spoiled meat breath in my face? Those were things I'd never forget, no matter how badly I wanted to.

If I was being completely honest with myself (which was not exactly my strong suit), I didn't really want to forget the horrible things I had seen. I didn't want to deal with the reality of it, sure, but I also didn't want to stick my head back in the sand. I was scared and felt more helpless now than I had ever before—but I was also one hundred and twenty-seven pounds of pretty freaking pissed off. I was far from thrilled to have had such a strange and alienating responsibility thrust upon my shoulders, but wishing it away wouldn't keep me safe from the monsters. Worse, it wouldn't keep the people I loved safe either. Maybe I had already made up my mind to help them on the cab ride over; it just took my brain a little more time to catch up to my heart.

My choices were dwindling. It was time to roll the hard six. "You said the other night that you needed me to help you locate a 'secret keeper.' What is that?"

She perked up. The naked relief I saw in her face embarrassed me. "Does that mean you will help us?"

"Maybe." I loaded the word with all the impartiality I could muster. We both knew that, to stand any chance of stopping all this weirdness from overtaking my life, I would be forced to bargain with them. Still, my father had raised me better than to throw my lot in with strangers without getting the full story first. "I want to know what I'm getting into before I make any promises."

A smile brightened her face like the sun breaking through storm clouds. "Secret Keeper is a title, much as you would be considered a Warder or I a Healer. It is given to those who possess a gift my people call the Remembering. This Gift gives the Secret Keeper an infallible memory. They have been privy to many things now long forgotten, passed down through others of the bloodline. Their touch unlocks many secrets in the minds of those they connect with. Sometimes they glean things that even the quarry has forgotten. Like Warders or Guardians, they once served our rulers exclusively.

"The man we are seeking calls himself the Lynx. He has long resided in this world. His glamour is incredibly strong, and thus we have not been able to locate him. He was trained by one of the foremost lore keepers in Tír na nÓg, who himself trained under the High Court magi. It is our hope that the Lynx will know how to break the banishment that keeps us from crossing back into our own world. Of course, first we need to find him."

I digested that with a nod. "And that's where I come in."

"Yes. We need your Warding to break through his glamour, once we find him."

"That's all well and good, assuming this Gift of mine works on him, but what's the plan here? You just tote me around the city playing fae-detector?"

She nodded. "In a sense, yes. Mairi and Gannon—Kaine's Guardian, whom you have not yet met—have been searching the city for any trace of the Lynx, but he is incredibly elusive. He himself was banished from our realm some years ago, and it is said he has not trusted another soul with his whereabouts since earning the High King's ire."

"So you're working off rumors?" That did not sound promising.

"Yes and no. We do have some friends willing to aid us here in the city, though they must do so indirectly lest they find themselves named outlaws. They pass along any worthwhile tips they hear to us and if the lead proves promising, Kaine chooses someone to investigate it. If you agree to help us, you will accompany them and become a more reliable set of eyes. Should you see someone that they do not, that person may well be the Lynx, hidden from our sight."

I wanted to pace, but I couldn't find the energy to get to my feet. My bottom lip stung from the vigorous chew I was giving it, but the angst had to come out somehow. This whole thing sounded insane, not to mention a bit dangerous. The last thing I wanted was to be dragged around the city, seeing all sorts of freaks in sheep's clothing, looking for the one freak in particular that no one else could see. "And I'm expected to do this for free?"

She sized me up with a glance. We both knew I wasn't talking money here, though to be honest I wondered for a moment if that was such a bad idea. She said, "Of course not. While I cannot say for certain that all you desire will be agreed to, you are free to set forth your terms for negotiation before the pact is struck."

"Pact. My, that's official sounding. I don't think I'm dressed for the occasion." I giggled and gestured to my little velvet flats and low-cut top. I could tell my usual default-to-sarcasm wasn't going to go over big here. Seana was the most approachable of the three—or four, if I had heard her correctly—and my attempt at humor appeared to be lost on her. With my last ditch attempt to dissuade myself through avarice down, I was out of excuses. In the end, what choice did I have?

As if she was reading my thoughts, she said gently, "Caitlin, you do not have to do this."

That was a lie. She was trying to be kind. "You don't believe that. If I don't help you, what chance do you have of finding the Lynx? And without the Lynx, what chance do you have of finding your way home? And if you don't find a way home, who else is going to stop those things from coming here?" She remained silent. It was all the answer I needed. I looked down at the floor and took a deep breath. Like ripping off a bandage, it was better to do this fast than draw it out any longer. "So where do I have to sign?"

"I myself cannot make such a contract. You will need to speak to Kaine."

Curiosity gnawed at my soul. "I get that he's the head honcho around here but who is he, exactly? Obviously he was important enough to piss off the king and warrant this whole banishment business, so don't try to tell me 'nobody.' I ain't buying that."

"I am not at liberty to discuss his personal matters. Suffice to say that Kaine once stood against the High King and his growing madness, and paid dearly for his sense of honor."

Damn. That just made me all that much more curious. That he was highborn and influential was already a given. The way the two ladies had deferred to his quiet, detached presence in my apartment earlier in the week had assured me of that. I was dying to dig, but I knew better. Seana clearly considered him her leader and respected his privacy. If I tried to wheedle more information out of her, it wouldn't end well. Guess that meant it was time to roll the dice. "Fine. Then where is the big guy?"

She let my flippancy pass but it earned me a warning glance. She nodded in the direction of the staircase behind me. "He is upstairs, in the study." She rose and gestured for me to follow her. The butterflies in my stomach were instant. I had the urge to yell, "No, wait!" but it was too late to back out. I knew what had to be done; what demands I had to lobby for if I was going to get through this alive and ever have a hope of living a normal life again. Heart beating in my throat, I followed her up the stairs.

She stopped me with a gentle hand on the second floor landing, nodding her head in the direction of the closest door, open just a crack to reveal a warm, golden light from within. "Wait here for just a minute, please." She slipped inside and closed the door behind her.

I stood there, feeling lost. I looked around, admiring the dark wood and ivory stucco around me. There were few personal touches in this hall. It was just a long corridor of closed doors and a runner of deep chocolate brown that matched the carpet in the living room below. At the end of the hall, beneath a high-set window, was a small, round table. Calla lilies filled a long, fluted vase on its surface. They looked real from the distance I was standing at. For some odd reason, the sight of fresh flowers comforted me. It made the people I was throwing my lot in with seem more relatable to me. More human.

Of course that was probably just a stupid excuse my alcohol-soaked brain made up to keep me from bolting. I wavered and reached out to steady myself against the wall before I could do something stupid, like topple backwards down the stairs. The longer I was on my feet, the more my body reminded me that it was approaching 3 a.m. and I was no longer a spring chicken. Thankfully only a moment or two passed before Seana slipped back out into the hall, leaving the door cracked behind her. I couldn't read her expression, but I wanted to believe I saw something like concern in her eyes. "He will see you now."

Wow; they were making this a proper audience weren't they? Not trusting myself to open my mouth without something smart-alecky coming out—and I didn't really want to sass the only one of them who had treated me with any sort of understanding—I settled for a nod. As I went to step past her, she stopped me with a hand on my arm. Her lips were so close to my ear I could feel her breath as she whispered, "Be careful. Remember: your words are your bond."

I wanted to ask her what the hell that meant, but she headed down the stairs without another glance. It happened so fast I wondered later if my weary brain had made the whole thing up. I took a deep, centering breath and steeled myself for the worst. I stepped into Kaine's office and closed the door behind me.

CHAPTER EIGHT

I stepped into Kaine's study and was greeted by the most normal, cozy looking office I had ever seen in my life. It was something straight out of an HGTV special. The whole thing radiated masculine warmth, from to the deep green carpets to the honey-colored wainscoting. To my right lay a dormant fireplace; in front of me, a large mahogany desk. The wall behind the desk was lined with bookshelves. They were overflowing with everything from neatly tucked sheaves of paperwork to ancient looking leather-bound books.

The desk itself was the focal point of the room. Two plush looking armchairs faced it from my side, their upholstery matching the carpet. Kaine was seated on the far side in his own throne of a chair, head bent. There was a piece of paper centered on the blotter before him, which he was writing on with—I shit you not—an honest-to-God quill. Fluffy white plumage, graceful golden nib; the whole shebang.

I took in the sights, thinking yet again that I would kill to have their accountant cook my books, and waited. Something about the deference Seana showed him told me this was a "don't speak until you're spoken to" sort of situation. That level of patience wasn't normally my forte, but I had the feeling it would be a struggle to get this partnership get off on the right foot as it was. I didn't need to further stack the deck against me.

Besides, I was nosy. I scanned the bookshelves and picked out what titles I could. It seemed that my host had a taste for Greek philosophers and Irish poets. Not exactly my cup of tea (I preferred losing myself in a brain-numbing bodice-ripper any day), but I admired his spirit.

I was musing over one title whose foreign string of letters baffled my brain when he finally set his "pen" aside. He folded his hands on the blotter and looked up at me. I was struck again by how arresting his gaze was. It was like staring into a bottomless pool of some sort; deep and calm yet subtly unsettling. They were unnaturally bright, like turquoise come to life. There was an inhuman sort of beauty about him, a rugged edge to perfect Calvin Klein model features that spoke of something wild and, well, fae. I let my eyes drop to my feet. It was disgusting how poetic I got whenever I laid eyes upon him.

"Seana says you have changed your mind about aiding us."

Sweet baby Jesus, I was mortified by how deeply this man affected me. Something in his deep baritone resonated with me, setting all my nerves buzzing. No one had ever been able to send my thoughts spinning to unabashed lust with such innocuous words before. Yummy or not, there was no excuse for how flushed that single sentence made me. Resisting the urge to try and cross my traitorous legs, which would look pretty ridiculous while standing, I cleared my throat and tried to sound a lot more confident than I felt. "Perhaps. I think I understand what it is you're asking me to do, but I have some requests of my own before I agree to anything."

It might have been my imagination—I was busy feeling pretty proud of myself for sounding so calm despite my quivering insides—but I thought I saw the corners of his lips rise in the faintest of smirks. He swept out a hand out and gestured to the chairs set before the desk. "Of course. By all means, sit. Let us discuss the venture before us."

Well, there was certainly nothing sexy about that statement. Good. Talk of business kept my panties from dampening any further. I took the chair to the right. Once seated, I did cross my legs. I gave my libido a stern reminder that this was a very serious enterprise we were entering in to and not the time to be fantasizing about how silky Kaine's thick hair would likely feel running through my fingers. We compromised: I promised it free reign to muse over such things once we got home, if it left me alone while I was trying to appear composed. I threw in the extra incentive of a hot bubble bath, because I'm just generous like that.

When I was seated, he asked, "What are your terms?"

I tripped over my tongue for a moment, surprised by the lack of preamble. Watching so many documentaries on the History Channel over the years had made me expect some sort of long, drawn out pomp and circumstance before we got down to the nitty-gritty. Lack of social puffery aside, he sat there behind his grand desk and watched me with the calm, expectant gaze of a man holding court to his lessers. His face was all but unreadable—and, really, I couldn't meet his eyes without some very unsettling tremors in my lady bits—but I could tell he already thought of me as just another vassal looking to join his merry band of minions.

Lucky for me, I had also watched a lot of Law and Order in my day. I cleared my throat again and said, "First, I would like you to explain to me just how you expect me to help you."

"As Seana has told you, the Lynx's glamour keeps him hidden from us.

He resides here, in Riverview, and we have ears listening for any hint of where he might next turn up. We will use your immunity to that glamour to help us locate him. One of us will accompany you when searching for his whereabouts." His stone-cold expression went grim. I thought I saw him heave a small sigh. "There will, regrettably, likely be some trial-and-error to this course of action. While we are yet unclear as to how successful it will be, it is our best—and last—hope."

Grim indeed. High stakes rode on one in a million odds, and Kaine knew it. I said, "I hope you don't expect me to be trolling around the city night and day, looking for the invisible man."

He sat statue still, not even a tremor of a smile crossing his lips. Perhaps my brand of smart-assery was foreign to him. He said, "No. Most of the leg-work will be done by Mairi, Gannon or myself. You will be free to live your life as normal, until we have need of you. When we have an idea of when and where he may make an appearance, we will call you."

Yeah; no. That was not a pit I was falling into. I sat forward in my seat, imitating his ramrod straight posture, hands crossed over one knee. "That's one thing we need to clear up before we go any further. I do have to keep living a normal life, as you yourself just said. That means I can't drop everything and come running every time you think you've got a bead on this guy, especially during my everyday 9 to 5. If I agree help you find this Lynx, I will do so to the best of my ability. But if I can't make it, I need you to respect that."

That did not earn me a happy face. Steel entered his voice. "This is a matter of utmost importance, Ms. Moore. We need the Lynx found as soon as possible."

"Upending my life will not motivate me to find him any quicker. My world has been jacked upside down as is, with trolls and Shades and satyrs frolicking in and out of it. I need some assurance that my life isn't going to become one long, fucked up fairytale."

Those turquoise eyes glittered with disgust. "I assure you that this is no fairytale, nor am I Prince Charming."

"That's just fine by me. I'm not Snow White." I had to grit my teeth to hold back further snark. I took a few slow, deep breaths, and said, "Kaine, I will work *with* you but I don't want that mistaken as me working *for* you. I will aide you when I am able, and you will respect the boundaries of my schedule. Is that clear?"

His gaze continued to bore into me. I had overstepped my boundaries and the Lord of the Manor was not pleased. He was clearly not used to someone talking to him straight. Especially if their brand of "straight" bordered on rude, with a side of defiant. Though my insides were quivering in a whole new (and much more unpleasant) fashion, I stood my metaphorical ground. I kept my chin high.

Finally, after what seemed like an eternity to my aching neck, he nodded once. His mouth had compressed to a thin line, but his tone remained unchanged. "Agreed. We will give you as much notice as possible when we require your assistance, and we will do our best to remain respectful of the schedule you must keep to maintain the life you currently live. In return, you will make yourself as open and available to our needs as humanly possible."

If that hadn't been said with such frostiness, I might have slid out of my chair. Seana's warning echoed in my mind, so I pushed for fine print. "Until the Lynx is found."

This time, I thought I saw another one of those ghost-smirks. "Yes; until the Lynx is found."

"Agreed, then." Kaine wasn't happy, but his feathers didn't seem quite as ruffled as they had been a moment ago. I warmed a little inside at that. I had stood up to the Grand Poobah and lived to tell the tale. More importantly, I proved I had a backbone, for all the good it might actually do me. Time to roll those dice and use that new spine. "In return for my help, I will need a few things. First, I will need you to teach me about the fae." His raised eyebrow made me stutter. "Well, maybe not *you*, per say. One of your entourage or something. I need to know what's going on here. If you want me at my best, I need to be forewarned. I can't keep bumbling around in the dark, running into these things with no idea of what they are or how to handle them."

He nodded. "A fair request. Of course, it would be impossible for you to learn all there is to know about my kind and our ways, even should you live two lifetimes."

His tone made me feel like a pet who had just done a particularly clever trick but I let it slide—as much as I could, anyhow. There was no keeping all of the tartness from my reply. "Because the fae are vast and varied. I get it. I don't need to know everything. I couldn't give a rat's ass who ruled your kingdom five hundred years ago or what fork I would need to use for the cheese course. I want to know what's here, in Riverview; roaming the streets and preying on my people. I have the feeling that I'm going to see more than my fair share of crazy over the next few months and I want to know what to do when I do."

This time, he cracked a faint smile, however quickly it was smothered. I got the feeling that there were very few people who dared use such colorful sarcasm in front of him. He inclined his head. "Understood. Between Seana and Mairi, I believe we can bring you up to speed fairly quickly. Is there anything else you require?"

My mind raced. This was it. I was throwing myself in with this lot of crazies, for better or for worse. If the gravity both he and Seana gave this yet unwritten pact meant anything, this was serious business I was getting into. Seana's warning continued to haunt me. If my word was my bond, so was his. If I wanted something else from him, be it a flush weekly stipend or a goddamned ham sandwich, I had to say so then and there.

"Teach me to defend myself." The words tumbled out of my mouth before they registered with my brain, but they made sense. I was sick to death of feeling like I had no choice in the course of my future. If I was going to play Lynx Detector, I wanted something out of it, consequences be damned. I thought I saw a flicker of surprise in his eyes, the slightest break in that stoic condescension, but wishful thinking was not out of the realm of possibility. I don't think he had expected me to agree to this deal in the first place, let alone make demands of my own. I was proving to be something of an anomaly in the eyes of the rigidly structured fae—and that was a point in my book. I sat up a little straighter. "Teach me to defend myself against those things and I'll help you find your Lynx."

An unbearably long minute ticked by before he said, in the most deadpan voice I had heard from him yet, "That is your price? You will locate the Lynx, but only if we teach you to kill our kin."

When I heard it put like that, it certainly sounded a little off color. Backtracking would be a sign of weakness, however, and that was certainly not the foot I wanted to start off on in this relationship. I nodded and hoped my face was as calm as I was aiming for. "Yes. If they're going to feed on us, I see them as fair game. I want to protect myself and those I love from those slimy creeps when all of this is all said and done."

"I suppose that is a reasonable request." He looked me up and down, brow furrowed. I was aware I didn't look much like the fighting type, big talk aside. "Do you have any foundation to build upon?"

"No, not really. My daddy took me to the range a couple times and I've been to a couple turkey shoots but that's about it." I swallowed hard and refused to let his blasé gaze of incomprehension shake me. I clarified, "I've used a gun a few times, but I'm no expert."

He sneered and waved a dismissive hand. "Modern machinery is often foiled by those skilled in magic, the fae especially. Cold iron is a vastly superior weapon. You will need to learn swordplay and physical combat skills if you truly want to protect yourself."

"Then teach me that. Whatever it takes." For me to walk down the street at night again, I added silently.

"I cannot guarantee you will learn all that you wish," he warned. "As I have stated, time is of the essence. Should you find the Lynx as quickly as we hope, this may prove an unfair bargain."

"I'll take that risk. I'm a fast learner when properly motivated."

He nodded, lips pursed. He sat back in his chair, fingers steepled beneath his chin; the image of deep consideration. Sweat beaded on my lip as I waited out his silence, itching to beg, to plead. Two more seconds and I would have screamed in frustration. But, when he finally responded, I was blindsided. "Agreed. Your requests are sound, however crudely they may have been put forth. Yet, I find it odd that you have made no mention of the troll that played such a key role in the crossing of our paths."

Well, shit.

I realized my jaw had dropped and shut my mouth with an audible click of my teeth. How in the hell had I forgotten Goliath? He had seen me—but worse, he knew that I had seen him. Shades and satyrs were all well and good, but he was the biggest threat to my safety. Kaine could train me to be a super solider, a one-woman fairy-killing death squad, and that wouldn't make one lick of difference if Goliath went home and told all his buddies (and their crazy king) about my nifty little Gift. No skill in the world could protect me from the onslaught that would bring crashing down on my doorstep.

It was too late to hide my surprise, but I tried to play it cool. "I need your help with him as well, yes."

A slow smirk spread across his face. His eyes positively twinkled. "Define: help."

I swallowed down the fury that bubbled up in my throat and tried not to sound like I was choking on my carefully worded request. "He can't let the High King know about me. I want you to hunt him down and make sure he can never tell the High King about my Gift."

"And by that you mean…?"

"Dead. I want the troll dead." Anger blazed inside me like a wild, demonic thing. All the fear, all the confusion, all the god-damned helplessness that I had been feeling all week long exploded. "I will never be safe so long as that monster walks this earth and I want you to help me kill him."

Kaine sat back in his chair, looking relaxed and human for the first time all evening. "Is this your final request?"

"Yes," I ground out, teeth clenched.

"I will take you under my wing and my retainers will teach you as much as they are able about faekind and how to defend yourself against my bestial brethren. We will do all in our power to hunt down the troll and make sure he can never tell the High King about you gift, agree to dispatch of him once and for all when he is found. This is my solemn oath to you. In return, you agree to remain bound to me until you have helped us locate the Lynx and learn the means with which to break Tiernan's banishment. Do we have an agreement?"

"Yes."

Kaine stood and gestured for me to do the same. He took an ornate dagger out of the top drawer of his desk. Without so much as a blink, he slashed his right palm on its razor sharp blade. He flipped the knife over in a one-handed movement that defied logic and offered it to me hilt first with his uninjured hand. I must have been gaping like a carp again, because he said, "All fae pacts are sealed with blood."

Now Seana's warning made sense. This wasn't some drawn up contract, signed and sealed with fancy wax. This was a magical binding in its own right. I didn't know enough about my Gift to know if this magic would work on me or not, but I had the feeling Kaine would not have purposed it in the first place if it wouldn't. Too late I realized my mistake. Why hadn't I asked the pertinent questions? Like, what would happen if either of us broke this bond? I had the feeling it couldn't be anything good. Was there an escape clause in there, in case this Lynx proved to be a myth, or was I going to be bound to this man until the day I died? Something told me it wouldn't be that easy to walk away, not if we were sealing the damn thing in bodily fluids.

Shit.

He waited, hand extended, with blood pooling on his palm. It was too late to back out now. It was now or never. I took the dagger with a trembling hand, nearly dropping it when its weight proved much more substantial than I had anticipated. The golden hilt was cool in my grip, the wickedly sharp silver blade already wet with blood. I stared at it for a long moment, stomach churning. My heart hammered so fast I thought I could hear it in my ears. There was no other way. I had already made up my mind. I turned my head away and squeezed my eyes shut as I drew it across my left palm. The steel was so sharp I barely felt it cut my flesh.

He took the dagger from my hand and held forth his bleeding palm. I let him clasp my own wounded hand, gasping as the string flared to life under his crushing grip. I met his eyes, blinking back tears. He said, "And so the pact is made."

I echoed, "And so the pact is made."

A surge of burning pain ran up my arm, like the stinging bites of a hundred fire ants. I cried out, jerking my hand from his grasp. I stumbled back, catching myself on one of the chairs before I fell to the ground. My head spun. It took me a minute to realize that the hand that I had caught the arm of the chair with was the one I had cut—yet there was no pain. My arm continued to tingle, like it once had when I tried to stick a plug into an ungrounded socket (let's just say I wasn't the smartest child), but my palm should have been screaming in agony of its own. I looked down at it and saw smooth, unbroken skin. No gash; not even the faintest trace of blood.

I looked back up at Kaine. He was once again seated behind his desk. The dagger had disappeared back to wherever it had come from. He held the quill in his hand once again and it moved in deft strokes as he finished up the letter he had been writing when I first entered. He was the perfect picture of nonchalance.

Good god. What kind of devil had I just bound my soul to?

CHAPTER NINE

The next morning, I awoke in a strange bed. I hadn't thought I would sleep well in a house full of strangers, especially since one of them had apparently just become my blood-bound buddy. Maybe it was sheer exhaustion or the super high thread count of their expensive sheets, but I couldn't have lasted more than five minutes before passing right out. I could hear birds singing outside when I next opened my eyes, curled up on my side, wrapped in a little cocoon of soft, warm blankets. I hated to admit it, but my own bed was not nearly as comfortable.

I yawned and rubbed the sleep-crusties from my eyes. The curtains were drawn but a digital clock on the nightstand told me it was almost noon. The sky had been starting to lighten as I was shown to my borrowed bedroom, so I couldn't have slept all that long. All things considered, I felt pretty good, despite the harrowing night I had had. It took a moment for the feeling of being watched to penetrate my sleepy haze. The hairs on the back of my neck rose. I rolled over and sat up, gasping at the sight of Mairi perched cross-legged on the foot of the bed. I wasn't a deep sleeper. How the hell had she gotten there without me noticing?

"Sorry. I didn't mean to scare you," she said. She gave me a shy smile, like the new kid at school who was unsure of her welcome on the playground. I didn't know what to say, exactly. It was pretty creepy to wake up and find her staring at me, but that was hardly the worst thing that had happened to me lately. Technically, it was her home; not mine. Instead of making a fuss I just smiled back and made a noncommittal shrug.

While the thought of the things she could do still scared the holy bejesus out of me, in her human form she was rather normal. She reminded me of a sixteen year old dead set on disobeying her parents, with the bleached blond hair and a hole frayed in one of the knees of her black skinny jeans. Her heavy eyeliner matched her sparkly purple tank top and the black nail polish on her short nails was artfully chipped around the edges. She was cute and harmless, in that rebellious punk rock sort of way. I smiled as I thought back to my own teenage years, chock-full of black clothing, burgundy lipstick, and endless hours of listening to Type O Negative. Ah, the good old days of my misspent youth.

I ran my fingers through my tangled hair and regretted my lack of a comb. And a flat-iron. Maybe a fresh shirt. And, while I was at it, I added a clean change of underwear to the wish-list. She watched me with a mix of curiosity and defiance, toying with the stringy edges of the gap over her right knee. Perhaps she was just as unsure of me as I was of her. That was a thought. I broke the silence before it could get too uncomfortable. "Did Seana send you to check up on me?"

Her nodded. "She was worried. We don't sleep much. She wasn't really sure how much sleep a human would need."

"Luckily I've never needed much either." As soon as the words left my mouth, I remembered her offhand question about my humanity at our first meeting. Not wanting to go down that road again, I quickly changed the subject. "I assume you were told that I made a pact with Kaine last night, to help you guys find the Lynx?" At her nod, I continued, "Great. Only, Kaine wasn't exactly chatty when it came to explaining just what this 'pact' thing means. Do you know more about it?"

"Pacts of blood are very serious," she said. "They're only invoked in extremely important matters. Bad things happen to either party if they try to back out of it without fulfilling their end of the deal."

Bad things. Well, that was just great. Everything from being chased by the slavering hounds of hell to being subjected to endless hours of Dr. Phil on loop sprang to mind. I didn't think I had the gumption to have her elaborate while I was on an empty stomach. Topic number two, then. "So, Kaine said one of you will help teach me about the fae. Should I assume lesson one will be taking place today? Perhaps over brunch?"

She shook her head. "Kaine wanted you to meet with Gannon first."

Ah. So Lesson One would be fairy kung-fu. I had meant every word about wanting to learn to defend myself from creatures like Goliath and the Wax-Man. I just hadn't expected that first thing in the... I glanced over at the clock; twelve o' five. Well, not exactly first thing in the morning, but; still. That was a lot to spring on a girl at the crack of noon. Maybe the lack of clean clothing wasn't so important after all. I had the feeling I'd be covered in sweat by the end of the day, given my rather soft physique.

Mairi unfolded herself with a teenaged grace I envied, and picked a small tote bag up off the hope chest at the foot of the bed. It looked familiar; much like one I had at... I fixed her with a very perturbed stare. She looked sheepish as she said, "Kaine asked me to get you something more comfortable for you to train in. I grabbed some stuff from your bathroom too. And I put your keys back in your purse."

I took the bag with a tight smile. Longing for clean clothes aside, I was a bit annoyed that they had taken it upon themselves to go through my things while I slept. I guess this new lack of privacy was something I was going to have to get used to. Something told me this wouldn't be the last time our fae/human sensibilities clashed. I rifled through the bag. The items she had chosen was more like lounge-wear than real clothing. Stretchies and a tank top were all well and good for working out, but I certainly wasn't going to feel very comfortable hailing a cab in them later on. Then again, they were probably the closest thing I had to appropriate gym attire. Getting all sweaty with a fairy hadn't been high on my list of priorities thus far in my life.

When I looked back up, Mairi had paused in the doorway. She nodded her head toward the hall beyond. "Come on. I'll show you where the bathroom is. Seana will make you something to eat before I take you to Gannon." She paused, looking me over. I hope I didn't look as panicked as I felt. "Something light, maybe. Not gonna lie. Gannon is pretty tough. You're in for a workout today."

Just what a girl wants to hear. For the hundredth time I wondered just what the hell I was doing. I extricated myself from the sheets and followed her down the hall, my tote clutched tight in my arms. I reminded myself again and again that I had asked for this. I'd be damned if I was going to back down. Kaine's obvious expectation of my failure was one thing; that I had pretty much expected. Seeing that pity mirrored on the face of a rail-thin girl who looked half my age? Nuh-uh. That wasn't going to fly.

I was going to show them both up.

After all, how bad could it be?

~*~

Me and my big fucking mouth.

You would think, in my thirty years of walking the planet, I would have learned somewhere along the way not to tempt fate. Or maybe, at the very least, not to goad it on so damn much. Yeah—nope.

Sunday night found me unable to move off of my couch. There wasn't a single inch of my body that didn't feel gross. Or sore. Or, more likely, both. My hair was sweat-crusted and scraggly and my scalp was itching for a shower, but I had no motivation to move. I was sprawled in an awkward half-slump but that position only made a handful of my numerous bruises ache. That was good enough for me. I didn't care that I reeked like holy hell or that I hadn't eaten since brunch. I was pretty sure I was dehydrated from losing half my body weight in sweat too, but the kitchen was just too far away. My thighs trembled at the thought of standing. I still wasn't sure how

I had made it up the steep staircase to my apartment in the first place. There was a distinct possibility that I might have stopped halfway up, arms wrapped around the banister for dear life as I wept like a little baby. Of course, that might have been a hallucination. I wasn't sure I had enough moisture left in my body for tears.

The stubborn itch along the nape of my neck finally won. I reached back to scratch it and swore at the pain that radiated down my arm. My muscles were worn well past the point of exhaustion. I was too weak to hold a pen, let alone the stupid wooden rod I had been tortured with all day. The succession of bruises along my forearm didn't help. They were ugly yellow-blue reminders that I was shit when it came to blocking a blow.

Lesson One had not gone in my favor.

Just thinking about it made bile rise in my throat all over again. From anger, of course; not from the excruciating pain that had made me think I was going to hurl on Gannon's shoes multiple times throughout the day.

Gannon.

Ugh. I wish I *had* hurled on his stupid shoes. It would have served him right.

Seana had watched me throughout breakfast with the troubled eyes of a mother sending her child off to their first day of kindergarten. It had made eating difficult, but I tried to smile and kept the conversation light. Mairi sat across from me at their quaint kitchen table and watched me with those strangely luminous eyes the whole time, which didn't exactly add to my sense of ease. I had no intention of showing either of the women just how piss-scared I was, but after ten minutes of chatting about the weather and traffic patterns, I finally just shut my trap and focused on putting fork to mouth.

After I had forced down enough orange juice, buttered toast, and eggs over-easy to placate the cook, Mairi had taken me back upstairs. In what I had assumed to be a broom closet across the hall from my former guest room, there was actually a narrow staircase leading up to a third floor. Perhaps it had been meant as an attic at one time, but now it was clear of any clutter. There were no boxes of Christmas ornaments or old baby clothes up there. It had clearly been outfitted to be a training room (a.k.a. my personal hell).

It was one large rectangular room that ran the length and width of the house. Huge skylights had been set at regular intervals in the ceiling, flooding the room with natural light. The hardwood floor was spotless, except for a large red ring painted in the middle. A long wooden bar that looked like it belonged in a ballet studio ran along the wall to the left. I saw a weight bench and matching punching bag tucked in the back right corner, as well as stacks of faded blue padded mats that reminded me of my elementary school gym class. A few shelves rounded out the room and ran along the far wall, damn near overflowing with a hodge-podge of sporty looking items I couldn't even begin to identify.

Those run-of-the-mill home gym bits weren't the worst of it. It was the rack of neatly placed wooden rods closest to the door gave me pause. The one next to it containing sheathed swords caused the knot in my stomach to sink even lower. What the hell had I been thinking, asking for this? I didn't have a lick of combat training, unless you counted the one-day self-defense seminar we had had in my senior year of high school. Hell, I couldn't even keep a gym membership in good faith. Ten minutes on the treadmill was my highest achievement and I'm pretty sure I had stopped for ice cream on the way home.

Me and my bright ideas.

I didn't even notice the man standing in the shadows next to the stairwell door until he moved away from the wall. To say I jumped out of my skin would be an understatement. I nearly bowled poor little Mairi over as I stumbled back, a hand pressed to my chest. I managed to strangle my scream, biting my tongue in the process. Not the first impression I wanted to make by a long shot. I had expected some hulking brute with battle scars and stacked muscles the size of a professional wrestler, with all the hush-hush hype they had spoken of him with. Instead, Gannon turned out to be only a head and a half taller than me, with a lean frame much like Kaine's. Perhaps faeries didn't bulk up like human meat-heads. Even the cold-eyed, sword-wielding ones.

And man, those eyes were cold. Where Kaine's were that weird shade of turquoise and filled with heat that made me feel every inch a woman, Gannon's were the startlingly clear blue of the winter sky. Like that frigid sky, there wasn't a drop of warmth in them. He wasn't an unattractive man. Quite the opposite, really. Not too tall, well-muscled, flat stomach that promised washboard abs. He hit every item on my man-candy wish list, yet the vibe I got from him was much more "watch your back" than "come hither." There was something undeniably predatory—almost feral—about his face, with its high cheekbones and thin nose, surrounded by dark hair that was cropped short on the sides, yet tousled on the top. The calculating stare didn't help. My eyes skidded away from his, to escape that chill. He wore loose black track pants, a matching sleeveless shirt, and worn trainers: the uniform of every jock who had ever laughed at my scrawny ass in high school. His crossed arms were taut with wiry muscle. I did not doubt the rest of him was likely as strong. Something told me someone with the title of Guardian wouldn't be a push-over.

Mairi giggled behind me and I elbowed her in the stomach without looking. Gently, of course. Gannon's eyes never left me. His scowl hadn't budged. I took a deep breath and hoped my face wasn't as red as it felt. I straightened up, squared my shoulders, and extended a hand. "Hello, I'm

Caitlin."

He didn't return the favor. Instead, he jerked his head in the direction of the ring at the center of the room. "Let's see what you can do."

I let my hand drop. The rebuttal stung. I wanted to call him out on his rudeness, but swallowed my pride. Maybe the fae were immune to what we humans called "common courtesy." I found my eyes drawn to the center of the room. My mouth went dry. I had no clue what he expected from me, but I had the feeling I would be glad that Mairi had chosen yoga-pants and sneakers when raiding my wardrobe. I strode toward that evil-eye painted on the floor with my head held high, but inside I was shaking. When I looked back, Mairi was gone. Gannon had two of the wooden rods in hand, his feet braced shoulder's width apart in a fighter's stance at the edge of the ring. How he had moved so quickly and silently was beyond me. The only coherent thought I remember having at that moment was *I am so screwed*.

He tossed one of the poles at me with an easy underhand. I grappled with it as it came my way, nearly dropping it in the process. I cringed. This was going to be a train wreck.

I didn't miss his deep sigh. My face lit up like a bonfire. His voice held a note of condescension. "I see that Kaine wasn't kidding when he said you had no training."

I whipped my head up. He smirked. My mind flashed back to the memories of schoolyard bullies and stupid football jocks. So, he found amusement in my clumsiness, in my embarrassment, did he? I knew without him saying a word that he expected me to quit right then and there.

Well, fuck that.

Being discounted out of hand was a big pet peeve of mine. I would be damned if I was going to take that from some asshole who had known me for all of five minutes. I didn't know what this Guardian could do—maybe he shot laser beams from his eyes, for all I knew—but I wasn't going to let him intimidate me. I straightened up, hefting the pole to get a sense of its weight. It wasn't all that heavy, but it was long and would make for an uncooperative dance partner. I had no doubt it would wear on my scrawny chicken arms after a few swings, but I didn't plan on letting that stop me. Instead, I summoned every memory of movie magic I could and positioned myself so I faced off with him on an angle. I held the staff catty-corner in front of me with two hands and met his unimpressed stare with a frosty glare of my own.

He tilted his head to the side, amusement gone. I didn't see one bit more of respect in his eyes but at least I had wiped that smirk from his face. He came towards me with the loping grace of a jungle cat and I knew a moment of true fear. This man was dangerous. I had been right to think him predatory; he moved like an animal on the hunt. I knew that Kaine had ordered him to train me but that didn't mean much in the long run. He wasn't my enemy but he wasn't my friend either. He wouldn't kill me, sure, but that didn't mean I wasn't going to get hurt. In that training room, we were alone. Not ten minutes in, not a single swing taken, and I already knew that in that space, Gannon called the shots. Worse, Gannon would be the one *taking* the shots, at me. I had the feeling he would revel in me learning each lesson the hard way.

Boy, was I right.

Even home, sprawled on my couch, the anger flared up inside me again. My fists clenched and my face flushed with embarrassment. The first few minutes hadn't been so bad. He had corrected my stance with clipped directions and a firm hand here and there. I tried not to stiffen every time we made contact but it was hard. I trusted him about as much I would have trusted a starved back-alley mongrel. Probably less, honestly. Still; that had been tolerable. I saw the wisdom in his guidance and though the stance made the muscles in my shoulders and calves burn with new use in no-time, I was grateful that Lesson 1.1 was something I didn't fail at immediately.

The same cannot be said for Lesson 1.2 through 1.5.

I couldn't block a blow to save my life. The "gentle" first taps he gave my staff to help me get the rhythm of the blocking maneuvers sent shockwaves of vibration up my arms. My initial fears were correct: after only a few minutes of slow mock fighting my arms started to shake. I gritted my teeth and kept at it, following the tempo as he counted in a droning monotone. After another few minutes he stopped mid-count and stepped back. I fell back to the starting stance as quickly as I could, just as he had instructed. It was sloppy as hell, but I got there.

"Have you had enough for one day?"

There was no need for him to tell me he thought I was pathetic. It was clear from his blasé disdain. I strengthened my grip on the staff, ignoring the sweat dripping down my neck. My muscles were burning but adrenaline surged through me. I thought I had a pretty good handle on the different positions. "Hardly." I tossed my head to get the damp hair out of my eyes. "Is that all you've got?"

I *really* needed to do something about that smart-ass gene.

When Gannon pulled off the gloves and started to come at me for real, I realized that I had never stood a chance. Even my best block was far too slow. I lost count of the raps I took from his lightning quick strikes. I gave up on watching his feet to anticipate his next move. He was just too damn fast. Trying to keep up with his unnatural speed made me dizzy. Maybe I got lucky and fended off a strike here and there, but they were followed up by counter-strikes so blindingly fast I couldn't fathom how he was changing his trajectory so quick. Every time my staff went spinning from my hands and clattered to the ground, I saw disappointment in his eyes. It was humiliating.

Each bout ended with me the loser. Every time he stepped back and fell into the starting stance without the slightest hitch to his breath, I felt a piece of me die. He just stood there, looking composed without the faintest sign of strain, and let me stop to catch my breath—sometimes hunched over holding my knees, other times laid flat out on the sweat-slick floor. While I wheezed he would ask me again if I was ready to quit. He stopped saying "for one day" when one bout ended in a split lip. It was clear that he expected me to walk away, never to return—but that just made me angrier. I was slower to rise each time, and my staff was held lower and lower, but I refused to give up. I scraped myself back up, posturing as best I could, and let him shame me.

Again, and again, and again.

The last time, I could barely feel my fingers and every part of me ached worse than I had ever felt before. His final blow hit me square in the stomach. It knocked me flat. I fell face-first against the floor, all the breath driven from my burning lungs. My staff skittered away as I lay there, blood smeared across my chin from my reopened lip. I gagged and gasped for air around the pain. The world spun. Out of the corner of my eye, I saw his sneakers come within an inch of my head. He stopped. I couldn't muster the strength to look up at his face, let alone stand.

"We're done here."

I was too exhausted to search for the scorn in his deadpan voice. I was revolted by my poor performance; I had no doubt he was as well. He walked away, his even footsteps stopping once by the door; probably to put away the practice weapons. A few more echoing steps brought him to the top of the stairs and then he was gone. I laid there for a long while. I might have even passed out for a bit. When Mairi finally roused me from my stupor, the room was nearly engulfed in shadows. My face was wet with tears when she helped me to my feet, but she was kind enough to pretend not to notice.

"I should've puked on his fucking shoes," I spat as I forced myself up off the couch. Each movement made me wince. I was sore and tired but also so angry that sitting still was impossible. Maybe it was the rage or maybe it was the day's exertion catching up with me, but I realized I was also powerfully hungry. I shuffled down the hall to the kitchen and rummaged around until I found bread and peanut butter. I kicked the fridge door shut—with a muffled curse at myself—after I put the grape jelly away. Taking my anger out on inanimate objects was the best I was going to get. I didn't want to go through the fun of maneuvering myself into a chair again, so I ate standing with my back against the kitchen counter.

Sandwich finished, I lingered in the same spot, transfixed by the playback in my head. I was furious with Gannon for his casual dismissal of me. For his mocking smirk. For his contempt. He hadn't taught me a damn thing. All he had done was use me like a personal punching bag! That downright enraged me. But even more, I was furious with myself. I had goaded him on, like an idiot teasing a tiger with a big, raw steak. Maybe I would have stood a better chance if I had been nice or, god forbid, respectful but; no. Instead I had run my mouth, like always. I could resent how hard he had pressed me, how hard he had beaten me, but the truth was that I had asked for it. I had hurt his ego from the word go, and now that was damage I would constantly be struggling to undo.

That was bad enough. But the ease with which he had taken me down again and again? That stung ten times worse than any blow I had taken, even the one that had split open my face. I sucked at fighting. If there was a word beyond sucked, something even worse, I'd be that. I felt like a fool for having signed on for this; for having demanded it be part of the pact.

Whatever delusions of grandeur I had entertained about playing avenging angel on the darkened city streets seemed stupid in hindsight. Now I was at the mercy of a man who I had not only offended but one that was amazingly good at what he did, while I could barely get out of the way of my own feet. Fantastic. I was only beginning to realize how deep over my head I was—and I had the feeling the bottom was still a long way off.

I don't know how long I stood there in my kitchen, replaying the awful day over and over in my head. When I finally mustered the energy to drag myself away from the counter, shuffling toward a much needed shower with stiffness that made me limp, my face was wet again. I was thankful there was no one around to hide it from this time.

CHAPTER TEN

By mid-week I started to feel human again. The first couple of days were a rather unpleasant adventure though. I was so stiff from Lesson One that I moved like an arthritic grandmother. On top of that, each day required spackling on a ridiculous amount of foundation to keep from being asked just what I had done over my little vacation. Luckily my co-workers had accepted my tale of boring relaxation: shopping trips and Mad Men marathons on Netflix were a perfectly acceptable use for PTO as far as they were concerned. I had thrown in an anecdote about having signed up for a self-defense class at the gym, just in case anyone noticed the shoddy job I had done of covering up my fading shiner.

No one had.

Marc avoided me. Our paths crossed once, on Monday morning as I went to grab some paperwork from the copier by his department. He had looked away just as quickly as I had, hiding his snout in a pile of paperwork. I didn't think he had any clue that I could see him for what he really was, but there was no mistaking the tension between us. Maybe he felt guilty for having gossiped about my mental meltdown around the office.

Little did he know that he was doing me a favor. I much preferred the awkward silences over his previous flirtations. The last thing I needed was a daily dose of his furry face, while I was trying so hard to act normal. Then again "normal" was pretty hard to achieve, given that I was touching up my makeup every hour to keep the whole world from asking questions I didn't have very believable answers for. So, maybe I was screwed either way.

Trying to fit back in to the workplace had made me doubly appreciative that Seana had taken the time to stop by my apartment to check on me on Sunday evening. My lip had swollen up three times its usual size, oozing whenever I tried to eat, and my nose had been looking a bit off kilter as well. It had seemed silly, at the time, to go through the trouble of getting all doped up for something so little. After all, Seana couldn't just wiggle her fingers and work her mojo on me, like she would on anyone else. Oh no; thanks to the Warding I had to knock back a truly foul tasting concoction that I was damn near certain contained all sorts of icky twigs and berries. I had to give it to her though; whatever that putrid smoothie contained, it worked quicker than a double dose of NyQuil. I had barely had time to curse its tongue curdling flavor before I slipped off to la-la land. It also hadn't left me feeling the least bit groggy when she roused me a little while later, my nose straight and lip whole once more. Bonus.

Unfortunately, there had been nothing she could do for bruising. She said that there were some things the body just had to take care of in its own time but I had the feeling that was a load of crap. The disapproval in her eyes as she treated me had been fairly obvious. Maybe she thought I deserved the ass whooping I had taken as much as I did. The memory made me groan. I was tired of replaying the embarrassing spectacle in my mind, but my brain seemed to have it on permanent repeat.

Ugh. Whatever. I still hated Gannon with gonorrhea-like passion and daydreamed of the day when I could knock him flat on his back, but I had awoken that morning with the resolution to put him and my crushing embarrassment from my mind. I didn't know how I would handle our next meeting, in or out of that cursed practice ring, but that was another bridge I'd burn when I came to it. It was Wednesday, which meant that the workweek was half over and I was on the mend. All in all, it was too nice a day for me to waste on dark thoughts.

I met up with Jenni for lunch at a cute little café down the street from my office. The day was crisp but not yet unbearable and the sun was shining. All morning long I had thought of little other than some fresh air, shared gossip, and a hot fresh mozzarella and roasted red pepper panini. As soon as I rounded the corner into the little nook of outdoor tables, I spotted her and waved. I threaded my way through to where she was sitting, the smile wiped from my face as I was greeted with a wide-eyed stare and an exclamation of, "Jesus Christ, Cat! What the hell happened to your face?"

Leave it to your bestie to see through five layers of makeup.

I hung my purse on the back of the chair and sat down. "Gee, nice to see you too."

Jenni reached across and took my hand, squeezing it hard in the lazy friend's version of a sit-down hug. She was still searching my face with concern. "I'm sorry. Seriously though, what's with the black eye?"

Before she could start to make guesses—which would inevitably lead to another round of guilt over what had happened at Gilroy's on The Night of the Troll—I thought it best to throw her off the trail. I stuck to the same glib half-lie I had used around the office. "It's no big deal. I started taking a self-defense class." I threw in a self-deprecating laugh. "Obviously I'm not very good yet."

Her look softened to something like pity, mixed with smothered amusement. "Awww, Cat..."

I picked up my menu and busied myself reading it to hide my guilt. "Don't you 'awww' me! Go ahead, laugh. I know you want to."

"I'm not going to laugh, I swear. It's not a bad idea, you know. Remember when I took that one at the Y a few years ago? Parts of this city have gone to hell. A girl should know a couple moves." She paused. I was sure she was giving me a knowing look, but I studiously avoided it. She hated the neighborhood I lived in. Part of me knew it was because she was jealous of my solitude, but there was an equal amount of concern for the safety that solitude cost me. Especially given what had happened recently. There was just no avoiding it, was there? It was like I had that damn pink elephant on a leash and it followed me everywhere. All I wanted was to forget about faeries and special destinies and trolls.

When I continued to act like the wrap list was the most interesting thing in the world, she sighed and continued, "You should have told me. I would have signed up with you."

"I'd rather flail around like a spider-monkey on Ritalin by myself, thanks." That came out a lot more snarky than I'd intended. I forced another laugh I wasn't feeling. I knew she would see right through it, so I quickly added, "Sorry. You know how much I love looking like an idiot Maybe once I learn to stop running into people's elbows instead of away from them you can take the advanced level course with me."

I tried not to let the troubled smile that earned get to me. Three minutes into lunch and I was already failing miserably at trying to be normal. Thankfully the waitress came and rescued me from the awkward silence I had caused. I ordered my panini and an iced tea, gathering my thoughts while Jenni hemmed and hawed over the menu at the last minute, just like she always did. She finally settled on a diet soda and tuna on white toast. Just like she always did. She didn't notice my dewy-eyed smile as she checked the email that had just come through on her phone. I don't know why her predictable behavior made me want to bear-hug her and start bawling—but damn, did it ever. Maybe Gannon had knocked a few screws loose after all.

"Jason just emailed me. He got a job at a museum in NYC," she said, beaming. "He's moving back to Riverview in a few months!"

I made an appreciative noise. Jason, Jenni's little brother, was the same age as my sister Emma at six years our junior. He and Jenni had been pretty close all through our lives, where Emma and I had been anything but. The sibling bond was another of those family intricacies that was pretty much lost on me. "Good for him. Bet your mom will be excited."

"Oh yeah, I see a huge Fisher family reunion in the immediate future." She laughed and gave me a saucy wink. "I bet Jason would be pretty excited if you came too."

I groaned, letting my head fall back. Jason had had quite the thing for me in his later teenage years, though that childhood crush was an awkward phase of my life I'd rather have forgotten about completely. When I said as much, it seemed to hit a nerve. Jenni's eyes went all squinty in the way they did when someone said something off-color, making me wonder if she was playing at being offended or if I had stepped in it. She said, "Jason's a good kid. Polite, handsome, and apparently set up with a really good job on top of it all. You could do far worse. Are you saying there's something wrong with dating him?"

Shit. She really was offended. I held up my hands in the patented gesture of "what do you want me to say" and said, "There's nothing wrong with him. I'm sure a hundred girls out there would be lucky to have him. The problem is the idea of me dating him."

"And why is that?"

"It just squicks me out, okay?" I caught my bitchiness too late, once again. I backpedaled. "I mean, he's your little brother. We grew up with him and Emma tagging around behind us. I remember him crashing our sleepovers in his ThunderCats footie pajamas for Christ's sake! The whole idea of it would just be far too… Weird."

She laughed. "Well, okay. When you put it like that, I guess I get it."

Before the awkwardness could re-descend—or she could back track to ask questions about the pretend self-defense class I was supposed to be taking—I said, "So, get this. I get in this morning and hear those two bitches in HR gabbing while they're getting their coffee. It sounds like that new girl they hired is supposed to 'shadow' Karen for the next week and a half. And they want to call Karen in for a 'meeting' next Friday, which just so happens to be payday."

Jenni's eyes lit up with a familiar mischievous fire. She never could resist some juicy gossip. It didn't hurt that Karen was the snotty bitch who had treated me like a lackey for the first three months I had been with the company. Jenni was not forgiving to those who had made her bestie cry into her ice cream, once upon a time. She broke out in a particularly smug grin, cooing, "Oooo! Sounds like someone is about to get fiiiiiired!"

We made some vicious, catty speculations about Karen's general character throughout lunch and Jenni had me laughing so hard my eyes watered. The hour passed too quickly. I hadn't felt so much like myself in longer than I cared to remember. We were lingering over our nearly empty drinks when my phone rang. I didn't recognize the number, but it was a local area code. While Jenni flagged down our waitress for the check, I propped the phone on my shoulder and dug around in my purse for my wallet. "Hello?"

"Hi, Caitlin?"

I froze. It was Mairi. I had to remind myself to breath. Damn, that elephant was persistent. Apparently an hour of being a carefree, ordinary person again was all I got. I swallowed the sour lump in my throat and made myself sound casual, "Oh, hey. What's up?"

"Can you meet me tonight?" Her voice was so calm and even that I couldn't get a bead on what was going on. She seemed to sense my hesitation and clarified, "To look for the Lynx."

"Tonight? Oh, uh—yeah, sure; sure." My insides felt like they had turned to acid. My stomach churned and made me regret the heavy dose of crushed red pepper I had begged the waitress to put on my sandwich. Jenni's head was tilted to the side in the puzzled way that ensured there would be more questions waiting when I hung up the phone. I couldn't figure out how to draw more information out of Mairi without asking things I would rather Jenni didn't hear.

Instead, I pulled the check from her hand and started counting out bills, trying for all the world to act like that phone call was the most normal thing ever. "I get out of work at 5. Is that okay?"

"Sure. Kaine wants us to start rotating through some of his more likely haunts. Tonight will be a good trial run, so we can get a method down."

"That sounds... Fun."

"Great. Are you ready to take down an address?" I didn't know what to say. How could I respond to that without sounding like a nut-job in front of Jenni? Mairi must have noticed my pause because after a moment she asked, "You're somewhere where you can't speak about this, aren't you?"

This time my burst of laughter was real, though it had a hysterical edge. "Yeah, you got that right!"

I thought I heard a muffled chuckle echo through the earpiece. At least it was muffled; that proved she had some tact. Maybe not every faery got a thrill out of playing Embarrass The Human. There was still a hint of amusement in her words. "Sorry. Next time I'll just shoot you a text. I'll send you the address in a minute. See you tonight."

The phone went silent as the call ended. Thank god Jenni didn't know that. I pushed out another laugh. "Sounds good, Em. See you later."

I shoved the phone into my purse. Jenni had sat back in her seat, eyebrows raised but her curiosity visibly dimmed. She had bought it; she thought the call had been from my sister. Thank god she didn't question the coincidence of us both hearing from our younger siblings in under an hour. I threw in a roll of the eyes and a huffy sigh to seal the deal. "Like I don't have better things to do than help her look through stupid graduate school stuff."

"Why doesn't your mom help her?" Jenni asked, slupring up the last of her soda. "I mean, doesn't she realize your advice about higher education is probably the advice she should run screaming in the opposite direction from?"

I stuck my tongue out at her but shared in the laugh. "I know, right?"

Hopefully the thick layer of foundation was hiding the flush I felt in my cheeks. There were no words to describe the level of terrible I felt when lying to my bestie. We hugged goodbye and made promises to get together for drinks over the weekend. I wasn't sure where exactly we would do that, as I was quickly ruling out all the decent bars in Riverview with my weird encounters, but I agreed nonetheless. I shoved my hands in my jacket pockets as I made my way back to the office. I had left it only an hour ago with so much pep in my step. That was gone. The energy had been drained right out of me.

All I had wanted was to enjoy a casual, normal lunch with a friend and I hadn't even been able to do that.

CHAPTER ELEVEN

It turned out that I was meeting Mairi at the big Barnes and Noble downtown, only a stone's throw from my office. It wasn't a place I frequented; I preferred to spend my last buck at the dying mom n' pop shops rather than the massive two-story corporate edifice that was choking the life out of those shops. Still, it was close and had the added bonus of a coffee shop inside. Both facts were much appreciated once I realized I'd be spending my usual dinnertime hunting for a ghost.

Mairi met me there and waited patiently by my side in the long line so I could grab an overpriced latte and a blueberry muffin. She declined my offer to get her a beverage, which I was secretly glad for. Payday seemed eons away to my nearly empty wallet.

Bookstores have always been a happy place for me. Something about the smell of ink and paper was soothing; comforting yet filled to bursting with so many possibilities. I could still remember how exciting such stores had seemed to me when I was a child. My father and I had often made early morning trips out to them when I was younger. I would inevitably come back to him with a stack of books when it was time to leave, and he would bluster over how I couldn't possibly need all of them. That was just dad being dad. He'd buy them despite his grumbling and we'd find ourselves back there in a week or two. I had always been a big reader and it was something my parents had encouraged.

The adult in me didn't approve of the corporate greed of the big box stores but I guess there was a remnant of my inner child frolicking around somewhere in there. I couldn't help but feel that familiar old serenity descend upon me the minute my feet crossed the threshold. Even standing on a line ten deep for overpriced snacks didn't seem to faze me. The reminiscing felt good. It made me feel grounded, and that was something I hadn't much felt lately.

With food and drink were finally in hand, we took the escalator up to the second floor and found a relatively secluded spot by the railing that overlooked the ground. We had a clear view of the door, which I guess would have come in handy if I had a clue who we were looking for. Mairi leaned back, resting on her elbows, and watched the flow of the crowd behind us with typical teenage detachment. When the rumbling of my belly was put at bay, I said, "I'm not sure what I had expected when you told me we were going hunting, but hanging around by the cooking section really wasn't it."

"Secret Keepers love knowledge. They're drawn to it. Bookstores, libraries, museums—they love them all. Not a lot of people know much about the Lynx but from what we've heard, he spends a lot of time trolling them." She twisted around with lithe grace so she too was overlooking the lobby below. "They have a weakness for gossip too, so it's a good thing you like coffee. We'll be hitting up every Starbucks in the city limits. On Kaine's dime, of course."

I glanced at her askance. "Seriously?"

She shrugged. "You'd be surprised what you can overhear while people share a cup of coffee."

"Makes sense, I guess." I swallowed another bite of muffin and washed it down with another swig of cooling, sugar-laden caffeine. My eyes roved the faces below, but they all looked blessedly normal to me. "So what exactly am I looking for? Does this guy have horns or wings or something?"

"Nope, he's Aos Sí. He should be pretty normal looking by human standards, like Kaine and Gannon are."

"Well that's a start." Hearing that name soured my stomach. I swore I felt every bruise on my body twinge at the mere mention of it. I crumpled up the wrapper that had held my snack and jammed it in my jacket pocket. She turned her head and regarded me with those freaky eyes and I thought I saw my reflection in them. The fae penchant for having to have every tiny bit of information pried out of them with a verbal crowbar was exhausting. I mentally counted to three to keep my temper in check. "Then what's the plan here? Do we have any idea what he looks like beyond 'pretty normal'? Because that's not exactly helpful."

She pulled out an old picture, which I took with care. It was worn, the corners rounded and the front faintly creased. The finish of the print was smooth and matte, nothing like today's glossy computer printed photos. It focused on a man sitting at a small outdoor café, much like the one I had eaten my lunch at. He was dressed in a dark brown overcoat with an orange and brown striped scarf wrapped around his neck; looking down at a paperback book resting against the edge of the table. His eyes were shaded by dark, round wire-framed sunglasses.

There was nothing memorable about his long face and wind-tousled sandy brown hair. He looked like a run-of-the-mill guy catching up on some Steinbeck while drinking a coffee. There were empty tables in the background and leaves on the ground. The whole scene had an autumnal feel to it, which made me wonder what month it had been taken in. For all I knew, it could have been taken on the very same day so many years ago. I felt like I was looking back in time, at something long lost. The thought made me shiver.

"He may look older now," she said. "Fae don't age as quickly as humans, but we do age. His clothing will likely be updated." Her eyes slid across the photo. "I mean… It might not actually even be him. The naiad who gave it to us swore that it was, and she seemed pretty sincere but we don't have any real proof. We know the Lynx can be seen if he wants to. Kaine thinks this is him, taken years ago on one of the rare occasions when he had his guard down. Those were safer days for all of us."

I let the naiad comment slide. I had no interest in finding out what that was just yet. I handed her back the photo and watched it disappear into her voluminous purse. "Well, that may or may not be helpful. This is all assuming we ever happen across him in the first place. If he blends in with the crowd like any other suburban soccer dad, what's the chance I'm even going to notice him?"

"We discussed that at length last night and I think I came up with a solution." Her smile was shy, like a child awaiting praise. She jerked her head in the direction of the shelves behind us. I followed her lead, falling into step beside her. We walked at an unhurried pace, stopping before the first shelf we came to. She scanned the rows slowly, like she really was searching down a particular title on pressure cooking. Her voice was so soft I almost had to lean in to hear it. "See that young boy to the right, sitting by the wall with the graphic novel?"

My eyes darted right. I saw the young man in question and confirmed it. "Yeah, so?"

Her smile grew bolder. "And that big blond lady across the way, on the left? And the older gentleman in glasses who just came around the corner and is giving her dirty looks for blocking the shelf?"

Again, I confirmed. She had picked a rather empty section of the store, so it wasn't all that hard to see who she was talking about. "Of course, but how is this supposed to help—"

She shushed me with a wave of her hand. Her voice was still so low that I could barely hear her. "Is there anyone else around us?"

"No, just those three. But why…" I trailed off as the light-bulb went on.

The astonishment must have shown on my face. She grinned. I had never seen such an open and genuine look of joy overtake her. "It was my idea. Granted, it's not exactly high techy-tech but I think it should work. It might take us some time to get the rhythm down, especially to where we're in sync and quiet enough not to sound like crazy people, but I think we can do it."

I nodded slowly. It was a good plan. Simple, but good. My handler could point out the people around us and I would keep my eyes open for someone they missed. Even the most powerful glamour wouldn't keep the Lynx safe from my eyes—and if I saw someone my companion did not, whether he looked like the lone picture we had or no, we would finally have a lead.

When Mairi bumped my hip and steered me down the aisle toward the next section of the store, I followed. It was hard to keep up with her skipping pace when my own was still the limp of the walking wounded, but I did an admirable job. Even as we fell into a unhurried rhythm of quietly identifying each passersby, I couldn't escape that nagging feeling that everything wouldn't be peaches and roses forever. For the moment, however, it felt good to be doing something useful. Bat crap crazy, but useful.

After all, the quicker I helped these people find their quarry, the quicker I could be rid of them. And I, for one, would have jumped for joy never to see Gannon's smug face ever again.

~*~

An hour later, we had done two passes through the store and found ourselves back at the second floor railing. Our search yielded nothing, but we had gotten into a good rhythm quicker than either of us expected. I wasn't sure I'd have quite the ease with my other hunting companions the first time out, but Mairi and I had found a way to seamlessly blend our queues into banal chit-chat. I regretted my snap decision of her character upon our first meeting. Appearance aside, she was a funny, quirky little spitfire of a girl. Had our outward ages not been so disparate, I probably would have befriended her immediately.

"—and I knew Kaine would need me. So, I left and here I am," she said. She heaved a heavy sigh that appeared too large for her tiny frame.

The story of her involvement in the exile that had trapped her here in my world boggled me. How one who looked so young and flippant could have such an unexpected depth to her truly took me aback. She was dressed in an ankle-length, layered black skirt and a long-sleeved fishnet shirt over a pale pink tank-top. Her shit-kicker boots were old and scuffed, their laces half tied. She looked so young—so much like me, trying to rebel at sixteen—that it was hard not to treat her like a child.

My jaw had damn near hit the floor when she had told me she was about to turn forty. She had laughed long and hard at my cold coffee snorting shock, until tears had streamed down her face. Little brat. After she had composed herself, she had kindly taken the time to explain how the full-blooded fae aged differently from humans. For all intents and purposes, she was little more than a teen by their standards.

That didn't change how brave her actions had been. She had walked away from everything she knew, everything she had ever been taught, to help a stranger all on the strength of a single vision. That was more conviction than I had ever showed anything in my life. The thought humbled me. I mirrored her sigh. "Won't they miss you? And what happens when you go back?"

She shrugged again. Her eyes were far away, looking at something beyond the physical. "They'll get over it." She smiled at my burst of laughter. She had a wicked sense of humor, which I appreciated. "Besides, I'm hardly the prodigy they were hoping I would be."

"How so?"

"I have a lot of premonitions; little visions about inconsequential things. Helpful from time to time, sure, but not exactly what they expected from an Oracle of my family line. Some of them blamed it on my father being a shape shifter. Muddied the bloodline or some crap like that." She rolled her eyes. "Whatever. Either way I've only ever had two of the real big 'grand mal' type visions in my life: the one that landed me in the cloisters and the one that got me back out."

I was intrigued. "The one that told you Kaine would need you during his exile."

She nodded. "Yeah. So, I'm sure they'll punish me for leaving without permission, but I don't think anyone was all that sorry to see me go. It's not even like I'd be the first to run off to follow a vision. Happens more often than you'd think, actually. My granddame was one of the most reputed Oracles in her generation and they still tell stories about all the rules she broke. A lot of Oracles have come from my family."

"You must be proud."

She shrugged. "I guess. I never met her. She passed away before I was born. People used to tell me I looked a lot like her though."

"Do you miss your family, being stuck here?"

"Yes and no. I was young when I was sent to the cloisters. Sometimes I hardly remember them."

I rifled through my purse for some gum as I asked, "They're not allowed to visit you?"

She took the piece I offered her, folding up the silver wrapper into a tiny square. "They are. My parents came a few times at first. I think I embarrassed mother, crying and asking to be taken home each time. Father came once or twice without her, but the last time was years before the exile." She was still focused on the crowd below us, though neither of us had taken back up the game of calling out faces since we had returned to the banister. Something told me she was seeing a whole different gathering in her mind. "It hurt when they stopped coming, but only at first. Mother and I were never close. I think she was jealous that the Gift skipped over her." Her laugh was hollow. "I think my resemblance to granddame upset her. With me cloistered away, she didn't have to look at me anymore. Sometimes, I think she's forgotten I exist."

Well, that hit uncomfortably close to home. Mommy issues were something I could completely relate to. Without thinking, I reached an arm out and slung it across her shoulders, squeezing her tight. She stiffened at first and I questioned whether I had overstepped a boundary. After the initial surprise faded, however, she leaned against my side. I wondered when the last time someone had hugged her was.

Hell, if not for Jenni, the last time someone had hugged *me* would have been a distant memory. Maybe I was projecting, desperate to feel some sort of kinship with someone in a world gone crazy, but I felt a connection to the strange little fae girl at my side, occasional whiskers aside. We just stood there for a few minutes, listening to the dwindling bustle of the shoppers around us, breathing in the paper-and-ink smell that permeated the air.

"I'm glad you turned out to be the Warder," she said, so softly that I almost missed it. "You're a good person. I like you."

I'll be damned if my eyes didn't well up when she said that. I knew she couldn't read my mind, but she had an uncanny knack for knowing just what I was thinking. Maybe her heightened intuition could still brush against my psyche just a bit. I didn't care how she did it. At that moment, it just felt nice to be complimented; to feel wanted. I hadn't been feeling that much since the night Goliath crashed into my life. A tiny piece of my heart twinged at the thought, as if I were betraying Jenni by making a new friend—one I wouldn't have to keep secrets from. One I wouldn't have to lie to. I firmly told that part of my heart where it could shove that guilt.

I squeezed her again, before I let my arm drop. "Thanks. I like you too."

She fixed me with a sly sidelong glance. "All of us?"

"Hardly," I snorted. A scowl jumped to my lips like a diva who had been waiting in the wings, ready to take stage. Mairi cracked up at my expression, laughing harder the narrower my eyes got. I stuck my tongue out at her. "Ha, ha; laugh it up there, chuckles. You wouldn't find it so funny if your body was the one aching like an arthritic granny's."

"Oh come on, lighten up." She wiped her eyes and nudged me in the ribs until I cracked a sheepish smile of my own.

"I like you and Seana. Kaine is…"

"Kaine."

I chuckled. "Exactly. I can't quite get a handle on him, but that doesn't bother me so much as I thought it would. It's like work: you don't need to *like* your boss, you just need to respect that he *is* the boss." Although the overwhelming urge to drop my pants every time my "boss" walked into the room was a problem I had never had before. Budding friendship or no, that was certainly not something I intended to reveal to Mairi. That left me with only one more; the one I was trying my best not to think about. I fought to keep the scowl from reemerging. "Let's just say that Gannon is far, *far* from my list of favorites."

Mairi's pout was far too cheeky to be sympathetic. "I told you he was tough."

"Tough does not begin to cover it." I distinctly remembered lying awake the night after Lesson One, feeling like my body was one big top-to-bottom bruise. I hated nothing more in the world than a warm pillow when I was trying to fall asleep but I had been too sore to consider reaching up to flip it over. That, my friends, was hell.

"He was pretty rough on you." She sounded clinical, like she was examining the issue with a professional eye. Maybe there was a hint of mild concern in there, but not much. I strongly reconsidered our new found rapport in that moment. "Seana was absolutely livid, you know. She really laid into him that night at dinner." My eyebrows must have shot up in surprise, because she assured me, "She can be quite the momma bear when someone hurts her cub. Healers don't approve of fighting in general, but she was especially pissed at him for being so rough on you that night."

That cheered me up a bit. "Good. I know it's my own stupid fault for asking for the lessons in the first place, but… He could have lightened up on me just a bit when he saw how badly he was beating my scrawny ass—literally."

Mairi leaned her head on my shoulder. "Yeah," she drew out the word, "Gannon isn't really the 'lighten up' type. He's really good at what he does though. There's no better teacher this side of the Veil. It won't be fun, but he'll make sure you can take care of yourself by the time he's through with you."

The thought alone made me groan. I didn't want that maniac making sure of anything. In fact, I wanted nothing more than to punch him in his stupid, smug face the next time we crossed paths. A time that I sincerely hoped would be the day after never, however impossible that was. I said as much to Mairi and concluded with a bitter, "—assuming he ever lets me step one foot in his precious ring again. I think he made it pretty damn clear that he sees me as a lost cause."

She shifted, leaning one elbow on the railing as she fixed me with something that was stuck half-way between a pout and a scowl. Her eyes were on the floor as her fingers fiddled with the strap of her purse. I knew that look, those fidgets; I had similar ticks. She was dreading telling me something. I stiffened. "What?"

She took a folded piece of paper out of her bag and held it out to me. "Sorry."

I took the note with the tips of two fingers, so delicately you'd think I was handling live explosives. I unfolded it and read the short letter, written in deeply grooved, decisive cursive, aloud. "Saturday morning. 9am. Same place."

My eyes darted to Mairi's face. She nodded, still looking chagrined for being the bearer of bad news. That alone answered the question I hadn't asked. She really didn't have to. I already knew who it was from. I don't know why it surprised me. Maybe a part of me really had thought he'd refuse to waste his time trying to train me. My deal was with Kaine, after all; his lackey hadn't smeared my hand with blood. Granted, he had smeared his own hands with plenty of mine in the ring last week…

The pit of my stomach settled somewhere around my knees. Remembered pain and embarrassment made me flash hot then cold. I couldn't decide if I was angry or scared out of my pretty pink panties. Maybe it was an equal measure of both. One thing was certain though. I was pretty damn screwed.

CHAPTER TWELVE

I dreaded that next Saturday morning like none ever before.

Saturday and I have been bosom buddies since childhood. I wait for it all week long, counting down the days until it comes back around like someone anticipating being reunited with a long lost lover. All through the week I day dream of spending the morning curled up in my bed with my favorite fuzzy blanket, lost among the pillows. There are few things in life that make me happier than sleeping in, especially on a cold, dreary late October morning in New Jersey.

This time? Not so much. Instead, I found myself growing antsy for an entirely different reason as the week drew on. My desire to stop the nasty fae bottom feeders out there from snacking on the people I loved hadn't changed but now I knew how high the deck was stacked against me. I didn't have an ounce of enthusiasm for my next meeting with Gannon, but there was no way I could think of to avoid our next play-date without losing face. Never mind that I was the idiot who had demanded it be included in Kaine and I's bloody pinky swear in the first place. I sure as hell wasn't going to be the one to break the pact first. I didn't know what would happen if I did, but I didn't want to find out.

The thought of the ass-whooping to come consumed me. I kept trying to force it from my mind, but it came back again and again until it was all I could think about. I could see my growing distraction reflected in the obviously perturbed face of my boss while I mopped up the coffee I had spilled across my desk, ruining a stack of paperwork. I could hear it in my mom's voice when she called to remind me that my grandmother's birthday was coming up and it took her three tries to get an answer out of me as to whether or not I could attend the family dinner party. I saw it in the annoyance on the pizza delivery guy's face when he came to drop off my white pie with broccoli... only for me to realize I had two dollars in my wallet.

Worst of all, I could hear it in each of Jenni's repeated inquiries into my state of being. We talked daily and those conversations wore the worst on my heart. When I begged off of our Friday night tradition of drinks and gossip—something I rarely passed up, especially given the week I had just had—I could tell she was shocked. A full minute of silence passed while I panicked and tried to come up with a feasible reason for avoiding her. My quickly spun tale of monstrous laundry piles and dust bunnies the size of stray cats was weak. *Soooo* weak. She laughed at the dramatic delivery of the lie, like any good friend would, but I knew she wasn't fooled. My sworn promise to make it up to her at her upcoming gig mollified her, but it did me no good.

I still felt like a world class heel.

Friday night came and with it that restless, sort-of-sick feeling that made me aimless and irritable. It was the kind of restlessness that I knew would keep me awake well into the night but was powerless to stop. I couldn't even get in to any of my favorite shows, a true sign of how low I had sunk. Instead of flopping around on the couch, I headed to bed in hopes that sleep would claim me but, nope; no dice. I lay awake for hours, tossing and turning. It was creeping up on 2 a.m. when I found myself musing over the fact that I really did have a Sasquatch sized pile of dirty clothes in the corner of my bedroom. I couldn't quite escape the merry-go-round of trepidation and guilt.

I don't know how long I laid there, sleepless, but when the alarm went off the next morning it was far too soon. I dragged myself through a shower and breakfast with all the enthusiasm of a teenager on the first day of school. I threw together another leggings and old t-shirt combo, suitable for the beating I was about to take. No sense in dressing to impress. I was pretty sure there wasn't a single thing I could wear—or do—to impress my teacher (cough*nemesis*cough). If I had been a religious person, I might have said a prayer before walking up that third floor staircase. As it was, I doubted that would do me one lick of good. I was pretty sure whatever god was up there was getting a kick out of me eating my words.

I'd like to say the second session with Gannon went better than the first but that would be a big, fat lie. The day started off horribly awkward. I don't know who was more uncomfortable: me, who had to struggle not to cringe away like a kicked puppy every time he took a step toward me, or Gannon, who obviously was no more enthused about teaching me than the first time we met. I suppose Seana's verbal chastising had done some good. He wasn't exactly bubbling with warmth, but this time we started off the day with a slow, step-by-step lesson in form and the basic functions of hand-to-hand combat. I was immeasurably glad not to see those stupid sticks come off the rack. Not that I was looking forward to getting pummeled with fists either but, hey; a girl has to take what she can get, right?

He drilled me on different fighting stances, punches and kicks, all of which I struggled to keep from going in one ear and right out the other.

From what I could gather I was a terrible mess; my stances listed too far to the left, my punches were weak, and my kicks flat-out sucked. His instructions were curt, his expression so deadpan I could only assume he was running me through the exercises on the toddler level difficulty. I guess my performance from last time had earned me a demotion to the kiddie class. Great.

By the time he was through with his coaching I was drenched with sweat. My hair was plastered to my neck and forehead. I was so out of shape it was disgusting. My arms felt like limp noodles and my legs hadn't fared much better. While that made my ratty gym attire justified, it did nothing for my confidence. I desperately wanted to sit down and catch my breath but he didn't offer and I certainly wasn't going to ask. Instead, he returned to the ring with two sets of padded gloves. He let me fumble around with them for a moment before yanking them out of my hands and strapping me in.

He put his own pair on with ease. Showoff.

As he took his position across from me, I was filled with that good, ol' righteous anger. His expression remained passive but that smug spark was back in his eyes. That haughtiness made my stomach acid curdle. I don't think I had ever hated anyone more than I hated him in that moment. I'm sure my loathing showed in my narrowed eyes and clenched jaw. I forced myself back into first position, quivering knees bent and noodle-y arms raised to protect my face.

Then the games began and I was reminded that I could hate him far, far more.

While I didn't take quite the beating I had the first time, I was still the obvious loser. Every. Single. Time. I just didn't have the coordination or the stamina that he did. It was glaringly obvious that he was pulling his punches yet, again and again, he blew past my weak-ass guard and connected. My lip got split open again when I failed to move fast enough to cover my face. A square hit or two to the gut knocked the wind from me as well. I wasn't the black-and-blue punching bag I fully expected—and, quite frankly, deserved—to be, thanks to his going easy on me. My ribs were glad but my ego was not.

I was on my hands and knees, wheezing and trying not to dry heave from a third punch to the stomach, when I knew I had lost our final match. I just didn't have the strength to get back to my feet. All the fight had drained out of me. He stood there, towering over me for a moment. I don't know if he was eyeing me with some more of that pitying disdain he liked to dish my way. I didn't want to look up into his face to find out one way or the other. Instead I sucked in another burning breath and kept my eyes glued to the floor. I was pretty sure the blood splattered to the left of my hand was my own. It sure as hell wasn't his. I had managed to block the odd shot here and there, but my gloves had never touched skin. Besides, my chin felt warm and wet. That damn lip.

"We're done."

His footsteps rattled in my brain like war drums as he stalked off, leaving me there in my puddle of shame once again. I sat back until my ass hit my ankles, my arms burning. I folded myself into a huddled mass that somehow felt good, and wrapped my trembling arms around my knees. I closed my eyes. I was as exhausted as I was humiliated. At least we had started the torture early this time; the room around me was flooded with the sunlight. The sky outside was bright and blue; the cool, sunny kind of autumn Saturday that felt full of possibilities.

I felt like the beautiful day was mocking me.

This time, I was pretty sure only a few minutes passed between Gannon's exit and Mairi's soft footsteps coming up the stairs. It was an effort to lift my head. The concern in her eyes made me wish I hadn't. I waved off her offered hand with a still-gloved fist and dragged myself up to my knees. While I completed the arduous task of getting to my feet on my own, she asked, "Should I get Seana?"

I wobbled a bit but managed to stay standing once upright. Good god damn I hurt. Still, I ignored my screaming muscles and shook my head. I'd have another shiner in the morning and my lip would continue to bleed every time I smiled or sneezed over the next day or so, true. For some reason, I didn't care. Maybe I didn't want to drink that disgusting sleeping potion again. Hell, maybe I *wanted* the pain; wanted the reminder. Maybe I wanted to look at myself in the mirror and see what I had so foolishly begged for. Maybe I wanted to hate myself for ever thinking I could handle this new rough-and-tumble world I had stumbled into.

Then again, maybe I had just taken one too many blows to the head and needed to lie down. I used my teeth to pry the Velcro fastening of one glove open, ignoring the incredulous look Mairi gave me when I refused her help. The longer I stood, the more in control I felt. My muscles burned like hell and I felt as strong as a newborn kitten, but my pride wouldn't give an inch. I finally made it out of one glove and let it drop to the floor, a nasty little spike of joy buzzing through me at the thought of disrespecting Gannon's spit shinned sanctum of cruelty. I let the other glove join its mate, kicking them away like they were the cause of all my problems. I wished I could kick him as hard as I kicked them.

I caught a whiff of myself in the temper-tantrum process and cringed. Apparently I had yet to find a deodorant that could stand up to two hours in the ring with a fae prizefighter. Maybe what I really needed was a bath. It was an effort to put one foot in front of the other in an orderly fashion, especially with Mairi hovering by my side the whole way, but I persevered. Picking up my purse from the table by the door was like lifting a ton of bricks. I think I groaned aloud. I apologized, "Sorry I'm not much for conversation. I think he might have deflated a lung."

"Wouldn't be the first time." When I shot her an alarmed look, she winked. I managed to smile at her dry humor, but even that hurt. She bit at her lower lip, shifting from foot to foot. "Are you sure there isn't anything…?"

"No. I'll be okay. I'm just gonna head home. Take a bath. Apply a gallon of Icy Hot. Eat a pint of ice cream. Wallow in some self-loathing. You know: the good stuff."

She chuckled. "Sounds fun. Want some company?"

~*~

"—and, seriously, who the fuck does he think he is? He's supposed to be teaching me. Teaching me fight; teaching me to defend myself. Some fucking *teacher* he is! All he does is beat the piss out of me. He can see I have no clue what I'm doing. I clearly don't know the first thing about any of this fighting crap—that's why I asked Kaine for help in the first place! Do you think he'd take it easy on me? *Nooooo*, he barks at me like I'm a freaking cocker spaniel that peed on the floor every time I do something wrong, but it's not like he ever really showed me the *right* way. Hell, the first time he just threw that damn stick at me and expected me to come at him. Who the fuck does he think I am—Xena?

"And I know he gets off on wiping the floor with me. I just know it. He keeps that stupid stoic face of his on the entire time but I *know*. I can see it in his stupid eyes. He's just so fucking… *Stupid*." I spat the last word like it was three-day old sushi and it seemed to echo off the tiled walls. I stopped my tirade to take a deep breath and then an equally deep gulp of Pinot.

I was chin deep in lavender scented bubbles but they weren't doing a damn thing to calm me. The warm water beneath was doing wonders for my aching body, though I'm pretty sure the wine helped just as much. I balanced my glass on the edge of the tub and sank back down to my chin to stew in my indignation.

Mairi was seated cross-legged on the closed toilet, listening to my outburst with an ongoing litany of mumbled agreements and understanding nods. It didn't really matter what she did or said, although I was thoroughly enjoying her silent understanding that it was time to be a chum and refill my glass whenever it got low. What really mattered was that I could vent. Finally!

How we had wound up having a girlie bitch-fest in my bathroom, with me submerged in the tub and gulping down my third glass of wine, I couldn't really remember. I certainly hadn't expected her to come on in and stay for a spell, when she first checked in on me and offered to fetch me a drink. I couldn't even remember how we had gotten on the topic of Mr. Stupid Eyes in the first place. I just knew it felt good to finally be able to say something to somebody.

That tight, sour feeling had lodged itself my stomach. Like homesickness, even though that made no sense. I *was* home. Maybe I had never realized how dependent I was on being able to use Jenni as a brain-dump for just about everything in my life. I sucked at keeping secrets (revisit my pathetic laundry excuse), so it had become easier to avoid her all together. If I couldn't share my current woes with my bestie, I certainly wasn't going to share them with anyone else. That had made me a hermit. I had never been given much to maudlin displays of emotion (cough*liar*cough), but the weight of the last two weeks had really settled quite heavily on my aching shoulders. I hadn't meant to launch into such a tirade but Mairi was the first person I had been able to be candid with—and as much as it hurt, it felt equally good to finally let off some steam.

"He's not so bad once you get to know him," she said softly. The look I gave her must have held quite an edge, because she sat back a bit and backtracked quickly. "Not that I've ever had to train with him. I don't think I'd last two seconds against him. You've got some balls, even getting in the ring with him."

"Good save," I mumbled, glaring at some stray bubbles as I flicked them off of one wrist.

She gave me a sly grin. "Sorry. I guess it's not a good time to try to convince you that he's actually a good guy, given that he's currently at the top of your shit-list. That's kind of like siding with the dude and talking about logic after a break-up, isn't it?"

I snorted in an unladylike fashion that would have horrified my mother. "Yeah well the only 'break-up' I'd ever like with that particular asshole is the breaking up of his stupid nose." I grabbed my glass and gave its contents a stern look when they threatened to slosh out of the glass. It stopped it's crazy dance under my death-glare and allowed me to knock back the reminder with practiced poise. I might have sucked in the boxing ring, but I was a true champ in the world of lightweight alcoholics.

"Seriously, though? He's usually very patient and kind. Stern, yes, but never cruel. I don't know why he's pushing you so hard. It's not fair. There must be something else going on. Something I can't see, and it drives me mad." That whisper-y far-off quality was back in her voice; the one that made me think an old soul lived in that punky teenaged body.

She was such a strange juxtaposition; one moment a brash, funny girl who reminded me of my younger self. The next, she was an otherworldly, all-knowing creature who kind of scared the shit out of me. The sudden swings back and forth between her personas truly weirded me out.

I was glad the bubbly water hid my shudder. I cleared my throat, "Yeah well, whatever his deal is, he has it out for me." Before I could lose my temper again and go on a tirade about how stupid his eyebrows were, I said, "It's probably my own fault. This is karma coming due. I mean, I asked for this. It was in my part of the pact. I'm just paying for my own stupidity in a very painful and visible fashion."

"Still, it isn't right." She looked down at her lap, her fingers fiddling with the hem of her shirt. "You've had enough to deal with lately, with us turning your world upside down. You shouldn't have to take his crap on top of that." I didn't know what to say, so I stayed quiet. She finally looked up and I saw guilt written across her face. "You must really resent us for all the crazy we've brought into your life. I'm sorry we've made you so unhappy."

I opened my mouth to refute her. You know, to give her one of those banal dismissals we give friends when they say something that is right on the nose but hurts them so much that we don't want to admit it's true to their face. But the words never came. In that moment it struck me like a bolt of lightning and I was glad the metaphor didn't take use of my bubble bath to fry me alive.

I hadn't been happy before they had barreled into my life. Hell, I couldn't remember the last time I had been all that satisfied with life. The growing pains of becoming an adult hadn't lessened as my twenties passed in the rear view. In fact, they threatened to drag me down on a daily basis. I had been lost and bored, feeling alone more often than not, for so long that I could barely remember *not* feeling that way.

My family life had been crap for as long as I could remember. Distant was the kindest way to describe those relationships. Jenni was the only true friend I had. The other girlfriends from my high school and brief college years were long gone; moved away, grown up, married and popping out kids at a pace I didn't even want to try to keep up with. I couldn't even remember the last time I had taken stock of my life and realized how lonely I was.

Had I missed them? Was I avoiding reconnecting because I was jealous of their success, their stability? Maybe. I loved Jenni to pieces and she was like a sister to me. We had plenty of adventures and fun antics, but even those good were a struggle to maintain. Constantly teetering on the brink of eviction-level poverty had me stressed out more often than not.

Even on the days where I wasn't a ball of nerves, I wasn't really happy. Not miserable, per say, but I certainly hadn't been skipping along, whistling Dixie and counting rainbows. How long had I been just getting from day to day without thinking; without feeling?

When had I settled for surviving instead of living?

Had I done anything other than bemoan the hardships Kaine and his buddies had piled upon me over the last two weeks? Oh, right: I had spent a good deal of time moping around, droning on and on about my bad luck until I got on my own nerves too. And let's not forget my short stint as crazy shut-in either.

Yeah okay; no one liked having the veil ripped off their eyes, but that wasn't really their fault. As far as I knew, they hadn't worked some freaky fae mojo on me. My "awakening" had happened all on its own. If that chain of events had kept going the way it had that night *without* their intervention, who would have stopped Goliath? If Kaine hadn't come to my rescue, there was no doubt in my mind he would have smeared me across the concrete but had I ever thanked him for that?

Had I thanked Gannon for taking on the task of teaching me to protect myself either?

I had been so lost in my own whirl of emotions that I hadn't taken the time to really think a single thing through. I had been scared out of my wits, like I had never been before. I had been angry to the point of spitting acid and bewildered as all get out. I had felt an aching distance growing between myself and the friend I had always considered a sister; but I had also found the new surprise of a fresh start. In the worst of it, I had been taken down to my very lowest, made to feel like I was an insignificant little fly—but I had also felt a little jolt of victory every time I had knocked away a punch aimed for my face.

I couldn't remember the last time I had felt so alive.

Suddenly, the magnitude of what a whiny pussy I was being hit me. Instead of dealing with things head-on, I'd been dragging my feet and looking backwards; wishing things could go back to normal. Never mind that "normal" sucked and had for such a long time. It was what I knew and that made it that safe kind of suck. The kind you no longer loathe because loathing requires passion, which has been drained right out of you by that point. The kind you grumble about when it's not looking instead of telling it to take a hike so you can make room for something more useful.

Here was that "something" I had been looking for all along. It certainly wasn't what I had expected. It wasn't ideal either, and it certainly wasn't going to give me a chance to make the slow, baby-steps transition I preferred—but it was *something*. It was a change; a purpose. I could do something that no one else in the world could do, and I could use it to help others; Kaine and his friends, the people I loved, even complete strangers who would never know any better. I had the chance to *do* something with my life instead wasting every freaking night sitting on the couch, watching another mindless TV show while counting down the hours until bed-time. Just so I could get up the next morning and do it all over again.

Well, fuck that.

Fuck me too while I was at it. I'd been an idiot and that needed to stop. Water sloshed over the side of the tub as I sat up. Luckily the bubbles continued to hide my lady bits. Mairi and I weren't quite that close yet. From the alarm on her face, I had a feeling she wasn't used to my normal dramatics, so that was a level of intimacy we really didn't need in our budding friendship. I flung an arm out toward the door. "Toss me a towel and go turn on my laptop!"

"Wha—I—ah, okay." She unfolded herself and stood, but hesitated; wavering. "Are you okay?"

"Fine, fine," I said, waving a dismissive hand. "Moment of humbling clarity is all. Need to strike while the iron is hot and the ego is pouting!"

She continued to stare at me with wide eyes. "Uhhh, yeah… I don't…"

"I'll explain when I'm less naked. Laptop, living room, coffee table—go. I'll be out in a minute." She turned and was halfway out the door before I exclaimed, "Wait! Towel first!"

The look she gave me was bemused, to say the least. She tossed me my towel—which I, amazingly, caught before it landed in the tub—and shut the door behind her. I kicked up the tub drain and stood, toweling off the bubbly residue. I caught a glimpse of myself in the mirror; my hair balled up in a messy bun atop my head, my cheeks still flushed from the steam. I was scowling something fierce but there was a crazy glint in my eyes. I could see why she had looked at me like I was a madwoman. I kind of looked like one. Oops.

I had meant it though. Maybe I hadn't realized it until the words had spilled out of my mouth, but I *did* need to strike while the iron was hot. I needed to make a move now, before logic and laziness kicked back in and I wasted another night eating Chunky Monkey in front of Sex in the City reruns. I had asked for their help, but I hadn't really been pulling my weight. Maybe I had been drifting along for so long, letting life blow me wherever it wanted, that I had become complacent in my misery. Complacent with my penchant for failure; for my tendency to give up when things got too hard.

Yeah; screw that.

It was time I stepped up and took control.

CHAPTER THIRTEEN

"You know, we probably should have measured the room before we brought this damn thing home."

Mairi's words of wisdom earned her a wrinkled up nose and a stuck out tongue. She was right, of course, but that wasn't what I wanted to hear. I ignored her giggles and hauled myself to my feet, dusting my hands off on my pants.

It was dark outside and a glance at the cable-box told me it was almost 7pm. Not late, really, but a good deal later than it had been when we started our current adventure. I guess that made sense. What home improvement project ever ends before you're exhausted and in no mood to clean up the wreck you inadvertently created?

I surveyed the damage with a deep sigh. The living room behind me was a disaster area. My coffee table was lost under boxes and my couch—oh, my poor couch. It was littered with discarded Styrofoam, swaths of packing tape and other assorted bits of packing material. The floor would need a good sweeping too. The adjacent dining room hadn't fared much better. It was a small offshoot of my living area to begin with; little more than a table, four chairs and some abstract art I had found at a thrift store. I hadn't really stopped to think of its size when the need for a home gym had struck me. The table had been pushed into one corner, the chairs tucked in tight with no room to be pulled back out.

Oh well. I ate at the tiny counter in the kitchen more often than not. No longer being able to host my non-existent dinner parties was a travesty I would deal with later. (Boo-hoo.) Luckily, there was a decided lack of mechanical odds and ends among the mess. It had taken us nearly an hour to assemble the accursed treadmill, but I was pretty sure it wasn't going to explode when I turned it on.

My credit card may have melted in my wallet—and I was pretty sure I'd have a similar meltdown when the bill came in—but I was pretty happy with the self-betterment binge I had gone on. My new workout clothes were in the dryer and a fresh pair of sneakers awaited me by the front door. The treadmill was parked in the center of the room. I didn't think I had the strength to move it now that its monolithic majesty was all put together, so there it would likely stay. An adorable set of graduated dumbbell weights sat on their little stand by my entertainment center. I figured placing them there would remind me of my new commitment every time I was tempted to veg in front of the TV. (Score one for guilt!) I had no idea where I was going to put the yoga mat or the huge, blue balance ball that had rolled down the hall.

Honestly, I wasn't even 100% sure what was I even supposed to do with either of them. I was sure the pile of fitness DVDs stacked on the table would help, but the reality of what I had just done sort of sucker punched me in the gut.

"Great. Everything is put together and we're all finished..." The amount of cheer in my voice didn't at all match my words. "And now I don't have a clue where to start with all this."

A poorly stifled giggle made me glance back over my shoulder. Mairi was doubled up on one corner of my couch, hands pressed over her mouth in an attempt to keep me from hearing her laughter. Her face was red with the effort, however failed it was. I pursed my lips and gave her a squinty-eyed glare of Not Amusement, but that too failed. Instead of being chastised, she just pointed at me and flailed about more, letting loose a peel of laughter. I stood there, hands on hips, and tried to appear stern for a moment or two before giving in to the hysterics. I shoved aside a Styrofoam brick and a swath of weird foamy wrapping paper and flopped on the couch beside her.

We laughed until tears streamed down both our faces. I gasped more than breathed between fits. I don't know what, exactly, we found so funny but each time we would quiet down, one would look at the other and the giggles would start all over again.

Finally the giggle fit ran out of steam and left us sprawled among the debris on my couch in a sort of boneless stupor, panting as if we had both just run a marathon. My sides ached, yet it felt good. Not like earlier, after my second ass-whooping. This was a pleasant kind of ache that defied logic or explanation. I was surrounded by shiny new contraptions of debt and enough trash to fill a small dumpster, but I felt content. Peaceful. Relaxed. Dare I say, accomplished? That felt kind of silly, since I really had no clue what to do with all the expensive goodies I had just bought on my shopping spree. "One of these days I'll get the hang of planning past step one."

She seemed to know what I was talking about without me having to explain. "Well, you got those DVDs, right? I'm sure they'll help." She had tucked herself back into the far corner of the couch. "I know you'll probably throw something at me for saying it, but if you ask I'm sure Gannon could give you some pointers too."

That was the first time hearing the devil's name hadn't evoked an immediate snarl from me. I must have been truly exhausted. I shrugged, "I guess that couldn't hurt."

Her jaw dropped, mouth forming a surprised little o, complete with wide eyes. I was about to rip into her for mocking me when I heard the familiar creek of my front door opening. Jenni's voice echoed down the hall, "Hey, Cat, did you leave your phone on silent or something?"

My heart jumped into my throat as my eyes bounced around the room. It still looked like a Sports Authority bomb had gone off around me. Never mind the wide-eyed, teenage looking girl sitting next to me. I didn't even want to think of how hard that would be to explain. This was not a good time for a surprise visit from my bestie. I leaped off the couch and stumbled my way through packing material land-mines, nearly tripping over the half-hidden coffee table. I came around the far side of the couch and skidded to a halt in the hall, nearly colliding with Jenni.

"Jesus Cat!" She had a hand to her chest, the other outstretched to catch herself against the wall as she stumbled back. Her comical expression of surprise rapidly morphed into a scowl as she literally looked me up and down. "What the hell? Why aren't you dressed?"

For a few seconds I stood there staring at her dumbly. What was wrong with what I was wearing? Granted, faded jeans and an equally ratty old Wonder Woman t-shirt were far from the epitome of high fashion, but I wasn't exactly slovenly either. Well, maybe just a tad if you counted the messy knot my hair was in and how I had sweated most of my makeup off hours ago. Even if I hadn't been playing assembly technician for most of the evening, it hardly mattered what I wore to knock around the house. Especially since I wasn't planning on going out...

Shit. The panic I had felt a moment ago was nothing compared to the cold, sick feeling that pooled in the pit of my stomach. She was dressed to the nine's in a little black dress and to-die-for red patent leather pumps. Her makeup was flawless. It looked like she had even splurged for a blowout. Tonight was the night of her show. She had been going on and on about this gig for weeks, about how excited she was and how some scouting agency or something would be stopping by to see her. I had even pinky promised to be there, come hell or high water, to show my support for her just a little over a day ago. How could I have forgotten?

The guilt must have been written all over on my face. She said, "You forgot, didn't you?"

"Oh my god, Jen, I'm *so* sorry, I don't know how I got my dates mixed up. I thought it was next week and I..." I trailed off, hands flapping helplessly in the air. She gave me a look one normally reserved for someone who had just run over a beloved pet. Her shoulders dropped, the chunky silver bangles on her wrist jangling accusingly. Damn it. I knew how important this was to her; how big of a step it was for her dream. I wilted, feeling the last of my new found confidence drain out the soles of my bare feet. I was a horrible friend. "I'm an ass."

"Damn right you are!" Her eyes burned through me, her crimson lips set in a hard line. She looked like she wanted to stamp her feet or hit me. Probably a little of both and, honestly, I blamed her for neither. She blew out an angry breath. "How could you forget this?"

"I know! I feel terrible. I can't believe I let it slip my mind." I fidgeted from foot to foot. I didn't know what else to say. "I really am sorry."

She crossed her arms. I wasn't getting forgiven that easily. "What's going on? This isn't like you."

I had let guilt cloud my mind for a minute there but her words brought me back to the present—and to the secrets I had hidden not five feet away in my living room. I gaped, my jaw working up and down as I stuttered, trying to think of a good response. I could hardly tell her I had gotten all tied up in sniffing out an invisible fairy like he was a prize-winning truffle. Fate gave it to me good yet again as her eyes finally went over my shoulder and found the hulking monstrosity of the treadmill. You would have thought I had turned my living room into a crack den from the look of astonishment she turned on me. Her voice was a shrill squeak, "What the hell, Cat?"

Good god damn. I loved Jenni to pieces but at that moment, I really resented how deep our ties went. Years had passed since the time when my mom's scolding tone could make me quake in my boots, but my bestie could still make me feel like a dirty pervert caught trolling an underage chat room with four words. I scuffed my bare feet and chewed at my bottom lip. I couldn't meet that accusatory stare. It made my brain short circuit. When the moment drew out uncomfortably and nothing witty came to mind, I tried to look charmingly befuddled and mumbled, "Its a treadmill?"

"No shit. I can see that! I mean, what the hell is it doing in your living room?"

I looked over my shoulder, dying a little more inside with each passing second. "I, ah, figured it was time for me to get in shape. I'm tired of getting my ass handed to me so I thought a home gym would help." I tried not to choke on my words and hurriedly added, "You know, at my, uh, self-defense class."

The set of her jaw told me that was the wrong answer. "So, let me get this straight. Even though you keep getting the snot beat out of you at this 'self-defense class' of yours—nice lip, by the way—you refuse to consider switching to my gym, where I've never seen anyone leave with a black eye. On top of that, you suddenly decided that you needed to run out and buy yourself a home gym today, of all days. And *that's* why you forgot the most important night of my life?"

I took a deep, shuddering breath and counted to ten. I didn't blame her for being mad. I would have been, had our situations been reversed. To make it worse, when spelled out that way, it really sounded like I had fallen off my damn rocker. So, yeah; she had every right to be angry. The hysterics were a bit much though, and they grated along my last nerve. I didn't need her to make me feel like I was the worst friend in the whole world; I was doing a fine job of that all on my own. I took another deep breath. That sinking, swirling feeling gripped me again. Normal seemed so very far away and I just didn't know what to say to get myself out of hot water this time.

At that moment—at the worst possible moment—a clatter rang out from my living room.

Jenni jumped, eyes wide. "What was that?"

It sounded like the precariously stacked pile of DVDs on my coffee table falling to the floor, but how the fuck did I even begin to explain that? Instead, I sputtered and panicked. I took far too long to think of an excuse. With an angry sound that was half snarl, half sigh, Jenni pushed past me and stormed toward the living room. I tried to grab at the arm of her jacket, a strangled sound of alarm caught in my throat, but she evaded me. My chest seized up as I stumbled after her, waiting for the next outburst when she saw Mairi sitting on my couch.

She stopped just inside the doorway and jerked back a step. She combed back her hair with one hand, sounding more baffled than irritated when she said, "Now I know you've lost your mind. When, and more importantly *why*, the hell did you get a cat?"

I froze my face before it could betray me. Instead, I poked my head around the corner and faked a cough to stifle a chuckle at what I saw there. Peeking out from beneath a tent of cardboard upon my sofa was a curious-looking little calico. She looked back and forth between me and Jenni, giving us that squinty-eyed look I think was supposed to express feline affection. She even rewarded our continued attention with an adorable little "*mrrrow*."

Jenni gestured to the cat and gave me an expectant look. I shrugged. "Well, after that night at the bar I was a little uncomfortable being all alone at night, so…" I trailed off, hoping that she would let such a sensitive issue drop. (God, I was a shitty excuse for a friend.)

My ruse worked. Instead of harping on the crazy depths of my current behavior, she fell silent. She put her purse down on the end table and leaned over the couch, offering an outstretched hand to my new "pet." Mairi played along, slowly creeping forward to sniff at it before accepting some light scratches behind her ears. "What's her name?"

"Cali." Not incredibly original, but I was proud that I managed to respond without stuttering. Score one for the home team.

"It does make me feel better knowing you're not all alone here," she said. "Not that a cat is really much protection."

"Well the landlord would have had a kitten of his own if I got a dog, and I'd hang myself before getting a bird. It was the best I could do."

Jenni patted Mairi on the head and picked her purse back up, tucking it up high on her shoulder. "She's a cutie. I bet your mom will go bonkers when she hears you got her."

My mother was one stray shy of being her neighborhood's crazy cat lady. I had long bemoaned her penchant for taking in every bedraggled creature that crossed her porch. The I-told-you-so smugness would never end once she heard that I had adopted a four-footed friend. The thought made me groan out loud. "Yeah, I haven't told her yet."

Jenni snorted. "I figured. I ran into her at the mall the other day. She would have said something if you had."

"I can only imagine."

She tucked her hair back behind one ear. She had straightened it for the show; it glimmered like gold. "She said she hasn't heard from you in a week or so."

That was as close to a chastisement as she had ever given me. I let it slide thanks to the overwhelming guilt I was wallowing in. Jenni knew my history with my mother. To say that our relationship was rocky was like calling a hurricane "a little rain." It was true though. My strained weekly phone call to hear mom complain yet again about how loud the neighbors were or how she had caught my father sneaking midnight snacks despite his diet had fallen by the wayside in the previous weeks. "Yeah, I know. I haven't had much to say. I'll call her soon. Promise."

"Okay."

That awkward silence stretched on between us. Mairi did a good job of pouncing and stalking through the garbage on my couch, giving us something to focus on. Still; I couldn't just stand there forever, feeling like shit. "Jen, I'm really so, *so* sorry for forgetting about tonight. It was terrible of me and I hate myself for it. I hope you know that."

"Yeah, well, it's fine. Shit happens, right? Besides, you've had a lot on your mind." Her smile was weak. I guess I wasn't the only one feeling the chasm stretching between us. I wanted to cry. She glanced over at the clock. "I really need to get going."

"Okay. Do you want to grab some brunch tomorrow? You can tell me all about it over mimosas. My treat."

She nodded. "Sure. I'll call you in the morning." She gave me a quick hug and headed out the door. I stood in my living room doorway and watched her go, my throat tight. It occurred to me as the front door clicked shut that she had never urged me to throw my ass in a quick shower or asked me if I was going to show up later, to catch any bit of her performance that I could. She already seemed to know what the answer to either of those questions would have been: another half-assed excuse.

I was a world-class heel. I heard rustling behind me as Mairi untangled herself from the packing she had been curled up under. She said, "I'm such a klutz! I was trying so hard not to make any of the stupid cellophane crinkle that my fat ass took out half the table."

Fat ass, my ass. She looked like she weighed ninety pounds, soaking wet. "No need to apologize. My stupidity caused this mess in the first place. Quick thinking with that whole cat thing though. Thanks."

"Seemed like that would be easier to explain than things mysteriously falling over by themselves." I could see that she had perched herself on the back of the couch, human-looking once more, out of the corner of my eye. "You're not the greatest at this double-life thing, huh?"

I cracked a smile that I didn't really feel. "Nope. I'd make a terrible secret agent." When I turned around, the sight of my destroyed living room sucked the last of the energy right out of me. I just wanted to leave it that way and let "Future Caitlin" deal with it, but I'd hate myself even more in the morning if I did. If that was even possible, of course. I hated myself pretty bad at that moment.

"You okay?"

"I'll be fine. I feel like shit for letting her down but I'll make it up to her. Somehow. The sooner we find that damn Lynx and I can get back to my normal life, the better." I didn't believe a word of it. Mairi's lopsided smile didn't meet her eyes. That look told me I wasn't exactly convincing her either. Whatever. I didn't want to talk about it and the only other thing I could do was ignore it. I heaved a deep sigh and gathered up an armful of bubble wrap. "Come on. Let's get this place cleaned up and then I'll take you home."

There'd be enough time for self-loathing later.

~*~

It was hard for me to follow Mairi back into the fae house later that evening. Humility is not something naturally coded in my DNA. If my mother's overly dramatic tales were to be believed, I had been stubborn from the cradle on. I was known to hold onto my pride longer than was necessary, even in the face of having been proved unequivocally wrong. So, knowing full well that I was going to have to swallow that pride not once but twice made each step up the walkway to that house incredibly hard. It was a small favor when Mairi hung back with Seana in the living room, after the latter directed me toward the kitchen. It was hard enough to be contrite without an audience.

I stopped in the kitchen doorway, holding my purse on my shoulder with a sweaty grip. The scene before me was so commonplace that it struck me as bizarre. A large pot bubbled away on the stove, giving off the luscious scent of tomatoes and garlic. Kaine, seated at the kitchen table, had his head inclined over the newspaper spread out on the table before him. A sweating half-empty bottle of beer stood at his elbow and he was chewing absently on the capped end of a ballpoint pen. Apparently, the freaky fae Lord of the Manor who made blood pacts like they were nothing also liked to cook and to do crossword puzzles. While drinking Sam Adams. I stifled a chuckle. Okay. Nothing weird about that. Nope; nothing weird about that at all.

"Can I help you, Caitlin?" he asked, never looking up. That deep baritone shot through me like Cupid's arrow yet again, making all sorts of things inside me vibrate in response.

I hated how he could do that every single time he spoke. Bad enough that I felt like a moron for having to deliver a heartfelt apology to a near stranger, but the way he set my hormones buzzing was an added insult that set my teeth on edge. I traced the checkered pattern of the floor tiles with my eyes, face red. I cleared my throat and aimed for deferentially polite. "Is this a good time? I could come back another day, if you're busy."

I heard the rustle as he folded the newspaper. Out of the corner of my eye I saw him sit back in his chair. "No, no. Please; sit."

I pulled out the chair opposite his and sat; clutching my purse in my lap. It gave my hands something to do other than fidget. I knew he had me fixed with that calm, unwavering stare; those eerie eyes like calm waters in some Caribbean sea that I had only seen on the Travel Channel.

Okay, scratch that; I hated how poetic his eyes made me even more than I hated his voice's panty-dropping properties.

He chuckled softly. I wondered how much my expression was giving away. "Is there something on your mind?"

"Uh, yeah. Sort of." I cleared my throat—far too aware of how awkward I sounded—and dove in. "I just wanted to say I'm sorry. I never thanked you for saving me, that night the troll attacked me."

I glanced up at him from beneath my eyelashes and saw that he had his head cocked slightly to the right; a smile playing on his lips. He looked amused, which tickled my libido's fancy just fine. He held up a hand to forestall any further rambling apologies I could make. "There is no need to thank me. I acted as any man worth his salt would, seeing a lady in peril."

I swallowed a reflexive snort at his Shakespearean gallantry. He probably would have taken that as rude. I still couldn't get over how quickly my internal pendulum could swing from horn-dog to know-it-all bitch with this guy. I shook my head. "Yeah, well, maybe where you're from they do. Here? Not so much. Strangers don't just go risking their lives for one another."

"They do not?"

Now his head was cocked full force, something troubled rippling in his eyes; like wind ruffling the stormy seas. (There was that goddamn poetry again.) I bit my tongue and gave myself a sharp reminder of where I was and who I was with. This was so not the time or place to get sappy. I released it so I could continue busting his chivalrous bubble. "Ah, no. Not generally."

He frowned, brow deeply furrowed. I had never seen him look so disturbed, so confused, so…Human. For some reason, that bothered me on a level I couldn't even begin to explain. He said, "I could walk this world of yours for a hundred years and understand it no better. Is that not a lonely way in which to live?"

"Uh… maybe? I'm not really the one to ask. You kind of get used to it when it's all you know, I guess. In any case, I'm pretty sure I would have become sidewalk pâté if you hadn't come along that night, so thank you."

He inclined his head, every inch the stately lord once more. I had to resist the urge to drop into a curtsy. Not wanting to get into a debate about the miserable mess that was modern day humanity, I threw myself to the wolf and asked, "And where would I find Gannon tonight?"

~*~

I really hated that back staircase.

Every time I ascended it my heart leaped in my throat, pounding so hard I felt like I would choke on it. Kaine made me uneasy, with the way he sent my thoughts spinning and had some primal part of me panting like a dog in heat from a sideways glance. That was bad enough. Yet somehow that particular uneasiness seemed oh-so-much more manageable than the foreboding I felt at the mere thought of entering the same room as Gannon. Maybe the inherent moral code I had sensed in Kaine from day one, even before his genuine dismay at the folly of man, had made him feel safer, somehow.

Gannon? Nope. No safety net there. Not even a bungee cord to pull me back. When I was left alone with him I felt like I had been thrown into the pit, an impromptu gladiator with a blunt stick facing off against a hungry lion. There was something about him, something feral and downright dangerous, that made my insides quake on a completely different level. I sensed anger in him; a seething force that bubbled just beneath the surface every time we traded blows. Hell, I saw a flash of it every time our eyes met.

Still, if I didn't nut up and face that fear, I knew I would never be able to walk into that training room without a cloud of defeat hanging over me. Eau de Failure was not my preferred perfume. I truly wanted to learn what he had to teach me, if I were capable, and we would never get past Lesson One if I didn't make some sort of an attempt to salvage the rapidly crumbling rapport between us.

Just as Kaine had promised, Gannon was in his little inner sanctum of torture. I'd promised myself I'd stop calling it at the bottom of the stairs but, well... Shit happens. Only one of the overhead lights was on, its beam focused dead center in the middle of the room. Moonlight flooded in from above, creating wide swathes of pale silver across the floor.

He was seated in the center of the Red Ring of Doom, nothing but a small square cushion between him and the floor. He was dressed in one of those white uniforms straight out of a Karate Kid movie; legs crossed, hands resting palm up on his knees. I teetered in the doorway, mentally cursing. Interrupting his midnight meditation seemed a piss-poor way to start making amends. I had nearly turned to go when he said, "Is there something you need?"

His voice was deep, steady; unruffled. For a heartbeat, I thought I heard an echo of Kaine in that voice. Maybe all that meditation mumbo jumbo wasn't the steaming load I had always thought it was. Of course, that could have just been his normal speaking voice too. It wasn't the gruff tone I had grown used to hearing as we sparred, but as the few words we had exchanged hadn't exactly been pleasant ones, it was possible that my opinion was slightly skewed.

Okay; it was likely that my opinion was more than" slightly" skewed.

"I'm sorry to interrupt you." I tried to aim for that same deferential neutrality I has used with Kaine, but I'm pretty sure I came off sounding like I was two seconds away from cowering in fear instead.

He unfolded himself from his seated position in one slow, fluid movement. Once on his feet, he turned with practiced grace and crossed the distance between us. He stopped a foot away from me, feet spread in an even stance; arms crossed. He was so close that his hair looked black in the low light and I could see that his high cheekbones shimmered with a faint remnant of sweat. He waited, his blank expression never wavering. Not another word was spoken.

I took a deep breath. It was hard for me to find my train of thought when his presence brought up a wellspring of emotions: awkwardness, resentment, nervousness, embarrassment. I hated, hated, *hated* the way his mere presence intimidated me. He made me feel like a child asking a parent to indulge some frivolous whim. As much as I loathed facing him, I hated fearing the walk to my car every evening and the nightmares over what could be lurking in the dark outside my door each night even more. I swallowed the lump in my throat along with my pride. "I came to apologize."

I finally summoned the courage to meet his eyes. It was like having a bucket of cold water dumped over my head. I had grown so used to seeing them regarding me with calculating ferocity, when they weren't narrowed in anger or rolling in disappointment, that to see them emptied of all that exasperation shocked me. Instead, there was a deep, centered sense of calm there. It was unlike anything I had ever seen before. I'll be damned if it didn't make me instantly jealous.

He compounded my astonishment when he said, "There is no need for you to apologize."

I snorted. "Uh, yeah there is. I made a deal with Kaine and you got roped into it. I never thanked you for agreeing to teach me and I certainly didn't show you the respect any teacher deserves. We got off on the wrong foot, and that it was largely my fault. I'm hoping I can change that."

He smiled, the first real smile I had ever seen on his face. "I am Kaine's Guardian, Caitlin. I do as he bids; it's my duty. There is no need for you to make amends for him."

For a moment I wondered if I had been better off with the hostile, aloof Gannon. He was speaking civilly to me—and I was both surprised and pleased to hear how normal he sounded when not barking orders or swinging a pole at my head—but the casual dismissal of everything I had agonized over all day long was a bitter pill to swallow. "Still, I feel the need to do so. If not for having made the bargain in the first place, then at least for my bratty behavior." He watched me, not budging a single step in the direction of accepting my penitence. I wanted to scream. I let a small growl of frustration slip out. "Come on Gannon, for Christ's sake, I'm *trying* here. Will you give me just a little back, please?"

He remained calm, eyes never wavering. The bastard. I held his gaze and hoped mine said everything I was thinking—including just a little bit of "stop being such a shit." After a few agonizing seconds, he let his head loll back; slowly rotating it from side to side until it cracked. He sighed and seemed to relax, just a tad. "And just what, exactly, would you like me to give you?"

A million responses rushed to my mind—some sarcastic, a few of them dirty. I wanted to spit, I was so frustrated. "Accepting my apology would be a good start."

He scratched at the nape of his neck, running his tongue along the edge of his teeth. "I already told you: an apology is not necessary. Apologies are just words, and in the end, words matter very little to me."

This was not at all how I had expected this confrontation to go. Granted I hadn't thought we would become bosom buddies after a little chat, but I had at least expected some sort of common ground would be found. I think my jaw dropped open again. I gaped at him for a moment. "Are you freaking kidding me?" There was an undignified squeak on the end of those words. "You mean to tell me that I dragged myself all the way up here to apologize for being a brat, just for you to tell me it doesn't even matter?"

"I said *words* do not matter. The sentiment behind them is appreciated, but I value your actions more." He turned and walked away, leaving me standing there.

I couldn't believe his nerve. Everything in me seemed to vibrate, like a taut bowstring let loose. I was shaking, my fist clenched so hard around the strap of my bag that I was pretty sure the imprint would remain on my palm for the rest of my life. He had gone back to the center of the room and dropped back down into his meditation pose without another word. Livid was too gentle a word to describe the fury that was vibrating inside me. I clenched my teeth. Oh, I would show him actions, all right.

Just as I turned to storm off, one hand already gripping the door frame, he called out, "Caitlin."

The sound of my name on his lips made me want to whack him in the head with my purse. I spun around and spat, "What?"

"Monday, 7pm. We'll put together a workout regimen you can do during the week. Then we'll start with basic grappling and floor work, before we give weapons another try."

Goddamn, I was getting tired of my mouth hanging open like a fish. I spluttered for a moment, torn between a dozen different thoughts. Luckily, before I could spout off again with something stupid (which was pretty much my default setting), a little light-bulb flickered to life in the back of my mind. He knew about the monstrosity that had taken over my dining room. Mairi must have told him about my sudden shopping spree this afternoon and my subsequent doubts about how to make the best use of it all. She couldn't have had much time to do so. My conversation with Kaine had lasted all of ten minutes. And what's more, whatever she had found the time to say had obviously made enough of an impression on Gannon for him to extend the olive branch.

"Sure, that sounds good. See you then." I took a deep, slow breath. Perhaps he hadn't been too gracious concerning my attempt at humility, but he had made the first overture into helping me step up my training. It was step in the right direction.

And that was something.

CHAPTER FOURTEEN

By late November, I wanted to throttle the crap out of the Lynx the moment I found him.

Because, of course, I had not found him. In fact, I had begun to doubt the slippery shit's entire existence, faded photograph aside. My grumbles of dissension were met with promises that he was indeed real and out there, lurking somewhere in Riverview. "People" had seen him, I was told. That pretty much amounted to someone's cousin's sister's hairdresser swearing it was the god's honest truth. Sure; I knew Kaine & Co. had a network of friends. I didn't have the foggiest clue who they were, but I believed that they were out there nonetheless, feeding us little tidbits of information when prying eyes couldn't catch them in the act and rope them into whatever treasonous charge hung over Kaine's head. Knowing that they existed and that the Lynx existed, however? Those were two entirely different things.

My belief was wavering. Night after night, we cased bookstores and cafes and museums—even making a couple day-trips into good old NYC just in case our prey had decided to hop the Hudson—all with the same result: nada. Zip. Zilch. Not even the tiniest glimpse of someone whose presence couldn't be explained. I didn't think it was unreasonable for me to start questioning how long we could go on, chasing the invisible man. My companions, however, remained resolute. I guess they really didn't have a choice.

We hadn't found Goliath either, but everyone seemed to take that in stride like that was no big deal. (Thanks, dicks.)

Seana tried to calm my fears, reassuring me that Kaine had scared the troll off my trail. (Not that anyone would tell me just what Kaine had said or done after I blacked out, to make said troll turn and flee in terror.) When that hadn't worked, Mairi had suggested that—trolls being rather dull-witted to begin with—the damn thing may never have realized what a prize he had held in his ham-fist in the first place. Maybe he wasn't looking for me. Maybe it had just been a one-and-done type of attack. Their platitudes were appreciated, on that "aww, my friends are trying to comfort me" level that lurked deep down inside, but it didn't make me look over my shoulder any less.

In that time, I had also learned a lot about myself and just how well I handled stress. Unfortunately, the answer to that was badly. I had never spent so many nights tossing and turning. I was bone weary, literally aching from head to toe, yet unable to catch more than an hour or two of fitful sleep at a time.

Lying had also become second nature. I didn't mind it so much when it was to my boss or a co-worker. I was pretty sure no one was buying my frazzled PTSD routine anymore anyway, but I could hardly blame them. That shtick wore a bit thin pretty fast. Problem was, with all those late nights (and the zillion cups of coffee I consumed on them), the alarm clock and I had quickly grown weary of one another. My former punctuality had gone out the window, earning me one write up already. I probably should have tried to care a little more. I just didn't have the energy.

Hell, when you got right down to it, I didn't even mind the few little white ones I had to slip my mom every now and then, just to keep her off my case. It was lying to Jenni that cut the deepest. I had never grown comfortable feeding her lame excuses for my increasingly erratic behavior. I wondered how much self-hatred one could build up in so short a time. I'm pretty sure I was setting a new record.

Even though life was weighing pretty damn heavy on me, I can't say that nothing good came out of the time I spent with my new fae buddies. They had turned out to be a pretty good bunch, freaky backstory aside.

Mairi reminded me so much of myself at a younger age that she quickly became the little sister I had never had (which I'm sure my real little sister would have *loved* to hear). We had so much more in common than I ever would have guessed, from our secret love of crappy sci-fi movies to a shared aversion to the wiggly slime that was Jell-O. (Ugh.) Even on the nights when we weren't hitting the pavement on another wild goose chase, I found myself in her company more often than not.

It made it easier to pretend that Jenni calling me less and less didn't hurt when I had someone to sit on the couch with, watching whatever terrible movie was playing on Syfy that night, sharing a pint of rocky road.

Of course, I was living in a crappy sci-fi movie of my own, so who was I to judge?

It had taken a little more time and effort to get to know Seana. She was reserved and quiet; a bastion of calm, with a motherly vibe that clearly said she was the caretaker of the group. She never accompanied me to look for the Lynx. That wasn't her style. Instead, she became my professor of Fae 101. I came to enjoy the quiet evenings we spent at the kitchen table with a seemingly endless supply of tea—a nice jasmine-infused green that I had oh-so-thoughtfully provided, just so I wouldn't have to grimace through another swig of her favored bathwater brew. She would tell me tales of the world they came from and the ways of her people, which proved both educational and fascinating. The variety of faekind boggled my mind and the list of powers they possessed ran nearly as long. I didn't see how there was a chance in hell I could ever acclimate to being somewhat attached to their world, but I tried to take it all in. Sometimes I regretted not taking notes.

Once or twice a week Mairi was given the order to stay home and, instead, I would be accompanied by one of the boys. Fun times, those. Kaine still made me incredibly uncomfortable by just being there. It was hard to scan a room when my eyes wanted to run back to that chiseled chin and high cheekbones. Conversation with him was, in a world, terrible. Or, more to the point, terribly awkward. I couldn't shake the feeling that I was a filthy street urchin addressing some fancy highborn aristocrat. I couldn't figure out what to talk to him about, let alone *how* to talk to him, so I constantly found myself tongue-tied. While he was kind enough never to point it out, his patronizing me only made me blush brighter.

Ugh.

Those nights were not my idea of fun, but the nights on the town with Gannon weren't any better. Where I felt compelled to try and make faltering small talk with Lord Fancy Pants, I was perfectly fine with maintaining the bare minimum of conversation with the latter. Aside from following the plan and calling out our cues, we rarely exchanged more than a dozen words. We had gotten to a less-hostile place in our relationship since the night of my apology so it wasn't an unbearable silence anymore. It just wasn't much fun, either. We were far from being buddies, but at least I felt comfortable around him. We had settled into an acceptable student-teacher dynamic.

Of course, as he knocked my feet out from under me and sent me crashing to the mat, I revisited the fantasy of choking the shit out of him.

I had improved in my defense training over the past few weeks, thank God. We had started over from ground zero after my heartfelt (and summarily rejected) apology. He certainly wasn't the nurturing type but at least he had started fresh. When I asked, he stopped to explain things—over and over again, if need be—and guided me through each new task slowly. It was still glaringly obvious that it would take me awhile to meet the bar he had set for me, but at least I could see that bar this time around.

My personal markers for improvement were a lot less impressive, but I was proud to have reached them. I could go an hour without falling down in a wheezing heap. I hadn't taken a punch to the face in well over a week. I had even managed to throw a couple of my own that made him duck out of the way at last second. I wasn't letting that make me cocky. I knew he had to be holding back with me but it felt pretty good nonetheless.

Truth was, I highly doubted I could have stood two minutes against him if he came at me for real. I wasn't exactly sure what super special skill-set a Guardian possessed but I had a feeling "fast as freaking hell" would have shown up somewhere on his character sheet. Maybe one day I'd work up the courage to ask. That would probably be on the same day that monkeys flew out of my butt, but hey; anything was possible. For now I had found it in me to be okay with the kid gloves.

I still had a long way to go, but I didn't fear my treadmill and weights quite as much as I had on the night the moved in to my home. I loathed the quality time spent with them, maybe but, come on, who really enjoys getting all sweaty and icky? At least I didn't loathe my time in the ring with Gannon quite so much anymore. My position on the floor, cursing like a sailor, aside, I mean.

"Hold," I groaned, rolling to the side so I could push myself into a sitting position. He instantly fell back, giving me space. Had I known it was that simple to catch my breath from the get-go, maybe I wouldn't have spent so many nights cursing his eyebrows.

"Do you know how you got there?" His voice was even, calm; so monotone I half-wondered if he was a robot running the same recording over and over. It was his usual way of making me work through why I had just gotten embarrassed and, as much as I hated it, it worked.

I rubbed at the back of my head and pulled my hand away, wincing. My wrist twinged when I moved it, a reminder of how awkwardly I had landed. I hadn't learned to stop trying to stop myself from falling yet. "I was watching your eyes again."

He lowered himself down into a squat. "And?"

I sighed. "The eyes lie."

He grunted his agreement and took my hand, the one that was throbbing. He turned it over slowly, first one way and then the other. I had to resist the urge to pull it back. Something about his touch always made me go all squirmy inside. I pressed my lips tight and tried not to freak out like a little girl when his ran his thumb up my wrist; slow and methodical. I gasped when he found a tender spot right behind the ball of my thumb. Dang, that smarted.

"You should have Seana look at this." I looked up from where my hand was held in his, and drew back an inch. His face was only a foot away from my own, his lips pursed; brows drawn down. I might have mistaken that body language for concern in a less aloof person. He glanced up and our eyes met. For a moment I thought I saw some flicker of emotion, some moment of *connection*. It was gone in a heartbeat. The wall that slammed down was damn near palpable. He let my hand go and stood, face covered by that maddeningly blank mask once more. "I don't think we should continue today. You may have sprained it."

I kept my gaze trained on my wrist. It did look a bit puffy. By tomorrow, it would likely be a mess of black and blue. I ran my fingers over the tender flesh, trying to feel what he had felt. Was it some secret warrior's intuition? Training to aide his fallen comrades on the battlefield of some fae-Valhalla maybe? Then again, for all I knew, it was so obvious a Boy Scout with his first aid merit badge might have been able to figure it out. I was the gal who had been too squeamish to dissect a frog in high school biology; I certainly wasn't winning the Florence Nightingale award. My mouth took advantage of my distraction to muse, "You're pretty handy with the first aid, huh?"

He had started to fold up the floor mats, his back to me. If he had reacted to my nosiness, I couldn't see it. "Healers aren't always around when you need them. A fighter needs to know how to take care of themself."

I couldn't explain it, but something deep inside me wanted so damn bad to figure the guy out. Yet, every failed attempt to root out the humanity in him—for lack of a better term—was thwarted. *So* frustrating. I draped my arm across my knees to take some of the pressure off of my wrist. I wasn't about to let that opening close without sticking my foot in it. "So you've been in battles then?"

A fluid shrug made his shoulders ripple like water. "Battles? No. Nothing so dramatic as that."

God forbid he elaborate without me egging him on. The breadcrumb comments were igniting a familiar irritation but I tramped it down. I would never get anywhere with him by getting snotty. Like I was coaxing a wild animal out of a corner, I kept my tone neutral. "But you have been in fights?" Before he could give me another noncommittal answer, I clarified, "Like, the life-or-death kind of fights?"

"Yes."

Such an inadequate answer, yet it was the first time he had ever given me even that tiniest piece of insight into himself. I rooted deeper. "Were you a Hunter?"

He turned his head slightly, so that I could see one blue eye regarding me over his shoulder. "What do you know about Hunters?"

"Not much, honestly. Seana mentioned them. She said they take care of fae problems, over here on this side: the Shades, trolls, other nasties that break the law. I kind of got the impression they were like fae bounty hunters, only a bit more... Final."

"Close enough, I guess. And, no; I'm not a true Hunter. That has become part of my job while we are stuck here, but it is temporary." Did I detect a note of bitterness in those words? He had stacked the mats—all but for the one my butt was still parked on—along the wall. He turned, leaning back against them, and scratched at the back of his neck. "I'm

Kaine's Guardian. It's my duty to protect him and him alone."

No surprises there, though his response provoked more questions than it answered. Here we went again, with the pulling of teeth. I sighed the sigh of one long in suffering. "Care to elaborate a little?"

His eyes seemed to glow with an inner radiance of their own as they bore into me. A trick of the light, but one that made the hair on my arms raise nonetheless. His jaw was set at a hard angle, his lips thinned into something just short of a scowl. I glowered right back at him, challenging him to dismiss me. After a long moment, he heaved a sigh and said, "Guardians do not only protect the race. Many do; it's likely where our Gifts came from. We were bred to be killers. But some of us are assigned a specific charge at birth, as I was."

I'll be damned if that didn't make me itch with curiosity. Kaine had to be someone important. *Had* to be. Would any regular Joe Schmoe off the street get another soul bound to his for protection? No, nu-uh, no way. But I knew better than to ask that question. Gannon would shut me out the moment I started digging into the personal life of his Lord and Master, just like Seana had.

Instead, I tried my damnedest to feign a sort of bored-yet-mildly-curious impartiality, absently rubbing at my aching hand as I said, "Sounds pretty important. I already know firsthand your damned good at what you do though, so I guess that's no surprise."

I glanced up at him through the fringe of my eyelashes to see him smirking. "Flattery will get you nowhere with me."

I tried to look adorable and innocent. "Can't blame a girl for trying, right?"

He walked towards me and I was struck dumb by that loping, feline grace of his once again. I had meant every word I said about his prowess. My brain still compared him to a panther, all lean muscle and savage grace. Maybe all fae men had the inborn ability to make a girl get poetic. Either way, it bothered me less when my thoughts went all lyrical over him than over Kaine. Go figure.

He reached out and I took his hand with my good one, feeling its callouses against my palm. He hauled me to my feet like I weighed nothing at all. I managed not to stumble into him, though his chest was only inches from mine. I was a good head shorter than him and had to tilt back to see his face. Up close, I could see the stubble along his jaw and how long his eyelashes were, framing those eerie pale blue eyes as they searched my face.

He let go of my hand and I backed up a few steps. He broke into a slow smile. I liked it when he smiled, which so far had been a rare occasion. He looked much younger; much more human. "I don't like games, Caitlin. If there is something you want to ask me, just to do it. I may choose not to answer, but I will never lie to you."

My face warmed. He was always saying my name when he spoke to me. It made me feel weird. Unwilling to be put off, I stood my ground. "Who are you?"

He bowed. "Gannon Aonghus, firstborn son of Éamonn and Murine; Guardian of Kaine."

His answer challenged me to cross a boundary I knew better than to step over. Instead, I crossed my own arms—careful not to jar my injured wrist too much—and considered my options. After a moment I asked, "Why are you Kaine's Guardian?"

"He is my brother."

My brows shot up. "Really?"

His smile turned sly. The twinkle in his eyes mocking me ever so slightly. They lent a little bit of humanity to those icy cool orbs, so I was willing to forgive it—this time. "We are not brothers by blood," he said. "We were born within days of one another and our families had a long-standing friendship. I was chosen be his Guardian and my twin sister was chosen to be his bride."

Ah-ha, a betrothal! Further proof that he was—

"Wait, Kaine is *married*?" The last word came out as a squeal. My jaw dropped. I'm sure my eyes widened to comical proportions, because he let out a long, loud laugh. Flustered, I slapped his arm, though that only earned me a stinging palm. "Stop that! This isn't funny."

He ignored my weak punch but he did swallow the last of his laughter. Some of his former seriousness had hardened his face; his eyes narrowed ever so slightly as he teased, "I am sure my sister would *love* to see such a reaction. Sorry to ruin your amorous fancies."

"Hey, I didn't have those fantasies on purpose, thank you very much!" My face felt hot enough to fry an egg. *Why* had I just said that? I could feel the incredulous stare I was getting. I groaned, covering my face with my hand. "Okay, fine. Maybe there was an impure thought or two here and there—but I didn't want to be having them! That's completely unlike me, I swear."

He chuckled. "Don't take it too personally. There's succubus blood in his family line. He has that effect on most women." I peeked at him from between my fingers, my expression confused enough that he generously elaborated, "Succubi control the powers of seduction. Their Gift tends to...*leak* out in their aura, even when they aren't using it."

"Thanks. That makes me feel both better and worse." I scrubbed at my face with my hands and then straightened my sweat-spotted t-shirt, like that made me look more respectable. "You know, since fae Gifts aren't supposed to work on me at all."

He grinned. "That's the problem. He's not 'using' it on you."

I blew out a hard, frustrated breath. "See, this is what I don't get. What good is this Warding? Some things work on me, some don't. Seana swears I'll be Super Woman one day, but I just have to grow into it. What are the freaking rules here?"

"Seana is right. Every Gift needs to grow to full strength. When yours does you will be incredibly powerful, in your own right. You will be impervious to any fae Gift that needs to impress itself on your will to work."

I glared at him. "Yeah, that right there? Not at all helpful, since it doesn't make a lick of sense to me."

He sighed and held his hands up. "Gifts work in two ways." One hand jiggled. "Some Gifts need to be used on another person to have an effect. Let's call those mental Gifts. Healing, seduction, reading thoughts, enchantment, manipulating emotions—Gifts like those need to affect another person, in their mind, to have power. Right now, while your Warding is new, there are workarounds that let some of those Gifts reach you, but in time you will become immune to them." He wiggled the other hand. "On the other hand, there are physical Gifts—such as my speed or, say, a Fury's strength. Those Gifts affect the one who is Gifted and are not something you will ever be able to rebuff, unless you somehow match that physical power."

Huh. Put that way, it made a whole lot more sense. I said as much and earned another chuckle. He said, "As for Kaine, I assure you he isn't trying to impress his will upon you. His Gifts are naturally very strong—stronger than most, really. That residual energy just happens to be amplifying your thoughts and feelings."

"I don't have any such feelings, buddy!"

"Hate to break it to you, but yeah—you do. If those urges weren't there already, however small, he likely wouldn't affect you so strongly, or perhaps even at all."

Good goddamn, did my face feel red. Radioactive, solar flare strength, beet red. "Well, isn't that just great. So, now that we've figured out my starved libido is the problem here, I think it's time for me to go get this wrist looked at. And then maybe, I don't know, find a nice, dark corner somewhere to go die in."

I bowed to him, though god only knows why, and grabbed my purse from the table by the door.

"Caitlin."

A shiver shot up my spine. I looked back over my shoulder. In the ten seconds it had taken me to gather my things, he had folded up the remaining mat and returned it to the wall His footsteps were so quiet that I had never even heard him move. He had his back to me again, framed in the dying light of the setting sun. "You did well today. I think you've got defense down. On Wednesday, we'll start on offense."

"Awesome." I broke out in a silly grin and ducked my head to hide my joy as I skipped down the stairs. I didn't know what was making me more giddy—my success or his approval. Both were firsts and felt pretty damn great.

~*~

Lucky for me, the sprain to my wrist was minimal. One quick infusion of Seana's special (i.e. gross) herbal brew and a short nap later, I was patched up, wrapped up, and left with only a trace of tenderness. She had promised I would be as good as new in a day or two when I asked how soon I could get back to training, but her disapproving stare reminded me that she still wasn't keen on my current curriculum. I didn't know if she was opposed to our gender getting down and dirty in the training ring, or if she had a distaste for all fighting in general, but it wasn't an issue I was going to broach with her. We got along well otherwise and that was some awkwardness I didn't need.

There was no way in hell I was going grocery shopping or cooking after such a long, tiring day. I had changed back into normal clothing before leaving the fae house so, while I wasn't going to find myself a hot date, I at least felt presentable enough to have a quick, quiet dinner. A few blocks from my apartment sat a little dive with a killer bar pie, and that sounded like heaven to my empty stomach. The atmosphere of the place was a bit on the shabby side, being more bar than restaurant, but I could overlook that in favor of a thin, crispy crust, greasy pepperoni, and plenty of gooey cheese. Paired with a frosty beer, it was my idea of carb pig-out heaven.

I requested a table in the back corner of the side dining room, giving myself a bit of privacy as I chowed down. The waitress was nice enough to check on me from time to time, talking me into a second beer, but for the most part she left me alone. That was fine by me. I was still feeling pretty grimy under my quickly applied social veneer and, honestly, in the age of smartphones, who feels alone at dinner anyhow? I kept myself amused with Pinterest until I was on my final slice and the last inch or so of my second beverage.

The guilt I normally felt for inhaling all that greasy goodness was hovering just around the corner, so I picked the toppings off that last piece (because that somehow made it better) and looked around for the waitress. She was nowhere to be seen. I sighed. That always seemed to be the way of things at that place, a downside of its catering more to inebriated regulars than infrequent diners. Once you decided you were ready for the check, all the servers were mysteriously sucked into a black hole. I sat up straighter and combed my eyes through the throng that had built up by the busy bar, hoping to spot her.

Instead, I found a heart attack.

On the edge of the crowd loomed an all-too familiar behemoth. He wore the same shabby, black trench coat that he had on the night he attacked me, with the same stringy mane of black hair trailing down his back. As I watched, he slowly scanned the room with those piggy little eyes. My heart jacked up to warp speed. I felt lightheaded. Holy fuck. Was he actually there looking for me? It certainly seemed like he was looking for someone.

A small circle of space had cleared on either side of him. His glamour might have made him look acceptably human, but there was no hiding that foul aura of his. The people around him might not have known why he made them so uneasy (aside from his incredible stench, of course), but I was willing to bet dollars to donuts that everyone nearby could feel the *wrongness* of him. Scratch that; all but one, it seemed. A man, who seemed to be of normal height and build from my vantage point, had stepped up to the troll, his back facing me. Goliath stooped down to listen when the man leaned in.

Great. My nightmare had a friend.

I slid down in my seat and grabbed my phone. My hands were shaking so bad it took me three tries to unlock the home screen and another two to open my contacts. I stabbed at the screen, trying to get it to dial as fast as possible. Each ring on the other end made my heart stop, and I whined softly to myself, "Come on, come on, come on! *Answer* dammit!"

Mairi sounded distracted, the murmur of voices in the background nearly drowning her out when she finally picked up. "Hey, Cat. What's up?"

I almost sobbed with relief. "He's here! Goliath is fucking here and I think he's looking for me!"

"Wait, wait—slow down! Who's where?"

"I stopped for dinner at the Peddler. That place I took you for burgers the other day, the one a few blocks from my apartment?"

"Yeah, I remem—"

I talked over her. "He's here, Mai! Goliath is here!"

"Wait—who?"

"The fucking troll!" I hissed. "I don't know how he found me but he did. I think he's got someone with him too. They're at the bar, between me and the door. I don't think I can get past them without…" The weight of my words hit me. Dinner turned to a churning whirlpool in my stomach. "Fuck! What if they follow me home?"

"Wait; wait. Calm down." Her voice turned into a mumble. It sounded like she had pulled the phone away from her face and was talking to someone else. I couldn't make out what she said, but it felt like an eternity before her voice was strong in my ear again. "Is the place busy?"

The dining room I was in was only half full, but the area surrounding the bar was packed. There was a football game on all the TVs and the night-time drinking crowd had filtered in. "Yeah, busy enough I guess."

"Good. Don't move. You're safer there. I don't think he'll cause a scene with that many witnesses."

"That's not exactly comforting, Mai." I could barely swallow. My throat felt like it was packed with tomato sauce flavored cement.

"Just hang tight. We're on our way. We'll be there as fast as we can. Promise."

I put the phone down on the table and gripped its edge. I squeezed my eyes closed and took a deep, shaky breath. I could do this. She was right. There was safety in numbers. I could stay tucked away in my quiet little corner until the cavalry arrived. I wasn't sure exactly what the plan would be once they did, really; but I couldn't dwell on that.

"Anything else I can get you tonight?"

I jumped, startling the waitress nearly as much as she had startled me. I forced out a shrill laugh. "Sorry! I was daydreaming for a minute there. I think I, uh, saved a little room for dessert after all. What do you have?"

She rattled down their list of desserts, each one sounding more unappetizing than the last in my present state. I finally settled on some rice pudding, figuring I could force a spoonful or two down while I waited for my rescue. I felt like a rat, trapped in a corner, knowing the cat was prowling out there, only feet away.

Why hadn't I sat in the main room on the other side of the bar? That room was usually packed with families and their squealing brats, true—but it also had a clear shot at the door. Of course, it was possible that I might never have noticed Goliath's ugly mug in the first place had I sat there. I pondered that for a moment and couldn't decide if that would have been better or worse, him getting so close without my ever having realized it.

The waitress dropped off my bowl of pudding along with my check for whenever I was ready; no rush. I pushed it around with my spoon, unable to take even the tiniest bite. I kept looking at my phone, refreshing the screen when it threatened to go dark, counting each second. I wondered where they were. I should have asked them where they were coming from. Was traffic holding them up? The long moments and useless thoughts drew on until I couldn't take it anymore. I pushed myself up and sneaked a peak back over the wall into the bar area—and immediately wished I hadn't. Goliath was closer; just a few feet away from the low wall that separated us. He still appeared to be looking through the crowd; searching. I shrank down, cursing softly under my breath.

"See something you like over there, sugar?"

My head whipped around. A man stood at the edge of my table. I had never met him before and nothing struck me as being particularly fae about him, but I knew he had to be Goliath's friend. He looked out of place. He had good ol' Southern boy written all over him from his worn jeans and gaudy Lone Star State belt buckle to his button down plaid shirt. He looked to be in his mid-thirties, attractive enough with his close cropped blond hair and former high-school jock build. It was his eyes that made me go cold. There was no life in those eyes. They were two flat, hazel marbles; like the cold gaze of a dead fish. The fear must have shown on my face, because his smile stretched into a leer. He leaned casually against the wall like we were old friends chatting. In all actuality, he had just neatly trapped me in my seat.

"Back off, buddy," I snapped. "Who the hell do you think you are?"

"That ain't important, sugar." He kept his voice low, so the couple at the nearby table wouldn't be disturbed. I wanted to scream for help, but something in those dead-fish eyes told me that would be a very bad idea. "What is important is that you had a little run in with a friend of mine a few weeks back. Big fella. A little hard on the eyes. Not from around these parts, if you know what I'm sayin'?" He pointed up, across my table. I followed the line of his arm.

Goliath was less than a foot away, on the other side of the wall, watching me through the glass divider. Our eyes met and his maw split into a toothy grin that turned my bowels to water. I couldn't look away. I croaked, "What do you want?"

"Well, last time you had a few friends break up the party just as my friend there was getting to know you," he drawled. "And he was so brokenhearted, he just had to find you again and tell you how gosh-darn pretty he thinks you are."

I flashed hot and cold, torn between anger, fear, and embarrassment. I felt like I was spinning. The room was starting to feel oppressively warm. It took every bit of willpower I had to turn away from the troll but I fixed his buddy with my best "back the fuck up" stare. "I've got news for you, asshole. You think you're funny? You're not. You're the furthest fucking thing from it. So why don't you and ugly over there piss off. Find someone else to harass."

The faux friendliness drained away, his leer becoming a silent snarl. "I don't think you should go calling strangers names, Warder."

Fuck. Me.

My chest tightened so much that I could barely take a breath. All my thoughts were scrambled, sent tumbling by a tidal wave of fear. All this time I had held on to the hope that Mairi had been right; that Goliath hadn't marked me for what I was that night. I had hoped that my secret was safe. Each day that had passed without us finding him—without him finding me—it had gotten easier to tell myself that lie. As usual, I was wrong.

It took me a few seconds too long to recover and pull myself together. My retort rang hollow, even to my own ears. "And just what the hell is that supposed to mean?"

He laughed. "Awww, sugar, you're a terrible liar."

I wanted to slap that smug expression off of good ol' Texas Pete's face. I gripped the edge of the table so hard my healing wrist twinged in protest. I considered leaping over the table and making a run for it, but even if I managed to get out of the restaurant after causing such a scene, that would only leave me even more screwed. I couldn't run home and hide, when they could so easily follow me. The realization that I was trapped and helpless made me want to throw up. Where the hell was my back-up?

While I was wrapped up in the hell of my mind, my new friend helped himself to my dessert. Around a mouthful of it, he said, "You may think those new friends of yours can protect you, but you're wrong darling. Me and my buddy over there found you once. Took us some time, true; but we can do it again now, easy as pie. A girl with skills like yours should have known better than to go showing off like that, calling in her fancy back-up and whatnot."

I couldn't look at him. I could feel Goliath on the other side of the wall, slavering at me like a starving dog just begging to be let off its leash. Every muscle in my body ached; tight and ready to shake to pieces the moment I let go. I felt my eyes sting, desperate to water. Voice cracking, I asked one last time, "What do you want from me?"

"We just wanted to let you know that we know. We know what you are. We know who you are. And now?" He dropped the empty bowl back down on the table with a clatter. "We know *where* you are."

He stalked off and I lost sight of him as soon as he turned the corner. I pushed myself up and looked over the wall. Goliath was gone too, though how someone so big and distinct could have melted into the crowd so fast was anybody's guess. I thought I caught a glimpse of him by the door, but it was gone in a flash. I leaped to my feet, a couple of twenties thrown down on the table. I couldn't give two shits about over-tipping at a time like this. I grabbed my bag and coat and ran, pushing my way through the crowd and tossing out apologies as I went. I burst through the doors and nearly tripped over my own feet as I stumbled down the single step to the sidewalk. The street was busy enough for a chilly fall night, but the troll and his crony were nowhere to be seen.

Footsteps pounded up behind me. I whirled around, falling back into the fighting stance Gannon had taught me, fists raised.

"Whoa, Cat, it's us! Stand down!" Mairi skidded to a halt, skirt fluttering around her striped stockings. She was panting nearly as hard as I was, out of breath from her own sprint. Gannon and Kaine were hard at her heels, both looking like they were spoiling for a fight.

Their anger had nothing on mine. I strong-armed Mairi out of my way. "Where the hell were you guys? What took you so long?"

Kaine frowned and looked around, making a shsshing motion with his hand. "We got here as fast as we could—"

"Well you weren't fast enough! They're gone. Did you hear me? *Gone*!" I was a hairsbreadth away from screaming. Tears streamed down my cheeks, though from fear or anger I couldn't say. I was shaking so hard I couldn't keep my purse on my shoulder. Passerbys hustled along, looking over their shoulders at the scene I was making. I didn't care.

"We couldn't get here any faster." Gannon took the fore when Kaine turned away, displeased by my display of emotion. He sounded angry too, but not nearly repentant enough for one making such an inadequate apology. He spread his hands in entreaty. "We were all the way across town. There was nothing we could do."

"You don't get it, do you? They know who I am. They know *what* I am. They were looking for me and they found me. This might have been the one chance we had at stopping them from letting all their little friends know I exist! You promised to keep me safe but the first time I needed you—" I couldn't continue. I turned away and buried my face in my crumpled jacket. I trembled, trying to keep my legs from giving out. I should have known all along that something like this would happen.

Mairi came up behind me and wrapped her own coat around my shoulders. Her words were soft in my ear. "Come on. Let's get you home."

I wanted to push her away. I wanted to cling to her and sob. My whole world felt like it had been shaken to the foundation. All the fight drained out of me. I fished my keys out of my purse and handed them to her. I didn't spare Gannon or Kaine a single glance as I let her lead me to the car. I just couldn't.

All this time I had been convincing myself that I was strong; that I was a fighter. All it had taken was ten minutes to rip me down and prove that I was a silly little girl in over her head. I had thrown my lot in with strangers—dangerous strangers—and expected them to live up to their word when it counted. Silly me.

Stupid, silly me.

CHAPTER FIFTEEN

The alarm went off for a third time on Tuesday morning. I slapped at it again, this time aiming for the kill switch instead of the snooze. I rubbed the sleep crust from one eye and glared at it. My digital adversary told me I should have stumbled into the shower twenty minutes ago but there I was; still entangled in my blankets, with my hair frizzing out in a halo around my head. I felt safe in my warm little cocoon. Safe and sleepy, even though I had spent the better part of the previous day dozing on and off in the very same place.

In fact, I had spent the last few days shut up in my apartment. Unlike the last time, where I had indulged in a bit of crazy after my world was rocked, this time I had spent a good amount of time crying and stamping my feet. I'm pretty sure there was a hefty amount of bemoaning my fate and rethinking all of my life choices as well but, who can tell? By Monday I had stopped spending time in the living room, where the treadmill glared at me with accusation, opting for quality time with my bed and laptop-turned-DVD-player instead.

My phone had been on perma-silent, making it easier to ignore all calls. Mairi had checked in via text a few times, but she seemed to understand that I needed a bit of space to come to grips with the emotional upheaval the other night had caused. The fae-house had also rung me twice. I had let both calls go to voicemail, where they remained; unchecked. I wasn't ready to deal with them just yet.

I had forestalled Jenni with the claim of a nasty stomach bug. It was the same lie I had told to my boss yesterday morning before turning over and falling back into a sleep often interrupted by bad dreams. I wasn't ready to cop to all-out depression just yet (that wasn't really my thing), but I had no motivation to get out of bed, let alone face work. I was running out of sick time, and the boss would be super pissed if I called out a second day in a row, but I couldn't bring myself to care.

I looked down.

The cellphone was already in my hand.

When the automatic system picked up on the second ring I punched in the numbers that would direct it to Allison's extension. I could remember, once upon a time, when I had hated calling out sick. Loathed it really, to the point that I had often gone into work when legitimately ill just to avoid making that awkward phone call in the morning. I guess those days had faded into the past with the rest of the normalcy in my life. I didn't feel the overwhelming guilt and panic I once had, but I still wasn't looking forward to the disapproval I would hear on the other end either. I held my breath and hoped it would go to her voicemail.

I should have known I wouldn't be that lucky.

"Good morning, this is Allison speaking. How may I help you today?"

The amount of chipper in those words hit me like a brick. I pulled a face like I was dying, sticking my tongue out even if no one could see it. Petty, sure, but it made me feel better at a time when so little did. I didn't bother trying to clear the sleep fog from my voice. "Hi Allison. It's Caitlin."

I could almost hear the frost crackle as it settled over the line. "Good morning Caitlin. What's up?"

Yeeeeah, there was nothing "good" in that greeting.

The me of a few months ago would have started having heart palpitations over the impending lie after such a chilly reception. Present Caitlin? I don't think my heartbeat even sped up. I said, "Nothing good, unfortunately. Still feeling pretty terrible. Thankfully, I'm not glued to the toilet anymore, but I think I'm gonna need another day of tea and toast to get back on my feet."

When in doubt, hedge on the side of TMI. It discourages too many unpleasant questions.

There was a moment of silence and I could picture the sour pucker I was getting on the other end of the line. I threw in an "I'm sorry" though I didn't think either of us really believed that I was. It was just another of those social niceties in the angry boss/contrite employee game but, hey; I tried.

Finally, she graced with me a small sigh—possibly more of an angry nasal exhale—and said, "Fine. Feel better."

The call ended.

I stared at the screen on my phone, searching myself for any hint of surprise, but found none. I didn't care and it was pretty impossible for me to pretend otherwise. I knew that I should be feeling some sort of remorse or worry over the hot water I was wading into with her but... I didn't. I couldn't. Facing a pissy soccer mom and her verbal reprimands hardly seemed frightening after looking into the eyes of a fairytale creature who wanted to eat my spleen.

I tossed my cell back onto the nightstand and rolled over. The blankets followed, enveloping me in a warm, downy cocoon. I snuggled in until I found a cool spot on my pillow, hoping the physical comfort would quiet my mind and lull me back to sleep.

~*~

A few hours later I had gotten out of bed just for a change of pace. Not that parking myself on the couch, still in my pajamas, was much of an improvement. The TV was on but I wasn't paying attention to it. I was using the cooking channel more to mark the passage of time than for entertainment purposes. Whenever one overly cheerful hostess was exchanged for another, I knew another half hour had passed.

On some level, it irked me that I was wasting a perfectly good mental health day. On the other hand, I just couldn't find the energy to do anything. I was in dire need of a shower and I hadn't even managed that. The most energetic thing I had managed was a PB&J for lunch, so preoccupied at the time that I had hardly tasted it.

My thoughts just kept chasing themselves around in circles. One moment I'd be fuming over Kaine's failure to keep his promise and get my bad guy. The next, I'd be wallowing in crushing despair, certain that said bad guy (now guy*s*, actually) were going to find me, no matter what I did. The worst part was that I knew I was being overly dramatic. I knew, deep down, that Kaine et al. had tried to come to my rescue. Unlike the romance novels I had grown up reading under the covers, the hero didn't always swoop in at the right moment to help the damsel in distress. That was just real life. Real was a vague term, considering I was talking about a life that involved trolls and faeries—but, still.

I knew I shouldn't be taking it so personally, but I couldn't help it. I didn't want to help it. Maybe it was the timing. I had just finally started to feel like I was stronger than the mess my life had become; like I had a handle on it all. Being, literally, cornered by those cretins had taken me right back to the square one. They had left me feeling like that scared shitless, powerless, vapid girl who had thought things like designer purses and the season's hottest shade of lipstick were oh-so important. The one who had honestly believed that everything in life would work out, one day, and that being a little lost was no big deal, so long as I had a good time doing it.

They reminded me of the innocence that night had taken from me and I hated them for it.

I rolled over onto my stomach and buried my face in a throw pillow. I kicked my feet like a child, screaming until my throat went raw. Thankfully, the pillow muffled it enough that I didn't expect the owners of the business downstairs to come check on who was being murdered. When the frustration had drained out of me, I lifted my head and pushed the tangled mass of hair out of my face. I scuttled back into the corner of the couch, pulling my blanket around me like it would somehow protect me from that aching empty place inside me. I looked around the apartment.

Nothing had changed, of course. The TV chattered on in front of me, the chicken sizzling happily in a skillet making my stomach turn. The faint sound of traffic echoed outside the window, interspaced with a few honks and the wail of a far-off police siren. There was nothing new, nothing special, to mark my emotional breakthrough. The world was oblivious to my anguish, just as it always had been. Getting to the heart of the issue didn't lift any of my sadness; it just made me feel more alienated. Suddenly, I didn't feel quite so much like being alone anymore.

I fished around under the blanket until I found my phone. I stared at it, cradled in my palm. There were only a few people I talked to regularly, and none of them really fit the bill, considering what I was going through. Even as irritated with me as she was, I knew Jenni would still drop everything to lend me an ear if I called her in the middle of the day. I even considered it for a moment, before deciding that doing so would likely cost a price I wasn't up to paying. She would have more questions than solutions for me, and, honestly, I didn't have any answers for her. The only other one I could turn to was Mairi. She would actually understand the issues that were at the heart of my impending breakdown, but I didn't really want to go there with her either. Not yet.

I took a deep breath. I already knew I'd regret the urge later (as I always did), but I gave into that primal instinct every girl has when she's feeling lost and vulnerable.

I called my mother.

As it rang, I wondered if I had finally lost my mind. Conversations with my mother never went in my favor. Don't get me wrong; she was a sweet, loving woman—just not particularly so with her eldest offspring. It had been that way from the cradle, if family lore was to be believed. My maternal grandmother had been more of a mother to me than my own during the first few years of my life while my mother suffered through some undiagnosed post-partum depression. That may have explained some of the coolness between us, but it hadn't made accepting it any easier. I only had the alienated, often hurt, feelings of my teen years to go on. I remembered more screaming matches (which I had usually started) and slammed doors (which was how my younger self had preferred to end those verbal battles) than hugs in my lifetime.

As the years went by, I continually knocked my head into the same wall over and over, trying to forge some sort of common ground, adult-to-adult relationship. Sometimes I tricked myself into believing it was working.

"Why aren't you at work?"

Sometimes even I couldn't be that deluded.

The disapproval was evident in her voice, like I was still thirteen years old and being caught playing hooky from school. I swallowed a sigh. "Hi to you too mom. I called out of work today. Had a little stomach virus or something."

"Oh." I could hear the television on in the background. She was probably watching The Price is Right while she ate her lunch. She had done that pretty much every day since as early as I could remember. I bet her lunch had been a ham sandwich with mayo too. She had always been a creature of habit. She asked, "Something going around the office?"

I don't think she really believed me, but it was nice to be humored. "Stomach trouble" had always been her go-to excuse to beg off of something she didn't want to do too. I was probably a lot more like my mother than I cared to admit. I shrugged, knowing full well she couldn't see me do so. "Maybe. Kinda hit me out of the blue."

"Diane had some sort of flu last month. Everyone has been getting sick on and off ever since." Mom droned on about the Great Plague of the Year and its effects on her office for a bit. I made the appropriate sounds of encouragement to keep her going every now and then. I didn't really care about any of what she was saying. It was just nice to hear another voice that wasn't coming out of the television.

When her tale of woe had run its course, she took a noisy drag on her cigarette and asked, "So what else is wrong with you?"

I'm not sure if the timing of the question or its phrasing gave me pause, but for a good thirty seconds I was left dumbstruck. Finally I managed to slap on some sarcasm to hide my guilt-ridden surprise. "Gee ma, love you too!"

She laughed, in her wheezy-wet smoker's way. "Not with you personally, dingbat. I mean, what's going on that has you calling me on a Tuesday afternoon?"

I sucked in my cheeks, counting slowly to five. "Why do you assume something is wrong? Can't a girl just want to say hi to her mother?"

"You never call me in the middle of the day, Caitlin Marie." I shrank back into the pillows reflexively. Hearing my middle name was never good. She chided me, "Hell, you hardly call me at all these days. Something must be going on. What is it?"

Had I wanted to talk about the deep, dark issues that were eating away at my soul? Maybe—but only on that "never actually going to happen" level. Really dishing the dirt with my mom was something I hadn't done since, well… Ever. I felt betrayed by her sudden interest in my life. I pulled the phone away from my ear, giving her little digital image on its face an accusatory stare.

Have you ever had one of those moments in a conversation where you realize you really have nothing to say? Like, not even small talk? A moment where the words have literally dried up in your mouth and you just want it to be over, so you start to panic while trying to think of a single freaking thing to say? You know; one of those times where you just sit there, feeling dumb and listening to the silence drag on, wondering why the hell you ever picked the phone up in the first place?

Suddenly I was wondering just what the hell I had been thinking. Calling my mother had been some deep seated little-girl-in-need-of-comfort instinct but I had remembered too late that there was nothing comforting about our relationship. Her putting me on the spot like that left me slack-jawed, feeling more and more anxious by the minute, until the words finally spilled out of my mouth, unbidden. "I'm lost."

"Come again?"

Tears had already sprung to my eyes. My voice wavered, threatening to crack. "I'm lost, ma. I feel like nothing I do is ever right and I just keep spinning my wheels trying to figure out how to make tomorrow better—but it just stays the same or gets worse." I took a deep breath, swallowing a sniffle. I scrubbed at my traitorous eyes with a balled fist. "I just don't know what to do to fix my life."

I don't know what I expected her to say. I wasn't really expecting an earful of sage wisdom. Mom had never been big on doling out wordy life lessons. Maybe I was hoping for a nugget of advice. Perhaps even some sort of commiseration; a promise that every woman went through this stage in their lives and that mine too would pass. At the very least, a sound of sympathy would have been nice.

"Really, Caitlin." The word was drawn out almost into a drawl, heavy with disgust. Or maybe it was exasperation. The two kind of sounded the same when coming from mom's mouth.

I felt like I had been slapped. My eyes welled up again and my cheeks burned, missing only the sting of a physical blow. My stomach did a sickening somersault, chastising me for expecting any sort of empathy to have come through from the other end of the phone. I felt like an ass, and that made me snappish. "Yes, *really*, mom."

She heaved a sigh, like I had asked her to move mountains. "I mean, come on. What do you want me to say to that?"

She said "that" like it was a dirty word. I hated the way my voice shook. "I was hoping for some sort of advice, maybe."

"Advice?" She snorted. Her tone turned snide. "What kind of advice could I give you? By the time I was your age, I was married with two children and a full time job. I didn't have time to sit around feeling sorry for myself."

Feeling sorry for myself.

The words burned.

That's what it always came down to with her. Every problem, every complaint I had ever had in my life could be laid at the feet of my selfish and all-consuming need for people to pity me. I don't know what I possibly could have done as a child to warrant such immediate distrust from the woman who birthed me, but I couldn't remember a single time in all my years that she had taken a single concern of mine seriously.

I didn't want to believe that she went out of her way to alienate and hurt me—who wants to think such things of their mother?—but I couldn't forget all the times she had dismissed me or out-right laughed at my ideas. The worst memories stuck out most, of course. What teenager would ever forget her mother refusing to take her shopping, because she was ashamed to be seen in public with a rebellious little goth?

After so many years of being put-down, I should have lost the ability to be burned her coldness. Instead, each time we butted heads, it just bit into the old, familiar scar tissue and added another weal. I felt cold inside, like I had swallowed ice water and it had frozen as it trickled down my throat.

Calling her had been a mistake; maybe the biggest I had made yet. The cold reminder of the aching distance between us hurt more than the memory of Goliath hoisting me into the air, ready to devour me. Maybe my life had gotten crazy and weird. Maybe I needed a little dose of normal to help me get my feet back on the ground—but I sure as hell wasn't going to find that in mom.

"Thanks for the pep talk, mom. I've got to go; stomach is ready to act up again."

She was still talking as I hung up. I didn't care.

I lowered my phone into my lap. My fingers were clenched so hard around it that my knuckles ached, but that was nothing in comparison to the ache in my jaw. I couldn't explain why, after so many years, I still let her get to me but each time it was a new surprise. I hated how much it hurt, but I hated myself even more for expecting better of her. I'm not sure how long I sat there, lost in my own private darkness, but by the time I finally found the strength to force myself up off the couch, my cheeks were dry once again.

~*~

To say I didn't accomplish much that day would be a gross understatement. Well, I guess if you consider moping and staring at the wall "something," I had reached pro status by that evening. Since I don't, I pretty much just chalked the day up as a loss.

After the heartfelt chat with my mother, I shambled around the apartment for a good ten minutes or so, trying to find something to lose myself in. The effort of working out was straight out right off the bat, but little things like doing some laundry or taking a shower were given a cursory perusal. I had even briefly considered taking a walk and getting some fresh air to clear my head but that had just seemed too damn complicated.

Despite the restlessness crawling around like ants under my skin, I just didn't have the energy to *do* anything. And, let's be honest; if basic hygiene was difficult to manage, there was pretty much no chance I was stepping out into public. Instead, I wound up back in bed with the solace of my pillows once again.

After a few hours of tossing, turning and fitful napping, I was forced to emerge from my cave of despair by my grumbling stomach. Melancholy or no, it wanted to be fed. It was already a fitting pitch black by 6pm, but turning on the lights just didn't seem worth it either. The fridge was near bare, leaving me with only a handful of frozen dinners as viable options. I still had some wine left, so I didn't think it was worth the effort to go grocery shopping either. I may have considered that such thoughts were dangerously close to that of an alcoholic, but it took all of two heartbeats for me to decide that I really didn't give a flying fuck.

So, by the glow of the television, I sat on the floor behind my coffee table watching—you guessed it—more Food Network as I ate an unsatisfying, nuked Swedish meatball dinner for one, accompanied by a full-to-the-brim glass of Chardonnay.

Let me tell you, I had crazy in the bag.

I had just drained my glass when my phone rang. Mairi. For a moment I considered letting it go to voicemail, but she had been really good about letting me wallow in my funk without interruption thus far. I didn't want to alienate her as much as I had everyone else. I sighed and picked up the phone. "Hey."

"Good evening, doom and gloom. You sound like shit."

A startled bark of laughter erupted from me. I had to admire the kid's style. "Thanks, bitch."

She made one of those slightly patronizing sympathy noises. "You still in your funk?"

My lip twitched like it wanted to smile. "Yup."

"Figured as much. You want some company?"

I considered how to answer that for a minute. I certainly wasn't in the receiving mood, being all sleep-ruffled and slightly ripe. On the other hand, I was lonely as hell. Oh, the conundrum of the hermit. What it really came down to was, would I ever escape my misery if I just kept hiding from the world while letting myself feel alienated and victimized? Finally, I shrugged, feeling stupid for doing so when I knew damn well she couldn't see it. "Not really, but I wouldn't kick you off my porch."

She chuckled. "Figured you'd say that too. Come let me in."

Funk or no, she reminded me so much of the brash, ballsy teenager I had once been that I couldn't hate on her. When I opened the front door, she was leaning against the wall of my vestibule, one hand slipping her phone back into her purse. The other held a bottle of red wine. She smirked at my raised eyebrow. "I didn't think you'd mind me bringing a friend." I took the bottle when she stuck it out at me. The devious look of glee on her face made me smile. "I liberated this guy from Kaine's personal stock. I know dick about wine but something tells me it's probably a damn fine vintage."

I had never heard of it which meant it was a likely a higher price point than the bargain basement booze I was used to drinking. I ushered her into the hall and locked the door behind her. I stopped to grab two fresh glasses and my corkscrew from the kitchen. In the short time it took me to make that detour, she had thrown her jacket and purse onto the loveseat, removed her boots, commandeered a corner of the couch, and changed the channel to some wacky cartoon with a talking bespectacled dog and a kid who looked like he was wearing a white hat with bear ears. Already the room felt less oppressive.

I parked myself on the opposite corner and poured us each a drink.

"Thanks," she said as she took the glass. She settled back into her corner. She was watching me, her lips—sporting a bright fuchsia lipstick that matched some streaks she had run through her messily knotted hair—pursed. "You mad that I came by?"

As much I hated to admit, her presence had already begun to make me feel better than I had all day. I couldn't let myself think too hard on that. Realizing how close the odd little fae girl had come to replacing Jenni in my life would bring up those swells of guilt again. Instead, I took a slow sip and shook my head as I swallowed. "No. I think I've done enough wallowing for the week. It lost its appeal right around the time it forced me to a Lean Cuisine for dinner."

"Gross." She broke into a grin, which I couldn't help but mirror. Her mirth was infectious. She sobered a bit as she asked, "You still mad about the other night?"

"Part of me wants to be." I swirled my glass, admiring the streaks the wine left on the side of the glass. I wasn't normally a red kind of girl, but she had done well in her selection from Kaine's cellar. "I know you guys tried to get there."

"We really did," she said, almost pleading with me to believe her. "I was yelling at Gannon to drive faster the whole time but we hit every freaking light and..."

I held up a hand and cut her off. "I know it's not your fault. It wasn't something that could be helped. I'm sorry I freaked out the way I did but..." I balled my fists. "It's just so damn frustrating! It's like, every time this asshole has found me, there's been nothing I could do about it. I just have to sit there like some dumb-shit and hope he doesn't tear my head off. I hate feeling so...*vulnerable*."

I don't know why that was the magic word, but it was. Saying it was like lancing an infected boil. Immediately I felt all of the anger that I had bottled up inside drain out of me. It wasn't like that was a new revelation. I had had a pretty good idea of why I was so upset the whole time, but saying it out loud—to another living being—seemed to make all the difference. I almost felt dizzy with the relief of having admitted it.

"We'll find them," Mairi promised. Her face was stone cold serious. "Gannon has been searching high and low, trying to find out who they are and where they could possibly be hiding. I swear to you, Cat; we are doing everything we can to find them, fast."

I felt my face warm. For some reason, hearing that made my insides go all squirmy. "Really? Gannon has been searching for them?"

"Yeah, he has. He felt horrible that we missed those creeps." She tried to hide her smile by taking another sip of wine and failed. She winked at me, leaving me feeling like I had missed some part of a joke. When I stared at her blankly, she heaved a sigh. "Of course, he might just be scared that you'll take it out on him next time you're in the ring together."

I ran through a quick mental calendar and groaned.

Shit. Tomorrow night was our next lesson.

"You think you can emerge from Château de Misery in time for that?"

I threw her a nasty look, complete with scrunched nose. Tomorrow was shaping up to be a hell of a day to try and re-enter the normal world. I knew I was in for a dressing down when I went back to work, and the thought of fighting rush-hour traffic to cross the city and get all sweaty with some fae-fu right after wasn't exactly appealing.

Although, if Gannon was true to his word, our next meeting would finally be time for me to start learning to kick some butt, instead of just defending my own. If that were the case, then maybe the next time Goliath and his cronies tried to make me feel like a scared little girl, I wouldn't be quite so helpless. The thought sent a fission of warmth through me; tingling along all my nerves.

I gave Mairi a sly grin of my own. "Wouldn't miss it for the world."

CHAPTER SIXTEEN

I hated all life by the time 6pm rolled around Wednesday evening.

Work had been the hell I had expected it to be. Allison was clearly on her last nerve with me. I had been called into her office even before I could put my purse down to be told, in no uncertain terms, that I was out of sick time. Any and all future absences would be held against me. Her frosty attitude I could take, but knowing that I was one misstep away from another strike shook me a little deeper. I didn't like my job but I did have a love of gas in my car and food in my belly. I also didn't think the landlord would accept teary-eyed apologies in place of the rent check, no matter how pathetic I looked while doing so.

So, I spent the next eight hours on pins and needles. Allison made so many trips past my cubicle that I couldn't tell myself it was mere paranoia. She obviously wanted me to feel like every moment held the potential for a cataclysmic screw up. Her syrupy sweet tone and Cheshire cat smile told me the bitch would use just about any little thing she could to put that nail in my coffin—and she had her eye on me hoping to find it.

After that abysmal workday, I had to fight my way through the special hell of forty minutes of bumper-to-idiotic-bumper traffic to get to the fae house. You can guess how much fun *that* was. Not wanting to add time on to my trip by stopping for food, my dinner instead consisted of two granola bars fished out of my back seat, which I scarfed down while stuck at a red light. Of course, since I was having such a wonderful day already, the second one decided to explode from its wrapper in a cascade of oaty bits and minuscule chocolate chips. All over my lap. I was pretty sure I had missed a few and would be finding embarrassing melty smears on my clothing at inopportune times in the future.

Great day.

Thankfully, Mairi and Kaine were out on the town. I only encountered Seana on my way into the house. She seemed to sense my foul mood, giving me a quick hug followed by a wide berth. They had been nice enough to bequeath me with unlimited use of the spare back bedroom. I stored some workout gear in a dresser there, which made the changing process much less of a hassle. Seana was even made sure they were washed and ready for my next meeting with Gannon each time. My own mother had never been so reliable.

Dressed, I sat down on the bed to tie my shoes—also kept by the bed—and paused. It no longer felt weird to simply walk into the house and putter around it like it was my own. I couldn't remember having ever felt so comfortable in a stranger's home. I hadn't really let myself think about it, but it was fast becoming my home away from home. I wasn't sure why that bothered me quite as much as it did.

I threw my hair up into a sloppy bun as I jogged up the attic stairs. I was actually looking forward to a little confrontation. My blood was singing with indignation at the affronts the day had heaped upon me. I could use a physical outlet. I could already envision Allison's smug face floating before me, just begging to be punched. Maybe I could get Gannon to let me tape a print-out of her ugly mug to the punching bag, for a little creative incentive.

When I passed through the door and into the training room, I paused. I was used to the shelves along the left wall being well stocked with the tools of Gannon's trade: an array of hand weights, some wooden staves in varying length, padded gear to protect the head and legs; boxing gloves, maybe a stack or two of towels for when we—I, really—worked up a sweat. They were the sorts of things you might see around any old gym, so I had never thought to bat an eye at their presence. While I hadn't been anywhere near up to snuff on the accoutrements of physical fitness, everything there had seemed to have a logical purpose even to my beginner's brain.

So, I was pretty surprised when I saw that side of the room had been converted into a medieval arsenal. Two long tables had been laid out end-to-end. Each was covered in a black tablecloth, filled with weapons of all shapes and sizes. I walked toward them in a daze. I came to a halt in the front of them, speechless.

Well. Shit had just gotten real.

Gannon stood at the end of the first table, closest to the door. His stood at attention with his arms crossed, as usual. I was too busy gaping at the arsenal before me to notice his expression as I approached. There was no emotion in that butterscotch smooth voice. "Good evening."

"Not particularly," I responded with a snort. I hadn't meant to sound quite so bitchy, but the day had taken its toll. I waved a hand at the display before me. "Though something tells me it has the possibility of getting better."

He chuckled. "Perhaps. Are you up to starting offensive training tonight?"

That was a loaded question. It was a shade too late to consider backing out, really. I rubbed my hands together and felt how damp my palms were. "Sure. Where do we start? I'm not going to need to use all of these, am I?"

I was too busy scoping out the goods laid out before me to get a good gauge on his expression, but I heard the smile persist in his voice. "No. We'll focus on one, to get you started. Take your time. Look them over. Pick them up, give them a try. Really handle them and get a feel for their weight. See what feels right in your hand."

I gave him my best deer in the headlights look. "Wait, you mean *I* have to choose which one to use?"

"I like to think it's more the case of the right one choosing you, but yes. You play a large part in where your training goes from here. Like I said, take your time." He stepped back from the table, jerking his head in the direction of the stairs. "I'll be back shortly."

All-righty then.

For a moment I just stood there, unsure of what to do first. I chose one end of the table and began the slow walk down its length. Some of the things before me were familiar; I had been to enough Renaissance festivals in my life to know what a sword was, even if I had never handled one. I had also had a penchant for knives during my angsty goth years, so those weren't entirely unfamiliar to me either.

It was the dizzying variety of either that astounded me. Swords and knives of all shapes and sizes seemed to go on and on for a mile. Some more exotic items were mixed among them, though I couldn't name more than a handful of them. I touched a few lightly as I passed, feeling the chill of their metal beneath my fingertips. I was too overwhelmed to consider picking any of them up just yet. They all seemed so big and heavy, just from looking at them.

I was no closer to choosing my weapon by the time I reached the far end of the table. I bit my lip and did an about-face, gazing back the way I had come. My mind was whirling. None of the weapons looked new; well taken care of, yes but certainly not new. Gannon had told me to pick one at random, which meant he likely felt comfortable teaching me any of them. The implications of his skill grew by leaps and bounds in my brain. Goddamn, Mairi was right. I really couldn't have found a better teacher.

On my second pass, I strove for confidence. I ruled out the big, unwieldy items straight off. I was pretty sure the double-headed battle axe was lacking the discretion needed for my day-to-day life. Hell, that was assuming I could even pick it up! My strength training routine had begun to sculpt some teeny tiny guns, but I was a long way away from swinging a massive hammer above my head like Thor. I finally made myself pick up a piece here and there. It was hard not to be disappointed every time a cool looking sword proved to be too much for me—a single swing of a moderately sized one nearly spun me to the ground. The trial and error was made easier by my being alone in the room. Had I had an audience, my cheeks would have been flaming red. I would have to remember to thank

Gannon for his forethought.

By the time I was on my third journey down the aisle, I had ruled out all of the larger weapons. The array of swords was awesome, but—weight and length issues aside—they failed the discretion test just as much as the big, badass monstrosities. If I was learning to defend myself against creepy faeries, I needed something I could potentially keep near me. Otherwise, what was the point?

I settled myself in front of the knife section and slowly picked them over. Some were as small as my palm—which didn't do much to instill courage in me—while others were as long as my forearm. I ruled out the big, thick ones (and giggled to myself as I thought just that), sticking to the thinner blades that I could potentially hide in a purse or boot. A few felt nice in my hand. I finally whittled the selection down to a wicked looking cousin of the bowie knife that seemed to fit my grip well. It was doubled edged, with a decent weight and a good balance to it when I mocked some punches and stabs. I stood there, holding it, and gazed down at it for what seemed like a long time.

I placed it back down in its original spot on the table, biting at my lip. It was nice but there was just something missing. It didn't have the *umph* I was looking for. I don't know what I had been expecting. Maybe, when Gannon had given his little weapon choosing the wielder speech earlier, I had expected some crazy Excalibur like moment when the perfect one found its way into my hand. That was silly, of course, but it lingered in my mind. I just hadn't felt that click yet and it was damn frustrating.

While I chastised myself for my dreams of grandeur, my eyes roved the table and finally came to rest on a pair of long, tapering blades laid by the far end of the table. I had discounted them as being too dainty to give me the sense of security I was longing for, in favor of the heavier, more familiar shape of the other knives. Certainly a sturdy blade would be more useful than something thin and sort of flimsy looking, right? After my extensive trolling of its kin, I was having second thoughts.

I took a blade in each hand, holding them up to admire them. They were indeed thin, but a bit heavier than I had anticipated. The blades were twice the length of the handle, each coming to a wicked point. I resisted the urge to test it with a finger; I already knew they would draw blood. The handles felt good. The soft, black leather of their grips felt smooth against my palms. The bar that crossed over—and I assumed, protected—my knuckles was ornately wrought to look like curling ivy. The girl in me appreciated that bit of flair.

I went through my awkward stabbing routine, only to find it wasn't quite as awkward with these knives. They followed my motions effortlessly, seeming to fit each move without much adjustment on my part. I felt a chill run up my back and smiled.

"I see we've found a winner."

I startled and whirled around, falling into the ready stance. Gannon's slow smile and appreciative nod made me blush. Truth be told, I was pretty proud of how instinctual protecting myself had become too but he didn't need to know that. I straightened up with a forced cough, feeling awkward standing there with the knives clenched in my hands. A slow smile spread across my face, until I was grinning like an idiot. "Yeah, I think I did."

He crossed the room and I let him take the blades when he held out his hands. I tried to ignore the little twinge inside me that didn't want to give them up so easily. He took his time examining them; turning them this way and that, giving one an experimental flip in the air which he completed with far too much ease. "Good choice. These will suit you well."

I took them back, clasping them in sweaty palms. "You think so?"

"These are stilettos."

"First kind I'll play with that aren't patent leather," I said.

He ignored my sarcasm. "They're intended for stabbing, which I think will suit your style. This particular pair has quite the history. They belonged to Kaine's mother. She trained many warriors in her day." He looked down at the blades, then back up to me; something curious playing in his eyes. "You have a bit of her spirit about you."

"Oh? How so?"

"She was quite the smart-ass as well." He broke into a grin when I stuck my tongue out at him. "You'll do them justice, I think. I'll show you how to take good care of them."

I gaped at him for a moment. "Wait, you mean I get to keep them?"

"It would be pretty silly for me to teach you to use them and then take them away, don't you think? Besides; every blade is different, even if only in the most subtle way. I would feel better that you stick with them, for the time being."

I gazed at them in wonder, like they were about to spring to life in my hands. "Won't Kaine have an issue that? I mean, will he be okay with me taking something that belongs in his family?"

"Don't worry about Kaine." Was that an annoyed tick at the corner of his lips that I spied? It was gone too soon for me to read further into it. He said, "He wasn't too happy with the idea of you going on the offensive, but he agreed to put the reins in my hands where your training is concerned. As long as you keep your skills here, in this room—"

"Say what?" I clenched my fists around the hilts of my daggers. "Nu-uh, no way. I need real-world experience if I'm going to stop choking up when these assholes come at me. I'm going hunting with you."

"No, you're not. It's too dangerous."

"Why? Because you might lose your Lynx Detector?" The discomforted look that earned me said I wasn't far from the truth. I scowled. "Yeah;

that's what I thought. Well, fuck that. I'm going hunting."

He heaved a great sigh. This argument didn't seem to surprise him. I don't know if he had expected my level of stubbornness, however. Silly man. He said, "Caitlin, this is serious. Hunting is a dangerous job. It's a lot to handle, even for a Guardian."

My smile might have showed a little too much tooth. "Don't worry. I can handle it."

A skeptically raised eyebrow confronted me and I stared it down like a champ. "It's one thing to say you're prepared, it's another to be so. Killing stains your soul in a way you cannot ever anticipate. Think hard before you say yes. Are you ready to have blood on your hands? Even in the name of justice, every life you take will stay with you for the rest of your days."

"Then that's something I'll have to learn to live with." I hoped the impassioned stare I leveled him with showed him everything I was feeling, even as I struggled to put it all into words. "I didn't ask you to train me just for vengeance, Gannon. Those creatures are a threat not only to me, but to other innocent people. I know I'm not going to be some super badass warrior, wheeling and dealing justice like a real Hunter, but if what you've all said is true, those guys? They aren't exactly doing their job these days. *Someone* needs to do something. People who have no clue what is out there are getting hurt and I might be the only one around here who knows the truth."

Where had that come from? I hadn't intended to go all avenging angel, but sure, why not? I was sick of feeling lost and vulnerable. I was done with being scared. Maybe if I had stopped and given it some thought earlier, I would have realized that sooner. I needed to stop being a passenger in my own life, but more so I needed to stop the outside world from getting bigger and scarier. I needed to *do* something.

If there was one lesson that my time with the fae gang had taught me, it was that sometimes you had to say the words aloud for everything to click into place. In that moment, it all made sense. The words just spilled out of my mouth, hot as lava. "There's no saying if you'll be able to fix shit once you get home. If you can't, I may be the only thing Riverview has between it and the monsters for a very long time. I'm not asking you to teach me this for fun. I *have* to do something."

He raised his hands, throwing up the white flag. "Fair enough. I'll speak to Kaine and work something out. But hear me now: under no circumstances are you to go looking for trouble by yourself. You wait until I say you're ready, and when we're out there on the hunt, you listen to my every word. I need to know I can trust you. Arguing here, in training, is one thing. Out there, it could get one or both of us killed. If I tell you to fall back, I need you do it immediately. Are we clear?"

"Yes, sir. Crystal." From the mildly frightened and wholly unconvinced look he was giving me, I must have been grinning the way I had when I opened up my Barbie Dream House on Christmas morning as a child. I felt that excited, so it made sense. I dialed it back a bit and tried to look suitably somber. "I have no intention of winding up in a back alley with an angry centaur just yet. I promise I'll follow your lead and I won't go looking to test out these bad boys"—I held up my new best friends—"without you. I am perfectly aware that I am little and squishy, and the things out there are scary and may have horns. I don't need a repeat of the other night."

I don't think he was buying it. He certainly didn't look all that convinced. He sighed, rubbing at the back of his neck. A shadow passed over his face. "Caitlin, about that night..."

I cut him off with an upheld hand. Shit. I should have known better than to bring that up. "I'd rather not talk about it, if it's all the same with you. I got upset and freaked out and lost my head. I shouldn't have taken it out on you guys. You were doing your best to help. Besides, there's nothing that can be done about it now. I'd just like to move on and get done what I need to get done—okay?"

Goddamn, his stare was intense. I fought the urge to shimmy away from his gaze, like my insides tried to do whenever we locked eyes. Instead I held that stare and lifted my chin. I was done letting anyone intimidate me. It was so damn frustrating, trying to get a read on where his head was at. I couldn't tell if I had said something to piss him off, or if there was some sort of gallant wellspring fueling his anger. I didn't want to guess and I sure as fuck wasn't going to ask.

I let some of the bitch drain out of my tone. "Mairi said you've been hitting the street looking for those bastards. You said it yourself once; that means way more to me than any apology."

We both stood there for a moment and I think he was as uncomfortable as I was. Why I had brought that up, I don't know. I hadn't been looking to create an awkward, touchy-feely kind of moment but I had. I jumped a little when he reached out and clapped my shoulder with a firm hand; squeezing it. "Understood. Why don't you start to warm up while I put those—" he jerked his head in the direction of the discarded weaponry—"away? Then we'll see just what you can do with those."

I found myself grinning back, my hands flexing eagerly around the hilts of my new toys.

Finally, something was starting to feel right again in my life.

CHAPTER SEVENTEEN

January

The blood would never wash away.

My hands would be stained with it for the rest of my life; a reminder of what I had done.

I'm not sure how long I sat there, letting the shower rain down over me until it was little more than lukewarm. It didn't matter. I had scrubbed and scrubbed until my skin was raw but I could still see the blood there, staining my hands. I could still feel it, hot and sticky; could still smell it. My stomach flipped and threatened to make me retch all over again.

Time had lost all meaning to me.

I had lost all meaning to myself.

Life liked to remind me of my place, whenever I got a bit too cocky. I don't know why I had ever let myself think that that would change. I should have known better. I *did* know better. I'd never been lucky, not even from day one. I was the kid who never got one past her parents without it coming back to bite her in the ass, for Christ's sake—how did I ever think I could lie to the Universe at large and get away with it?

Maybe I thought that the revelation of my super cool, mystical Gift had somehow transformed my luck as well as my humdrum daily life. Maybe I thought I could change by pumping iron and learning how to hold a knife. Maybe I just thought that if I wanted it badly enough—if I just tried hard enough—I could break become something different. Something stronger.

Who did I think I was kidding?

I wanted to be tough; to be a badass. The past few months had filled me with a longing to be anything other than the soft, weak little human I was. Anything other than the little girl lost, who was so far over her head in fae shit that she could barely breathe for the stench of it. Maybe there was a part of me that had thought a little too long on Mairi's offhanded question about my lineage; that had dreamed a little too much in the dark of another sleepless night. Maybe, just maybe, that little part of me had started to believe that she could be part of their world, where things were different and exciting and strange.

The truth was no amount of wanting, no secret longing, would ever make me anything but what I was: a little girl trying to roll with the big dogs. I couldn't be one of them, no matter how hard I tried. I was stranded worlds apart from them, and no amount of knife-throwing and cardio workouts were ever going to level that playing field. Being badass came with strings attached and I hadn't stopped to think of what those strings were attached to or how hard they would tug when tested.

Life reminded me of that fact the first time Gannon agreed to take me on a hunt.

I ducked my head down to my knees and hugged my elbows to my ears, trying to block out the moaning. It grated along my nerves; that horrible, endless groan. It was the warble of something in pain. The last gasp of a dying animal. My attempts to block it out didn't help.

The sound was coming from me.

Something inside of me was dying.

I was pretty sure it was my innocence.

What had I been thinking, insisting that I play a part in dealing out fae justice? What had I expected to happen, when I took another being's fate into my own hands? Who the hell did I think I was? I couldn't even hold my every day, mundane little life together. Work had become a joke; I was out more than I was in. I had no lifelines left there. One more screw up and I would find myself out on my ass. I should have been taking the initiative to look for another job—or maybe another living arrangement, for when everything finally went south—but I hadn't. I wouldn't.

Jenni hadn't called or texted me in over a week. I could hardly blame her. I was living a life apart from everything she knew now. Our conversations had become more silence than words, hers stony while she waited to hear whatever poorly concocted lie I had for my increasingly unexplainable behavior, mine thick with guilt. I think we had a date set up to have lunch, but I couldn't remember when. I hoped I had written it down somewhere but doubted I had. Soon, I would be making another round of ill-received apologies.

I was pretty sure my family hated me far worse than Jenni at the moment. I had missed my grandmother's 91st birthday, forgetting not only the fancy dinner my mother had planned, but the day in question all together. Of course Grandma had said it was no big deal when I called to make my tearful apology two days later, but I wasn't buying it. As her oldest granddaughter, I had the responsibility of remembering something as important as that. I could hardly tell her I had gotten caught up in another wild goose chase, scouring some crappy little off Broadway theater in the city because a sylph had told us that her djinn buddy had promised that he had heard, on good authority, that the Lynx had purchased tickets to the show that night. Big ol' waste of time that had been.

Perhaps mom and dad would have forgiven me that transgression (even if I would never forgive myself), had I not missed Christmas too. I had no excuse for that one, save for the wear and tear on my body had finally caught up to me. That disaster was all me. Having the day off from work, training, *and* Lynx-hunting had been a rare gift. Maybe the day had started with the impromptu baking of semi-edible gingerbread cookies and present wrapping, but the temptation of a nap had wrecked all those good intentions. I had slept the sleep of the dead, straight on through morning, oblivious to alarm and phone both.

Jenni had remembered to stop by and see my parents, of course. She had come by on Christmas evening like clockwork, ever since we were teenagers. My mother's abrupt message on my voicemail had tartly informed me that she had left my Christmas present with them too, having expected me to be there. Once, I had found my bestie's love of my parents endearing. Now it was just another thorn in my side, reminding me of what a shitty daughter I had become. It was par for the course I guess. I wasn't just a shitty friend and an even shittier daughter; I was a horrible person.

I had taken a life. I had felt that life spill out over my own two hands and watched the light fade from a living creature's eyes. Yes, those eyes had been luminous green and more reptilian than human—but that hardly mattered.

My life was falling apart and I had no clue how to keep the pieces together. Everything felt wrong; *was* wrong. Every time I tried to shore up another weak spot, a leak sprung clear across the way and left me scrambling. With everything falling down around me, I had clung to the stupid hope that I was making strides toward becoming a new me, a *better* me. I told myself that when the fae went home I would somehow be better off for having met them. I let myself believe that I was learning something valuable; something that would shape my future. I wanted so damn bad to find my place in the world that I had jumped on in, thinking "Yes, *this* must be it!"

And what had that gotten me?

Nothing.

Worse than nothing, really. Instead of finding some sense of self, some confidence or whatever the fuck I had thought learning to knock off nasty fae would have given me, all I had learned was that my tough-as-nails attitude came with a price. Facing down a Naga in a dark back alley had revealed something even uglier than its snake-face living in my soul. It wasn't the fear I had felt, grappling with scaly hands that wanted to lock around my throat. It wasn't the panic that had done me in, in that moment when it bore down on me and I was sure as fuck that I had forgotten all

Gannon had taught me. It wasn't even some enlightening, angelic revelation that told me I was destined to be the god-damned protector of the human race.

It was the exact opposite. It was a cold and terrible fury that had taken me over when I stood above that thing, its eyes gone blank and its limbs still. It was the horror, the regret, that I had expected—*wanted*—to feel… only to never have it come.

I had stood there, searching myself for some sign of revulsion, while Gannon congratulated me on a job well done. It had been a clean kill, in his estimation. Could have fooled me, with the grime and blood splattered all over me, making my skin crawl and my hair stiff. His pride in me hadn't made the situation any better. In fact, the smug glow I had felt at his praise only made it that much worse.

I had killed a man. Someone's son, perhaps someone's brother or father. He wasn't human and he had killed innocent people—my people—but a life was a life, nonetheless. And I had ended it, without a second thought. I had watched Gannon load the corpse into the trunk for disposal, with the sickening realization that I was calm; controlled. I wasn't in shock. I felt no regret. I was at peace with what I had done, though every shred of my humanity was screaming that I should be anything but.

Too late I understood Gannon's warning. I had thought he was warning me that I couldn't handle the internal struggle that would come with taking a life, but now I knew he had been saying the exact opposite. I couldn't reconcile my lack of regret with the morals I had been taught to uphold all my life.

How could I ever face them again: my family, my best friend, even my co-workers? Seeing the mute horror in Seana's eyes had been bad enough. How could I look another human being in the eye again, having seen what I had seen; knowing what I knew; having done what I had done? How could I pretend to be normal, when there was a part of me so dark I would never be able to reveal it to another soul? Was there any going on with the pretense of a normal life?

How could you kill a monster without becoming one?

I had become something so far removed from everything I once knew. I had seen the monster that lurked deep inside me and it had smiled. I pressed my face into my palms.

I was more lost than ever.

CHAPTER EIGHTEEN

March

"Hello? Earth to Cat. Are you even listening to me?"

I jerked back to attention. That familiar flush of shame heated my cheeks. Shit. I had drifted off again. I kept losing myself somewhere between the feigned interest I had been so carefully cultivating and the bone deep exhaustion I had been fighting for days. Jenni was giving me that pursed-lip duck face of disapproval, meaning I had probably been bleary eyed for quite some time. At least we were sitting on her couch with some pizza and wine, rather than out in some public place where her impending wrath would leave me looking like a bad girlfriend to dozens of strangers.

Man, I sucked so hard at the double agent bullshit.

I heaved a deep sigh that was 100% real and put the half-empty wineglass that had been lolling in my hand back on the coffee table. "I'm sorry. I didn't mean to space out there." I scrubbed at my face, remembering too late that I had tried to be normal and wear makeup for our get together. I hoped I hadn't just given myself raccoon eyes. "I'm just so god-damn beat. It was a really long week."

I caught the eye roll she didn't quite try to hide. "Seems like you're always beat these days."

I didn't know what to say. I couldn't very well tell her my nights had become busier than my days. Aside from the futile Lynx hunts, I now had the Baddies After Dark routine to fulfill, which kept me roaming the streets with Gannon until the wee hours of the morning two or three nights a week.

I still wasn't sure how my soul would reconcile the new roll I had taken on—and taken on so damn well, at that—but I had learned to push down those difficult emotions like a champ. It was that or spend the rest of my days locked in my apartment, hiding behind my sofa while eating rocky road straight form the tub with a wooden spoon.

Repression aside, I was burning the candle at both ends. It was getting rough to keep my head up by mid-day without a dozen cups of coffee. This night had been slated as a night to catch up, to reconnect with my humanity like in the old days—only that wasn't working out so well. I would have preferred to spend my night off zonked out on my own couch, asleep before the ten o'clock news.

I hated myself for feeling that way, so I had made myself keep our dinner date, feeling like I should have wanted to spend time with Jenni more. Granted, the catching up had been pretty lame on my side. What could I tell her? Mind-numbingly boring stories about the office and watered down versions of my training routine wrapped in the guise of a gym membership that had sucked up my free time? That didn't exactly fly.

Instead I had encouraged her to tell me about all the mundane antics I had been missing out on: her job woes, her exciting new skin care routine, anything. I wanted to care, *tried* to care. I just… Couldn't. I couldn't get myself into that mindset of girlie gossip about boys and shoes and pipe dreams we probably should have given up in our twenties. It all seemed so damn inconsequential now, when my every waking moment had become so saturated with death and danger. What did stories of Anthony's impending homecoming mean to me now, when I saw monsters lurking around every corner? I spent my days worried that some terrible nightmare creature would catch her, or my sister, or the nice old lady who lived down the block from me, on a lone street corner and suck their brains out through their eye sockets. How could I relate to her musings on whether or not she should get a new couch?

I couldn't even pretend to be normal anymore. I wanted to. I really, *really* did. I wanted to care, I wanted to connect—I wanted to feel like Caitlin again; the goofy, gawky fuck-up who got excited about sales at Saks and thought missing the newest episode of Game of Thrones was the end of the world. God, how I wanted to be her again.

Maybe that was why I had dragged myself off my couch for this sad little shindig. It was a last ditch effort at proving to myself that the old, normal part of me was still in there somewhere. Not because I wanted to see Jenni. Not even because I wanted to fix our failing friendship, but because I needed her to find that part of me I knew I was losing touch with.

Wow, did that ever make me the worst kind of bitch. If I was too far gone to even maintain a series of nods and mumbles of encouragement as she told me about all the stuff I had been missing in her life, what hope was there for…

"Cat, seriously. What the hell?"

I blinked, realizing that I had done it again. I rubbed my face with my hands, makeup be damned. Why was I finding it so hard to keep it together? "I'm sorry! I really just… I can't help it. My mind just keeps wandering off and thinking about…stuff."

"Care to elaborate?" She lounged on the opposite corner of the couch, her position casual though her expression read anything but. I could see the tension in the way she held herself. A twitch of the thumb told me she was fighting down anger, resisting the urge to make a fist. I couldn't help but read every nuance of her body language, calculating; planning.

My stomach felt tight, the pizza within doing a flip flop. It didn't matter how much I wanted to be normal old Cat. I wasn't. Not anymore. The realization made me nauseous. I looked away, focusing on the fuzzy blue afghan thrown over the back of the sofa. I picked at a loose thread, noticing for the first time how ragged my nails were. They weren't painted and my cuticles looked like hell. When was the last time I had gotten a manicure?

"Are you just going to ignore me?" she asked, words sharpening.

"I'm not ignoring you. I just don't know what to say."

Her laugh wasn't the least bit friendly. "You say that a lot these days. You know, this is the first time we've hung out in, what, two months? Three? We used to spend, like, every single weekend together until you started disappearing all the time. I don't know why you suddenly pushed me away but I tried to be cool with it. I tried to give you your space until you worked through whatever the hell has been going on with you. Tonight was your idea but the whole time you've been acting like this is some big sacrifice for you, to be hanging out with me. So what gives?"

What the hell could I say to that?

"Well, Jenni, there's been a lot going on that I haven't been telling you. On my birthday I was attacked by a troll because—surprise!—apparently I'm not 100% human. And because my great-great-grandma got frisky with a faun or something, I can see faeries. These faeries aren't the cute, dress making Sleeping Beauty type either. Some of them are evil and nasty and just downright gross. They've been feeding off us in secret for years. Since their nut-job king went off his rocker and stopped paying attention to what they do over here on Earth, they've even been killing people.

"That's why the good faeries need me. I've got to help them track down this Lynx person who no one but me can see, so they can get home and stop that wacko from ruining both our worlds. So I had to learn to fight like Xena: The Warrior Princess and start killing them off too. You know; for the safety of mankind. Don't worry though, I'm actually pretty good at it. Freaky good, actually. The buff-and-handsome faery man I've been hunting with says I have more natural skill than he's seen in a hundred years. How cool is that?"

Yeah, that sooooo wasn't going to happen. The truth was so far from believable that I couldn't spill the beans now, even if I wanted to. The skulking around museums and book stores and freaking coffee houses in search of a phantom stranger was bad enough. How would I ever look her in the eye again, once she knew I was a killer? Human, fae, hamster; it didn't matter. I had taken lives, plain and simple. How would she ever *trust* me, once all that I had hidden from her over the past few months came to light?

I felt my eyes start to water. I looked away, gaze roaming the room to look at anything but the hurt, accusatory stare that was being leveled my way. Something inside me was trying to curl up and die. It hurt to take a breath. What a fool I was, for ever having thought that my life would be normal again, when all this passed. Had I really ever believed I could go back to being boring "sits at home drinking wine and watching Netflix on a Saturday night Caitlin" again?

Weird was my normal life now.

It was who *I* was now.

A deep, shuddering breath finally filled my lungs. I stared up at the ceiling, tracing the uneven stucco lines as I blinked hard to stop myself from crying. "I'm sorry. I'm really, really sorry Jen, but… I can't."

"You can't," she repeated, deadpan. "You can't what? I mean; Christ! We haven't kept secrets from one another since we were kids! I just don't understand what is going on with you. What is with all this running off and keeping secrets like you're afraid to let anyone know where you are anymore? Were you recruited by the goddamn CIA or something?"

My lips twitched, trying to smile. I chuckled, but it sounded hollow. "Yeah, I wish. At least then I'd be making some bank."

"I'm worried about you."

I let out a low, long breath and tried to stop that horrible shaking feeling that was spreading from the inside out, all through me. There wasn't even a watered down version I could conjure up now. "I know you are and I'm sorry. I hate that I'm worrying you. It's not that I want to keep secrets from you, I swear. It's just that things in my life have gotten really… Complicated."

Her laugh was bitter. "When haven't they been?"

Once upon a time, that would have been the opening for some banter. I would have tossed out a playful insult, maybe, or came up with something caustically witty to diffuse all the tension around us. Sadly, I was as low on wit as I was on lies. "These last few months have given that 'complicated' a run for its money. I swear, Jen, if I could tell you more I would."

The look that earned me was one I would have saved for someone who had kicked my puppy. I hated myself for hurting her. She looked like she was going to chew through her lip, trying to keep all that anger in. She let me hang for a minute before asking, quietly, "Why can't you?"

I felt trapped. This storm had taken me by surprise, though I should have seen it coming, and now I was caught in the downpour without an umbrella. I rubbed my hands over my knees, watching their clamminess dampen the denim. I wanted to bolt, to grab my things and run out the door, but I just couldn't. My bestie deserved better than that, even if my heart was telling me we wouldn't be besties for much longer. I leveled her with as apologetic of a look as I could muster. "Because you wouldn't understand, even if I tried."

Wrong answer.

She surged to her feet, a throw pillow sent tumbling to the floor. "Really? *I* wouldn't understand? We've told each other everything, from the first day of pre-school. I understood when we were nine and you cut your own hair with those stupid plastic scissors and then freaked out, making *me* take the blame so your mom wouldn't yell at you. I understood when you kissed Bobby Green and got mono, knowing full well I liked him. I even understood when you asked me not to tell anyone you were cutting yourself all through junior year of high school, even though it scared me to death every single day, thinking I was going to lose you. I have understood every stupid, fucked up thing you have ever done in your life. So, tell me, Cat. Tell me just what, exactly, is it that I wouldn't understand now?"

I could feel the emotions coming off her: the anger, hurt, confusion. They whirled around me like a gale-force wind, yet I felt strangely untouched. It was like I was watching everything from a distance; like life had become a TV show and I couldn't quite understand what the characters were making such a big fuss over. Maybe a part of me had been waiting for this, building up some sort of shield around my heart. Maybe part of me was relieved.

She stood there, trembling; staring at me with tears in her eyes. It was seeing them there that made me realize I was crying too. I probably had been for some time. My hands were gripping my knees so hard my knuckles were white. A sob threatened to burst from my chest. The realization slammed into me. This was it; this was her last, desperate grab to hold on to me. She wanted so badly for me to let her in, but I couldn't. There was just no way. All this time I had felt like Jenni had been growing apart from me but, really, I had been the one slipping away.

"Me," I said. "You wouldn't understand me."

In that moment, I knew nothing would ever be the same between us. Time might heal some wounds. Maybe one day we would be able to laugh again, to catch up over a random cup of coffee—but never again would I feel that sister-like bond we had shared for so many years. I had pushed her away until that bond had broken. My heart felt like I had dropped it into a pile of jagged glass, but this was what was right. This way was better for her. She would be safer without me.

I stood slowly, feeling like I would fall to pieces if I moved too quick. I felt robotic as I leaned forward and took my purse from the floor and pulled my coat off of the arm of the couch. Jenni was sobbing. I think she was saying something too, but I couldn't hear it over the buzzing in my ears. She deserved a better goodbye but, well, maybe it was par for the course that I didn't have one to give her, seeing how shitty of a friend I had become. I felt like I was strangling as I said, "Goodbye."

I couldn't tell if her voice shook more from anger or sadness. She waved her hands in the air, turning to watch me as I headed for the door. "That's it? You're just going to say that and leave? Cat, come on; what—"

I let the door close behind me, cutting off her words. I fell back against it, my whole body wracked by a sob so strong it wanted to pull me to the floor. I struggled to catch my breath, to force the strength back into my legs. I wanted to let the pain cripple me, but I couldn't.

I still had a job to do.

~*~

"Skinny guy with the stupid hat and hipster glasses two tables over?"

Mairi's eyes skittered to the left over the top of her second cappuccino. She was a pro at the not-looking glance. "Check. And I happen to think that hat is adorable, by the way."

"Damn." I pushed my mostly empty cup away from me. "I thought he kinda looked like the picture. If I squinted. Maybe." I shot her a wary look. "And if you think mustard yellow plaid is cute, we need to get your eyes checked."

She scrunched up her nose—which was sporting a new stud in the left nostril—and stuck out her tongue, making me chuckle. That was probably her intent, of course. She could always be counted on to perform as my one-woman cheering squad, warming my stone-cold heart. Only an hour ago I had pushed my oldest friend away for good, yet it already seemed like it had happened a lifetime ago. I was dry-eyed and hyper-focused, scanning the crowd around me with a strangely frenetic energy.

Of course, that could have been thanks to the two caramel macchiatos I had sucked down in that time frame but hey; I was going to take my focus any way I could get it.

"I'd really hoped he'd be here," I said, ashamed of how dumb the words sounded as soon as they left my mouth.

"Me too." She sighed deep enough to make me do a double-take. On one hand, it was nice to know she shared in my frustration, but it also bothered me to see my plucky little buddy downtrodden. When I said as much, I earned myself a wry twist of the lips and a shrug. "I don't think this is any more fun than you do. I like hanging out with you, but—all the same—I'd much rather be doing it at a spa or something."

"That sounds lovely. I can't remember the last time I had a little 'me time.'"

I was scanning the room again, without even realizing it. It had become second nature. My eyes roamed every nook and cranny; counted every head. The faces around us hadn't changed much in the last ten minutes, but I was searching them again and again, hoping that something out of the ordinary would catch my eye—but, nope. Nothing. I leaned back in my chair and stretched until my spine popped. I was beyond tense. "It's just so hard to keep doing this, night after night, never even catching a glimpse of him. I know Kaine said we have the word of some people he trusts but... How long are we going to keep this up?"

She shrugged again. "As long as it takes?"

I scowled. "Not a great answer. I didn't sign on to be doing this until I was old and gray, chicky."

"Just think: we were doing this for a few years before you came along, and that was when we didn't really have any idea of how to tell if we did cross paths with him. Hell, we might have been in spitting distance of him a dozen times without ever having realized it. How's that for depressing?"

"Touché." I winced at the thought. Talk about perspective.

"I wish I knew where he was. I wish we could end this tomorrow, but no one has that golden ticket." She looked chagrined. "Not even me."

The bleak truth threatened to suck the last of my willpower right out of me. Suddenly, I felt another thirty years older and so damn bent I was all but broken. The words slipped out. "I don't know how much longer I can keep doing this, Mai."

I gazed down at the table, crestfallen. She reached over and placed her hand over mine. "You know, the myth about my kind being vulnerable to cold iron has some truth to it. It doesn't make us turn tail and run screaming for the hill or anything, but it hurts us. Wounds made by it are slow to heal, if they heal at all. No one has ever been able to figure out why it affects us so badly, but it does. It's one of the reasons Kaine was so insistent on you learning to fight with knives, instead of just pointing a gun at someone."

I looked up into her old soul eyes, puzzled. What on earth had brought that on?

She continued, "The old legends used to say that the Warders earned their Gift by slowly immunizing themselves to magic. For centuries, they drank a potion imbued with iron, enduring incredible pain and sickness, until they had iron in their very blood. They passed that blood down to their children, and many say that was what made them immune to all other fae Gifts." She squeezed my hand. "That might be a bunch of bull of course. But you? *You* are iron. You are stronger than you think and this will not break you. You can do this."

For someone who swore she couldn't read my mind, she certainly had the uncanny knack of always knowing what I needed to hear. Her unshakeable faith in me chased away some of the darkness. I smiled and squeezed her hand back. "Thank you."

She picked up her cup to take a sip. Her gaze roved the shop. "So yeah; this sucks. But this is all we've got at the moment. And, really, is there anything worse than the alternative?"

Images flashed through my head. Goliath's gaping, Rottweiler toothed maw. The Wax Man's hollow eye pits. The barely identifiable remains that had been strewn about the lair of the Snake Man. While I had grown more comfortable in my hunter's skin, I still couldn't face the memory of that night; of that first hunt. Just the thought of it made me shudder. She was right. Stopping the High King was the only choice. If this was only the first stage of a feeding frenzy rebellion by the bestial fae, I didn't even want to imagine the dark days that could lay ahead. Once they really started moving in on us in force, there wouldn't be much chance that I—or anyone else that I loved—would make it to old and gray.

I hadn't sacrificed my bestie's trust for nothing.

I took a swig of my lukewarm coffee, grimaced, and let my eyes trace a path back to the farthest table from the door. "Moon-eyed blond with the ridiculously low-cut purple sweater?"

"Check."

"Disinterested playboy boyfriend paying more attention to his phone than her?"

"Check."

My eyes skipped to the table to their left. "Soccer mom powwow. Snooty brunette to the left; L'Oreal redhead to the right…"

CHAPTER NINETEEN

"Shit, shit, shit!"

The Bluetooth in my ear crackled to life and the sharp note of Gannon's concern pierced into my brain. "Everything okay down there?"

"Yeah, yeah. Everything's fine. Just stepped in some literal shit. A Great Dane-sized load, from the looks of it." I shook my foot hard, scowling at the excrement that dislodged itself from my heel. I had called my lovely new combat boots shitkickers, but I hadn't meant that literally. Besides; they were brand new. Gross.

I resumed my slow creep, sticking close to the wall of the dingy building but I glanced down far more often than before. Why couldn't the murderous fae assholes ever go to ground in a nice, clean area? Nothing residential of course; that would pose too many problems. But a nice secluded park or maybe even an upscale business district that cleared out and got quiet after dark? Noooo; of course not. They always skulked back to their freaking waterfront lairs like creepy comic book villains, which meant that my nights were spent tiptoeing around gross old warehouses and wallowing through the—apparently literal—shit of the earth. I skirted a moldering pile of something I couldn't and, from the rank smell it gave off, didn't want to identify. I covered my nose and mouth with a cupped hand. "Goddamn, this town really is fucking disgusting."

He chuckled. "Welcome to the seedy underbelly of New Jersey."

"Oh, bite me." Easy for *him* to say. He had rooftop duty. I was the one down in the trenches, struggling to see two feet in front of me. It was foggy and dark between the looming buildings. The moon was hidden by clouds and I didn't think its light would have helped even if it had penetrated through. The streets were still damp, with puddles forming in a hundred different pot holes and crevices that spider webbed the cracked pavement. The air had that moldy smell that the dark corners of the city gave off after a long day of cold rain, obscuring all else.

Aside from the foul reek of the remnants on my shoe, of course. Stupid dog.

It was close to midnight. We had been canvasing the network of buildings for near an hour without ever laying sight on another living soul. Gannon had been tracking this particular baddie for almost two weeks, so he was sure that it had gone to ground somewhere between here and the river. The problem was mathematical: two hunters, fifteen city blocks of warehouses, gross nooks, and garbage-filled crannies. While I was happier at the lessened chance of complication—a random person wandering into a hunt was not something I cared to deal with—the slow, methodic pace was beginning to wear on me. The thrill of the chase had turned into the irritation of the chase.

I edged my way into another intersection. Lookie, lookie; more of the same. Another inroad into the labyrinth of buildings lay to my right, and—from the potent perfume wafting over me—a dumpster filled dead end loomed to my left. How exciting. I started to call the all clear but sucked in my breath.

Something in that dead end rustled to life.

I whipped around, dropping into a half-crouch as I spun so that my hands were a hairsbreadth away from the stilettos tucked into my specially made, dog shit tainted boots. I barely breathed the word. "Contact."

"On my way."

The alcove before me was damn near pitch black. I could only make out the hulking bulk of the industrial sized dumpsters and nothing seemed to be moving. I had half convinced myself that a rat was responsible for nearly making me piss myself when I finally saw one of the shadows shift. Two amber discs flashed in the darkness. A low, rumbling growl warned me that I was in someone's territory, and that someone wasn't happy about it.

A god-damned dog. I started to relax back but something inside me remained taut; vibrating like a bowstring. Far be it from me to ignore my Spidey senses. The damn thing could be rabid, for all I knew. I stayed crouched. "Come on out sweetie, I'm not gonna hurt you." I made those ridiculously friendly cooing noises one reserved for babies and frightened animals. I held out one hand—the other never straying from Leftie's pommel—and waggled my fingers in what I hoped was a friendly gesture. "I don't have any Milk Bones, but maybe we can find you a nicer snack than you'll find in that smelly old garbage, huh? Would you like that, boy?"

"Update. What's going on down there?" His breathing had quickened. He must have wandered further away than I had thought. Well, good. Let him haul ass to get to my rescue. What if it had been our baddie, instead of some stray? Served him right for giving me the legwork while he moseyed around up top.

"Stand down. It's just a do—" The words dried up in my mouth.

That low growl rose sharply, its tremor near-deafening as the body it was attached to detached itself from the shadows. Those eyes flashed like heat lightning, set in the head of the scariest fucking animal I had ever seen.

Never mind a Great Dane; the damn thing was the size of a pony.

Had I been standing, he easily could have laid his head on my shoulder—not that I had any intention of letting that vicious looking snout come anywhere near any part of me. His lips were drawn back from teeth the length of my fingers, the jowls below slick with ropes of drool. Long, mangy black fur matted with all sorts of filth covered him like a shag carpet, and an equally disheveled tail snaked down to the ground. As he snuffled at the air and caught my tasty human scent, that tail sprang into action and whipped from side to side like a bullwhip. Trash went flying in all directions. A snarl echoed around me, vibrating deep in that massive, barrel chest.

"Holy hell!" I yanked my hand back and wrapped them both around the girls' hilts. My chest felt tight; my lungs compressed so high that I could barely draw a full breath. Things fell together in my mind like dominos: click, click, clack. I let out a low, shaky breath. "Gannon, please tell me that 'black dog" was some sort of bullshit fae honorific. Like, you know; how you call the Lynx 'the Lynx.' Do *not* tell me we came out here actually looking for a big, angry black dog that now wants to disembowel me."

His curses rang in my ear.

Well, fuck was right.

"That's information I could have used hours ago!" I backed away as slowly as I could in my awkward crouch. The beastie matched me step for step; stalking forward, his head low and ears back. I looked him up and down, drawing a big ol' blank. How the hell was I going to fight Cujo on steroids? I could grapple my way to victory with something bipedal, but I was clueless at how to incapacitate something with sharp, pointy teeth and four clawed feet that looked as strong as 2x4's.

"I did!" I could hear him grunt as he stuck a landing. His breathing had quickened considerably. I no longer found it amusing. Irritation made his words sharp. "Didn't you read the dossier I gave you?"

My mind scrambled back to the printout on my living room coffee table, likely still under this morning's cereal bowl. And a stack of mail. Where it had been for the past three days. Part of me wanted to tell him not to feel bad, that it was keeping good company with the stack of musty old fae history books I had been promising Seana I would get to for the better part of three months—but something told me he wouldn't appreciate that. I'm sure I would have snapped back with some witty and bold-faced lie, had time not run out.

Cujo has sized me up and found me wanting. Or maybe he just wanted to see if I had the tasty insides of Tender Vittles. His reasons didn't matter when he burst into action and lunged at me with preternatural speed. I wasn't sure how intelligent he was, but I didn't have time to try and reason with him. In that split second when he pulled back on his haunches and readied himself to spring, my mind emptied. I wasn't sure how I did it, but that didn't really matter: I did it. My eyes darted to and fro, calculating the situation unfolding in the blink of an eye—faster than I would have ever have thought possible. There was no more than twenty feet or so left between me and Cujo. If his strength was at all proportionate to his size, he would be on me in seconds.

I wasn't sure how much mass was hidden beneath all that scraggly fur, but he had me beat three to one, at the very least. Even if I managed to find a weak spot and connect in the final, Hail Mary moment, the sheer weight of that damn thing could crush me. I needed something bigger; something with more force, to take it out at the knees or brain it into submission. Too bad the streets around me were bare.

My odds were not looking good so I did the only sensible thing a girl can do, when facing down a gigantic, vicious faerie dog in a dark alley: I turned and ran.

I darted back the way I had come, hoping the sharp turn would throw the damn thing off a step or two. A wild baying erupted behind me, echoing off the buildings around us. I heard a crash that vibrated up through the soles of my boots but I couldn't turn to look. The scrabbling sound of nails on concrete and guttural snarls told me all I needed to know: Cujo was hot on my trail. I needed to maneuver it into some sort of position where I could gain the upper hand. I had no clue how I was going to do that, mind you; I just figured it was my best shot at not getting dead.

I tilted forward and aimed for the next corner, hoping I wouldn't wipe out myself. I made a grab for the nearest wall, feeling its sharp edges bite into my palm as I gripped it tight and propelled myself into the next cross street. I stumbled but kept from hitting the ground. I mapped out the roads ahead in quick succession. A few more turns or the straightaway to the pier. Dammit. Neither of those options worked for me. What if I took a turn into a dead-end? I still wasn't sure how I was going to stop this thing when we inevitably locked horns.

Another crash resounded behind me. It sounded like Cujo was ricocheting itself off the walls in its attempts to get to me. Come morning, there were going to be all sorts of a mess left behind to confuse the dockworkers. Another angry snarl rolled over me. The air was humid but I was sure, somehow, that I felt his fetid blow past me. I needed to gain more distance, but my calves were already starting to burn. This was not good.

"Shit, shit, *shit!*"

Gannon crackled to life in my ear again, an unwelcome note of panic raising the pitch of his voice. "Caitlin, what the hell are you doing?"

I gulped in air. "Running like hell!"

"Dammit! I can't get to you if you're moving in the opposite direction!"

"No time. To argue," I panted. Talking was not going to work. I wasn't built for this kind of sprint. I could barely catch my breath around the words.

I ignored the long, loud string of curses in my ear. They weren't conducive to staying alive, at the moment. Instead, I bolted around another corner. I was coming in too fast and went skidding through a large puddle. Unable to slingshot myself as I had before, I gritted my teeth and prayed for the best as I mimicked Cujo's method for myself.

Let me tell you, bouncing off of a solid brick wall wasn't as easy for squishy human flesh as it was, apparently, for a large, angry canine. I lost precious air as I collided with the wall, grunting as the wind got knocked right out of me. My bounce wasn't nearly as controlled as I had hoped and I found myself tumbling to the ground. I fell into the roll and let the momentum carry me forward. It was easier to spring back up than to land flat on my face, but I lost a few seconds doing it. At least I'd still have a nose.

Splashing and scratching and snarling exploded in a cacophony behind me, all crawling up my ass once again. I guess worrying about my nose was pretty stupid. It wouldn't matter much if I had my entire face chewed off in about ten seconds.

Dredging up whatever will to live I had left, I pushed myself up, hard, and bolted. I ignored the stinging on my palms and the ache where my shoulder had met wall. Hell, I ached from top to bottom. My chest burned like all get out and my lungs threatened to seize up with each breath. This was my last dash. I didn't have much left in me.

"Update." It was a bark; a command. Was that an echo I heard? I couldn't tell if he was close, or if my scared shitless brain was playing tricks on me.

"Gaining. On me," I rasped. "Crossing. Seventeenth street." God, each word hurt. My eyes darted right, then left. The building just ahead to my left had a rickety looking set of rusted metal stairs leading up to a second story entryway. The landing they lead up to looked equally dubious but it was the best shot I had. "Corner lot. Second floor landing. Going for it."

I barreled ahead with all I had left, taking the stairs two at a time. They shuddered in protest. I felt their pain. I threw myself up the last two steps and collided with the railing. I hung there for a few breaths, every muscle in my body shaking. Finally, I could look behind me. Finally, I could see the demon coming at me in the dark.

Another long, loud bay resounded down the alley as the damn thing straight up *charged* down the street. He was a surging mass of teeth and fur, tail streaming out behind it like a banner. When he caught sight of me, those flashing eyes burned with a savage hunger. He never slowed. He would be under me in a moment. The sight of that mad beast bearing down on me lit a fire within me, filling me with a cold, familiar rage. I yanked one of my stilettos from its sheath and gripped it tight in a sweaty palm. I stepped back from the railing and backed up as far as I could, praying I wasn't about to kiss pavement as took a literal leap of faith.

Good lord, I hoped this worked.

My timing was spot on, but the landing wasn't nearly as soft as I hoped. My chest collided with a solid mass of writhing fur, knocking the wind out of me once again. Though I was gaping like a fish, I knotted my free hand in a mass of musty pelt and scrabbled for purchase. I managed to get myself astride the beast and gripped its wide back as firmly as I could with my knees. Immediately, Cujo ground to a halt, which nearly succeeded in sending me sailing over its massive head. My face bounced off its thick neck. Blood filled my mouth and a metallic burn shot up my nose. I held on tight, retching from the combined stench of garbage-y, wet dog and the vile taste of the blood in my mouth.

The black dog squealed, spinning and lunging in a crazy dance as he tried to throw me off. I wrapped the arm attached to the hand holding the blade around the beast's heaving neck. It was all I could do to not stab myself as I held on for dear life. I had never ridden one of those stupid mechanical bulls you see in hick bars in movies and such, but I had the feeling the ride I was being taken on was about the same.

"Almost there. Hold on!"

Gannon must have sighted us. While part of me soared at his reassurance, it did little to help me in that very moment. Cujo and I were getting too close to a wall for my liking. All I needed was for the dim light in that massive skull to go on and have him realize he could scrape me off his back like a barnacle. My nifty little Kevlar cat suit offered me some measure of protection in a fight, but it wouldn't do dick against that tactic. I wheezed, "Hurry!"

I paid dearly for every jerk and whirl. I barely knew which way was up anymore and it felt like my teeth were going to rattle out of my head. I couldn't see Gannon arrive, but I heard the thunderclap as he landed behind us. Cujo spun around, skittering to a halt when faced with my reinforcement. My head was spinning, my stomach heaving from my wild ride but there was no time for weakness. I took the shot.

I reared back and drove my blade down hard, aimed at the base of the beast's skull. With a shriek, Cujo bucked and sent me flying, the blade ripped free from my hands. I tumbled hard, managing to protect my face as I rolled, but it wasn't fun. Every bone in my body seemed to get jarred by the impact. The world around me dimmed for a moment, but I stopped short of passing out. Instead, I lay still, dirty water soaking into my hair; my chest struggling for each fiery gasp. My breathing was so harsh and heavy that it took me a few minutes to realize how quiet everything around me had gone.

I rolled my head to the side. Even that took Herculean effort. Gannon crouched beside the still mass of the black dog's body, just a few feet away from me. He pulled my knife from the corpse and wiped it clean against the beast's fur. Even as battered as I was, as close as I had come to losing that fight as I had, a strange trickle of pity welled up inside me. Cujo looked a lot less fierce, drained of that primal fury. He looked a lot more like a feral stray than a horrific monster. Now, in hindsight, the whole situation felt wrong. Unfair. I had killed him without ever a word spoken between us. It was the first time I had killed a fae that was more beast than human.

Was it still justice, if the killer hadn't known what it was doing was wrong?

I closed my eyes. It didn't really matter, did it?

Nothing was fair anymore.

~*~

"You're upset."

I didn't even open my eyes for that question. Gannon, Mr. Magnanimous that he was, was driving me home after a quick pit stop to see Seana. She had fixed me up as much as possible, healing my cracked ribs and torn skin with tight-lipped disapproval. As usual, the good doc's nasty green sleepy-time concoction had knocked me out cold but for once that had been perfectly fine by me. I had a hunch she had added an extra dose of pain killers to the mix. Even after I awoke, a pleasant fuzziness remained on the edges of the world. It wasn't making me stupid, per say, but I had found it a lot harder to pay attention to the world around me until Gannon had spoken.

It was nice to not be bleeding all over his nice leather seats and I was thrilled to be able to take a reasonably deep breath without wanting to vomit, but I wished she had been able to do a bit more for me. I was as shocked as she was to learn that her Healing hadn't been able to reach most of my ills. I don't think anyone had expected my Gift to adapt quite so quickly, least of all me. That didn't bode well for future hunts, unless I learned to stop getting knocked around so hard.

As it stood, I was exhausted, with muscles aching in places I hadn't even been sure muscles existed before my wild sprint through the back alley labyrinth. Though my ribs were mending, my abdomen was a patchwork quilt of bruises and my right side ached like hell. I had gauze wrapped around both hands and half way up my arms, mummy-like, to protect the tender new skin Seana had coaxed over my raw, scraped palms. I felt every pot hole and rumble-strip the city roads had to offer with aching clarity.

So, no; I wasn't exactly a happy camper. But upset? Considering I had insisted on being given the fae hunting responsibilities that had caused all my wounds in the first place, I couldn't say that I was. I shrugged and gritted my teeth for the effort. "No, not particularly. Should I be?"

He didn't respond. For a few minutes, all I could hear were the ambient sounds of the late night city around us. Curiosity got the better of me and I finally cracked an eye and rolled it in his direction. To say he looked pensive was an understatement. His dark brows were drawn down over his eyes, dagger-like; casting them in shadows. His jaw was set like stone with a slight tick being the only indication that he wasn't carved from marble. He gripped the steering wheel with white knuckles, as if we were driving in the Indie 500 instead of doing forty down a nearly empty street on the far side of midnight.

I scooted myself up to a more alert and upright position in the passenger seat, which took a hell of a lot more effort than I had expected. "Uh, are *you* upset, maybe?"

He shot me a glance, something troubled and strange flashing in those eyes before he turned them back to the road. The passing streetlights made it hard to tell, but I thought I saw that tick along his jaw get stronger. I didn't need Mairi's freaky mind-reading to tell I had hit a nerve. "Wait, are you upset with *me*?"

"You could have been killed." The words were sharp and to the point.

My jaw nearly dropped. Had I heard him right? Could it be that Mr. Grim & Serious had been worried about me? About *my* welfare? Be still my heart! Something fluttered in my belly at the thought, making me feel all warm and silly inside. I quickly told the tittering teenager that apparently still lived somewhere in the depths of my soul (and the other lady bits that might be listening) to cut that the fuck out, fast. Those were not feelings I wanted to nurture, especially not about my hard-as-nails sparring partner. Narrowly escaping death could wreak all the havoc on my endocrine system that it wanted; I wasn't going to be suckered into playing along.

Resisting the urge to coo and make puppy dog eyes at him was hard, despite my iron will. I managed to put on my best serious face as I said, "I appreciate your concern but…"

"Kaine was against you walking down this path from the start," he snapped, giving me another lightning quick dagger stare.

I stopped, jaw sawing wordlessly for a moment as I fought to find my train of thought. "I know that, but you said yourself that I'm good—"

"It doesn't matter how good you are if you're reckless! We had an agreement and you broke it. You didn't prepare for this fight and you weren't ready for what you found. You put us both in danger." The heat in his words made my ears burn. "On the hunt you are on my watch, under my command. You follow my orders and you do not ignore my leads again—are we clear? If you act that foolishly again, it will be your last hunt, whether you walk away from it alive or not."

My mouth snapped shut with an audible clack. I swung my head around to stare out the dashboard, my face burning like the tenth circle of hell. Silly me. He didn't want to be the one to disappoint his lord by losing their precious fae-detector. Why had I even thought for a single second his concern had been for any reason other than that? I swallowed hard, feeling my saliva slither down around the lump my throat, and ignored the hot sting in my eyes. "Sorry. It won't happen again."

I heard him heave a sigh. "Look, Caitlin, I—"

"Don't." The word shook. I gathered up my anger, letting it strengthen me. "You made your point."

We lapsed into one of those terribly awkward silences I previously thought were reserved for the moments following a lover's spat. Shit, even then some angry-resentment-nookie could be had to break the ice once the two parties were done hating one another's guts. Not that *that* had a snowball's chance in hell of happening. Smoldering good looks or no, my naughty bits had gone Hoth cold after that lovely little moment of brutal honesty, thank you very much.

The truth of it was that I had put us both in harm's way. I knew that. I should have read that damn dossier. There was no good reason for me not to have. I had just been tired and lazy. I had put it off until later—like so much in my life—and later had never come. If I had done more than glance at the title of the stupid thing, I wouldn't have been caught with my pants down in a dark alley, thinking that creature had just been some poor, harmless stray. I had been careless and lazy and thanks to that laziness one—or both—of us could have died. But I sure as fuck didn't want him to know I was filled with guilt. So we endured the rest of the ride in silence. That was just about as much fun as you'd expect it to be. I wasn't sure who I hated more: him or myself.

Thankfully it was only a few long, soul-sucking minutes later before we pulled up in front of my apartment. I wanted to bolt from the car in a grand, dramatic gesture complete with a car-rattling slam of the door. Instead, when I swung the door open and my feet hit the pavement, I nearly fell backwards into my so recently vacated seat, bowled over by a wave of dizziness. I caught the edge of the doorframe with my swaddled hand, realizing a second too late that it would have been better to fall on my ass. As fire exploded across my palm, I let out a paint-blistering string of obscenities that insulted the parentage of everything from the higher powers above to those of the nearby fire hydrant.

Gannon appeared in front of me, still wearing that peevish look of concern. He held out a hand. "Let me help you."

God, how badly I wanted to be a mulish bitch and push his hand away, stalking into my apartment of my own accord. Unfortunately, I couldn't even find the breath to speak around the pain of my poor, throbbing nerves. Swallowing my pride—and nearly choking on it—I let him steady me as I stepped away from the car. He shut the door, then looped one arm around my waist to keep me steady. I swung an arm around his shoulders to further balance myself, but man oh man, did I really just want to hit him upside the head with it.

It was a difficult journey, despite only being a few feet. I didn't want to lean against him both out of bitchiness and because my ribs ached at the slightest touch, but holding myself rigid wasn't much better. Every step up to the second floor was a nightmare. Visions of a hot bath and soft mattress spurred me on. The promise of being Gannon-free and able to let loose the torrent of emotions whirling around inside me was also a great motivator.

My willpower shriveled up and died when we finally reached my door. It was partially open, the edge splintered where it had been forced in and broken upon its own lock. I felt Gannon's arm stiffen around me. He was on high alert immediately, while my brain got stopped up trying to process what I was seeing. He maneuvered me against the wall and said, "Wait here."

I couldn't do anything but listen. I leaned against the worn brick wall, suddenly numb to the pain in my side and hands. All I could feel was the wiggly-legged sensation that threatened to pitch me forward onto my face if I so much as moved a muscle. This couldn't be happening. Not my home. Not my one safe haven. My mouth had gone so dry that I couldn't swallow.

It was only a few seconds before he appeared in the darkened doorway, looking grim. "It's empty."

With him firmly grasping me at the elbow to help me keep my balance, I took a few teetering steps into the long hallway. Even from the door I could see the destruction of my living room at the end. The loveseat was tipped over, some of its cushions torn. Stuffing and papers and the remains of my destroyed treadmill littered the floor. My bedroom door stood open a few feet to my left. I made myself get there, stopping in the doorway as my stomach sank. The bed had been torn to shreds. My clothing was strewn across the floor. Here and there something metallic glinted among the mess. I had left my laptop on the bed that evening, when I left for the hunt. Now it was an expensive paperweight, with the screen shattered and the keyboard smashed in. I saw a few of the missing keys scattered here and there on the floor.

I started trembling so hard that Gannon once again looped his arm around my waist to keep me upright. I careened my head to look over his shoulder and into the kitchen across the way. Shards of glass and ceramic littered the floor in a crazy mosaic. Bits of dry pasta and crushed potato chips frolicked among them. A wretched, desolate sound somewhere between a wail and a moan forced its way up out of my throat. I felt like every muscle in my body was turning to water. "He found me."

Gannon tightened his grip. It made my ribs throb but I didn't care. "Calm down. We need to go. Let's get your..."

"Calm down? *Calm down?*" I don't know how I managed to sound shrill and snot-garbled all at once. "That thing broke into my home. My *home*, Gannon! He knows where I live. He trashed every single fucking thing I own but he didn't *take* anything." I flung an arm in the direction of my laptop and jewelry, lost in the wreckage. "He wanted me to know he could do this. That he could find me and hurt me, any time he wants. So don't tell me to calm down!"

He didn't argue. I saw the conviction in his eyes, in the grim set of his jaw. The troll had found me. I couldn't stand anymore. I felt myself falling, but thankfully he was there to help lower me to the floor. He propped me up against the door frame and turned away, walking back out onto the landing with phone in hand. I could only hear the low murmur of his voice, but I didn't care. Eavesdropping held no appeal for me now.

I curled into a ball, right there in my bedroom doorway, gasping for breath around my rising panic. He had trashed my stuff. My things—*everything*—ruined. Tainted. I knew logically that I should be happy he had taken his aggressions out on my material items rather than my body but; still. These were the things I had worked so hard for over the years. Every little bit and piece I owned. It only made things worse that he had invaded my home to do so—the one place I had always counted on to be there for me, when I needed to retreat from the world. There was no safe place for me now. There was nowhere for me to go that he couldn't find me.

"Caitlin." Gannon had squatted down beside me. I peeked up at him through watery eyes. "We need to go. He might come back. It's not safe here."

"Go where?" I snapped. I could barely breathe around the knot in my chest.

"You'll stay with us," he said, still maddeningly calm. But why wouldn't he be? It wasn't *his* life that was scattered all around him in ruins. It wasn't *his* last bit of normalcy that had been ripped from his grasp. I tucked my head back down into the cradle of my arms, too ashamed of my breakdown to let him see my tears.

"I'll gather some of your things."

I stayed huddled in my little ball of misery. I had only begun to realize that my life could never return to the normal I had once known when I was forced to push Jenni away. Now, in hindsight, it was the best idea I had ever had. I couldn't imagine living with myself if she had been hurt by those monsters.

All that time, I had feared what evil lurked in the hearts of strangers; out there, passing by on the streets. I had feared being attacked, like the night

159

Goliath and I had first crossed paths. I had never stopped to consider what else he could take away from me, of how deeply he could hurt me, without ever laying a finger on me.

CHAPTER TWENTY

That bastard.

It was some time after midnight but I was wide awake, unable to find the blissful ignorance of a good night's sleep for the third night in a row. I refused to look at the clock on the nightstand out of pure spite. Instead, I stared up at the darkened ceiling, missing the familiar crack in the plaster that would have been there had I been in my own bed. Not that it was my bed, not anymore. Nothing was mine anymore. Everything I had once loved now carried that creature's foul taint.

My hands had curled into fists of their own volition.

I just couldn't let it go. I mean, how could I even try to? Goliath had tracked me back to my home. He knew who I was, that much was painfully clear. Those ham fists of his had smashed by last bastion of safety to little bitty pieces. The thought of that beast rifling through my things—the spiteful glee that must have come across his ugly mug as he ripped apart my life… My fists curled so tight my nails bit into my palms. The whole situation made me sick to my stomach.

I had been living with the fae for just about two weeks. The first few days had been strange, to say the least. It had been a sort of perverted Real World situation: me in the midst of a melt-down, forced to live among four strangers who weren't really strangers (but who were definitely strange). Lucky for me, Seana and Mairi had been incredibly supportive of my fragile state of mind. Being forced into such close quarters with them had turned out to be rather pleasant, kind of like having a mother and little sister by my side day in and day out. They weathered my alternating fits of rage and crying jags with grace.

My co-habitation relationship with the boys was another matter. Kaine had given me a wide berth from day one. Like most men faced with the prospect of dealing with a hair-triggered, hysterical woman, he opted instead to steer clear of me. He didn't go out of his way to avoid me, per say, but a suspicious number of other tasks seemed to come to his mind the moment I entered a room. That was just fine with me. I still couldn't get a handle on how to deal with him and, given the current shambles of my life,

I didn't even want to try.

Gannon and I, on the other hand, were clearly on the outs. We hadn't spoken a single word to one another since that night. He had gone out of his way to avoid me all together and wasn't making any attempt to hide it. Our paths hadn't crossed more than twice since my change of residence, and then for only the briefest of moments.

I supposed that would change soon, as Seana had cleared me to resume fighting, but in the interim I had done a good job of pretending our estrangement didn't bother me. Fuck him and his holier-than-thou attitude. Even if I had deserved some of the riot act he had read me that night, he could have softened up just a bit when he saw that my whole world had pretty much just gone to shit.

The image of my decimated bedroom flashed through my mind.

My stomach churned.

I hadn't been able to make myself go back. Filing a report with the police, knowing full well that it would be a fruitless search, had been hard enough. Going back there and seeing again the proof that my days of blithely pretending I was leading some cool, secretive double life were over? I just couldn't handle that. Not yet. Thankfully, Mairi knew and understood. She had gone back for me and had picked up a bunch of clothing without my even having to ask. Living in a borrowed home was bad enough. I don't think I could have handled having to wear borrowed underwear too.

I don't know how long I laid there, stuck on my internal merry-go-round of anger and despair, but I must have dozed off at some point. When a hand gripped and shook my shoulder, accompanied by a whisper of my name, I went into DEFCON 3 mode and nearly clocked the figure looming over me in the dark.

"Jesus, Caitlin, it's me. Stand down," Gannon said. He had taken a step back to avoid my wild swing. Damn his preternatural speed; I bet I had almost had him. He turned on the bedside lamp, as if I needed visual proof that he was who he said he was. I was momentarily dumbfounded to see that he was dressed in his hunting leathers, sword sheathed across his back and everything. It took me another moment to realize that if I was puzzling over his choice of pajamas, that meant he could also see me. In bed. In my lack of pajamas.

"Gannon!" I yanked the sheet up to my chin as I scrambled to pull my bare leg back beneath it. "What the hell?"

He started to say something, but appeared to think better of it; biting his lip. He barely kept the grin off his face as he said, "You're not... *indecent*, are you?"

I could feel the heat flooding my face. That boyish charm was like kryptonite, damn him. Something in that single word that went straight to the core of me. Traitorous core! We didn't like him much at the moment, remember?

Thankfully I wasn't; not really. I had fallen asleep in a ratty old V-neck t-shirt that had seen far better days and a slightly embarrassing pair of orange and black striped panties that said "Tiger" in gold across the rear. Not something I wanted anyone to see me in, but at least my naughty bits were covered. Since I had fallen asleep on my back and the sheets had remained largely at stomach level, my secret was still safe. I strove for indignant and ignored his question, countering it with one of my own, "Is there a reason you're barging into my room at"—I glanced over at the alarm clock, rounding up a smidge—"3:30 in the morning, dressed, quite literally, to kill?"

That earned me another one of those smirks; the ones where he eyed me from under one raised eyebrow, looking all confident. And cocky. And stupid. He jerked his head toward the open door, the hallway beyond dimly lit. "I found him. Get dressed. We leave asap."

I stared at him, slack-jawed, and tried to put two and two together. Maybe it was the remnants of sleep, or maybe it was just the distractions of my traitorous core and the thoughts that smirk of his made it think, but I kept coming up with five. "Him? Him who... Wait, do you mean the troll?" My voice rose to a squeak on the last word.

He waved a hand, shushing me. "Of course 'the troll.' Who the hell else have I been scouring the city for? And his name, by the way, is Argoth."

"He has a name?" I was still speaking in tones suited for dolphins, my adrenaline having kicked in to high gear. How dare a vile creature like that have a name? Knowing his name, rather than just calling him Goliath or Ugly or half a dozen other insulting nicknames like I had in my head all along, humanized the monster in a way I couldn't accept. My fists were balled up again, shaking.

"Of course he has a name. Now, come on. I found where he's been holed up but I don't know what his next move will be. He could make a run for it any time, so we need to do this quick."

There was no way in hell I was giving that beast a shot at getting away from us, not when we were finally so close to ending the reign of terror he had inflicted upon my life. I shot out of bed, scrambling to untangle myself from the sheets that tried to follow me. My mind was mind racing. Where had I stashed my leathers? Were my shitkickers in the closet or under the bed? Had I sharpened the girls before putting them away after the last hunt? I didn't know if I trusted my dexterity to do so in a moving car on the way. Hell, would I even be able to grip them again, now that my hands had healed? It would be my first time fighting since...

"Caitlin."

I froze; spine gone ramrod straight. There was something dangerous in the calm of his voice. I turned, hands still gripping the edge of the dresser drawer. He had his arms crossed, those icy eyes fixed on mine. "This could go bad real fast. I need to know you will listen to every word I say tonight, and will do every single thing I tell you to do. No arguing. No hesitation."

We could not have a repeat of the black dog fiasco. It was unsaid, but I heard it loud and clear. I nodded, lips pursed. "Understood."

He nodded once in return and turned toward the door. "Then get ready—and do it quietly. The others would have a fit if they knew I was taking you along on this."

Something smart-assy tried to make its way out of my mouth but I swallowed it down. I knew this hunt was out of my league. I had already seen firsthand how big and strong trolls were. I held no illusions that I was anywhere near a match for that, and it was no surprise that Kaine would have put the kibosh on me tagging along. Squatting at the fae house had made me privy to some very loud shouting matches coming from Kaine's office. The danger his treasured Lynx Detector had put herself in had not gone unnoticed by the Lord of the Manor. While I had secretly gloated over knowing that Gannon had gotten chewed out way harder than he had done me, it had to have left an impression on my teacher. Which made me wonder why he was sticking his neck out for me again at all. I had to know. "Why?"

The one word was enough. He paused, hand on the door-frame. I could only see him in profile. He was chewing at his lip again. "He's your nightmare. You need to see this through to the end."

As often as I wanted to kick him in the nuts, Gannon understood me in a way few ever had. I swallowed hard, my throat tight. My eyes stung. "Thank you."

He turned ever so slightly and smiled, the corners of his eyes crinkling. "You're welcome."

I yanked opened the drawer and dug for my gear.

"Meet me at the car in five, Tiger."

I whirled around, clutching at my butt like that would somehow help the situation, but he was already gone. A faint chuckle echoed down the hallway. My face was on fire again. I snarled; fuck him. I would get him back for that later. Right now, we had more important things to do.

I had a troll to kill.

~*~

"You're fidgeting."

"Of course I'm fidgeting," I snapped, glancing over at Gannon from the passenger's seat. "We're finally going to nail this bastard. How could I not be excited?" And scared damn near shitless. I left that part out but I was pretty sure he already knew. He kept his eyes on the road, never sparing me a look, so I tried to do the same. Companionable silence was a-okay by me. We were almost there. My frenzied mind was racing over the possibilities of what lay ahead of us again and again.

It was hard not to be equal parts excited and scared. I had been waiting for this very moment for so long. The promise of safety and the ability to breathe again were damn near at my fingertips. Yet, the danger we were walking in to was pretty damn frightening too. I knew how freaky strong that troll was. A girl didn't forget the night when she had been picked up by the scruff of the neck like a newborn kitten. I held no illusions: Goliath wasn't going to go down easy.

I refused to call him Argoth. Fuck him and his having a normal name and a life and a history. He didn't get that right, not after having ruined my life.

I took a deep, slow breath to steady myself. I gazed out the window at the slowly passing scenery, but that wasn't exactly calming either. We were trekking deep into Riverview's only truly "bad" neighborhood, a low-rent district not far from where the black dog hunt had taken place. It was a place the sunny little Caitlin Moore of six months ago would never have dared gone even in broad daylight, never mind at 4 in the morning, armed or no. The litter lined streets around us were dark and abandoned, lit only by the dull, yellowed light of the intermittent street lights. The storefronts here had no lighting of their own, though they had plenty of barred windows and heavy iron shutters. Bad mojo hung thick in the air. Swords and stilettos wouldn't be worth dick if we ran afoul of whatever gang called this block home. Gannon's dislike of guns wouldn't stop one from putting an end to either of us quick.

We pulled up half a block away from our target. I could barely make out the crumbling stairwell that lead down to the basement apartment below a closed and shuttered store whose faded awning promised fancy dresses at a deep discount. My heart hammered in my throat. I said a quick prayer to whatever higher power might be floating around up there. I just wanted us to get in and out quickly, with one less troll on my tail.

Gannon hadn't moved to exit the car. He sat very still, except for where his fingers were drumming lightly on the steering wheel. That was another of his nervous ticks that I had picked up on over the past few months. While I liked that I was learning to read him more and more, stoic expression or no, it didn't bode well that even he was nervous about what we were about to do. I kind of needed him to be my calm and unflappable rock.

"What's the plan?" I asked, licking lips suddenly gone dry.

"You're not going to like it," he said, voice low even though there was no one around to hear us.

"I figured that." A nervous laugh escaped me. "Lay it on me."

It was his turn to let out a long, low sigh. "I need you to go in first."

My jaw was literally hanging open as I gaped at him. Had he lost his mind?

He seemed oblivious to my shock as he continued, "I don't like using you as bait, but it's the only way we're going to get in there and not have this go down on the streets."

"He'll make mincemeat out of me."

Gannon shook his head. "No, he won't. You're more valuable to him alive. Dead? The King won't believe a word he says. It'll be just another tall tale told by someone trying to get in good with royalty. Tiernan would have him executed on sight. Trolls might be slow, but they're not stupid. Even Argoth has to know how fickle the King's moods can be. He needs proof the Warding is alive and well, and being passed down to descendants here in your world."

I took a deep breath and held it for a moment. That made sense. Damn. I scrubbed at my face and grimaced at how sweaty my palms were. "Okay, fine; I'm bait. I go knock on that door and then what? Sit him down for tea and cookies?"

"I'll be right behind you, as close as I can be without him being able to sniff me out. All you need to do is get in that door and distract him—and then get the hell out of the way."

"Whoa, whoa, wait a minute! I didn't come along just to do nothing! This is—"

He turned and fixed me with a hard stare. "Out of your league."

"Maybe, but I—you said—" I spluttered.

"I said you needed to finish this and I meant it," he snapped, words so hard they were almost a growl. He looked away and for a heartbeat all I had to see was the back of his head and its tousled hair.

When he looked back at me, my stomach clenched. The concern there took me out at the metaphorical knees. "Caitlin, you are not ready for this fight. I'm probably a fool for taking you along in the first place. I know how important seeing Argoth defeated is to you but, please, believe me: you'll only be a hindrance if I get distracted worrying about your safety. I'll stick to my word and let you have the killing blow if I can. But I also need you to hold true to yours. Promise me you'll stay out of the way until Argoth is down."

It wasn't a question. It was a command. My upper lip twitched, wanting to snarl but he was right. Again. I nodded. "Okay. Deal."

He reached for the door handle, then froze. "One last thing."

I already had my door open, one foot on the pavement. "And from your tone I take it it's not something I'm going to like."

"Probably not." He smirked that smug, infuriating, endearing little smirk of his but it didn't reach his eyes. He removed the keys from the ignition and tossed them to me. I caught them with a minimal amount of fumbling. "If it looks like I'm going to lose, run. Don't try to be a hero. Get the hell out of here, go back to Kaine, and tell him what happened."

I had known all along that we were walking a thin line, flirting with death in trying to take down a troll on its home turf, but in that moment the scope of just how badly the night could end became crystal clear to me. All the anger, all the snide, stupid little things I had ever thought about him suddenly melted away. I wanted to curse myself for having been an even bigger fool than Gannon ever could be. A hundred thoughts zipped through my mind and I wanted to say them all, but it wasn't the time or the place. We didn't have the luxury of distractions, no matter the possible regrets, so instead I nodded. "I promise."

I rounded the front of the car and froze, hands jammed in my pockets; eyes ahead. The street seemed darker than it had a moment before, every shadow cloaking evils beyond my worst nightmare—who, of course, lay just ahead. I was shaking and hated myself for it. I knew Gannon was fast. I had seen him move with breath-taking speed, yet that didn't do shit for my nerves. I couldn't stop trembling. Walking those last couple feet to that doorway became the hardest thing in the world. A hand pressed against the small of my back. It was impossible for me to feel its warmth through the layers of leather and cloth, but I swore I did. His voice was low, whisper close in my ear. "You've got this."

I nodded and flashed him a tight smile. The stoic mask was back on his face, and it gave my confidence the tiny bolster it needed. I took that first step forward and refused to let myself stop. I kept my head high. Sweaty palms or no, I wasn't going to let a rational little thing like fear stop me. I stopped myself from looking back over my shoulder as I approached those crumbling cement steps. Gannon had my back. I had to trust in that. All I had to do was find the opening; he would do the rest. I could do this. I *had* to do this. There was no room for failure.

The stairwell was dark and dank, far from the nearest street lamp. All sorts of muck lingered in the darkened corners, adding a cloyingly sweet note under the general stench of mold. Gross. I took the stairs slowly, careful to place each step so as not to slip or dislodge any of the crumbling mortar, ears straining to hear the slightest sound coming from within the apartment. There was no window, no porch light—just darkness and a silence that seemed eerie to a city-dweller like me.

I had no clue what awaited us inside, or if Goliath was even still there. I hated going in to something as dangerous as this blind. I stood in front of that door—so damn normal looking, that door—and closed my eyes, letting everything else fall away. You can do this, I reminded myself. This was what I had been waiting for; the moment I had been chasing for the better part of a year. It was time for ballsy, brash Hunter Caitlin to earn her keep.

My knock sounded like a gong breaking the silence.

For a moment I stood there, barely breathing, and wondered if we had missed our shot. I couldn't hear any movement from within. I bit my lip and raised my hand to knock again, just as the door swung open. Goliath stood before me in all his stooped, seven foot glory; still big, still ugly, still—now that we were up close and I was downwind—stinking worse than all the garbage lining his vestibule. Beneath his furrowed Herman Munster brow, those piggy little eyes went wide, mastif jaw slack in confusion to see my standing on the other side of the door.

Go time.

I put on my best shit-eating grin and said brightly, "Hello, Ugly."

I shouldered past him and strode into the apartment. It was a rundown pigsty, sparsely furnished with dilapidated dumpster dive finds and chock full of empty take-out containers as far as the eye could see. Three steps in I was bum-rushed by a dank, rotten stench that made it hard to suppress a gag. Oh Lordy, I was going to use every bit that single year of high school drama club had taught me if I was going to keep this act up. I cased the joint in a heartbeat: two doorways out, one behind me (most likely the kitchen, given the wafting odor) and another to the right, leading to a hallway; a dim light coming from beyond the open door of a side bedroom. No sounds of movement. It was unlikely anyone else was home.

Good.

I turned to face him. In the thirty seconds it had taken for me to get my bearings, he hadn't moved except to turn around and gape at me like a confused dog. My eyes flicked to his left, around one massive, muscled arm. Dumbshit had left the door open behind him. Good—I had been counting on that. Now, I just had to keep his attention. "Nice place you've got here. Smells a bit like ass and feet, but the ambiance is very you. What would you call this decor? Crack house chic?"

That seemed to penetrate his stupor. Goliath narrowed his eyes and snarled, revealing those huge, yellowed canines as he took a step toward me. I backed up a step, careful to shuffle so as not to slip on any of the trash littering the floor, and told myself to get ready to draw. Those meaty paws rose in the air and stretched out toward me, and the sight of them triggered all types of remembered panic. In that second I forgot every goddamned thing I had learned in practice; not a single form or move could get past the jibbering fear of those hands coming at me, threatening to hoist me up into the air like a sack of potatoes again. Fuck, this had been a stupid idea.

"Argoth." Gannon stood in the doorway; my avenging angel, heavenly sword drawn.

The troll turned. Seeing Gannon standing there, his shoulders rose, shaggy head lowering like a bull ready to charge. A rumble resounded deep in his chest. The gladiators stared one another down, each waiting for the other to make the first move. I was all but forgotten.

With Goliath's eyes off me, I was able to think coherent thoughts again. The first of which was, right—time for me to get out of the way before all hell broke loose. I didn't like the odds of getting caught in another room, should the worst happen, so I darted to the right, keeping an open path between myself and the door, and did so not a moment too soon. They broke the stalemate at the same moment, rushing toward one another to meet with a resounding crash in the center of the room. I cringed at the heavy thud of their impact. How Gannon could withstand running into that brick shithouse was beyond me; that alone would have broken half the bones in my body.

They bounced apart but sprung immediately back in to action, neither missing a beat. The fight was on—and it was breath-taking. My eyes darted to and fro, trying—and failing—to track Gannon's movements. It was like trying to watch the wind.

In the training ring, Gannon had moved like a panther; a predatory animal, sleek and primal. Now, he moved like a force of nature. He ducked and weaved around the monster's wild swings, seeming to anticipate the troll's every move. His blade whistled through the air and, again and again, I heard Goliath snarl as it broke his leathery hide. Gannon had been right—trolls were ungodly strong, but they were also slow. In close quarters, unable to get a good, running charge, the beast was at a serious disadvantage.

My adrenaline was pumping. I bounced on the balls of my feet, hands clenching and unclenching. The thrill was sizzling in my blood and I ached to leap into the fray, but knew better. I wouldn't break my promise. I watched Goliath lunge, hugely muscled arms scissoring close to Gannon's neck just as he spun away. I couldn't kid myself: what he made look easy was far beyond my reach. The chaos around me seemed to move at hyper-speed; beautiful and unreal.

Watching Gannon fight for real was both an epiphany and a god damn sock to the gut. I knew only then just how far he had been scaling back in the ring with me. For months I had secretly marveled over his speed, his strength, his grace—but nothing he had shown me came anywhere close to the truth of what he was capable of. Even when we hunted, the kills has come easy.

Now I realized that he had made sure of it. Those fae we had faced had been training wheels; a chance for me to get my sea legs, so to speak. Not a single one of them would have posed the smallest challenge to him, had he gone against them alone. I realized why he had been so furious with me the night we hunted the black dog. I had never—not once—been in danger on a hunt with him at my side. Not until I had put myself there.

A deafening roar broke my reverie. Goliath was not enjoying the fight nearly as much as I was from the sidelines. He was bleeding from half a dozen shallow wounds that would have felled a lesser creature, but he hadn't slowed one bit. A nearby lamp became a bludgeon in one of his meaty hands. He swung hard at Gannon, glass shattering as it met metal. Gannon jumped back, arm up to block against the broken shards as they flew through the air. Goliath threw the broken weapon aside, shattering plaster where it met with one water-stained wall, and lunged forward again, forcing Gannon back another foot.

My heart raced. How could a noise like that go unnoticed, even in squatter's row? Surely someone would call the cops. I jerked with indecision, going hot, then cold with the realization that no help—or hindrance—would be forthcoming. This wasn't my neighborhood, where screams still brought people running. It was quite the opposite. Here, domestic violence was likely all too common. Although the ruckus Goliath was making would surely wake and annoy some nearby sleepers, no one was going to risk their neck in something that was clearly not their business.

Still. This was taking too long. Gannon was too close to being backed into a corner. We needed to take the fucker down, quick, before it decided to use its sizable body as a battering ram, close quarters be damned. I had promised not to jump in to the fight, but that didn't mean I couldn't help—and I was getting ever so good at being a distraction. I drew one of the girls. Pitching myself to carry over the troll's growls, I yelled, "Hey, Ugly. Did you forget about me?" I threw the blade end over end and watched it careen into the back of Goliath's head; pommel first. I hadn't expected it to connect. All I had needed for it to do was exactly what it did.

Goliath spun on me with another wild roar. I backpedaled, retreating into the darkened hallway as he advanced on me. I screwed my face up in my best troll-like snarl and let loose an angry yell of my own. Goliath's attention remained focused on me as Gannon took advantage of my distraction and sprang forward. A few inches of steel, glistening with blood, protruded through the troll's chest. Goliath froze. I froze. The growling stopped.

I expected a bellow, a scream—some recognition of the pain he must have been in—but none came. Goliath was dead silent, panting heavily as he stared down at the sword blade. His hand trembled as he touched one thick finger to the edge of the blade and watched it come away, sticky and red with his own blood. He slumped to his knees, the floor trembling with the impact of his weight. I steadied myself with a hand against the wall, ignoring how moist it felt beneath my palm. Now I was the one gaping.

Gannon stepped up behind him. I saw a hand come up and take a fistful of the troll's matted, shaggy hair. He pulled his head back. Goliath let him.

"Now, Caitlin."

I drew my remaining knife and stepped forward. Face to face with my nightmare, cowed and dying, I felt no fear. He didn't move as I stopped in front of him, only inches away with a drawn dagger. He didn't struggle against Gannon one bit. All the fight had drained out of him. He was beat and he knew it. Not so stupid after all, I guess. I put one hand on his cheek, feeling the pebbled leather of his skin under my hand; feeling him tremble.

I stood there, looking into those wet, beady black eyes and saw fear in them. He was not fighting but, in those final moments as he felt his life slip away, he was scared. As scared as I had been for too many months on end. The rage inside me cooled. I leaned in close and whispered, "You can't terrorize me anymore."

The hide under his chin was softer than the rest; a vulnerable spot. My cut was deep and clean, made quick. This time, I didn't mind the hot, sticky rush that poured over my hands. Gannon loosened his grip and Argoth slumped sideways. For the first time in longer than I could remember, I felt like I could breathe again.

"Let's get out of here. I'll come back to deal with the body," Gannon said. He wiped his blade clean on the troll's shirt.

I nodded, cleaning my own blade before slipping it back in its boot sheath. "I need to find my other knife."

"I see it. I'll get it."

Gannon retreated back into the living room. I looked around for something to clean my now gore-covered hand on. The dimly lit bedroom to my right was likely the troll's, and I wanted nothing to do with anything that could be found in there. I pivoted and saw two more doorways behind me; a bathroom at the end of the hall and another room on my left, the door slightly ajar. Two bedrooms seemed pricey for a troll, even in the ghetto. Had Goliath worked from home, surviving on some dotcom income?

I crept forward and poked my head inside. I felt around for a light switch and flicked it on. It was another bedroom, complete with neatly made bed, book lined desk, dresser, and—from the looks of it—a recently ransacked closet. A few hangers hung bare and a discarded pair of sneakers lay forgotten on the floor. It appeared Goliath had had a roomie, up until very recently. I glanced over at the dresser. It was littered with random personal effects that had been too much of a hassle to take: a cheapo men's watch, a rather expensive looking bottle of cologne, loose change. Among the cast-offs was a single framed photo, and that made my blood run cold.

"Gannon!"

He skidded to a halt behind me only half a second later, my missing dagger in his hand and ready to strike. He let out a noisy sound of relief when he spied the empty room. He tucked my blade back into its home, muttering, "Good gods, you scared the… What's wrong?"

I pointed to the picture on the dresser, my hand shaking. "That." He nudged me to the side and slid into the room. I couldn't follow. The door-frame was keeping me upright. How could I have forgotten?

He picked up the frame, brow furrowed as he examined its contents. In it, a pretty red-headed girl with a smattering of freckles across her little button nose was gazing up a grinning guy; all lovey-dovey and sweet like. It would have been an endearing shot of a happy couple in love—if the grinning the jackass in it hadn't been Texas Pete.

"That's the other guy from the bar," I said, voice cracking. "The smarmy bastard that was with Ugly over there when they cornered me." Gannon cursed softly, but I heard it. All my muscles seemed to tighten up at once. That wasn't the sound of a coincidence. "What?"

"I know him."

"*What?*" The word could have peeled the paint from the walls.

Gannon put the picture back down. He rubbed at his jaw with one hand. "His name is Liam." He looked at me like someone had just died and he was delivering the solemn news. "He is Aos Sí, and was a Guardian."

"Was?" The word had to be forced from my dry throat. I felt like I would vomit if I tried to say more.

"He was cast out, years before my own exile. No one ever heard what happened, after he left. It was widely assumed he was dead."

I laughed, a dark, ugly sound, and knocked my forehead against the door frame, softly. "Yeah, well, apparently he's not. He's been living across town from me, making friends with creepy trolls and planning to sell my soul to the High King." I gasped, head whipping up so hard I nearly gave myself whiplash. My heart spasmed. "Oh my God! That's what he's doing, isn't he? He's going back—he's crossing the Veil and going to tell the King I'm here!"

Gannon hadn't moved. He wouldn't look at me. "There's no way to..."

"Really? Come on Gannon; be real. He's not here, is he? And it looks like he left in a hurry." It all made sense. Horrible, stomach churning sense. "This is what we missed. That's why Goliath was still here. We were wrong all along. The fucking troll was never going to run and tell. A goddamn Aos Sí, disgraced or not, would have a hell of a lot easier of a time getting the King to listen to him than a troll would, wouldn't he?" Gannon didn't answer, so I repeated, "Wouldn't he?"

"Yes." The word was a sigh; a resignation.

"And what better way to get back in the King's good graces, than to tell him right where to find a Warder?" I slumped back against the door-frame, eyes on the chipped wood above. I felt like I was back in another doorway, watching as my life was torn apart; my safety ripped away. I wanted to scream. "Fuck, fuck—*fuck*! It's like every time I take a step forward, I get knocked back three. This is just... I can't..." I closed my eyes tight to stop them from leaking.

Gannon's hands closed upon my arms like vice-grips, forcing me to open them and look him in the eye. "Caitlin, do you trust me?"

I hesitated, then nodded. None of this was his fault. He was one of the few people who had given a damn about making this right. I had him to thank for Argoth's death, after all. "Yes."

Fire burned in those ice-blue eyes. "Then trust me in this: I will find him. I promise you—I will find him and I will stop him."

CHAPTER TWENTY-ONE

I was awoken by a low, humming purr in my ear. I careened my head away from the fuzzy body pressed against the side of my face. I turned my head and found myself being regarded by a pair of luminous little cat eyes. Mairi always woke up when I started to get up. I had given up on trying to slip away without waking her. Feline senses were freaky, preternatural things.

She bumped her head against my forehead—which was cat for "good morning," I had come to learn—and took a leisurely stretch-n-stroll down the edge of the bed. I sat up, working some morning energy into my sleep stiffened muscles myself with a groan that was both pleasure and pain. She hopped down, padded over to the cracked door, and disappeared into the quiet hallway beyond. It was our usual morning routine.

Was it weird that I thought nothing of a shape-shifted fae girl sleeping on my pillow at night? Or, was it weirder that I didn't think that thinking things like that question was weird anymore?

It was Saturday morning. By all rights, I had no good reason to be awake at 7am. It was balls cold outside my warm, blanket cocoon. I had nowhere to be and nothing more important to do than shower. It was way too early to go searching for the Lynx, so what was I rushing to get up for? Another fae history lesson compliments of Seana? While I appreciated the hearty breakfast and endless flow of coffee that often accompanied her weekend lectures, I just didn't have it in me to get all excited about combing through another dusty old book, picking apart myths to find their teeny, tiny little nuggets of truth. I flopped back down on the bed and snuggled my face into a pillow.

Three days had passed since Gannon and I had taken Goliath down.

Three days with no word on Texas Pete's whereabouts, with my hopes slowly—but steadily—sinking.

Did it even matter now? I had wanted to fight the good fight to protect the people I loved, but couldn't remember why I had thought I could make a difference. I wasn't even sure why I kept trying, really. Maybe I was just too stubborn to give up. Maybe some masochistic part of me liked the pain of pushing myself through another day, just to see what else could go wrong. My life had been torn to shreds and I fully expected every day to bring another earth-shattering tragedy until there was just no solid ground left for me to stand on.

I held on to Gannon's promise like a beacon in the dark, but even then it was hard to resist depression's siren song. A large part of me was done with it all. That part really wanted to throw itself into a deep, dark despair—but the rest of me fought on. Giving up seemed like a big waste, after all I had endured.

So, despite the rain cloud parked over my head, I forced myself get out of bed each morning to soldier on. I left my faith in Gannon and tried to continue living life. I went to work, ate the food Seana so graciously put in front of me, and spent my nights drifting from one spot to another, looking for a man I was pretty much certain we would never find.

I made a long, low, unintelligible groan into my pillow. There just weren't words enough to express my frustration. I hated feeling so helpless. I hated drifting from day to day, like a kite dependent on the wind; no energy, no aspirations—just passively letting life choose my path for me. I had been fighting my own misery for so long. Maybe this new low was just my new normal. Maybe I had given in to depression and was just fooling myself by pretending I was fighting against it.

Mairi had called me iron, but I felt more like a lump of dog shit. She looked up to me like I was a big sister, like I would be the savior for all of them. And what was I doing? Lying in bed, moping. I sat up, kicked off the covers, and raked my hands back though my tangled hair. It felt scummy. I had to actively think to remember the last time I had washed it. It had been in a messy bun for that long. Gross.

I needed to get out of bed and into a shower. I needed to drag myself out of this funk, and force myself to put on pants and a bra—anything to try and to feel like a human being again. Lesson time with Seana wasn't exactly my idea of fun but what was, these days? Lying in bed all day, being dirty and sad? That had to stop. Whether or not I wanted it, this was my life; there were no take-backs. These fae were my partners, if not exactly my friends, and we were in this mess together, like it or not. I got to my feet and stretched, rallying every ounce of courage I had left.

It wasn't much, but it was something.

~*~

I was right about lesson time with Seana being no fun.

The more I got to know her, the more I came to realize that there were unexpected depths beneath that calm surface. As a Healer, she had cultivated her outward serenity to face the horrors she saw inflicted upon the flesh. That made sense, of course. No one wanted to be treated by a doctor who threw their hands up in the air and ran around in circles, wailing gibberish. She truly was a balanced, unflappable soul; the kind of even-keeled, generous-hearted person I admired and secretly wished I could be.

Beneath that unruffled calm, however, behind that sweet smile, there was the calculating mind of a woman, through and through. A relatable sort of mind, that disliked her opinion being ignored or discounted. One who would make sure that her displeasure was heard loud and clear, though she always managed to do so in a very polite way. Take, for example, the lesson she had so thoughtfully chosen for me when I finally rallied out from under my funk: Trolls—Breeds and Characteristics, with a focus on known weaknesses and fighting styles. It was a subtle dig but I got the message.

Obviously Gannon had told everyone that he had taken me along to dispatch Argoth, after the fact. She wouldn't come right out and reprimand me for it—that was Kaine's place, not hers. Instead, she made it very clear in her well-mannered way that I had upset her with my rash actions. As exasperating as I found her passive-aggressiveness, I couldn't hate on her too much. It was a valid lesson, even if that particular enemy was now past tense. I went along with it.

After breakfast we had moved into the small room at the back of the house that served as her office. It was cozy, in a meditative day spa kind of way. Gauzy curtains, cream colored walls, plush chairs, soft instrumental music playing; the whole nine yards. There was even a little rock fountain burbling away in one corner. I found the atmosphere relaxing to the point of distraction. When my head nodded toward my chest for the umpteenth time, Seana noticed. "I'm sorry, is the lesson I chose boring you?"

I snapped to attention. "No, no—not at all. Very interesting stuff here." I gave her my best endearing smile, complete with batted lashes, but I don't think she bought it. When she continued to level me with that knowing mother stare, I caved. "Okay, I'm having a hard time getting it."

She looked down at the book in her lap, brow furrowed. "I had not considered that. You've been a wonderful student. But if you're finding the material too difficult…"

"No, I didn't mean it like that." I gestured back and forth between the scribbles of my notes and her. "I'm having a hard time getting this whole scenario. You, teaching me about hunting. It just feels weird."

That look of mild bemusement continued. "How so?"

It was hard to find the words, without insulting her. I hedged and picked my words cautiously. "You just don't seem very fond of hunting, is all."

"Well, as a Healer, I am not fond of any violence. I wage my own war against death and injury all too often. To see brave souls putting their lives in such peril by throwing themselves between the monsters and innocents?

That upsets me on a level I cannot begin to explain. I wish it were a different world we lived in, one where such valor was not needed." She got a far-off look in her eyes. Her hands were clenched in a knot, resting on the worn pages of her ancient tome. She sighed. "But I know just how necessary the Hunters are to the safety of both our races."

I didn't need Mairi's creepy empathy to know she was thinking of a different time and place all together. It raised goosebumps along my arms. "You lost someone."

She nodded and looked away. "My son, Arland."

I was struck dumb. It had never occurred to me, in all that time, to wonder who Seana had been before the exile. It had shocked me shitless to learn that Gannon had a sister, and even more so to learn that his sibling was Kaine's wife—but I had never stopped to wonder about her. How had I never taken the time to ask her a single thing about her life before? I mean—how much did I really even know about her? I felt terrible. I fidgeted, torn between curiosity and anguish. "I'm so sorry, I never…"

"It was many years ago. A lifetime ago, now." The unbelievable sadness in her expression seemed to age her ten years. It made my heart ache. She said, "I was foolish and headstrong, in my younger years. Arland was the greatest gift to come from that dark time. He brought such joy to my life, such laughter. Moreover, he gave me a reason to find my path in my life."

The words pulled themselves out of my throat, slow and coarse. "What happened?"

"I had only just become a Healer, so we were still very poor. We lived outside of the city, on our own. It was a hard life, but we got by. He was only six when they attacked." She stopped, blinking hard, and gazed up at the ceiling. I wanted to tell her to stop, to shy away from bearing her pain, but I felt I owed it to her to hear her out. She continued, "Ogres. They had ravaged the countryside, though I had no way of knowing that then. My home stood between them and the nearby city. They came on us in the dead of night. I told Arland to run, but they were so fast. I heard him scream, before the pain of my own injuries overwhelmed me."

"Oh, Seana…" I didn't know what else to say.

"The High Queen's men found me. They had been tracking the ogres for some time. I was brought to the palace and cared for by the best Healers in the kingdom. Even so, I was lucky to live; they feared I would not for many days." She stared down at her hands, which still wrung together in her lap. "I did not feel 'lucky' for a long time afterward. I had no hope, no reason to go on."

I had no frame of reference for such terrible pain. I wanted to reach out to her; to empathize, somehow. I just didn't know how. "What did you do?"

"It was the High Queen who saved me then. She came to me, as I lay lost in grief, my soul withering even as my body healed. She apologized for her failing me as a liege; for not having stopped the monsters before they happened across my home. She knew well that there was no recompense she could make for the loss I had suffered. Her Healers had healed my flesh, and her coffers could rebuild my home bigger and grander than before, but nothing could replace the precious gift I had lost.

"She may have come to me, at first, as a Queen, but Isobail spoke to me then as an equal; as a mother. She herself had just given birth to Tiernan only weeks earlier. Instead of promising me reparation that would never be enough, she instead offered me something I would have never considered. She asked me to come live at the palace and train under her Master Healer, so that I could serve as nursemaid to her children."

My jaw hung open. "Wait, you mean you raised that wack—the High King?"

She nodded. "He and his brother both. Their mother was a wonderful woman; kind and strong, but often enraptured in the matters of state. I was their governess, as well as their personal Healer, from the cradle onward. Though nothing could ever replace Arland in my heart, raising them was a pleasure and a privilege."

I was floored. There was just so much I did not know, so much I had never so much as guessed at, hidden in the pasts of these people. I could have lived among them for a dozen years and I never would have expected such a bombshell revelation. Suddenly all my loudly exclaimed defamations of the Nutjob King echoed back at me. "What happened to him? How did he get to be…?"

"Tiernan was very different as a child. We were so close, he and I. Even then, he was mercurial and often taken by strange fancies. One moment he was a sweet, loving little boy who ran to me with every new discovery. A pretty stone or a flower in full bloom—oh, how such things lit up his face with a smile!" She smiled at the memory; a sad, sweet smile that made me want to hug her. "When he was like that, he was utterly enchanting; the perfect little Prince, full of joy and curiosity. He loved me like a mother, and I came to love him like the son I had lost.

"But there was a darkness in him as well. Overwhelming sadness would overtake him with no warning, or a terrible rage would fill every inch of his tiny body. At first, those terrible spells would only last a heartbeat, and everyone said it was just the temperament of a child—but I feared it was something much worse. Soon he was withdrawing from all around him when the moods overtook him, including me. He would rave about the monsters lurking in the shadows, saying we were all out to hurt him. He would spend long nights awake, screaming with terrors. It was terrible to watch. After his brother was born, the bad times came more and more often, lasting longer and longer.

"Those were very difficult years for all who lived in the palace. He seemed to grow out of it with time, though the joyful innocence of the child I raised was long gone. He became a quiet, reserved young man and many thanked the gods that he had outgrown his childish temper. I have long wondered if he had only learned to hide his sickness from those closest to him, but no one listened to my fears before it was too late. By then, the High Queen had passed and the throne was his. When I had held him as a babe, I had hoped he would be as great a King as his mother was a Queen, but somewhere along the way, I lost him too." She finally looked back up at me. A tear escaped and trickled down her cheek but it was quickly wiped away. "He was supposed to be a better man."

I didn't know which she wept for more: her lost child or the surrogate she had seen turn so very dark. I bit my lower lip. To hear my great, faceless nemesis had once been a happy go lucky child playing amongst the flowers was hard. Seeing Seana's heartbreak was even harder. How it must have hurt her, to be cast aside in the shadow of growing madness. Her little idiosyncrasies started falling into place in my mind, making a strange sort of sense now that I could see a little bit more of the bigger picture. "Is that why you've been teaching me, even though you don't want me out there risking my life? So that I can help stop Tiernan?"

Looking into her eyes was like staring into a pool of still, deep water. Even shimmering with tears, they exuded a primordial compassion that enveloped me. "I do all that I do in Arland's memory. If I could have my way I would never see another innocent die, especially as a victim of Tiernan's neglectful rule. While I may not be pleased to see you, a lovely, talented young woman, staining her hands with blood, I understand that these are desperate times. I would rather see you well prepared for what lies ahead of you on this path, rather than railing against the unfairness of a fate that cannot be avoided." She cleared her throat and wiped at one eye daintily. Her nose was reddened and her eyes glassy, but the naked glimpse I had gotten of her scarred soul well hidden once more. "Now. Shall we continue?"

I nodded, throat tight. How could I refuse her, after what I had just learned? I tried my best to be an attentive student for the rest of the afternoon. I was listening to her describe—far too graphically—a particular breed of swamp-dwelling troll and their hallucinogenic skin secretions when Gannon appeared in the doorway.

I looked up from the notebook that was once again spread open in my lap, my heart instantly ratcheting up to third gear. He looked exhausted, more so than I had ever seen him before. Deep shadows hung beneath his eyes. He watched Seana, who was absorbed in the passage she was reading, for a moment. His eyes flitted over to me and the sorrow in them hit me like a brick.

I sat up straighter. Seana paused, giving him a puzzled look.

His gaze dropped to the floor. He rubbed at the back of his neck with one hand. If what I had learned in his company over the past few months was true, he did that when he was uncomfortable. Not a good sign. He cleared his throat. "Sorry to interrupt, ladies."

He was hesitating. Gannon. Hesitating. That went against everything I knew to be true about the universe. Doubly not good.

Seana closed her book and set it down on the end table at her side. I could see that crease in her brow as she frowned, the healer's gears already turning in her head. "That's quite all right. How can I help you?"

"I'm here for Caitlin."

In that moment, I wanted to throw up. A million horrible, grisly things flashed through my head: my father coming home after work to find my mother slumped over in a puddle of blood at the kitchen table; my sister, decapitated in some dark back alley; Jenni's mutilated body being found in the dumpster behind Gilroy's. The panic must have shown on my face. He held up his hands, as if he was warding off my crazy. "No one has been hurt."

I let out a gasp of relief. That news was good—but it could only mean one thing. He had come to update me on the hunt for Texas Pete. My heart kicked into high gear, now for a completely different reason. Everything felt floaty and weird; my head spinning. I gripped my notebook so tightly that the metal spiral bit grooves into my fingers. Why wasn't he looking triumphant? Or battle hungry? Or even smugly satisfied, like he was about most things? He had solved the mystery, saved my sanity, and possibly even my life. Where the hell was that cockiness?

Something was wrong. Something was very, very wrong. The urge to throw up my bacon and eggs intensified.

I stared at his stricken face until he finally broke. "Liam is gone."

"Gone?" The word was a whisper that wanted to be hysterics.

He nodded. "Yes. Gone."

"What do you mean, gone? Gone from the city? The state? Are we talking, took a midnight train going anywhere gone?"

My feeble attempt at humor was lost on him but my rising hysteria was not. I loathed the sympathy I saw in his gaze. "Gone from this earth. You were right. He crossed back over the Veil, to our world."

He didn't have to say anything else. I already knew where he would go, now that he knew both who and where I was. Tiernan would pay highly for information on the last Warder. Gannon had done all he could, trapped on this side as he was. Until I found the Lynx—even if I had begged him to pick up the search, to stop that creature from ratting me out to the king—there was nothing else he could do now. Still, I had to try. "There has to be something you can do. Can't you send someone to stop him?"

The look I drew from both Seana and Gannon was an odd one. They both looked at me like I had lost my mind. Had I suggested something bizarre? It didn't seem all that strange to me. They got their leads on the Lynx from a source. I didn't know much about the shadowy network of informants that seemed to be at their beck and call and, to be honest, I had never really wanted to know. If they had some sort of crazy fae mafia connections, it was all the better that I kept my nose out of it—until now.

When I said as much, Gannon just shook his head. "We can't do that."

"Why the hell not?"

"Kaine would never ask that of them. This is not their fight."

Something hot and bitter roiled in my belly. I could almost feel the burn of bile in the back of my throat. "But if that bastard tells the king about me, he's going to come after me. Kaine promised to stop the King from finding out about me. You need to tell him about this. We can't just give up now!"

The quiet bit into me like a knife. Seana was looking down at her lap, refusing to meet my eyes. Gannon's jaw ticked, a sure sign of anger, though whether with me or something else, I couldn't tell. A long moment passed before he said, "Kaine is aware of Liam and his return across the Veil. He considers his end of the pact satisfied."

"Like hell it is!" I was on my feet, notebook and pen falling to the floor. My hands were balled into fists and I was five feet and four inches of righteous fury. "I'll show him 'satisfied!'"

I pushed past Gannon and made it less than two feet past him into the hallway before he caught me by the arm. "Caitlin, don't do this."

"Let go!" I yanked my arm away. He fell back a step. I was quivering with rage. "You promised me. You promised me you would find him."

He jerked his head to the side, as if I had slapped him. Good. "I tried."

Bitterness welled up in my throat. "Yeah, well, that's not good enough."

He didn't try to stop me again as I stormed down the hall. Livid was too shy a word to describe the rage that coursed through me. I was damn near shaking with that rage as I took the stairs at a machine gun pace. I was already having a knock-down-drag-out fight with Kaine in my head when I threw open the door to his study. I barely managed to keep a grip on the doorknob to prevent it from slamming into the wall. My teeth were clenched, my shoulders heaving in time with my breath.

Kaine was seated in front of his desk, for once, in a chair facing a merrily crackling fire. He had a book in his lap, which he looked up from slowly, not the least bit ruffled by my hell-hath-no-fury entrance. He closed it and let it rest on one knee. "Can I help you?"

Oh, that smug motherfucker. I was ready to spit nails and he was looking at me with the detachment of a psychologist dealing with a delusional patient. This was going to get ugly. It took every last shred of willpower I had in my body to gently close the door behind me, rather than breaking it clear off the hinges. I clasped my hands behind my back so he wouldn't see them shake. "Gannon told me Liam has crossed back over."

Kaine inclined his head, frowning in an oh-so-proper approximation of shame. "Yes. I am very sorry he was unable to locate him before he left this realm."

"Sorry is nice, but it won't keep me alive once your High King knows I exist." He did not deny my claim. His silence only made my blood burn hotter. God damn, it was hard to keep my temper. I wanted to rant and rave and throw his goddamned book into the fireplace, but instead I swallowed the lump in my throat and said, "You have friends here, fae friends who have been helping you. I need you to send someone back there, to try and stop him before my life is put in even greater danger. Please."

He looked back to the fire, lips pursed. My heart fluttered with hope for the briefest of moments before a curt shake of his head smashed it to the ground. "I cannot ask any who aid us here to risk their life." Maybe blood-curdling rage was the cure to his freaky fae wiles, because there was no inkling of attraction in me when that vibrant turquoise gaze met mine. "Our allies here are citizens of my realm; commoners who wished to live their lives out among humans. They are not warriors. To ask any of them to cross paths with a Guardian, even a disgraced one, would be far too dangerous."

I let my head loll back, my eyes locked on the ceiling as I took a long, slow breath. Put that way, I couldn't very well protest without looking like the most heartless bitch ever. Still; I wanted nothing more than to knock that demeaning calm right off his face. I didn't care what sort of noble blood he had or how important he was back in his home world—here, he was a smug dick.

"I am sorry, Caitlin. Gannon feels terrible, to have gotten so close, only to have his quarry slip away at the last moment."

"And what happens when we find the Lynx? If I get you home, will you let Gannon go after that asshole?" My mind was once again whirling, wondering how I could possibly step up the search, when we had had such little success for so long. If I could only find him, if I could somehow get them home soon, perhaps there was still a chance Texas Pete would be intercepted before my fate was sealed...

"No."

I stared at him, open-mouthed. I couldn't believe what I was hearing. "*What?*" I sputtered. "What do you mean 'no'? Why the fuck not?"

Again, that cool, detached gaze as he stomped on my hopes. "Gannon will have other duties once we are returned. I cannot spare him."

"But we had a deal!"

He spread his hands. "I have fulfilled my part of the bargain we struck."

"Are you kidding me?" My voice had risen to a screech. There was a damn good chance everyone in the house could hear my hysterics, but I didn't give a rat's ass. "You swore you'd protect me! You swore that you'd keep the King from finding out about me!"

"By hunting the troll down and making sure he could not tell the High King about your Gift, yes."

My mouth snapped shut so fast I nearly bit through my tongue. Those were the exact words I had spoken. I could remember him repeating them back to me, as clear as day. Suddenly, Seana's warning made the most awful kind of sense. At the time, I had taken her advice as caution against angering their sovereign lord. Now I realized there had been so much more weight to those words. The troll was dead. *He* could no longer tell the High King anything. I had never considered he would employ another to do his dirty work—and our pact had made no mention of friends.

I had been had.

I could barely speak. My jaw seemed to have fused shut in its attempt to keep a backlash of anger inside. I had never been good at dealing with authority figures and blatant abuses of power. This was no different. I adopted the sickeningly sweet passivity I usually saved for those smart-ass moments where I was about to get canned or dumped no matter what came out of my mouth. "I see. That must be terribly convenient for you. And now that your end of the deal is 'fulfilled' what, exactly, do you expect from me?"

"The same as before. You will help us find the Lynx." He never wavered. The fucker never so much as blinked. "That was your bond."

Good God damn, did I ever want to hit him. *So* hard. There was no malice in his response but that only made it worse. He had no compunction when it came to refusing me the help that might be the difference between my eventual life and death—but he also felt no remorse. He had lived up to the letter of his promise and was required to do no more. I, on the other hand, had no excuse to call off my end of the deal—which also suited him just fine, of course. My lips drew back in a snarl. "Oh yeah? And what if I refuse? What if I say fuck you and your backstabbing bullshit deal?"

He remained impassive, that steady gaze never wavering. He didn't have to say anything and he knew it. He knew I couldn't back out. Who would stand with me against the creepy crawlies if I walked away now? Sure, I could likely defend myself one-on-one—but what if they came in twos or threes? Argoth might be dead and Liam was beyond my reach, but that didn't mean they hadn't had connections here. Who knew who else out there might still know about me and where I lived? It didn't matter what kind of crazy faerie mojo might be waiting for me if I tried to break my end of the damned pact. Even that had become moot. I was completely dependent on him and the bastard knew it.

I stood there for another moment, dumbstruck. I wanted to scream. I wanted to cry. I wanted to stomp around in a crazy, stompy rage. It was all so incredibly unfair that I wanted to fall to the floor and never get up again. Instead, I curtsied at the lord of the manor—making it all that much more of a mockery in my tank top and yoga pants—before I turned and left. I only stopped long enough to grab my coat and purse from the alcove by the door before I headed down the front stairs two at a time.

No one tried to follow me.

I slid into my car and threw my purse into the passenger seat. I had the key in the ignition before I froze, wondering just where the hell I intended to go. Gilroy's? Jenni's? Home? The world around me was an unfriendly blur and all I wanted was something familiar. Something normal. Maybe that was just a pipe dream, but I had to believe it still existed out there, somewhere.

I don't know how long I sat there, staring off at nothing as the tears dried on my cheeks. The harsh light of day had finally pierced through to the center of me and I had no more lies to hide behind; no more fluffy dreams to shroud the cold truth of reality. There was no one else in this world that cared as much about my fate as I did. No one was going to save me. Perhaps I had always known that. I had been careless and stupid, letting my life get intertwined with that of these weirdos. Maybe I had wanted excitement and adventure, but I hadn't stopped to consider the costs. Didn't matter now, of course. It was too late for take backs.

Or was it?

My life in Riverview was in shambles, yes, but there was a great big world out there. What would I be leaving behind, really? A job I hated? People who didn't give a shit about me? The thought of never seeing my family again, however estranged we were, made my chest ache but perhaps that too would be for the best. They'd be safer. *I'd* be safer. Maybe that whole distance making the heart grow fonder crap would heal the wounds between us. Maybe I'd be able to drop in on them one day, when I had become less of a liability.

I didn't know what I'd do or where I'd go, but I could figure that out as I went. Surely the High King and his hordes wouldn't be able to find one little human among billions, right? Hell, even if they could, that didn't mean I had to sit around at the center of the bull's eye, waiting for them to strike. I wasn't sure which was making me lightheaded: the fear or the excitement. Either way, it was good to be feeling something.

For months I had been letting myself be lead along, like a passenger in my own life. Now there was something I could decide on for myself. There was no going back and I was tired as hell of sitting still. Why not shake things up? The contents of my life would fit neatly in the trunk of my car and, while I didn't have too much money squirreled away, I probably had enough to get me a few states away. I could find work, a cheap room for rent; something to pass the time, where no one knew me and there weren't soul-sucking creatures lurking around every corner. I pictured myself tucked away in some dusty, rural place where there were miles between houses, waiting tables at some mom-n-pop diner until I had enough money to move on to the next town. The picture wasn't that bad. I should have felt scared of such uncertainty but I didn't.

Goddamn. I let out a long, shaky breath. Was I really going to do this? Was I going to make a run for it and leave everything I knew behind? It was batshit crazy, but what in my life wasn't? Maybe another dose of crazy was exactly what I needed to fix the mess the old crazy had made of me. What was stopping me?

Other than a blood oath to a backstabbing fairy son of a bitch, of course.

I still needed to find them their Lynx. That elusive bastard was the last hurdle between me and a fresh break—a break I hadn't realized I wanted quite so badly until that very moment. I needed to find him, so I could put some distance between myself and the Caitlin Moore I had once been. I didn't know how long I had before Texas Pete spilled the beans and a host of angry fae came hunting for my ass but I didn't want to wait around to find out.

I fished my phone out of my purse. I didn't even wait for a greeting when the ringing cut off. "Mai, I'm outside. Get dressed. We've got work to do—and fast."

CHAPTER TWENTY-TWO

Another week of failure.

I tossed my purse onto the chair by the door and threw myself down on my borrowed bed. I screamed my frustration into the pillow until I was breathless and needed to come up for air, rolling over on my back to stare up at the ceiling. This sucked. I was exhausted, cranky, and just generally longing to throw things. Not even at a particular target, really. The wall would do. I was so frustrated. I might have made up my mind to take charge and get shit done but that didn't mean dick.

Fate wasn't letting me go that easy.

Every day felt like a lifetime. Each minute that passed was a step toward the gallows; another step Texas Pete made on his way to rat me out to the High King. Mairi had assured me that there was no direct passage from my realm to Tír na nÓg proper. It was marginally comforting to think that the smarmy bastard would have a long journey ahead of him before could even begin to seek an audience with the king. I hope it rained the whole time.

That didn't solve much in the long run, though. It only gave me a month or two of a head start, tops. Given how many failed attempts we had made to locate the Lynx, the numbers weren't coming in on my side. Seana had tried to soften the edges of my hysteria with a reminder that the king was indeed mad. There was a good chance that he wouldn't believe a word Pete said. My bloodline was supposed to be long gone, and a banished ex-Guardian's tale of a human girl in a far off city possessing it might be passed off as a wacky scheme to extort royal favor. That was all well and good, but what crazy, paranoid monarch would ignore the possibility of such a threat to his throne? No one had been able to argue against that point. Score one for me. (Yay.)

The truth was, no one could predict what would happen next. No one knew for sure how long it would take Pete to reach the king's realm. No one even knew how long it would take for him to get the king's ear once he arrived. Maybe news that big would get him an audience on the day he arrived. Maybe the King would have him tossed in the dungeons for telling ludicrous lies. Who knew? The vagueness of it all was killing me. Every day

I half expected to be told that the Lynx had "moved on" beyond our reach as well, crushing the last little bit of hope that remained. That would be my luck.

"Brooding again?"

I held up a certain finger in the time old gesture of "I don't find your joke funny." I was in no mood for, well, anything. I just wanted to sulk.

"Come on, Cat. Get changed and get moving."

I heard the muffled thunk of my purse hitting the top of the dresser. Damn. Mairi was clearing off the chair and making herself comfortable. That meant there was no hope of privacy for my sulking. "Maybe I don't want to get moving. Maybe I'd rather explore the full majesty of my misery."

I sounded pre-tween whiny even to my own ears.

"And maybe I want an all-expense paid trip to Fiji so I can work on my tan." My, she sounded tart tonight. She continued, "Maybe, if we're lucky, we'll both get what we want—but not until we find the Lynx. So, come on. Stop brooding and get up. We've got a fresh lead to check."

"What's the point?" I moaned, scrubbing at my face with my hands.

"The point is that all we can do is keep trying. You said it yourself—"

"Yeah, yeah. I know what I said." I pushed myself up on my elbows. She was folded up cross-legged on the chair by the door in that obnoxiously bendy way the young could still manage. Show off. I ached down to my very bones in a way that had nothing to do with sword-fighting and everything to do with sleep deprivation. The continuous rollercoaster of depression probably wasn't helping. "Stop reminding me."

She gave me her best look of disapproval, which really just came off as sassy duck-face. She mimicked me far too perfectly when she said, "'Time is of the essence, Mai. Don't let me get distracted by my funk!' We need to find him a.s.a.p., remember? So you can get your pretty little ass the hell out of Dodge."

She met me scowl for scowl. In hindsight, telling her my plan to run off into the setting sun the minute I had completed my bargain with Kaine had been a huge mistake. She hadn't taken it very well. While she hadn't come right out and voiced her resentment, the sudden swells of moody contempt spoke volumes. I didn't quite understand why she was so mad at me. We had become close over the past few months, but what had she expected? It wasn't like I had ever intended to join their merry band and follow them home once this was all over. Kaine could treat me like a lackey all he wanted—that didn't mean I was some sort of rare and majestic human pet. The plan had always been to find the Lynx, shake hands, and go our separate ways.

Whatever. I didn't have the energy to deal with her teenage snit.

She was right though. I had said just that. Continuing to argue with her because I wanted to wallow in self-pity would be futile. I scooted off the bed and started to riffle through the dresser for a clean pair of jeans. "What's the deal this time? Another stupid café with fancy, overpriced lattes? This city has more freaking cafés than I ever thought possible."

"A bar, actually. Word has it that he's a regular there. Surprise, surprise; all this time we've been hopped up on caffeine when we could have been pickling our livers." She pulled a folded piece of paper from her pocket and smoothed it out on one knee. "Let's see—its downtown, on the corner of Maple and Green."

"You've got to be shitting me." She didn't need to say anything else. My stomach had already dropped. *"Gilroy's?"*

"Huh—yeah, that's right. How did you…"

The silence was deafening.

I turned around and saw her giving me a wide-eyed stare, her mouth a charming little o of surprise. Things had just clicked into place for her. "I didn't make the connection when Seana told me. That's where we first met you, isn't it?"

I nodded. The place where I had met them. The place where the troll had attacked me. The place where my former best friend worked. The place I had once called a second home. The place where all I had known had died and everything since had been one long, fucked up nightmare. I leaned back against the dresser, covering my face with my hands like that would hold in the depreciative laughter. Oh, how fucking *perfect* was this?

Fate really kept giving it to me good, sans lube.

I knew she wanted to save me this pain, somehow—to tell me to forget it, to tell me we'd find him somewhere else—but she couldn't. Maybe her freaky intuition was telling her the same thing mine was: this wasn't a lead we could ignore. I stared up at the ceiling, not caring how the overhead light seared itself into my gaze. Going blind would have been preferable to dealing with this. "Does this source actually know the Lynx? Are we absolutely sure, 100% sure, that this is for real?"

"I don't know. They don't name names when they tell me things, but Seana seemed to think the lead was solid. Maybe this guy is a friend of the Lynx, or maybe it's just another random acting on rumors…"

No. I felt it in my gut. This was where he would be. This was the one stone we had never thought to turn over. I took a deep, shaky breath. I had come too close to freedom from all this to back away now. I had to face it all—my past, my mistakes, my fears—if I was ever going to get past this. I pulled a t-shirt out and shrugged into it, over my cami. "Then we'll do what we've got to do. No other choice, right?"

"Cat…"

As I turned she collided with me; arms wrapped around my waist and her head buried in my chest. "I'm so sorry we made such a mess of your life. I'm sorry I've been such a twat. I just don't want you to go! No one else gets me. No one else even acts like I'm in the room. They all treat me like a kid or a freak and I don't want to go back to that. You're the closest thing I've ever had to a sister and I don't want to lose you!"

I hugged her back, hard. I shushed her with soothing sounds, my throat tightened in a vice grip. Hearing her weep, I felt like a part of me was breaking loose inside. An avalanche of emotion I was powerless to stop threatened to bury us both. I understood her pain on so many levels. That part of her that felt different and powerless; hadn't I still been that very same lost little girl on my 30th birthday? I even understood her looming fear of abandonment deep inside, in that place that had always longed for the close, loving family that biology hadn't given me. I wanted to break down and rail at the unfairness of it all—only, we didn't have time for such things now.

Goddamn, I wanted to hate how much I had come to love the little weirdo. I resented the shit-storm the fae had made of my life, but they had given me the frustratingly entertaining little sister I had always wanted. I pushed her back, gently, and smoothed her hair back from her face. It was a riot of neon pink, orange, and yellow this week. It made me smile. "I know you don't. I wish I didn't have to leave you either." Her red-rimmed, watery eyes broke my heart. "Look, I don't know where I'm going when this is all over—but it's not over yet. Let's just get through tonight and see what happens, okay?"

She scrubbed at her face and put on a stoic façade. She nodded. "Yeah, okay."

I pushed her toward the door. "Give me ten. I'll meet you at the car. Let's find this asshole."

~*~

Walking up to the door of Gilroy's was as fun as approaching the guillotine. I hadn't been there since the night of my birthday. That was so many months ago that it now felt like a lifetime. I felt guilty for having avoided the place for so long, like my sudden absence might have somehow offended the very stones of the walkway my feet trod upon. That sounded crazy but, hey, what in my life wasn't crazy?

I hesitated, my hand hovering above the doorknob. Mairi was two steps behind me, cloaked in the glamour that would make her invisible to the other patrons. It was a necessary evil given her baby face. Unfortunately, that made my job a bit harder. Sitting alone, murmuring to myself was bound to attract some attention—especially if Jenni was working the bar tonight. I didn't know how I was going to do this without some sort of scene occurring. Hell, I was fully expecting this evening to unravel into an all-out, character damaging debacle.

Saying a quick prayer to whatever higher power might be listening, I whispered, "Show time."

Mairi took my hand and squeezed it briefly. "Right behind you."

That was small comfort for a gal who did her level best to avoid sticky situations like the one I was about to dive in to, but I'd take it. I opened the door wide and hoped she would be able to squeeze through behind me without too much fuss. As soon as I was two steps into the room, Rodrigo turned and looked at me, doing a double-take before a wide grin split his face. "Caitlin!" He stood up and engulfed me in a bear hug that lifted my feet clear off the ground. "Holy shit, it's been forever! Where you been?"

"Can't breathe, 'Rigo," I wheezed. His love was about to crush my newly healed ribcage.

"Sorry." He chuckled as he put me back down. He held my arm until I was steady on my feet. One of his huge hands squeezed my shoulder. His joy at seeing me was so genuine it made me feel all that much more a heel. "It's been months, girl. I was beginning to think we'd never see you again."

My eyes were already scanning the place in a frantically covert manner. Mairi had made it in. She picked her way through the room to an out of the way table that would still give us a good view without too many eavesdropping ears nearby. "Uh, yeah, I know. Sorry. I've been having a rough time lately."

His face fell. His hands clenched into angry fists. "Jen told me about what happened that night, on your birthday. I wish I had known. I coulda done something about that creep. I would have pounded that motherfucker into the ground for laying a hand on you."

His rage touched me. Sometimes I forgot I had friends in places I never thought to look. I smiled and patted his arm. "I know you would have, thank you. But, if it's all the same, I'd rather not talk about that right now. I'm just trying to work through it and get back to a normal life. Make amends for how shitty I've been lately and all that." The lies tumbled out, so natural that I hated myself for them. I forced myself to brighten, adopting a more cheerful smile as I asked, "Is Jen working tonight?"

He cocked his head to the side, one eyebrow skewed upward. "Nah, she's off the rest of the week. Tony came home on Tuesday. Didn't you know?"

I didn't, of course, but I couldn't let him know that. If Jenni hadn't broadcasted our parting of ways, I didn't want to be the one to break the news. I was filled with equal parts relief and devastation: glad that I wouldn't have to face her tonight, but oh-so-sad that I had had no idea her beau had finally returned home. In the old days, we would have planned a huge, overly complicated homecoming party and gotten rip-roaring drunk together to celebrate such a momentous occasion. Now, thanks to my own actions, I hadn't even gotten a cursory text. I wondered if my hunch had been right and if he had proposed yet. If he had, and she still hadn't reached out to me...

I fought to keep the smile on my face and waved it off like it was no big deal. "Oh, yeah. I thought she had said something about picking up a shift tonight. I guess I'll just have a drink and, you know, exorcise a couple demons or something. Gotta get back in the saddle."

Concern was clear upon the big man's face, making me feel like the most miserable shit to ever be shat upon the earth. "Yeah, okay. But, hey, if you want to talk it out or somethin' I could get Neil to watch the door. We could have a beer or two."

"That's okay. I'm probably not very good company right now anyhow. Maybe next time?" His sympathy was striking right through to the heart of me. My lower lip wanted to tremble and I was having a hard time keeping that traitorous fucker in check.

He grinned. "Okay. I'm holding you to that."

I threw my arms around him in a quick hug to hide the devastation on my face. "You're the best, 'Rigo. Thanks."

As we parted, he said, "It's good to see you back. We missed you."

I quickly wiped away the tear that had the audacity to make its way down my cheek and hurried back to the table Mairi had picked. I slid into the seat and gripped the edge of the table like it would keep me from sliding under the choppy waves of my emotions. I managed to act normal when the waitress stopped by to take my order. Thank god she was new and there were no uncomfortable questions or pleasantries to deal with.

When she walked away, my spine went limp and I slumped back into the seat. I raked my hair back with one hand. "Holy shit, this was a bad idea. A baaaaaaad idea."

Mairi squeezed my hand. "I'm sorry. I know this is hard."

"Hard doesn't even begin to describe it." I hadn't spared a single thought on Gilroy's or the friends I had made here over the years since the night Argoth had brought reality crashing down around me. That night, I had labeled the place as the "bad spot" in my memory banks and locked it away. All the happy memories had gone with it, buried deep in an attempt to forget my fear. Coming back now just made me realize how far I had strayed from the path of my old, everyday life. I was filled with conflicted emotions and just wanted to run away before they overwhelmed me.

I murmured my thanks when the waitress put my glass of Riesling down on the table in front of me. A big gulp went a long way toward settling my frazzled nerves. A few deep, meditative breaths brought me back from the edge. At least I no longer felt the overwhelming need to run, screaming, from the room. I tried to speak as low and slow as possible, moving my lips minimally behind my glass. "Let's get this done fast. Table closest to the door. Two college meatheads, both hopelessly flirting with the waitress?"

"Yup; check. The one in the Devil's jersey isn't so meathead-y though."

I stole a glance over at her from the corner of my eye. She was eying the male specimen in question with a particularly fond gaze. I smirked. This pretending to be alone thing was going to be tricky enough. I didn't need her sass making me laugh. "Cool your jets, kid. We're working tonight. Pick him up after we've cased the joint."

"Fine, fine. Proceed."

I went on to the next table. And so on, and so on. My heart sunk and my nerves ratcheted up with every one of her confirmations. This wasn't one of those leisurely café trips or a stroll through some mom and pop bookstore, where we could meander and chat. Sitting alone, for all anyone else knew, made me feel vulnerable. Not to mention I also felt more asinine with every passing moment, muttering behind my glass and hoping no one would report my odd behavior back to Jenni. I wanted so badly for us to find him. I wanted to know all the anxiety I was putting myself through being back here was for something. Instead I danced the old familiar two-step with futility.

Gutted and pretty much beyond hope, I flashed a quick glance over my shoulder. There was a smattering of tables set deeper in the corner, almost out of sight of the door. I hoped my look could be taken as casually looking around for the waitress, instead of the jerky, desperate thing it was. I had all the grace of a horny teenager trying to put his arms across the back of a date's seat at the movies. Thankfully, only two of the tables were occupied and my sad attempt at nonchalance was only greeted with one annoyed stare. The sad farce was coming to an end. Another sad, dead end.

"Two tables back. Two young professional types, likely on a date and now thinking I'm some sort of gawking homophobe creeper given the look the dark haired one just gave me."

Mairi smothered her giggle. "Yeah, he doesn't seem the biggest fan of you right now."

"It was just one little glance." I sighed. "Whatever. Last one then: table in the far back corner. Middle-aged loner reading Steinbeck, nursing a Guinness."

I gazed into my nearly empty glass, waiting for the final, crushing blow of disappointment. It took a moment for me to register that she hadn't responded. In fact, when my head snapped up, I found her eyes darting back and forth between my face and some unknown point behind me, so wide they had stretched to anime proportions. Her jaw was moving up and down but only a small, strangled sort of mewling whimper emerged.

I damn near shit my pants.

My heart, formerly lodged in the vicinity of my stomach, seemed to remember its job and began hammering in my chest. A chill ran through my body; hot first, then cold. The hair on my arms stood on end. I felt dizzy and sick and bounce-up-and-down excited all at the same time. I leaned forward toward her, when what I really wanted to do was whip back around to get a better look. I gripped the edge of the table and tried my damnedest to keep my face from showing my manic excitement as I hissed, "Are you *serious*? Is that him?"

"I don't know!" she squeaked. She fumbled around in her cavernous purse for, what I assumed, was her phone. "I can't tell you what he looks like if can't see him. But if I can't see him that says something!"

"Are you serious?" I repeated, my voice raising an octave. It seemed too good to be true. Too weird to be true. I had hoped to hear those words for so long that they now sounded fake coming out of her mouth. Some insistent little part of my brain wanted to make extra sure that it wasn't being screwed with, however dumb it made me sound. "There's really no one there?"

She fixed me with an incredulous look beyond her years. One of those "stop being intentionally dense, you sound like a moron" looks. "Would I lie about this?" She already had the phone to her ear.

I struggled against the urge to fling my arm out and point, like that would somehow help. "Wait! His beer is right there on the table. Right there, along the far side. Can't you see that?"

"No, I can't see that either! I don't how he's doing it, but he must have the whole table cloaked—sort of. I mean, not the table itself obviously, but himself and everything on it. Shit, that's scary powerful." Her attention went to the phone at her ear. "Seana, get Kaine! I think we found him!"

While she coordinated whatever the hell it was we were supposed to do next, I tried to calm down. That was hard, given how fast my heart was beating. If I didn't get a grip on my roller-coaster emotions, someone might have me carted off to Arkham for talking to people only I could see. It probably would have been helpful if we had planned out Phase II of the Catch the Lynx plan prior, rather than scrambling to do so in the heat of the moment.

Taking more of those slow, drawn out breaths to keep myself from bursting, I tried to relax back into what I hoped was a perfectly normal, bored pose. My wine was almost gone, so I picked up my glass and knocked back the rest. That gave me the perfect reason to risk Mr. Dark Professional's wrath by casually scanning the room for the waitress, ending my perusal with a penetrating glance at the table in the shadows.

I couldn't look long without drawing attention to myself, but I thought—just maybe—there was indeed a resemblance to the man in the old photo. His hair was shorter now, with some grey mixed in among the brown, but the shape of his face was similar. He had traded in his sunglasses for wire-framed reading glasses and his clothing was updated to the nondescript norm of the everyday man. A dark blue button-down shirt, perhaps paired with some khakis and loafers. A black satchel rested casually over the back of the vacant chair to his left, some papers peaking over its open edge.

For all intents, he was just some regular old Joe relaxing with a beer after a day at the office. Nothing special, nothing fancy—nothing memorable. Just the kind of get-up someone who didn't want to be noticed might adopt.

"Dammit. Kaine and Gannon left twenty minutes ago," Mairi said, pulling my attention back to her. "Seana is going to get in touch with them now, but she thinks they were headed into the city. I don't know how fast they'll be able to get here."

"So, what? We just sit and wait?" I hoped my exclamation hadn't come out loud enough for any of the nearby tables to hear. It was getting really hard to keep up my sitting alone act, when I was ready to bust out of my own skin. If she meant "city" like I usually meant "city", meaning New York City, who knew how long it would take them to get back. Traffic was always abysmal around these parts and even worse there. Those five or six miles could take almost an hour some nights, and the Lynx was right there! So close I could call out his name and get his attention—and instead we had to wait? That was downright stupid.

She looked as peeved as I felt. "She said to wait. We need to keep an eye on him and hope like hell he doesn't move."

I wanted to scream. All that work, all that wasted time, and now that we had finally found him, we were told to hurry up and wait for the big boys to come in and call the shots. The thought made my blood boil. His beer was more than half empty. It went without saying that if he left, we were screwed. She couldn't see him to track him and I wasn't sure I could maintain enough secrecy to follow a stranger through the city, even if he didn't have any other wily fae tricks up his sleeve to avoid just such attention. Sure, we could continue to camp out at Gilroy's and hope to stumble across him another time but that was the very last thing on earth I wanted to do. This night seemed fated to be the single best time to stumble upon him. Another attempt would likely draw unwanted attention and result in some sort of debacle.

"Like hell I'm sitting here with my thumb up my ass." I set my glass back down on the table with incredible restraint. She blanched at the look on my face. There must have been straight up evil coming out of my eyes. I pushed my chair back and stood up; deaf to her sputtered warnings. Nothing was stopping me. It was time for me and the Lynx to have a little chat.

I pulled out a chair at his table and sat down, facing the Lynx with the Handsome Professional Couple at my back. I set my phone down in front of me. Hopefully I could keep this from looking like I was having a conversation with an empty chair in a dark corner. If all else failed, I could always try and make it look like I was on the phone. Still, expediency would be my friend in this endeavor. The faster I got this over with, the less insane I ran the risk of looking.

Only problem was, the Lynx hadn't so much as looked up at me. One would think, that when a strange woman invited herself on over, you'd naturally look up—to give her a questioning glance of "what the hell do you think you're doing," at the very least. It disoriented me for a moment, to find myself being ignored. I was running high on adrenaline, so pumped to have finally, at long last, found this son of a bitch that I could hardly contain myself—and here he was, flat-out *ignoring* me?

I was about to lose my shit and, in all likelihood, blow any attempt I had at keeping this on the DL when it dawned on me that he had no clue that I could see him. For all he knew, I thought this table was vacant. Hopping to a different seat might be a bit odd but it wasn't out of the realm of possibility that I had switched seats for privacy. He had no reason to suspect that I knew he was sitting there, a few feet away from me.

Well, wasn't I about to rock his pretty little world?

"So, do you normally just ignore pretty ladies when they come take a seat at your table?" I asked, sugar-coating my sarcasm so heavily that it damn near dripped onto the floor in a sticky puddle. *That* got me a response. His head snapped up, eyes wide behind his glasses. The shock of our gazes meeting drove them wider still. His mouth opened a bit and then closed, as if he was stopping himself from saying something that might give away his presence. I leaned forward and smiled. "Let me save you some trouble. I'm Caitlin, you're called the Lynx, and yes, I can see you."

"Impossible." Even hushed, his voice was deeper than I had expected. It rolled over me, a low baritone that spoke of years I could only begin to fathom.

"Not for me."

He cocked his head slightly to the side, brow furrowed, and stared at me as if I were a hard math problem. I let the gears turn. Every second he remained in that seat was a win for the home team. Not that I particularly enjoyed being examined like some exotic new species on exhibit at the zoo. I had just begun to squirm when he finished his evaluation. He closed his book with care and set it down on the table. He sat back, folding his hands together over one knee. "This is quite a surprise. I was unaware there were any Warders in Riverview."

"It was a doozy of a revelation to me too." I scooched my chair just a bit closer and made sure my face was angled away from the view of anyone around us. "Look, I don't mean to be rude but this is as awkward of a situation as I've ever been in, and time might be of the essence here."

He tensed, a shadow crossing his face. I knew that look. That was the "about to make a break for the door to avoid the crazy chick" look I had seen on many human faces in this bar over the years. This was my first time *being* the crazy chick, thankfully, but I still needed to stall him. The words tumbled out in a rush, "Please; don't go. I've been looking high and low for you all over this damn city for months now. I know this is really, *really* odd, but I need you to hear me out."

He didn't relax but he also didn't bolt from his seat. I took that as an indication to continue only, in that moment, I realized I had no idea what to say. We really should have worked on Part II of the plan more. Oh well. In for a penny... "Some friends of mine need your help. They found me a few months ago and told me I'm the only one they've ever found with this Gift and that means I'm pretty much their only chance of finding you, too."

He nodded in time with my words, almost as if he was agreeing with me. "They are probably right. The Warding is so rare nowadays that many believe it has since died out entirely. I myself have traveled far in this world and even then have encountered very few with your Gift—the last, many years ago."

Oh man, that was tempting. I fought back a dozen questions and stuck to the task at hand, wondering all the while how far away Kaine and Gannon were, and what sort of hell might break loose once they arrived. Crap. Suddenly the images played out in my head like an old black and white movie: the boys bursting into the bar, the Lynx spooking like a feral dog, and me losing my one and only chance to get free of this mess. I didn't know this dude from a stranger on the street, but something told me that a man who went to such lengths to hide from prying eyes would not be pleased if he found himself starring down four-on-one odds.

So, screw it. I wasn't good at this fae politicking bullshit anyhow and I didn't know how much time I had before this all went pear-shaped on me. I dropped all pretenses and laid it out for him. "Believe me, I was just as shocked to find out I am what I am as you were. I had no idea anyone in my family could ever have been one of you, so there's a damn good chance you know more about what I am than I do. Hell, maybe I'll tell you that fun little tale over a beer some time, and you can tell me what you may or may not know about my fairy-banging ancestors. Right now, though, I don't have time for that."

"Fair enough." He chuckled. Was that a little glimmer of respect I saw there, lurking in those hazel peepers? He picked up his beer and took a long gulp of it. "I take it these 'friends' of yours warned you that I am not a man who likes to be found, hence my need for the glamour. While I am very impressed that you have managed to track me down, it does pose some...*inconvenience* for me."

Shit. That was not a point in my favor. I held up a hand in front of me, trying to keep it low to the table in an ultimately futile gesture of pleading. "I know, and I'm really sorry to invade your privacy like this. Truly, I am. I know that doesn't mean much, coming from someone who has you cornered in a bar, but please understand that I didn't have a choice. My life has gotten very interesting over the past few months, and by interesting, I mean bat crap crazy. I made a mistake. I agreed to help these people find you in return for their protection without realizing what a 'pact' meant."

That knowing nod again, complete with a long, low whistle. "Ahh. So, you really have found yourself in—forgive the phrase—quite the bind, haven't you?"

"Exactly." I let the pun slide. Let him rib me. It meant he hadn't shut me down or, worse, made a beeline for the door. "I know I don't have anyone to blame but myself. I was in trouble and I was scared, and I did something stupid. I should have listened when the one person who might have actually had my best interests at heart warned me against it, but what can I say? I was a stupid little human who thought she knew it all, and now I'm stuck.

"They've got me until I get you to them, and now that I've finally found you, I would really appreciate it if you could please meet with them. Maybe you can help them; maybe you can't. I hope you can, but if not; fine. I'll be free of my end of the pact, either way, and that's really all I'm asking for." I hoped I looked as desperate and pleading as I felt. I threw in an extra, "Please?" for good measure.

He sat statue still, one arm draped at an angle across the back of his chair. I could see that I had peaked his curiosity, if nothing else, but I wasn't sure how far that would get me. I was glad to see that he was no longer tensed to run, but I was not as thrilled to find myself being raked with that college-professor-ferreting-out-a-cheater gaze. It made my insides squirm. After a long minute, during which I thought I would die if he did not answer me, he said, "I can make no promises, Caitlin. To be honest, many think far too highly of a Secret Keeper's Gift. I am no miracle worker. I may not have the answers your friends are seeking."

That wasn't a no! My palms erupted like Vesuvius. "I completely understand that. They think you're the guy, that you know some magi mumbo-jumbo they need, but if not; cool. All I'm asking is that you meet with them. Please."

"I see." He had finished the last bit of his Guinness. He still seemed wary, but the pursing of his lips hinted at a teeming curiosity I hoped I could work to my advantage. "And these friends of yours, do they have names?"

Crap. Was I supposed to let those cats out of their respective bags? I didn't know if I would be stepping on toes here. After all, I just knew my gut said Kaine was someone important. I had no facts to go on. Giving his name could help or hurt me, but there was no way to be sure which until it was too late. Ah hell; I wasn't risking ruining this now, not when I'd come so far. Resolution aside, it was hard not to sound like a kid who had been caught sneaking out of bed past their bedtime. "Their leader is a man named Kaine. He is the one I struck the pact with."

A look of disbelief, shock, awe—I don't know, something surprised yet oh-so-much more—rippled across his face. It was gone in a blink but I was sure I had seen it. He wasn't meeting my gaze anymore. Instead, he opened his satchel and tucked his book inside. Was he reconsidering? Was he going to shove past me and run out into the streets? Would I—should I—chase him down if he did? My brain was about to melt from all the horrible possibilities. Just when I thought I was going to explode, he pulled a little notepad out. His face was unreadable. "And where shall I meet these friends of yours?"

It was all well and good that Kaine was on his way, but something told me quite strongly that Gilroy's was still not the place for this to go down. I didn't want to broadcast their address to a stranger either, even if that stranger could be the key to the end of my troubles and theirs. I scrambled for a third option. I stuttered for a moment until brilliance struck: I gave him the address to my apartment. It wasn't exactly home anymore, so what did I have to lose? It was as good a neutral place as any.

He jotted down the address and tucked the little pad back into his bag. "Very well. While this meeting was unexpected, Caitlin, I hate to see an innocent bound by the magic of my people. I make no promises that I can help them but I will be there, three hours hence, so that you may be released from your bond."

"Oh my god, thank y—" The words shriveled up on my tongue.

His seat was empty.

I twisted around and scanned the room, sputtering like a fool. He was gone. Just flat out gone. There was not one damn sign of him anywhere in sight. I sat there, mouth gaping; dumbstruck. Mairi was frantically waving to me, mouthing her concern, and all I could do was give her a stare of complete and total shock. My Gift was supposed to negate his and yet he had, somehow, managed to disappear from right in front of my face.

A chill ran down my spine.

Who the hell had I just invited home for dinner?

CHAPTER TWENTY-THREE

"What the hell did you think you were doing?" Kaine growled, for the seventh or eighth time. "We had him! We finally had him, and you might have ruined our *one* chance!"

I kept my head bowed, my eyes on where my clasped hands were tucked between my knees. I had never seen Kaine so angry before. Annoyed, perhaps, or exasperated by my sass, sure; but never full on, screaming, red-in-the-face mad. He paced back and forth between my coffee table and the spot where my TV once had been, fists clenched.

I sat on my couch, accepting his verbal abuse with uncharacteristic docility. Gannon lounged in the living room doorway where he could keep an eye on the front door, though I'm sure he was listening intently to everything going on behind him, and Mairi was folded up in my recliner, wide eyes darting back and forth between myself and her enraged master. No doubt they both expected me to flip shit any moment.

The trouble was, I couldn't really blame him for being so angry. My intentions had been good, but there was the distinct possibility that I might have fucked things up beyond repair, not only letting the Lynx disappear from my sight after long months of searching but also in giving him Kaine's name before he did so. In the ever perfect bitch of hindsight, I was questioning every move I had made and telling myself all the ways I could have handled it differently; handled it better. Of course, it had seemed like the best of bad options at the time, but...

Kaine and Gannon had nearly collided with me the moment I stepped out of Gilroy's. My having arranged a time and a place to meet with the Lynx in private wasn't the stroke of genius I had hoped it to be. They were far from pleased. Having had him in my grasp only to lose him was bad enough. Finding out that I had also shared their names with the Secret Keeper had sent Kaine off on a tirade that had lasted the entire car ride back to my apartment.

The conversation had consisted of little else while we were waiting for our guest to appear—or not. Three hours turned out to be an eternity when you had a very pissed off fae getting in your face. With each passing minute, the tension in the room thickened.

"One chance," Kaine repeated, smacking his palm with a balled fist. If he kept up that pacing, he was going to wear a track into my hardwood floor. "One chance, after all these years, and you blew it."

"I'm sorry," I said, not for the first time. I wanted to run from the room and lock myself in my bedroom, far from his accusatory stare, but that wasn't going to happen. I was pretty sure Gannon would stop me—and that would mean facing the wrecked remains of all I had once cherished as well. Someone had obviously come back and cleaned up the worst of the mess Argoth had left, but there was no filling the holes left by all that I had lost in the ransacking. That wasn't a disappointing reminder I had the stomach to handle, especially after the dressing down I had—and continued—to receive.

"Sorry doesn't fix this. You gave him my name. You've made it impossible for us to find him now. If he decides not to show up tonight all is lost!"

My head snapped up. "Hey, that isn't my fault! What was I supposed to do? Lie? He's obviously paranoid about being found. If I refused to tell him who was looking for him, do you think *that* would have made him stick around? No. He would have run then and there and maybe we'd be worse off! At least this way there's a chance he'll show." I shot him a scathing glare. "And how the hell was I supposed to know that he was going to disappear in the first place? You didn't tell me he could do that!"

Stony silence met my outcry. The horrible truth dawned on me. "You didn't know, did you? You had no idea he could do that." Suddenly, no one was meeting my eyes. Kaine stared out the windows, head high; jaw clenched. Mairi was white as a sheet, looking down at the hem of the shirt she was fraying between her fingers. Gannon kept his head turned so that his eyes were on the door. That cold certainty inside me grew. My voice was breathy with co-mingled rage and fear as I repeated, "You had no idea."

Kaine continued to stone-wall me. After a moment, without looking up, Mairi gave the minutest shake of her head. Acid roiled in the pit of my stomach. Fury, panic, confusion; I was one hell of a crucible for not-so-friendly emotions. I was on my feet thought I couldn't remember having stood. "So let me get this straight. All this time you've been sending me out after this guy and you didn't even know what he was capable of? You told me he was a Secret Keeper but you never once warned me he might have other Gifts! What if he had been crazy fast and or super strong, like him?" I thrust one arm out, pointing at Gannon. "He could have snapped my neck and left me dead on the bar room floor and I never would have seen it coming!"

"We can't know every little thing a fae can do," Kaine snapped.

"Oh yeah?" I sneered. "And here I thought you knew everything."

It was a battle of cold, hard wills between us. My guilt was overridden by anger. I wasn't going to back down. We were riding an ugly line and Kaine's furious scowl told me he knew that. Gannon spoke up from behind us, "The bloodlines have been intertwined for ages. Many fae manifest multiple gifts, inherited from their ancestors. It's impossible to know which have manifested until the subject is studied."

I seethed with indignation. I knew he was trying to diffuse the situation, but that did nothing to calm my outrage. They hadn't just used me. They had used me carelessly and I was furious. Through clenched teeth I asked, "And which bloodline, exactly, can teleport itself out of the room?"

Another round of silence gave me all the answer I needed. They had no freaking clue. Bile rose in my throat. I had been left in the dark, used, even betrayed—and, for what? That was the final straw. I had had enough. It was time for this to end.

I rounded the table and stood toe-to-toe with Kaine. I had to crane my head upward to look him in the face, given how much taller he was than me, but I faced him without fear. "You have no right to berate me for what I did. They might follow you without question—" I gestured to the others in the room, "—but I am done being one of your lackeys. *Done.* You kept things from me, important things, and endangered my goddamned life without a second thought. I did everything in my power to get you to the Lynx, just like you we agreed. You might not like how I handled this but that's tough. I found him and I made him agree to meet with you. I fulfilled my part of our bargain and this ends here. Agreed?"

Kaine glowered down at me, his face like chiseled marble. Who was I kidding? Statues of Greek gods had more expression than that. His furrowed brow cast his eyes in shadow. I didn't know what was going through his mind, but I had the feeling it was nothing good. Standing up to him was like facing down a feral dog. At any moment, he could choose to attack. A chill ran down my spine but I held my ground. I stood tall and repeated, "Agreed?"

He took an almost imperceptible step back, shaking his head. Something like disgust rippled across his face as he waved a dismissive hand in my direction. "Agreed."

A weight seemed to lift off of my shoulders, causing a wave of goosebumps to race over every inch of my skin. It was a small victory but a victory nonetheless. I was free of my bond. I had expected fireworks to mark the dissolution of the fae mojo that had been hanging over my head for so long, but instead all I got was that dizzying wave of relief. It was enough.

"My, my. It looks as if I am interrupting something rather important. Shall I come back later?"

I think we all spun around as one. The Lynx was leaning against the edge of my dining room table, hands shoved in the pockets of his khakis. He looked just the same as he had in the bar, which was a mild comfort. At least a different stranger hadn't randomly appeared in my apartment. My eyes darted over to the cable-box. Huh. It had been three hours on the dot. Couldn't fault the guy on his punctuality, at the very least.

"No," Kaine said, quickly. "You could not have arrived at a better time. We are grateful to you for coming."

"A beautiful young lady pleaded with me for help," the Lynx responded, ever so coy and just slightly mocking. He winked at me. My face quickly cycled through a dozen shades of red. "How could I ever refuse such an intriguing entreaty?"

Kaine the Sourpuss grunted and waved a hand in the direction of my empty couch. "Please, have a seat."

My temper soared to a fever pitch. Wasn't it nice of him, to offer up such glowing hospitality to a stranger in *my* home? Feeling like an ass for standing there between them when I was obviously no longer a part of the conversation, I took a seat on the arm of the recliner next to Mairi. She leaned in to me and butted her head up against my arm. I put that arm around her and let her settle in against my side. Maybe I wanted to gut Kaine with a spoon and smack Gannon into next Tuesday, but she wasn't on my shit-list. It was a minor comfort to know I still had one ally in the room.

Then again, the Lynx had agreed to this shindig for the sole reason of freeing my poor, stupid soul from the blood pact. That put him firmly on Team Caitlin too. He was still watching me with a smirk playing on his lips. He turned his attention back to Kaine, crossing one arm over his waist as he bowed deep. "As you wish, your royal highness."

Talk about a slap to the face.

I looked down at Mairi. She looked stricken. I demanded an answer with my eyes, to which she mouthed "I'm sorry" with a cringe. That clinched it. Months and months of unspoken hints fell into place. I was an idiot for not having put it together sooner. That aura of power, their unquestioning deference to him, his mysterious connections helping us out at every opportunity. Hell, even his all-consuming need to get home and rescue his people from the mad king. From his batshit crazy *brother*, the High King.

Son of a bitch.

The night we met—the night Kaine and Mairi had somehow scared off a huge, scary-ass troll with little more than a stern word—they had told me the tale of their woe. A homeland ruled by a unstable ruler who had even gone so far as to exile his younger brother for the horrible crime of being better loved by the people. And still, I had never put one and two together. Even when faced with the question of how important of a man would travel not only with a blood-bound Guardian, but his own personal Healer and an Oracle, I had remained blind. It had all been laid out in front of me from day one, but I had chosen to ignore it. Even Argoth's sudden disappearance on that fateful night made more sense now. Why would he have risked his head by striking down the King's little brother, exiled or no?

Goddamn, was I ever the fool.

The Lynx made himself comfortable on my couch. He stretched his arms out across it's back and crossed his legs, one foot swinging jauntily. He showed no fear, being outnumbered and in the presence of royal blood. Then again, considering that he had appeared in our midst without ever coming close to a door or window, I suppose he really didn't have much to fear from us in the first place.

"Caitlin said you were seeking my aid." Not one for preamble, that Lynx. "Please; tell me how can I be of service to you?"

For all his casual acceptance of the situation, there was an innate deference to his tone; a slightly stilted lilt I had come to expect from fae etiquette. For a moment I envied him his ability to appear so aloof yet so deferential at the same time. All these months running alongside them and I still had not managed to find that balance. Then again, given the formal parting of ways that had been struck only moments ago, I supposed that would hardly matter for much longer.

Kaine stood on the other side of the coffee table; spine straight, hands clasped behind his back. He looked confident. Or regal, one who had finally realized what had been staring her in the face all along might say. There was no trace of the angry, anxious mess he had been only minutes earlier. Then again, I guess a prince had to be used to being all stoic and shit, when addressing his lessers. "As you know, Tiernan has banished me from Tír na nÓg."

The Lynx inclined his head. "I had heard the rumor. It saddens me to see it is true. Almost as much as it saddened me to hear that the High King has become so—how shall I say it? Unstable?"

Kaine scowled. "The tales you hear are true. My brother is not well. He refuses the advice of his healers and advisors both. I had hoped to sway him, but as you can plainly see, even I was no longer able to get through to him."

"Madness often begets paranoia. Oft times, the one afflicted comes to see friends as foes."

"Aye, that may well be true, but it matters little now. He must be stopped. His rule has harmed our kingdom, and I fear that he will cause irrevocable damage if left unchecked much longer."

The Lynx sat forward, clasping his hands and balancing his elbows on his knees. "So you seek to depose him."

Kaine opened his mouth and closed it again. He resumed his pacing, hands still firmly clasped. We all waited in silence while the Crown Prince gathered his thoughts. Finally, he said, "It was never my wish to do so, no matter what Tiernan may think. I never held any desire to steal what was rightfully his, least of all the throne. But I fear it has come to that. He is unfit to rule and I am the only other left living with royal blood."

I sat still as stone, equal parts fascinated and appalled. So much time spent with them, and I had known none of this. I felt like I had learned more about Kaine in the past five minutes than I had in the six months preceding them. Then again I was only a human tool, to be used and discarded. What did I need to know of his fairy tale soap opera life?

The Lynx nodded. He looked thoughtful, in a distracted sort of way. "The situation certainly seems to warrant such a bold move. It may pain you to take a stand against your kin, but I think you will find few who will fault you, your royal highness. Tír na nÓg was a much brighter place in your mother's day. The people need justice. A justice only you may now provide."

"A justice I may only provide if I return home," Kaine said. He stopped in his tracks, fixing the Lynx with a hard stare. "Tiernan's power is absolute. His geis remains: I cannot cross the Veil. I have exhausted all efforts in trying to do so."

"Ahhh." A slow, knowing smile crept across the Lynx's face and, for just a second, I could see how he had earned his nickname in that Cheshire Cat-like grin. "So this then, is where you need my help."

Mairi was a ball of quivering energy beside me. I could feel her trembling. Gannon left the doorway, standing behind my loveseat; tense and gloomily serious. Even my nerves were jangling. This was the moment that we had all been waiting for, myself included. The million dollar question hung in the air, unspoken.

The Lynx was looking up at the ceiling, musing. "As you now know, there is little that can counteract the Word of the High King."

"You say little, not nothing." Gannon's hands were clenched on the back of the couch, his knuckles white.

"Indeed. The High King is as close to being omnipotent as any Aos Sí may be. Too close, some might say." I did not miss his dig, however subtle. He continued, "So long as your brother wears the Diadem of power he is nigh unstoppable. However, our ancestors would not have invested such incredible power in their sworn liege without ensuring that there was a fail-safe."

"Which you know of." It was not a question. An eager gleam lit Kaine's eyes from within. "You know of a way to break the Word."

The Lynx regarded them all in turn. After a long, lung-crushing moment, he said, "Yes. I know of a way you likely have not yet tried." He held up a hand to forestall any whoops of joy. There was a grave air about him. "But be warned—it is no simple task, nor one many would dare undertake. I cannot guarantee you success and it will not be without danger."

My heart bobbed like a buoy between elation and despair. Difficult often also meant lengthy. If this wasn't a quick fix, I could kiss my hopes of them getting home in time to stop Texas Pete goodbye. I knew I should be equally concerned for the fate of their realm and mine, filled with innocents on both fronts, but I was a little too preoccupied to spare much thought on that. The Lynx had made a very good point about madness breeding paranoia and I had held no illusions: the existence of a Warder would breed lots and lots of paranoia. My first concern was my own hide, however petty that was, and knowing it was not likely to be saved made me want to cry.

A look bounced around the room, shared by the three companions. It did not surprise me that no one raised dissent. They were willing to undertake any threat at this point—what choice did they have? Kaine nodded. "Understood. Any chance, however small, is one we must take."

"Fair enough. You must find the Claíomh Solais."

"The shining sword," Mairi whispered reverently.

Kaine didn't look nearly as impressed. "The Claíomh Solais has not been seen in many an age. It was lost to our ancestors long ago. Many believe it has been destroyed."

The Lynx smirked. "Many are wrong."

I looked over to Gannon. He knew weapons better than anyone I had ever met. Even he looked doubtful. A deep sigh welled up from the bottom of my soul. I guess I didn't find it surprising that this quest would be ongoing, or that it would require some kooky fae artifact straight out of Mythology 101. I had strongly hoped otherwise, but the truth of it all had always been staring me in the face: this wasn't an easy problem to fix.

Kaine said, "And this sword, it will break Tiernan's bond?"

"Yes and no. Possession of the sword alone will not allow you to break the geis, but it is the key. With it, you can challenge Tiernan's claim and petition one whose magic may override his Word."

An uneasy silence filled the room. The hairs on the back of my neck stood on end. A stronger magic than the all-powerful banishment of the High King? That did not sound good.

It was little Mairi who finally had the balls to ask the big question. "Who's magic is that?"

"The Morrigan."

A gasp rippled around the room. Even I tensed. The name rung distant bells in my memory banks, harkening back to my fluffy Wiccan days. Surely he couldn't mean the goddess from Irish folklore, could he? The scary tough-as-nails one of battles and crows and whatnot? The grim looks surrounding me made me believe he was. That sent a wave of the heebie-jeebies down my spine. Faeries and trolls were one thing. Gods were another entirely. Such a creature couldn't actually, physically exist... could she?

"You can't be serious," Gannon said. He looked angry enough to spit the aforementioned nails.

There was only a tiny bit of apology in the Lynx's words. "I'm afraid so."

Kaine had gone white. Straight up, sheet of paper, shaken to his core *white*. His arms hung at his sides, hands trembling. "Only a fool would dare summon Her. She long ago ceased to show any concern for her children."

"Perhaps. But She will answer the call of the sword."

"Madness," Gannon spat.

The Lynx spread his hands. "I can only tell you what I know. Did I not warn you it would be dangerous? She is the only being powerful enough to break the High King's geis. Like it or not, she may be your only hope for getting home."

"To fight one madness, we must condemn ourselves to another." Kaine's laugh was a cold, bitter thing. He scrubbed at his chin with one hand, gazing out the window. When he turned back around, he still looked shaken. "And do you know the whereabouts of the sword?"

"You are correct in saying that it was lost for many years. However, a few years back I crossed paths with one whose mind revealed to me that the Claíomh Solais had been unearthed once again. Humans have long held it, never knowing its importance. To them it is merely a relic of a bygone era—but to those of us who know the truth, it is so much more. I myself tracked the sword for some time. Our history's effects on this world are something of an interest of mine.

"Unfortunately, I never came in contact with it. The trail went cold and other matters took precedence, but before it I gave up I was able to trace it here to a private collector in New York City. I can point you in his direction, if you like. From there, I'm afraid you'll be on your own."

"Then that is where we will start looking," Kaine said, mollified. It was far from the happy ending we had all hoped for, but it was something. It was likely the best chance they were going to get.

The Lynx stood. He pulled that familiar little notebook from his back pocket and wrote down an address. He tore the page from it and held it out. "I'm sorry I don't know more. Truly."

With a jerk of his head, Kaine had Gannon step forward and take the paper. He held out his hand in the Lynx's direction, face solemn. "Do not be. The information you have given us may yet save our realm. You have done all that you can and, for that, you have my thanks."

Surprise was writ upon the Lynx's face as he clasped Kaine's forearm and shook. Something told me such familiarity was rarely wasted on the lower class. He said, "Good luck, your royal highness."

"Thank you. I fear we will need it." He and Gannon retreated to the far corner of my dining room, shutting us out of their private huddle.

Dismissed, the Lynx turned his attention to me. He settled himself on the edge of my coffee table, putting us fairly level. He regarded me with a look of wry affection. "You are a resourceful woman, Ms. Caitlin. You succeeded where I am sure many have failed."

For all the good it had done me. That was hardly his fault by any stretch of the imagination, so I strove for some small burst of decorum. "Thanks. If it's any consolation, you certainly made me work for it."

"Indeed. All the same, I must ask a boon of you."

"I've had shit luck in making promises with your kind," I told him, giving him my best don't-mess-with-me stare. "Forgive me if I insist on hearing the fine print before agreeing to anything."

"I would expect no less. Your Gift is quite possibly the rarest there is. This poses a unique danger, both to you and to myself. Many would seek to do you harm, to quell or possess your Gift—a fate I well understand. I too have many enemies and quite a few of them who would love to be able to find me, as you have. I ask for your word that you will never use your Gift to locate me at the behest of another again. In turn, I will keep your secret safe and never breathe word of your name to another soul."

I didn't think he would betray me, with or without my promise. He just didn't seem the type to sell me to the highest bidder. Still, it never hurt to have your tracks covered. I nodded, "Deal. I will not lead another to you, ever again—so long as you keep my identity a secret."

We shook hands, as Kaine and I once had. There was no exchange of blood this time and I wondered, briefly, if this pact was as binding as the one Kaine and I had struck. It didn't matter, really. I had every intention of keeping my promise. My honeymoon with the fae was over. Knowing that there was at least one person out there watching my back, even in the vaguest way, was a comforting thought.

When we broke apart, he smiled at me fondly. "You are an extraordinary lady. There are not many who would have adapted to this so well, so late in life. The Warding is a hard Gift to bear, and the danger you will face will be no easier. I wish you the best, in all that you do." Sadness overtook his smile. He reached out, his hand hovering in the air next to my cheek for a moment before it fell back to his side. "You have her way about you. She would be proud to see such strength in you."

I raised an eyebrow. "Who would be proud?"

"Your mother."

He grinned and then he was gone.

My jaw worked soundlessly, my wide eyes staring at the blank space he had occupied only heartbeats ago. My mother? He couldn't have been talking about Sarah Moore, the woman who had birthed and raised me. No one had ever compared me to my mother. We were polar opposites in just about every way, from looks to personality and then some.

I wracked my spinning mind but could not think of a single plausible instance where she could have crossed paths with such a man. Never mind that she was the most mundane woman on the planet; there was no way in hell she knew anything of the fae or had any idea of what I was going through with them. But if he hadn't meant her, then who?

Well. Didn't that just throw me for a fucking loop?

CHAPTER TWENTY-FOUR

My mother.

Those two words kept ringing in my head.

I sat on my bed, which was still stripped bare to the torn mattress, and stared off into space. An open duffle bag sat at the foot of the bed, with Mairi stretched out beside it. She was also staring off into space, though she kept her hands busy at unknotting one of my necklaces. I didn't think she was tearing herself up internally as I was, but I was glad for her company. It made the emptiness of the room feel a little less oppressive. I had been right about how depressing it would be, to sit here and look at all the stuff in my life that was now missing. Having some company, even the silent kind, made it hurt a little less.

We had left Kaine and Gannon to their private powwow in my living room. They had ignored us from the moment the Lynx had handed over the lead anyway. I guess I shouldn't have been surprised by that. They had never included either of us in any of their planning before. Since I had pushed Kaine to absolve me of any further involvement in his quest to return home, why would they bother to include me now? It had been easier to let them be, and run off to wallow in my own confused thoughts.

I had intended to pack up some more of my stuff when I had first stormed off. It made sense to get it over with and figure out if there was anything else worth taking. Then, I could be done with it and make the final break from this life. Once I was smack dab in the middle of it, however, it all suddenly seemed so much less important. What did it matter if I took more clothes or another pair of shoes with me? How would any material possession help me figure out the next step in my broken life?

I threw the shirt I was holding into the bag with a frustrated snarl. Try as I might, I just couldn't make myself stop thinking about what the Lynx had said. Those words rattled around in my head like a ping pong ball. I kept thinking back to the night I had met Kaine and the gang; the night someone had first questioned my parentage. I had thought them crazy at the time. Who wouldn't have? Only, now, I couldn't so casually dismiss it as being a ridiculous notion. There were too many questions I couldn't answer and, to be frank, I wasn't sure I wanted to answer them anymore. The specter of "what if?" loomed over my shoulder.

Mairi was the voice of reason. "He could have been lying, you know."

"And monkeys might fly out my butt." Oh, how I wanted to believe that. So much of my internal strife would be quelled if I believed that. Only... I didn't. I couldn't. I drew my knees up to my chest, resting my chin atop them. I was probably pouting, but I didn't care. I said it aloud, to make it real. "You don't believe that and neither do I."

She put the chain, kink free once more, atop the clothes in the bag. Her sad eyes only made me feel worse, so I focused on my feet. I heard her sigh. "Yeah; okay. I guess you're right. I figured it was worth a shot though. I'm fresh out of ideas to cheer you up with."

I shot her a grateful smile. "Thanks. Unfortunately, lying to myself hasn't gotten me very far. Might be better to just nut up and accept this curve-ball."

The Lynx had no reason to lie and we both knew it. I had already agreed to his terms; we had agreed to cover one another's asses and make sure no one used one of us to find the other. Why on earth would he lie to me? He knew something. It sounded like he knew or had known this woman, who he somehow thought was my mother. I had been too dumbstruck in the moment to find out more, and now it was too late. I didn't think I'd have much luck finding him again, even if I tried. Something told me he wouldn't be sticking around Riverview much longer, and I highly doubted he would ever cross Gilroy's doorstep again, just in case.

Maybe I was better off just letting it go, however hard that was. I mean, what choice did I have? My throat was tight as I zipped the duffle bag shut. There was no point in prolonging the agony any further. When I looked up at Mairi, my heart broke. Her cheeks and nose were red behind her tears, her bottom lip quivering. She threw herself across the bed at me and clung to me like it was the last time we would ever see one another.

It probably was, so I could hardly fault her.

Hot tears streamed down my own cheeks as I hugged her, my words interrupted by the occasional wet sniffle. "I'll keep in touch. As soon as I find a place to settle down, I'll find a way to let you know. I promise."

"I'll miss you so much." Her voice was a whisper.

It made me cry that much harder.

After a moment, she finally pulled away. She turned away from me, scrubbing at her face, and I knew there was nothing more to be said. Neither of us had any words to make this any easier. I grabbed my bag and tossed it over one shoulder. I paused once, in the hall, and looked back over my shoulder toward the dim light of my living room. I knew I should thank them and part ways on better terms—but I couldn't. I just couldn't face them and let them see me losing my shit, even to say goodbye.

I hurried out the front door and let it slam shut behind me. Even that sound cut straight through me. It was the goodbye to everything I had ever known.

Outside, the chilly evening air slapped me across the face. It was just what I needed to keep the shaking at bay. I took a deep breath and choked back a sob. I was nearly at my car when the stairwell door banged open behind me. Gannon called out, "So this is it then? You're just going to run away?"

I couldn't turn around; couldn't let him see the tears glimmering in my eyes. I popped the trunk and tossed my bag inside. "Yup, pretty much."

"Come on, Caitlin. This is stupid..."

My laughter was harsh and ugly. I hated how hearing my name fall from his lips shot a shiver up my spine. I snarled and slammed the trunk of my poor little Camry closed as hard as I could. "Well that's me, isn't it? The stupid, silly little human, running away and trying to save herself before the High King squashes her like a bug."

"I didn't mean it like that," he said, sounding exasperated.

"I really don't care how you meant it." I was being petty; whiny—but, who the fuck cared? Not me. "This is the one chance I have to get ahead of whatever that bastard sends after me and I'm taking it. Not like I have much to stay for anyhow. A shitty job? A family that hates me? A best friend that won't even speak to me anymore? Oh well. I'm sure I'll survive."

"You're being overly dramatic," he said, scowling. "Come back inside. Let's talk about this, before you make a rash decision."

"Oh yeah? Is that an order from your *prince*?" He looked away; his shame clear. I had to spit the words through clenched teeth. "You knew all along and not a single one of you told me—warned me!—who I was dealing with!"

He gave me one of those perturbed looks that made me feel like a petulant child. "All the signs were there. You should have figured it out."

That only made my face burn hotter. "Yeah, well I didn't, did I? I was in deep over my head from day one and no one thought to tell me. But I guess that's my own fault, because I was too *stupid* to figure it out."

He heaved a sigh. "I never said—"

I cut him off with a decisive wave of my hand. "You didn't need to. You've made your feelings about me pretty clear."

"Oh, have I?" The words were a sneer; a taunt. The little half smile that accompanied them made me want to punch him.

"Yes, you have; thanks. You've made it very clear, from day one, that you thought I was a fool for trying to live in this fucked up world of yours. And you know what? You were right. All it's done is fuck up my life. I haven't been able to walk down the street without jumping at every shadow for months. That was bad enough. Now the King is going to find out who and where I am. I'll never be safe as long as I stay here. It's too much, Gannon. I can't live with that kind of fear hanging over me. I have to go."

I tried to breeze past him, hopped up on righteous anger, but he grabbed my arm and forced me back around. I could see the concern in his piercing gaze as he searched my face and I hated him for it. It made me weak. I looked away; up at the dark sky and the blurry pinpricks of light I could make out beyond the ambient glow of the city lights. I couldn't afford to be weak. I couldn't let my resolve waver. I yanked my arm free of his grip and stood there awkwardly, still feeling the heat of his hand on my skin; like it had been a brand burned in to me.

His voice was lower, gentler. "I know you're angry. I get it. I'm not trying to say you don't have every right be pissed off, but we didn't have any other choice. We couldn't tell you who Kaine was. He's in hiding and we were protecting him because that's our job. It was nothing personal."

"It certainly feels personal," I grumbled, flashing between being angry and feeling stupid for being so angry. I hated it when he used logic on me.

"I assure you, it isn't." He fidgeted and rubbed at the back of his neck, clearly as uncomfortable as I was. Heart-to-heart chats weren't what we did. Neither of us knew where to go from them. Finally, he said, "Stop and think about what you're about to do. Out there you're going to be all alone. Who will you have to watch your back? Come back inside. Let's all sit down and talk about this. Running away isn't going to fix this. Let's figure this out."

Nu-uh. No way. Those were the opposite of the magic words. I had spent too many nights planning my escape; plotting my way into a newer, less scary life. I couldn't let this show of compassion undo me—and I was perilously close to letting it do just that. I held up my hands, key rattling as I took two steps back, warding him off. "No. I can't. I'm done, Gannon. *Done*. The pact is fulfilled and I'm finally free. I have to go now, while I still can; before they find me."

He ran a hand back through his hair, pulling it up at odd, spiky angles. "You don't need to run. We can help you; protect you, I promise—"

"Yeah?" A spike of rage ran through me. My laugh was an ugly bark; disappointment tainted by bitterness. "Like when you promised to find Texas Pete?"

Silence. He wouldn't meet my eyes.

My jaw clenched so hard my teeth hurt. I nodded to no one in particular. "That's what I thought." I turned and unlocked the door, throwing it wide.

"Caitlin." I froze, one foot in; hand still gripping the doorframe. My heart was thumping in my throat. He hadn't moved but his voice seemed to whisper in my ear. "Don't go. We still need you."

Inside, I wavered. I damn near *vibrated* with the need to turn around, to throw myself at him and beg to be held; to be told that this all could be fixed and that I could still be safe here. But it couldn't and I wasn't. So, I didn't. I didn't even turn around. "And when I needed you, you failed me."

I slid into the car and pulled the door shut behind me. When I turned onto the street, he remained standing where he was; a sentinel half lost in shadow, watching me disappear into the night. I made it to the highway by memory alone, so blinded by tears that everything was just about one big blur. Gannon's plea rang in my ears the whole way.

I was more lost than ever, and I was about to go off alone into the unknown. To be honest, I was scared shitless. Why wasn't I feeling elated; triumphant? I had done the impossible. I had found the Lynx; the invisible man. I had kept my end of the blood pact and had gotten away scot-free, severing all my ties from a fae Prince with my soul intact (except for maybe that shadowy corner that had realized it liked hunting down the monsters). I should have been jumping for joy. I should have felt proud, at the very least.

Only, I wasn't.

There were no streamers and confetti; no sense of accomplishment for having done something so incredible. Everything felt wrong. Instead of whooping with delight, I was breaking apart inside; trying to hold it all together when all I really wanted was to bawl like a baby. My life was a joke; a waste—a terrible cycle of fucking things up and having to choose the best next step from a batch of very bad options.

Finding the Lynx wasn't the grand achievement I had thought it would be. It hadn't solved any of my problems or theirs. Texas Pete was still beyond my reach and Kaine & Co. were still trapped in my world. Nothing had changed. What was running away really going to solve? I rallied against my fate; against the way *nothing* in my life ever worked out the way I intended.

The Lynx's face floated into my mind. That sad, sympathetic look on his face as he had almost caressed my cheek was going to haunt me for the rest of my freaking life. Why had I questioned him? Why couldn't I have just left things nice and vague and easily ignored? As it was, something about that admission just resonated too damn deeply inside me to disregard. I had never felt like I belonged in my family. I had never felt like my mother loved me as freely or deeply as she loved my sister. I had long ago blamed it away on our personalities being so poorly matched—but what if it was something more?

What if that lost, disconnected feeling I had had all my life was real? What if I was so much more than a girl who had inherited some ancestral power? Those "what ifs" were going to be the death of me.

...or would they? A chill coursed through me and I sat up straighter. I wiped the tears off my cheeks and the snot from under my nose. Maybe I just wasn't focusing on the right "what if."

Six months ago, I had wished on my birthday cupcake, hoping to figure out who I really was. What if the Lynx had just given me the first solid clue to the answer my soul was seeking? Maybe it wasn't what I had been hoping for, and maybe it had just made my life a hell of a lot more complicated, but, maybe that was just what I needed too. Hadn't I already proved that I fared the best in the face of adversity?

I hadn't gotten a handle on the big picture things I had once thought were so damn important, but maybe I had been wrong in assuming they were so important all along. Instead, I had found that I was much braver, much stronger, and so much more adaptable than I had ever thought I even had the capacity to be.

Maybe finding the Lynx hadn't brought about the ticker tape parade of victory that I had thought it would—but hunting did. Protecting people, saving innocents, stopping the bad guys? It went against everything I had ever thought was right or that I knew about myself, but I loved it. I lived for it. It brought a peace to my soul unlike anything I had ever felt had before. It wasn't the answer I had expected to find, but wasn't all that still something to be proud of?

The realization blazed through me like an electric shock. I *was* proud of myself, inner demons and all. I hadn't figured it all out, but at least I knew I was capable of so much more than the "me" on the night of my birthday had ever thought she could be. I wasn't the useless, broken little girl hiding inside the woman anymore. I was scared, but who wouldn't be? I wasn't sure what awaited me in the future—but who was? I didn't have all the answers but no one did. One thing was for damn sure: I was never going to find any more answers by sitting there; trapped by fear, feeling sorry for myself. That defining moment where I could stand up tall and fight or let myself shrivel with fear had come—and I hadn't let fear hold me down.

My grip on the steering wheel tightened. I was making my move. Maybe I wasn't sure who I was just yet—at least, not completely—and yeah, I still had a lot of questions to answer and a long road ahead to walk to find them, but I sure as hell wasn't going to stop until I found out.

CHAPTER TWENTY-FIVE

June

Gannon was right, of course. Smug bastard always was.

A life on the run was no picnic. Making a break from my past might have started off in exhilaration, but the luster quickly faded. Running was tiring, lonely, and crazy expensive.

I got as far as Ohio before the endless days of equally endless highways jaded my already weary soul. I spent a few penny-pinching nights spent sleeping in my car, spacing out my pricey motel stays, but in the end, it wasn't enough. My dwindling bankroll was being consumed by my belly and ever-hungry gas tank at an alarming rate. So, I stopped and settled in to what I figured was likely my first stop in a long series of get-up-and-go's.

I wasn't exactly enamored with my new life but it was good enough for the moment. I had found a cheap motel that rented by the week and had gotten a job waiting tables at a quaint but run down greasy spoon just off the interstate. It was something straight out of a 1970's stereotype; all white and red checkered linoleum and matching, cracked pleather seat cushions.

It was owned and run by a craggy faced woman named Maureen, an aged Southern belle with suspicious eyes and a two pack a day habit; the kind of woman who had seen some things and heard it all. I had no doubt she kept a loaded shotgun in that cluttered little closet she called an office. I don't think she trusted my flippant story of a wanderlust-lead life one bit but she asked blessedly few questions. I was pretty sure she thought I was on the run from an abusive ex and didn't dissuade her from that assumption. That was a lot easier to swallow than the truth.

The routine of my new life was pretty boring, compared to the stress of the fight-or-flight days I had left behind. Okay; scratch that. It was mind-numbingly boring. Mental Vicodin, if you will. Each day, I got up when the alarm on my phone blared to life, showered, slapped on some mascara, and headed over to the diner to wait on a spotty flow of tables for six or seven hours. My off the books employment deal included a charitable staff meal at the end of my shift, so I always packed away as many free calories as I could before heading back to my room. I didn't have much to do there really, except watch crappy network TV on a sagging, spring-punctured mattress, so that was the sum and total of my nights. Unless a rollicking trip to the nearest Laundromat to wash my grand total of five outfits was required, of course. Wild times, those.

The next morning I would wake from a night of nightmares and fitful sleep, to repeat the process all over again. It was the epitome of a mundane existence; one that demanded nothing of me and gave nothing back in return. I had no clue what to do next. Every option seemed just as soul-anesthetizing as the one I was living through, so why bother? If I had thought my old life was sad and pathetic—with my nights of drinking with my bestie, endless varieties of amusement on Netflix, and a kitchen full of whatever suited my fancy—I finally realized what a whiny little brat I had been. The old adage was true and I hadn't realized how good I had it until I was tossing and turning on a musty, strange mattress with only Jimmy Fallon for company.

Even those frantic months running around the city with the fae, expecting danger to find me around every corner, had been better than the hum-drum fake life I was living. I ached for the tear-jerking, deep belly laughs Mairi and I had shared while watching silly stand up reruns on my couch. I missed the sweet, motherly way Seana would brush my hair back as I scarfed down the mile-high stack of pancakes she had made me before a day of training. Hell, I even missed creeping through dark, stinky alleyways with Gannon; knowing we were righting a terrible wrong. Sharing that manic grin when we closed in on our prey. The way his eyes would sparkle in anticipation…

Perhaps Kaine's lying royal ass was the only thing I didn't miss.

A million times a day I found my cell in my hand, my fingers hovering over Mairi's name. I tried to accept my new life, my new loneliness, but the truth was, I was desperate to hear a friendly voice or see an encouraging text—only, I couldn't. The promise I had made to her went unfulfilled. I had to keep the break clean, even if it ached like hell. Reconnecting with the things I was missing would only make the pain last longer. I knew that; I did. It was just so hard to let go…

I was caught in one of those moments, phone in hand, resistance wavering, when Maureen's gravely drawl snapped me back to reality. "Hey, dollface, you wanna stop daydreamin' and help that fella over at table eight?"

I shoved my phone back into my back pocket, red-faced. "Yes, sorry! Going right now."

I weaved my way out from behind the server's station and down the aisle to the back corner booth, now occupied by a hulking brute of a man, his face buried behind the over-sized, plastic-sheathed menu. I stuck out like a sore thumb in the classic (cough*dated*cough) ambiance of the diner in my black t-shirt, dark washed skinny jeans, and suede knee boots. Still, I poured on all the fake charm I could muster as I leaned against the edge of the opposite booth and cocked my head, ponytail swinging. "Can I get you something to drink while you look that menu over? Cup of coffee, tea, soda?"

"Coffee sounds great. With cream, please." The menu lowered a fraction and I took a punch to the gut.

My new customer was a troll. Not my troll, obviously, but the features were frighteningly similar: the same sloped brow, wide jaw, and deep-set, piggy little eyes. This one was remarkably well groomed and well spoken, when compared to the memory of my personal nightmare. He wore an Ohio Bobcats jersey and a pair of jeans that had seen better days, his black hair buzz cut short atop his exaggerated, slightly misshaped skull. I was betting his glamour made people think of him as a big, broad former jock. Maybe his features bordered on the Cro-Magnon, sure, but they would overlook it because he reminded them of their high school sweetheart.

I, on the other hand, wanted to scream and run in the other direction. I ducked my head to avoid his gaze, snapping my gum in an obnoxious valley girl manner just to keep my expression from freezing. I scribbled down the start of his order on the little order pad in my hand, glad to have something to do to stop myself from staring. I hoped like hell I hadn't given myself away. I didn't think I had—trolls were notoriously slow on the uptake—but I still couldn't be sure. "Coffee coming right up," I said brightly. "You need another minute or two to look that over?"

He nodded, disappearing back behind the menu, and I took the chance to dart away. My hands were shaking as I picked out a mug and filled it with steaming coffee. It was a miracle I didn't spill any. Fuck, fuck, *fuck*. I probably shouldn't have been so surprised. It was more of a wonder that it had taken just over a month for any fae to wander across my path. But I mean; really, universe? It had to a troll, of all things? I griped the counter and took a deep, slow breath.

"You all right?" Maureen had come up alongside me.

"Yup, everything's fine."

Her gaze sidled across the way, to our lone patron. She didn't know what the deal was, of course, but she was already giving him one hell of a stink eye. "That guy givin' you any trouble?"

I shook my head. "No, no. Nothing like that. Everything is a-okay. Promise."

I plastered on my best smile but it wasn't fooling her. She accepted my lie with an affirmative grunt and walked back over to her seat, her crossword puzzle book spread open on the countertop before her.

I took New Troll his coffee and a little metal carafe of cream, careful to keep my cheerfulness at a realistic level as I served them up. "Here you go. You ready to order?"

He passed the menu to the edge of the table. "Yeah. Tall stack with bacon and sausage. Side of white toast too, if you don't mind."

I scribbled it down, hoping my quick pace hid how shaky my hands were. "Sounds good. Maple syrup and butter okay on the pancakes?"

"Yes, ma'am." He flashed me a toothy grin that I was sure was rustically charming to other people. It made me want to throw up in my mouth. I gritted my teeth and smiled back. A troll had just called me ma'am. I wasn't sure what to say to that, so I turned tail and went to put his order in. I stood by the counter, stealing glances in New Troll's direction. He was sipping his coffee and gazing out the window at the street beyond; the picture of nonchalance.

Even when his order was ready and I delivered it with another forced smile, all I got was a distracted thank you before he tucked in to the pile of meat and carbs. Not so much as a sidelong glance. He wasn't even giving me the time of day, really. No more than someone would give a server, at least.

I retreated to the counter while he ate, bewildered and on edge. If he were a spy of some sort, I'd have thought he would be been paying a bit more attention to me. I wanted to consider his disregard a good thing, but my brain was working overtime to read every little nuance. Maybe he was just lulling me into a false sense of security. Maybe he and a few buddies would be waiting outside for me at the end of my shift, just waiting to grab me.

My phone burned a hole in my pocket. I pulled it out and stared at the dark screen. I wanted to call Mairi so bad; to squeal and rant and lose my shit, with her telling me all the while to calm down and breathe. Granted she and the boys were much too far away to attempt to come to my rescue now, even if it did turn out that I was in danger, but just having someone who understood on the other end of the line would have calmed me.

"Marie, come over here for a minute, won't you?" Maureen called, using the fake name I had given her. I shoved my phone back in my pocket and hustled over, fighting the urge to toss looks back over my shoulder now that the troll was at my back.

"Sorry, sorry—I know I shouldn't have my phone out..."

"You ain't foolin' me, sayin' everythin's okay. I don't know what's weighin' on your mind today, but it's clear somethin' is."

I sighed, hands flapping about like two distraught birds. I didn't know what to say.

"You don't gotta tell me. Ain't none of my business. Why don't you take the rest of the day off an' deal with whatever's got you so bothered?" It was phrased as a polite suggestion, but we both knew it was an order. Maureen might have looked like someone's grandmother, but she was far from maternal towards me.

Fuuuuuuuuck. She was the source of money knowingly letting me live a shady double life; I couldn't risk stepping on her toes. I gritted my teeth behind yet another fake smile. "Okay, sure. Thanks. Just let me just go drop off his check and I'll cash out."

I tallied up the troll's bill—leaving off the up-charge for double meats, because fuck you Maureen—and strolled back over to his table. I dropped the check down behind his untouched water glass and said, "My shift is coming to an end. You need anything else, you feel free to ask Maureen, okay?"

"Sure thing. Thanks darling," he said, with another one of those toothy smiles. He reached into his pocket and pulled out two crumpled singles, sliding them across the table at me. I took them with a muttered thanks, clenching them in my fist as I made myself turn and walk away. There was no flicker of recognition in those beady little orbs; not even the slightest hint of subterfuge.

As I gathered up my purse and hoodie from the back, I was torn between relief and the nagging doubt that something about the situation stunk. Could our paths crossing really just be the most inconvenient of coincidences? I had a hard time buying that.

Not much in my life was a coincidence.

~*~

I waited outside, in my car, until the New Troll finished his breakfast and paid his bill. I felt like the world's worst creeper but there was no helping that. I had been played for the fool once too often for my taste. Better safe (and feeling like a homicidal maniac) than sorry (and dead).

My eyes darted to my pair of stilettos, chilling in the passenger seat next to me. I reached over and caressed one, the feel of its cool metal comforting under my fingertips. Having them close at hand made me feel both better and worse.

Better, because I was protected. Worse, because I was prepared to use them.

Eventually the New Troll ambled out the door, got in his battered pick-up truck and drove off; nary a split second of concern shown for my whereabouts. If he had been playing dumb to lull me, he had done a bang-up job. Part of me wanted to follow him. Another part wanted to storm back into the diner to question the hell out of Maureen; to see if the ugly fuck had sniffed around for so much as a hint about my private life—but I didn't do either.

I already knew I wouldn't be stepping foot back into that diner. My listless, lazy time in Ohio had come to a rather abrupt end. My gut deep reaction made it impossible to pretend I was anything but a Hunter, even tucked away out here in rural hell.

Maybe it was my mother's blood that made it so easy for me to become a killer. Whoever she was.

The thought made me flinch.

Problem was, I had no idea where to go next. That long ago daydream image of me decked out in red gingham, whiling away my days at Granny's Stop n' Chow hadn't quite lived up to my expectations. I had pictured myself waiting on lewd truckers and country bumpkin locals; slapping away some good ol' boy's hand if he got a little too randy. In my wildest dreams, I hadn't considered the appearance of a some slope-browed, sharp-toothed monster. And what had I done the minute the world reminded me that I was a Warder, like it or not? I had nearly whipped some knives out from under my apron and hacked his head off over a plate of half-eaten pancakes.

Talk about a health code violation.

I don't know why I had ever pictured myself in red gingham in the first place. I didn't even own any.

I laughed out loud, the long, hysterical kind of laugh that comes from the depths of defeat. Who had I been trying to kid? There was no charmed, simple life waiting out there for me.

I could run again and find a new spot to settle down in, but it wouldn't last. I couldn't hide forever. This was just the beginning of an endless cycle that I would never be able to stop. Gannon had been right about that too: out here, I had no allies, no network of strangers willing to shelter or help me. I was completely and totally alone.

I heaved a sigh and turned the key, letting the engine rumble to life.

There was only one thing left I could do.

CHAPTER TWENTY-SIX

When I pushed through the door to the fae house, I nearly knocked over a startled Seana. She froze in the doorway for half a moment at the sight of me, sputtering something unintelligible, but quickly stepped aside when she saw the determination on my face. I pushed past her and stopped in the living room doorway. Mairi was sitting cross legged on the couch, her iPad in her lap. Her cheeky little face—sporting a ring in one nostril and another through the adjacent brow—was nearly split in two by a humongous grin.

I found myself grinning back. I guess my grand return hadn't been wholly unexpected. "Where is he?"

There was no need for them to ask me who I was referring to. Seana continued to splutter and fuss about behind my back like I was a baby bird freshly fallen from the nest, but Mairi jerked her head in the direction of the stairs. "Study."

I nodded my thanks and took the stairs two at a time, leaving the girls behind in the living room. This was between Kaine and I. The study door was closed tight but I threw it wide open, earning myself a startled look from the otherwise unflappable prince. He was seated before the empty fireplace and he had dropped his book to the floor when I crashed through the door.

I stood before him, fearless. "This isn't over yet. I can't walk away from this, as much as I'd like to. I thought I'd be in danger until Texas Pete was stopped but it's worse than that. I, and everyone I know, will be in danger until Tiernan is dethroned and the laws are enforced again. We need to stop him. I want to strike a new pact."

To say the look that earned me was disbelieving would be charitable. He was looking at me like I was straight up crazy, his mouth opening and closing wordlessly. Maybe I was; I kind of felt it. After a moment of sputtering, he waved a dismissive hand at me. "Caitlin, it's not that simple. Let me explain to you how these sorts of things work. I—"

I cut him off with a sharp wave of my own hand. "Nu-uh. See that, right there—that 'Caitlin is a silly human who I talk down to all the time' shit?

That stops right now. You might be lord and master to everyone in this house and to the whole damn fae kingdom on top of that, but not to me. Got it? I am done being your lackey and I sure as fuck am not dumb enough to jump back into another lopsided deal with you. From here on out we deal with one another as equals or not at all. Are we clear?"

He sat back in his chair and regarded me with that regal stare of his. Perhaps he had thought I would show him more deference, having learned who he was, but that was going to be a long wait for a train don't come. Maybe it angered him; maybe it shocked him. I didn't really care one way or the other. I wasn't built for bowing and scraping. Instead, I said, "It's pretty obvious that neither of us has made much headway in our respective journeys this past month. I had to come back—and you're still stuck here. Maybe we're better off working together."

He looked like he wanted to deny that, and vehemently so at that, but he couldn't. If he had had any success in finding the sword, he wouldn't have been sitting in a Riverview brownstone, reading Yeats on a midsummer's Tuesday evening. He knew I knew and I could see that it was killing him. Jaw tight, he said, "Go on."

"I may not be part of your world but the search for the sword will be happening in mine. I think I can help you find it." I forestalled his doubt with a tart reminder, "I found the Lynx after all. I am offering to help, in whatever capacity I can. You don't know where this search is going to take you. Can you say, without a doubt, that you won't regret letting me walk away again, if I turn around and head back out this door right now? Because if I do, it'll be the last time. I won't make this offer again."

As much as he hated me in that moment for calling out his weaknesses, I could see that his interest was piqued. He stared past me and rubbed at his chin, brow deeply furrowed; the epitome of a lord deep in thought. Minutes passed in silence before he finally said, "Fine. We are in need of any help we can get. If I choose to agree, what will you expect in return?"

It was time to nut up.

I pulled one of my knives from its boot sheath and ran the blade across my palm. I held out it and my bloody palm both, keeping the bleeding hand carefully cupped so as not to mar his lovely carpet. My gaze had never wavered from his, not for an instance. "I'll help you get the sword and petition the Morrigan—and whatever else it takes to break the geis and get you home. In return, you swear to protect this realm and right the wrongs your brother has committed when you become High King. I will hunt down every last creature in this city that has harmed a human, if needs be, but once you are in power you will do your part too. You will put an end to the bestial fae coming across the Veil and hunting humans. Forever."

For a moment, I thought he would balk. I was asking a lot and I knew but; fuck it. In for a penny, might as well ask for a pound. I was tired of being scared and lost. I wasn't sure that throwing my fate back in with him was the best idea, but it was the only shot I had at getting answers to my questions and protecting those I loved. As with most things in my life, it wasn't a perfect solution, but maybe that was okay. Maybe an imperfect, challenging solution was just what I needed. It was better than running away. This was the time for me to take a stand; to be the strong, confident, decision-making person I had always wished I could be. He could deny my requests and turn me away, dashing all my hopes in the process, but that wouldn't change the fact that I had tried. That I had seen a chance and done something to right a wrong I felt so damn strongly about.

Thankfully, after a few tense moments, he stood and took the proffered blade. His turquoise gaze bore in to me as he ran it across his hand, never blinking. His grip was tight as we shook upon it. "Agreed."

"Agreed," I echoed.

Again the tingle; again the fire. When the flash of agony disappeared, so did the wound on my palm. He handed me back my blade, which too was clean of blood. Nifty trick, these blood pacts. I liked how they cleaned up after themselves. He sat back down as I sheathed the knife, already ignoring me in favor of Yeats. Despite having focused his attention elsewhere, he said, "Be aware that things will be different this time around."

I chuckled. "I should damn well hope so."

A flick of those blue orbs dried up my mirth. "I meant with you. How do you feel about me right now?"

Boy, was that a loaded question. I choked back the smart-ass answer and settled on, "Not particularly strongly one way or the other, really."

"Exactly."

It took a minute for me to catch that drift, and when I did a whole different sort of chill ran over me. I wasn't the least bit attracted to him anymore. Not even the slightest whisper in the panty department.

"The Warding is at its full strength now. That will protect you, but given your nature for trouble—and your ability to scrape yourself up once you find it—you must have more care. Seana will not be able to fix your ills any longer."

Did I detect a hefty dose of smug asshole-ishness in those words? Whatever. Let him be pissy and self-righteous. I let it slide. "Thanks for the warning."

He nodded once, in that perfunctory way he had, and continued reading. "That will be all."

Oh, how I hated being dismissed. I bit my tongue and dropped into an exaggerated curtsy. "Yes, your royal highness." My hand was on the doorknob before another thought gave me pause. Something about the night the we had all met up with the Lynx had been stuck in my craw for weeks—I just had to know. I looked back over my shoulder. "Kaine, when the Lynx dropped the mom bomb you didn't seem at all surprised."

He turned his head slowly, the flickering fire making his hair shimmer like gold. His eyes flashed. His face was a mask of indifference, the corners of his mouth hinting at the barest of smiles. "I wasn't."

I held that gaze for a long moment before returning that smirk with one of my own. Fine. Let him keep his secrets.

I had time.

~*~

Oh, that narrow staircase: my sworn enemy.

I thought back to another chastised walk of shame up those stairs, from months earlier. I had thought I had been filled with the pinnacle of self-loathing and anxiety then, but boy had I been wrong. They didn't hold a candle to the newest knot in my stomach. Facing Kaine had been clown shoes, compared to the confrontation that lay before me.

The memory of my last words to Gannon echoed in my head, bitter and filled with anger. I had made amends with Kaine, true—but I wasn't so sure this bridge would be as easily repaired, if at all.

When I crossed over the threshold into the training room, I found Gannon deep in practice. My presence didn't make him miss a beat. Watching him run through his flawless series of katas was breathtaking. He moved like the wind, like deadly poetry in motion as his blade flashed through the swathes of moonlight. It made my chest tight.

I had so much more to learn, so much more he could have taught me, but I wasn't sure that would ever come to pass. Truthfully, I wouldn't blame him. I had been cruel. I wasn't sure I deserved his forgiveness. I turned to leave, frozen in place by his voice as it rang out; somehow whisper soft even across the distance.

"Tuesday, 7 o'clock."

Tears stung my eyes. It was hard to get the words out around the lump that formed in my throat. "Wouldn't miss it."

I headed back down the stairs with a smile.

IF YOU ENJOYED *IRON*, BE SURE NOT TO MISS THE UPCOMING SEQUEL

FASTER

THE WARDING: BOOK 2

BY ROBIN L. COLE

CHAPTER ONE

There comes a time in every girl's life when she reassess the choices she's made so far.

I'm talking about the big picture choices. Not the little things we mull and obsess over every day, like "Was that skirt a bit too short for the office Christmas party?" or "Am I going to hate myself tomorrow for eating that greasy double cheeseburger—with a side of large fries…and a strawberry milkshake?" I'm talking about real choices. Those important decisions that have far-reaching consequences that you just know will come back to bite you in the ass, but you willfully ignore because you're all caught up in the moment. Like, "ignoring your better judgment and taking home that guy from the club because he's just too fine to pass up a night of naughty gymnastics with" big. Maybe even "quitting your horrible soul-sucking job without having another one lined up" big.

For me, that moment came as I hung upside down in a building along the Hudson River.

I didn't know what it had been home to in a previous life. Maybe some sort of a clothing manufacturer, given some of the odds and ends entombed within, but that hardly mattered anymore. It was a monument to disrepair: old, abandoned, and, if the scritchy little sounds I heard in the dark below me were any indicator, likely rat infested too.

Gross.

We had found enough suspicious scraps and discarded bones to confirm that our quarry had once called the building home. If it was still indeed in residence was the million dollar question. We had searched all three upper levels to no avail. Other than decomposing furniture, a shit-ton of dirt, and disgusting heaps of debris I didn't even want to try and identify, the building appeared empty.

That left the basement. The staircase leading down to the lower level had fallen away long ago. Was that the unfortunate side effect of time or a cunning move to make it impossible for intruders to stumble upon a private nest? Who knew? Not me, that's for damned sure. It didn't much matter in the long run. One way or the other, we were taking a look. It was a huge pain in the ass that needed to be circumvented.

The solution?

Lower Caitlin down into the dark, of course.

The cavernous space before me was pitch freaking black, except for a weak shaft of light coming from the stairwell above. Even with one wall perilously close to me, I felt disoriented. My brain just couldn't handle the overwhelming darkness. It didn't help that I was gently swinging back and forth, suspended from an honest-to-God harness like some trapeze artist. The damn thing was digging into my gut in all sorts of uncomfortable ways, cutting off the circulation to my legs. I guesstimated I was halfway between the floor above and the ground below, but it was hard to tell.

Maybe it was better that way. I really didn't need to know how far the fall to my death would be, should Gannon's grip fail.

The whole shebang was far from my idea of fun, but a necessary evil. Upper body strength and I had only recently become acquaintances, and though Gannon was all lean muscle, I had no faith in my ability to keep him aloft had our positions been reversed. Truth be told, I hadn't been too eager to let his strength by my sole anchor either, but—what could I do? One of us had to play spelunker and see if our unwelcome guest was still living below. Two little girls—twins, fresh out of kindergarten—had gone missing earlier in the week. Of course, the police were focused on tracking down the sicko who had taken them, but they were hunting for a run-of-the-mill abductor. We knew better. All signs pointed here and to a monster that needed to be stopped. Pronto.

"See anything?" Gannon's voice was pitched low but it reverberated in my brain, loud and clear thanks to my snazzy top-of-the-line Bluetooth earpiece.

I had finally stopped swaying. My face was starting to feel hot as all the blood pooled in my head, so I wanted to make the sweep quickly. I pried the flashlight from its pocket on my harness and said a silent prayer. We hadn't been able to come up with too clear a plan on what to do if the creature actually was hiding down there. I was armed with my trusty stilettos but they weren't going to be of much use to me while caught in mid-air. Gannon couldn't exactly come to my rescue either. Not without dropping me on my head.

I clicked on the light and shone it around in quick jerks, trying to cover as much of the room as possible. More trash, droppings galore, and some hulking machines I couldn't even begin to identify filled the large, high ceilinged room—but nothing moved, as far as the eye could see. I had to admit, when nothing leaped up at me from the dark, I let out a small sigh of relief. "Looks clear."

I heard him curse. It wasn't exactly the answer either of us wanted. Hours and hours spent on a futile hunt pleased neither of us.

"Hold on. Let me take a good look before you go yanking me back up." I slowed my search and tried to make my sweeps methodical and even, leaving no inch untouched. I held my breath, carefully cataloging every little sound I heard: the creak of the rope keeping me aloft, the faint drip of water hitting cement, that eerie ambient buzzing you get in your ears when things are just too damn quiet. Nothing out of the ordinary. Unless this thing was hunkered down behind something, holding its breath, I was pretty sure we were the only living things in the building.

An indignant squeak and the scratching of tiny nails on concrete echoed from somewhere to my left reminded me that was untrue. Fine then; it was just us and the rats.

"I'm not seeing anything. Want to lower me down? I can do a pass on foot." It was the furthest thing from what I wanted to do, but I didn't have any better ideas.

I could tell he was considering it for a moment by his pause, but he said, "No. Too risky. I wouldn't be able to get you back up and that harness is too tricky to manage in the dark, alone. I think we've seen enough. It's not here anymore."

Fuck. Who knew when—*if*—we'd pick up its trail again? The thought of those poor kids burned in my gut like a straight shot of Tabasco. I knew it was likely too late to save them—so likely that it was a pipe dream to expect anything else—but bringing them justice would have been something. Ever one to beat a dead horse, I continued to sweep the room as I was hoisted back up. I was dizzy as hell but determined. Unfortunately, that gumption got me nowhere.

Once the light began to return, I was able to gage my surroundings once more. The smell of marginally fresher air was a treat after spending so long in the damp cavern below. I tucked my flashlight away and reached up to grasp the rope with both hands. I managed to pull myself upright, wincing as the harness straps cut into my thighs in a whole new way. I was not a fan of the spelunking shit. I made myself a promise to start pumping iron. Next time, Gannon was going to be the one taking the plunge if I had anything to say about it.

The lip of the hole loomed above me and I reached out to get a good grip on it, helping guide myself up and over before the rope went slack. I flopped back on the concrete and laid there for a moment, waiting for my bodily fluids to redistribute themselves properly while trying not to think about all the dust and grime currently caking itself into my hair. Gannon crouched beside me, undoing the locks of the harness. It was the closest he had been to me in a long time, save for when we were kicking one another's asses in the training ring.

I shoved that thought away quick.

The whole situation really bugged me. We had come so close. The remains we had found on the lower floors proved some sort of bestial fae had certainly been living here. Who else could it have been, if not our serial killer? Given just how many stashes of picked clean bones we had found, the damn thing had called this shithole home for quite a while. There had even been a few suspicious looking piles in the basement, making me wonder where the damn thing had slept. Didn't that old adage of "don't shit where you sleep" apply in the fae kingdom? Actually…

I wondered aloud, "How would it have gotten down there in the first place, if the stairs are missing?"

Gannon paused for half a second. Over the last few months I had learned to read my teacher well. With him, that small tick was damn near an admission of guilt. He seemed to shake it off as undid the last strap and stood. "Kludde can fly."

"Fly?" I sat up. He had taken two steps away, back turned. I shimmied out of the remaining straps about my thighs. Those he had left alone. What a gentleman. Chivalry wasn't about to make me forget the bomb he had just dropped. The mental image of some feathered freak soaring up out of the darkness, beak agape, was emblazoned in my mind and would probably haunt me for days. "Gee, that's good to know. Nice of you to warn me before I went down there."

He shot me a look that was disbelief balanced by an equal amount of thinly veiled contempt. "Does it matter? One way or the other, one of us was going down there. You said it yourself; you weren't going to the one hoisting me up in this thing." He shook the rope for emphasis.

"Yeah, well maybe it would have changed my opinion just a little! I wouldn't have been so eager to be dangled in the dark like a worm on a hook, thanks." I shot him a peeved look, which earned me an eye roll. That was Gannon-speak for "stop being a drama queen," which only irritated me even more. I snapped, "Don't you think that's some information I could have used before we turned this place over from top to bottom?"

"Perhaps, but I didn't think it relevant."

"Oh yeah? And why not?"

"You've never showed interest in preparing yourself for a hunt before."

I might have recoiled visibly, if I had been on my feet. As it was, I froze with my mouth hanging open. He casually turned his back to me, as if he hadn't just given me a verbal five across the eyes. I glared daggers into his broad back. My face burned.

To say that our relationship was a rocky one would be something of an understatement. Gannon was my teacher and I was his unexpectedly capable student, but there the warm and fuzzies ended. From day one, we had run hot and cold with one another. We were usually civil and had found that we worked surprisingly well together when out on the prowl but beyond that, the lines of communication between us were a bit… strained.

They had become even more so ever since the night we had hunted down a black dog (which was pretty much exactly what it sounded like: a gigantic, slavering fae hound). I had acted like an ass and nearly gotten myself killed by blithely ignoring the dossier he had so painstakingly prepared for me the night of that particular hunt. The danger my laziness had put us in had led to one of the most severe dressing downs he had leveled upon me to date. The blow-out of that night made this insult seem almost flippant.

So, as much as I wanted to bite back after that not-so-subtle dig, I deserved it. Knowing firing back would just spark another war between us, I tried to be the bigger woman and swallowed my pride. Believe you me; that was hard for me. Really, really hard.

I climbed to my feet and picked up the discarded tangle of harness. It weighed next to nothing. He was on his own with the rope. I stalked off across the room, muttering uncharitable things under my breath once I was out of earshot. I needed to put some distance between us before I said something honest. No one had the power to infuriate me quite like Gannon. Even Kaine—whose princely ass remained at the tippy top of my shit-list—didn't make my skin itch like a wool jumpsuit.

I shouldn't have been too surprised, of course. Ever since the Warding had manifested in my life, letting me see through fae glamours in addition to being immune to their freaky magical abilities, my life had been one giant problem after the next. You would think that I would have adjusted to being around them damn near 24/7, but; no. Navigating the ins and outs of fae etiquette was nowhere close to being my strong suit.

My being the last known Warder left in the world—both mine and theirs—proved that some sort of fae blood was intermingled in my gene pool but I was still just a little human fish in a big, strange fairy pond. All I wanted was to protect myself and those I loved from the more savage fae who were slowly invading my world, but to do that I had to throw my lot in with the exiled prince and his buddies, like it or no. From day one, Kaine had made the hoighty-toighty royal decree that I not hunt the bestial fae without Gannon—his loyal Guardian, resident badass, and huge pain in my rear. That was just one more complication in my quest to save humanity from the monsters.

It wasn't like Gannon and I had exactly been chums before our little black dog spat, but I'd be lying if I said his prissy attitude didn't chap my ass. I had done him and his little coterie a huge solid by finding them their Secret Keeper, but when the Lynx's solution to ending their banishment hadn't proved a quick and easy fix, it had put further strain on our relationship. Which totally wasn't my fault but; whatever. I hadn't given their bat-crap crazy High King nearly omnipotent powers, had I? I didn't have anything to do with his having tossed their asses out of Tír na nÓg on trumped up (i.e. fake) treason charges, leaving them to rot in my world. And I certainly hadn't broken the news to them that petitioning a vengeful goddess using some near-mythical fae artifact was their only hope of breaking that exile. That was all on them, their crazy relatives, and the Lynx, thank you very much.

I snarled silently and kicked at a piece of discarded plaster, likely fallen from the crumbling ceiling above. Just thinking about it made me want to scream. I had thought I would be free of them as soon as I lived up to my end of the original ill-gotten pact with Kaine to find the Lynx. Instead, I had realized that I couldn't walk away from them any easier than they could from me. Until I saw Kaine returned home to usurp the throne from his crazy brother, there would be no stopping the bestial fae from crossing into my world to feed on humans. Forging another blood-bond with that smarmy, identity hiding royal bastard had been the only way to ensure my safety and that of the human race in general—but that meant that I was tied to them until they found that stupid sword and made it back home, come hell or high water. Finding the damn thing was proving to be another wild goose chase of a nightmare.

Good god damn, my life was a hot mess.

I heard the rustle of the rope being wound up on the other side of the room. I wanted to keep as much distance between myself and Gannon as I could until my temper cooled, so I chose to get some fresh air, relatively speaking. The door to the street was listing at half mast, a rusty length of chain still slung across it from the outside. If it was meant to keep out intruders if had failed miserably. Neither of us had had a hard time bypassing it. Not much of a surprise for my five-foot-four frame, but Gannon was a head and a half taller; lean but wiry with muscles I could never dream of having. Personally, I thought we should have taken bolt cutters to the thing, but Gannon had insisted we leave as little evidence of our search as possible. Whatever. Just another small way he annoyed the shit out of me.

I shimmied through the crack and emerged outside on the dilapidated front stoop. A few crumbling stairs lead down to the deserted lot below; the ground cracked, weeds sprouting up where employees had once parked their cars. The sun was shining bright in the sky and it made me squint. I was used to late night hunts; covert shit under the cover of darkness. We had risked the complications of seeking the kludde out during the day thanks to its nocturnal habits. Catching it asleep in its lair would have been much easier than tracking it at night. Had it still been calling this place home, of course.

Nocturnal and flying. How was that for a one-two punch?

I paced in small circles, too jazzed up to stand still. Just thinking about that thing still out there at large made my blood boil. It was an all-out predator, not just some crazy nutjob with a taste for human flesh. Having found no trace of it stuck in my craw even worse than Mr. High and Mighty's passive-aggressive bitchiness. Who knew where it was now? I could hope that it had moved on—but if those missing kids were any indication, it was still calling Riverview home. I didn't like the thought of something that vicious—that evil—residing in my city. Who knew where it would strike next? Who knew when it would swoop down, grab some unsuspecting innocent, and fly off to devour them in its new nest?

Fly.

I looked skyward. A bird was lazily winging along above, riding a nice breeze.

Son of a bitch.

We had been looking in the wrong place all along.

I spun around and craned my head back, shading my eyes with one hand as I scanned the side of the building. Sure enough, there was a rusty, rickety-as-hell-looking ladder jutting up from somewhere on the third story, leading to the roof above. Adrenaline surged through me. I sprang forward and shoved myself back through the cracked door, nearly colliding with Gannon on the other side.

"What the hell—"

I grabbed a fistful of his t-shirt and damn near spun him in the direction of the stairs leading to the upper stories. "The roof! We didn't check the roof!"

He gaped at me for a moment before the light bulb went on. A manic grin broke out on my face. I saw that excitement mirrored, crackling to life in his pale blue eyes. He dropped the rope by the door and sprinted toward the stairs with me in hot pursuit. We took them two at a time, sling-shoting ourselves across each landing to bound up the next flight. There were no words to describe the vicious excitement that flooded my veins. This hunt wasn't ready to be called a bust just yet. We slowed our pace as one when we hit the third floor, not wanting to alert anything that might be waiting above. I had to admit, our glaring differences aside, we worked in concert. We were one hell of a team.

The door to the outside was bolted shut; the lock long rusted. Gannon tried to shoulder-slam it into submission but it wasn't giving. I sacrificed the sleeve of my shirt to clear through the thick layer of grime on one of the window panes. Outside I could see a small ledge spanning the length of the building, hardly wide enough for two people to walk side by side. It had likely been a service walkway in its former life, long forgotten. An ankle deep layer of decaying leaves and God only knew what other matter awaited us. Ick. Hunting was far from being a glamorous job.

I looked around and found a hefty looking piece of wood among the debris surrounding us. I picked it up and tested its weight. It was on the light side—likely hollowed out by decay—but I had the hunch it would be enough. Gannon had stepped back, arms folded. He didn't have to ask. He already knew where this was heading. I really wanted to use my newfound weapon to knock the sly look of his face; devilishly high cheekbones and all. Instead, I took a deep breath and swung at the glass. The pane shattered with a satisfying clatter.

So much for keeping things quiet.

It took us a few minutes to clean out the frame and work our way through but we got there. The foul reek of rotting vegetation greeted us. He climbed through first. I heard the muffled snap of what I could only hope were rodent bones being crushed underfoot, lost among the rubbish. He reached in and helped me through, hoisting me over the edge so that the rough edges of the glass wouldn't snag on my clothes. Such a gentleman.

The ladder leading up to the roof looked no more stable up close than it had on the ground. The metal had long ago turned the red-brown of something rusted beyond repair, though it still seemed to be securely bolted to the wall. I slipped on a pair of thin leather gloves. I didn't know how much they'd protect me, but it was better than nothing. Getting a tetanus shot wasn't high on my list of things to do. I hoisted myself up and let the bottom rung take my full weight. It groaned and shook, but held. I said a quick prayer to whatever was watching over me and clambered up, as quick and quiet as possible.

I hopped over the lip at the top and moved off to the right, giving Gannon room to follow. I crouched and scanned the area. It wasn't very impressive. The surface was paved in gravel, though much of it had worn away in the years of disuse. Squat little chimney stacks popped up at regular intervals, each capped with a rusted metal hood. A cluster of metal towers and pipes dominated the far left corner, likely the remnants of the building's air conditioning system. I couldn't see what hid in that labyrinth, but my gut told me we were close. As soon as Gannon was up and over the edge, we crept forward. A few feet in, he stopped me with a hand to the chest. I followed his gaze to the ground. There was dried blood spattered among the gravel.

A lot of dried blood.

I drew my blades.

The world was scary silent up so high, with the building below us long dead. Even the traffic from the busy streets was muffled. We were only a few feet from first of the shed-like structures when I heard the rustle of something moving on the other side. We both froze; weapons drawn, and—personally—heart hammering. Belatedly, I realized I probably should have asked what exactly a kludde was earlier, instead of getting snarky over past mistakes. But that would have been the reasonable thing to do—a.k.a. not something ever entered Caitlin Marie Moore's mind until it was too late. (Why be logical when you can be bitchy, right?)

One day I was really going to get a handle on that smart-ass gene.

Gannon's hand grazed my forearm. When he had my attention, he jerked his head to the right and pointed straight ahead of us with his sword. I nodded, veering off on a path opposite of his. It was the luck of the draw to see who got the head end this time. I knew my luck. Something told me I was about to play bait once again. I pressed my back up against the shed when I rounded the corner, stilettos at the ready. Each step was carefully placed, my eyes never leaving that bend; that space where that monster might appear.

Until I stepped down on something that snapped with a loud crunch.

Until I remembered the kludde could fly.

ABOUT THE AUTHOR

Robin L. Cole likes to write, cook, and feed her voracious fiction reading habit through late-night splurges at Amazon. She is an indie urban fantasy writer who lives in New Jersey with her husband.

Iron is her first publication and she is hard at work on its sequel, *Faster*.

Visit her website at http://robinlcole.com
or
Follow her on social media:
Facebook: https://www.facebook.com/mrsrobinlcole
Twitter: https://twitter.com/robinlcole
Instagram: https://instagram.com/mrsrobinlcole